THE WORLD OF MARY MOYO

A STORY OF AFRICA

L. T. KAY

MJB

Published by [MJB]
ISBN [978-0-6482772-4-8]

This is a work of fiction. Names, characters, businesses, places, events and incidents are either the products of the author's imagination or used in a fictitious manner. Any resemblance to actual persons, living or dead, or actual events is purely coincidental.

Cover photo Copyright © by Frankie Kay

Typesetting services by BOOKOW.COM

To Maggie

With my love and thanks for your continued support and encouragement that enabled me to write this book

Acknowledgments

I am indebted to all those who helped me in writing this book. These include my beta readers who comment on grammatical and structural errors that have slipped through the net.

My thanks also go to Melody and Russell for their final line edit, picking up several small omissions and typos, and for their suggestions adding to the story.

I especially want to thank Maggie, my editor-in-chief, who read and re-read the manuscript several times, pointing out typos and other errors affecting the flow of the narrative.

Any remaining errors are entirely my responsibility.

Finally, I must thank you, the reader, for taking the time to read this book. If you notice any typos or errors of fact, no matter how small, please let me know through my website or my email address ltkay@ltkay.com, so I can improve the reading experience for those who follow.

L.T. Kay

Author website https://ltkay.com

How many brilliant minds,

gifted athletes,

and artistic talents,

have we lost through the lack of opportunity available to them?

L. T. Kay

CHAPTER 1

The White Cupboard

MARY Moyo stared in disbelief at the vacant space in her hut. That's where it stood until this morning. At first it brought her pride and status, but then led to worry and shame.

She remembered the day it arrived. Josiah, her husband, left before sunrise on the donkey cart with old Luke, Mechanic, and two of the village boys. He'd not said where they were going or why they needed the cart. But she guessed from his secretive manner he was up to something.

The only sign of village life was the familiar sound of buzzing flies in the suffocating, mid-afternoon heat. A sudden shout, and the excited voices of the villagers, drew Mary out of her hut. On the track leading up to the village, the donkey cart trundled nearer, with the two boys running ahead. Josiah sat in the front, exhorting the donkey to greater effort, and Luke and Mechanic stood on the back, steadying a large object between them. Excitement gripped the women and children as they ran out to greet the cart and view what it contained.

The tired donkey stopped in front of Mary's house, and a pleased-looking Josiah jumped down to greet her. The women and younger children stood open-mouthed and wide-eyed as the old men and the village boys unloaded the large object. Everyone thought it was the most beautiful thing they'd ever seen. In this remote part of south-western Zimbabwe, few of the inhabitants ventured farther than the neighbouring villages in the surrounding area. But now, the outside world reached them.

Josiah wanted it in Mary's hut, but they puzzled how to manage that. No matter how hard they tried, it wouldn't fit through the narrow doorway. It was too wide to fit through the narrow doorway.

Someone suggested putting it in the open-sided cooking shelter, but Josiah would have none of that. Mechanic, so named for his self-proclaimed mechanical prowess, offered to take it apart and reassemble it inside the hut. That might have sounded like a good idea, but Josiah remembered the time Mechanic took apart Alice's pedal-powered Singer sewing machine. With several false starts and lots of muttering and curses, he took a fortnight to reassemble it, but it never worked as well thereafter.

After much loud discussion with everyone putting forward their ideas, the villagers reached a consensus. Using a stick for measurement, they decided the best solution was to remove the door of the hut. At least, almost everybody, including Mechanic, would know how to reattach it. The good idea proved more difficult than it sounded. In the village, only Mary's door possessed a proper door frame and hinges. Sweat trickled down the men's faces as they took turns to undo the screws with an old Rhodesian tickey coin. Finally, after a half-hour battle, the door thudded to the ground. Now, carefully avoiding scraping the white cupboard, many willing hands carried the prize sideways through the narrow doorway and put it on an old piece of vinyl sheet Mary laid down.

'Where did you get it?' Mary asked her husband.

'I found it lying in the tall grass near the main road.'

'What were you doing in the grass?'

'I saw it yesterday when I got off the bus from Bulawayo.'

'But why would someone leave it there?'

'Perhaps they have a new one and didn't need it anymore.'

'We can store all our clothes in it, so they won't get dusty lying on the shelf.'

Two tall doors with sweeping handles gave it an elegant appearance. Behind the right door, removable shelves allowed for a hanging space below the top shelf. It would be just right for Mary's two dresses and

Josiah's three shirts, a tie, and his old, worn, charcoal suit. Useful narrow shelves lined the back of the door. The one with the cute little hollows would be perfect for storing her plastic rings, beaded bracelet and earrings, and Josiah's tie pin and cufflinks. The hollows would keep all these items separate, so they would not become jumbled. Mary put underwear and socks in the two bottom drawers: one for Josiah and one for her. Even their shoes could fit inside the cupboard. The left door opened to reveal several shelves, including more narrow shelves attached to the door.

'So much space!' said Mary. 'We will never fill it. This is the most beautiful cupboard I have seen.'

* * *

As the wife of the village head, Mary should have enjoyed her status. She was Josiah's number two wife until the death of Miriam, his first wife. Now, number one, she often felt the women in the village regarded her as a poor substitute in the role and didn't give her the respect she deserved. The new white cupboard would soon change that.

Nancy Ncube was the first to knock on Mary's door. 'Mary, can I look at your new cupboard, please? Everyone is talking about it. I saw it on the cart, but I would love to look inside it.'

Mary suppressed her first inclination to send Nancy away. She suspected Nancy to be the main instigator behind the coolness the village women showed towards her. Nancy had been Josiah's late number one wife's best friend. Here was Mary's opportunity to change things. 'Yes, come and look.'

Nancy's jaw dropped as Mary opened the cupboard doors. 'Ag-ag-ag! So much room, and so clean!'

'Yes, the doors are tight; no dust can get inside the cupboard.'

Nancy shook her head in disbelief as she viewed the wondrous cupboard. She put her hands over her mouth as she took in the hanging space, shelves, and drawers.

With all of Mary's and Josiah's clothes and other possessions inside, it still looked empty. Now, Mary disclosed the real magic of the white cupboard. 'Josiah said, if we lived in a big city like Bulawayo and opened the cupboard doors, a light would shine to let you choose what you wanted. But here, we don't have electricity.' The men talked of electricity in the towns along the main road, but the village women knew nothing of it.

Overawed, Nancy needed to sit down on one of the low stools nearby.

After she left, one by one, the women came to view the magic cupboard. There were many exclamations of ag-ag-ag, raised eyebrows, wide eyes, and open mouths. Mary's status grew and grew, and her popularity soared. She felt proud as she let each new visitor into the hut.

Nora remembered seeing a cupboard like that on her visit to Plumtree many years ago, but it was nowhere near as grand. She couldn't remember how and where she saw it and then wondered if, perhaps, she'd only dreamt it. Abigail told Mary, her husband, Mechanic, promised to get her one. The next time he went to the main road, he'd search the long grass for another white cupboard. Jemima, old Luke's wife, stared at it in silence for a long time. Then, overcome by the wonder of it, her eyes glistened with tears. Her village, alone, possessed such a beautiful cupboard.

Soon, word of the white cupboard spread, and women from other villages walked for kilometres to view it for themselves.

Mary's new best friend, Nancy, in the manner of a tour guide, ushered visitors to her door. The cupboard so impressed the visitors, they would stare at Mary, the cupboard's owner, as if she herself were something to behold. Mary swelled with a pride that grew in tandem with her celebrity. The visitors would leave in excited little groups, chatting about the cupboard and its owner.

After lunch one warm afternoon, two rather aloof women visited. Unlike all the other visitors, they sniggered and seemed to share a private joke. After they left, Nancy raised a troubling question. 'We must be careful about visitors. What if the president's wife hears about the cupboard? People say she takes anything she wants. If she likes something, she sends the police to get it for her. They say she has taken people's farms and even government land. The police evict people, black or white, out onto the road. They can destroy their houses and crops and take their property and animals.'

Other village women heard the same rumours, and now Mary was worried. She decided she would only allow the women of her village to visit the white cupboard. No one else would be welcome. Each day, from morning to evening, she periodically scanned the horizon for signs of the police or other unwelcome visitors. Josiah was sure the president's wife possessed an even bigger and better cupboard, but she was unconvinced.

* * *

One bright morning, when Mary thought the fuss over the cupboard was dying down, a cloud of dust appeared in the distance. Within minutes, a bakkie (ute or pickup) carrying four men raced into the village. The men jumped out, chasing the children, and hitting the women and shouting. Everyone trembled, fearing these might be the governing party's young thugs. It often happened around elections, but the villagers sensed a difference this time.

'Where is it?' the men shouted. 'Where is our fridge?' Who took our fridge? Everyone looked towards Mary's hut, and the angry men charged through the narrow doorway. They dragged Josiah from the hut and shouted, 'We will show you what happens to anyone who steals our property.'

'I found it in the long grass by the road,' Josiah wailed.

'Why did you steal it?' shouted the angriest of the men. 'Was there a sign saying you could steal this fridge? No, there wasn't. You stole, and now you must learn your lesson.' Josiah howled in fear. What an indignity, accused of stealing the white cupboard.

Three of the men dragged Josiah to the ground and hammered four large pegs around him. With strong ropes, they tied each of his hands and feet to a peg. Josiah struggled and shouted, but he was helpless against the young thugs. None of the terrified villagers came to his aid.

'I want everyone here to witness this man's punishment,' the leader shouted. 'We will punish anyone who tries to run away. First, we must all sing in praise of our government that allows us to live in safety and peace, in this, the second most developed country in Africa. We will punish anyone who doesn't sing.'

Josiah squealed in terror. His black face exaggerated the whites of his bulging eyes. A brave village woman stepped forward and covered his face with a broad-brimmed hat. 'No,' shouted the leader, 'he must face the punishment coming to him.' He held his knife up high, as if inviting the threatening dark clouds to strike it with a bolt of lightning. The villagers sang the songs they'd learnt at the time of the Gukurahundi —the government led genocide of the Ndebele people.

As the singing subsided, the leader lowered his knife and stepped towards the hapless Josiah on the ground. Mary wailed, fearing for her own life and helpless to do anything to aid her husband. 'Now we'll punish him and then set fire to his hut.'

* * *

Almost unnoticed, three police vehicles, a bakkie and two vans, pulled into the village. Six police officers with guns jumped out and shouted for everyone to stand still. The gang leader tried to run, but a bullet in his calf changed his mind. 'Lie on the ground,' the police commander shouted, and the thugs meekly obeyed. 'You stole a fridge from the removals van that broke down on the main road. Which one of you is the leader?' Almost as one, the thugs pointed to Josiah.

The police forced the thugs to bring the fridge out of Mary's hut and load it onto the bakkie. In their haste, they knocked the hut door off its hinges. They bundled their captives, including a protesting Josiah, into the van. 'I found it in the long grass. I didn't steal it from a removals van,' shrieked Josiah. 'These men stole the fridge and left it hidden, to pick up later.'

'We'll sort out everything at the police station,' said the commander, before jumping into the ute and driving off, followed by the two police vans.

So, thought Mary, the president's wife, must have sent the police to take her white cupboard, but at least she and Josiah kept their lives. As her misery grew, she suddenly realised their possessions remained in the cupboard. In the excitement, no one thought to empty it. Mary knew her husband to be an honest and truthful man, and she hoped the police would release him soon. But he'd have to walk the forty kilometres back to the village.

The village women melted away from Mary's side, and she suspected her status had fallen even below the level before the white cupboard arrived. She turned to Nancy for support, but her new best friend looked away, saying, 'A village head shouldn't lead a gang of thieves to steal another's property.'

Left standing alone, Mary turned and walked back into her hut. She stared in disbelief at the vinyl sheet where the white cupboard once stood. Mary hated the idea someone else would wear her clothing and jewellery, even if it was the president's wife.

Mary felt hurt and embarrassed. The friendship of the village women proved worthless, melting like hailstones in a summer thunderstorm on the veld. She consoled herself with her belief the friendship between the other women was likely to be as fragile as the friendship they showed her. It seemed envy and jealousy dominated emotions in village life. How did it come to this? Should not the village head's wife lead a privileged life?

If the news of what happened reached other villages, she'd be the area's laughingstock. It was too much to bear. If Josiah did not return soon, she imagined she might have to run away, back to her family. But Mary knew it would shame her parents, and they'd have to return the lobola (bride price). If her younger sisters miss their opportunity for an education, it would haunt her for the rest of her life. And what if her family sent her back? The entire village would then know she tried to run away, but her family didn't want her.

Mary decided it was Josiah's fault she was in these circumstances. If her silly husband didn't try to impress her with that stupid white cupboard, she wouldn't be in this situation. She would give him a piece of her mind when she saw him again. But then, what had changed? She was friendless before the white cupboard, and she was friendless now. Mary was like a caged bird. Would she spend her life in this trap? What could she do about it?

CHAPTER 2

The Price of a Good Woman

MARY worried she was being punished for her sins. She remembered what her mother told her when Josiah chose her as his second wife; 'Proud today, humbled tomorrow.' Josiah was a village head, and in the eyes of her family he paid a high lobola, and she revelled in the attention it brought her. Now she understood the true meaning of her mother's words. When she possessed the white cupboard, she'd been too proud, and almost without realising it, she became arrogant. The other women soon recognised this but tolerated the situation because of her newfound fame in the area. Mary became like the women she'd always resented. She now realised the glamour of the white cupboard blinded her. Shallow people often treat you differently because of your possessions.

* * *

Life was simple when she lived at home with her parents. She was the oldest and prettiest of their five daughters, and her sisters held her in awe. Mary helped her mother bring up her younger siblings, and she enjoyed caring for them. She never gave a thought her idyllic existence might not last. Like most young girls, she dreamed that one day a handsome young man might marry her and whisk her away to a glamorous life. But the distant future, forever away, did not trouble her yet.

One hot Sunday afternoon, an elderly fat man, sweating from a long bicycle ride, came to see her father. The visitor sat on the small stool her father offered, his ample bottom barely contained by the seat. Mary's mother brought a cool drink of water for the two men and then, along with Mary, left them to their discussion.

When Mary asked about the visitor, she got no straightforward answer, and her mother's evasiveness troubled her. The formality of the visit put a lie to her mother's claim the visitor was an old friend of her father. When they returned to the hut, they found the visitor gone. The murmured whispers between her parents made Mary suspicious. Everyone knew rumours of poor families who sold their children. Might her two youngest sisters be at risk? What if the stranger wanted body parts?

Later, after the evening meal, Mary's father disclosed the purpose of the stranger's visit. He came to discuss Mary's availability for marriage. Mary was aghast. She was not ready for marriage, and the elderly fat man didn't match the figure of her dreams. 'No, no,' her father reassured her, 'the visitor is the uncle of the prospective groom. Your prospective husband is a village head, and he will pay a high lobola for you. You would be his number two wife.' Mary's father's words did not comfort her, and she worried she might not like the village head. What if he looked like his uncle? And being a number two wife didn't appeal to her. Number one wives could be worse than stepmothers.

'He doesn't even know me. What if he doesn't like me? How did he find out about me?'

'Everyone knows about my beautiful daughters. News about such things travels fast.'

Mary turned to her mother for support, but she averted her eyes and said nothing. There was no prospect of her mother arguing against her husband's wishes.

On the second visit, Josiah, the village head and prospective groom, accompanied his elderly fat uncle. Mary studied him closely. Though younger than his fat uncle, she thought he was at least twice her age. Josiah was thin with a furrowed brow. Perhaps those furrows reflected high office rather than old age. As village head, he held a responsible position and would make important decisions. The prospect of mixing in that high company made Mary's head spin. But why was he so thin? Did he not get enough to eat? Perhaps he was not as rich as her father thought?

Mary overheard part of the negotiation between her father and Josiah's uncle. The debate surrounded the amount of lobola to be paid in cows or an equivalent amount of cash.

'My daughter is young and healthy. She is a virgin and worth at least eleven cows.'

'This is not South Africa, my brother. With the worsening economy in Zimbabwe, a lobola of four to six cows is common.'

'Yes, but you have seen my daughter. She is pretty with a smooth skin like a city woman. Nine cows might be acceptable.'

'You say she's never left the village? It is good she's still a virgin, but that also means she missed her schooling. My nephew might agree to five cows.'

'Mary is a good cook. She cleans the huts and has looked after her young sisters from when they were babies. She also works in the mealie field and looks after the goats. The educated ones think they are their husband's equals and make lots of demands. When we men drink beer under the trees and discuss important matters, they say we are lazy. Hard-working women are better than educated ones. A lobola of eight cows is a fair price.'

'Your daughter is pretty, but she is thin. Her hips are narrow, like those modern white women. She might not give my nephew many children. Once she proves herself, he might agree to six cows.'

The discussion flowed back and forth until an amount was agreed.

Mary's dreams of romantic love were not relevant to the negotiation, and she would have to do what her father decided. Her young sisters, thrilled at the turn of events, seemed more excited than she, but Mary enjoyed being the centre of attention in the village. She couldn't believe she was worth as much as six cows, but Josiah agreed to pay four up-front and two more after her firstborn. Josiah requested the wedding take place in Mary's village. It was an unusual request, and she wondered the reason for it.

Often, her mother told her they couldn't afford the school fees for the two youngest unless the three older girls found suitors who paid a high lobola. Mary never attended school, as her mother needed her help to look after the family. Now, her lobola would help pay for her two youngest sisters' education. A pang of disappointment stabbed at her, and she felt like a human sacrifice. Although she didn't understand what an education was and how it might help her, she'd heard others say it was something everybody should have.

* * *

Soon, the wedding day arrived, and friends and relatives came to join the celebrations. It was Mary's first opportunity to get a closer look at Josiah. He appeared to be a gentle soul, unlike his noisy, fun-loving young relatives. Just before the wedding ceremony, she received more 'marriage proposals' than any moral girl might expect in a lifetime. Mary learnt the flirtatious young guests travelled from Bulawayo, that great city one hundred kilometres to the east. How different from her simple family the young city folk seemed. Josiah was more like her relatives —conservative rural types. Mary's father eyed the young male guests, weighing up the prospect of suitable lobolas for his second and third daughters.

Mary wore a long white cotton dress her mother made, and a crocheted veil edged with beads. The veil looked like a tea tray cover, but Mary felt pretty in her wedding outfit. Her hair was styled in an intricate pattern of tight cornrows, and once she'd removed the veil, she attracted the admiring glances of all those present.

Josiah's uncle secured the services of a pastor from an African Indigenous Church. A small man with fiery oratory complementing a voracious appetite. The money saved on the pastor's modest fee was more than compensated by the cost of what he drank and ate.

For Mary, the day was a haze of eating, drinking, and meeting new relatives. Josiah, dressed in a smart black suit, looked younger than when she first saw him. Now Mary was more comfortable with the arranged marriage. Everyone drank too much and fell into a boozy sleep, and despite her excitement, exhaustion overtook Mary.

* * *

The next morning, the tired and hung-over wedding guests drifted away in small groups, some heading back to their villages and others to Bulawayo. A donkey cart waited to carry the bride to her new home. After a sad goodbye to her parents and sisters, it was time to leave. Mary bubbled with anticipation, despite a gnawing fear of the unknown. She hardly noticed the slow, bumpy ride over rutted and corrugated dirt tracks. The donkey cart travelled west on the edge of the road. In places, the degraded tar was indiscernible from the compacted earth verge. It disappointed Mary when they passed through the 'bright lights' of Marula village, without stopping. Next to Figtree, it was the biggest centre she'd ever seen.

They arrived, after dark, at Josiah's village, where a large, frosty woman greeted them and showed Mary to her hut. Miriam, Josiah's number one wife, seemed not at all pleased to meet wife number two. She'd not even attended the wedding, and Mary wondered how much opposition there may have been to Josiah's decision to take a second wife. Perhaps that was why Josiah requested to hold the wedding in Mary's village.

In the morning, Miriam took charge of Mary and put her to work, cleaning the three huts that comprised Josiah's home—one for Josiah and one for each wife. Miriam introduced her to the curious village women. Her off-handed manner made it obvious to all that she held Mary in low regard.

At the wedding, Josiah's relatives welcomed Mary into the family, and she built tentative bridges with the young women. Now Mary realised that none of those relatives who attended the wedding lived in Josiah's village, and they'd all come from elsewhere.

In her new home, Mary knew no one and felt isolated. Miriam appeared determined to keep it that way. 'He bought her for only four cows,' Miriam told the village women.

'No, Sister, it was six cows,' said Mary.

'Ha! You won't see the other two. First, you must give Josiah children. I gave him three sons, who all have good jobs in Bulawayo.' Miriam turned to the other women. 'When Josiah married me, he paid ten cows. That shows true respect.'

Mary didn't give voice to her thoughts. Ten cows for Miriam would be a fair swop if they set the lobola on her weight alone. These days, no woman would be worth ten cows. She'd heard rumours that rich people like the president could afford a lobola of forty. Perhaps the great white queen's family in London received even more cows, but these big payments were just rich people showing off their wealth.

'A lobola of four to six cows is common in Zimbabwe these days. The country is not rich,' said Mary.

'Eish! You are not even a real Ndebele. You are Kalanga. Even the president says the Kalanga are criminals and thieves, and too uneducated to have a proper job. Four cows! Too much!'

Mary gritted her teeth, and her hands trembled. Miriam's greater age and status as number one wife made it difficult for Mary to argue with her in any situation, let alone in public. At home, in front of Josiah, Miriam presented a sweet and innocent front. But now, her comments not only showed disrespect for Mary, but also for their husband. The lobola he paid did not concern the others. The value of the lobola showed a man's status and generosity, and his respect for the bride and her family. But Miriam launched an expanding circle of gossip like the ripples of a stone tossed into a still pool on the river's edge.

As time went by, Mary's isolation grew. Her status as the village head's second wife seemed to count for nothing. Josiah was attentive and kind, but Miriam seemed set on making her life a misery. One year later, Mary was still not pregnant. Miriam appeared triumphant in telling the other women Josiah would soon return Mary to her father and get a refund of the lobola. Josiah said nothing to Mary on the matter, and she worried he might have confided in Miriam.

When Mary first came to the village, Miriam gave her a cool reception and treated her like a servant, encouraging the other women to ignore her. Life as the village head's second wife was not what she expected. She missed her family and home village, but many kilometres separated them, and she wondered if she'd ever lay eyes on them again. Josiah seemed pleased with her and treated her well, but the more Josiah favoured her, the worse Miriam became. Mary feared talking to her husband about his number one wife because she worried he'd not believe her. She needed to resolve the problem. Something needed to change in her miserable life, but what?

Fate was about to play a hand. Late one afternoon, Mary accompanied Miriam to the river and guarded her towel and clothes while Miriam washed herself in the ankle-deep, still water on the river's edge. No one else was around, and in the peaceful surroundings, Mary daydreamed of her home village and wondered what her young sisters might be doing at that moment.

She noticed ripples on the surface, but thought nothing of it. Large fish in the river kept the villagers supplied with a varied diet. The village boys competed to see who would catch the largest barbel catfish in the river. They made tasty eating. More ripples disturbed the surface.

In the distance, she heard the young village boys practising on the drums. Squeals and laughter of the village women preparing the evening meal drifted down to the river on the gentle breeze as the sun sank low on the horizon.

'We should return to the village,' said Mary, 'or we'll be late.'

'We'll go back when I'm ready. Don't tell me when—'

Mary's heart jumped at the splash and the loud shriek. A crocodile clasped Miriam's right calf and pulled her towards the middle of the river, where the shallow ledge gave way to deeper water.

Mary jumped up, but stood there, stunned at the happening. Conscious of the beating of the village drums and aware they were alone, she worried she would be in danger if she entered the water. Everything seemed to move in slow motion.

'Help me,' shouted Miriam.

The young crocodile and the big woman engaged in a deadly tug of war. With Mary's help, the two women might have reached the riverbank, but Mary hesitated for a moment before rushing to Miriam's aid. Too late! Miriam slipped in the shallows on the rocky shelf of the river's edge and vanished into the deeper water. Neither of the women could swim, and the descending darkness made any rescue by Mary impossible. She rushed back to the village for help.

Soon the riverbank was lit with flaming torches, but the tranquil, slow-moving river hid any sign of the recent horror. It was the first crocodile attack in that part of the river in years. In African waterways, complacency was suicide.

Josiah was heartbroken, and Mary, more isolated than ever as the village women whispered their suspicions. The guilt ate away at her because she imagined if she hadn't dithered, she might have saved Miriam. She didn't intend for Miriam to die, but she'd fleetingly wondered what life would be like without her. That moment of hesitation might have cost Miriam her life, and Mary couldn't stop thinking about it.

Now, with her husband in jail, accused of stealing a white cupboard, Mary was friendless in the village. She feared things moved from bad to worse. Pride and humiliation contributed to the tragedy of Miriam and the crocodile. It was only a moment of hesitation. Might it have changed the outcome? But what if…? Doubt and guilt consumed Mary. Which way could she turn? What should she do? She determined that the only way to find peace would be to share her secret guilt with her husband on his return. But when might that be? How would she manage in the meantime? She'd no idea the troubles in the village would soon get worse.

CHAPTER 3

In Bed with The Lady

SINCE he sprung the news on Moira four days back, there'd been no peace of mind for Mark. He looked forward to camping with Robbie in the remote south-western reaches of Zimbabwe. The problem was he'd lied, and the guilt gnawed at him. He lied to Moira, and he tried to lie to himself, but it didn't work. His conscience pricked him. Mark hated it when things between him and Moira weren't smooth. They were a team, but now he'd created a schism he needed to repair fast. It would be several days before he was home and could resolve things. It niggled at him, but he'd have to bear it for now. When he got back home, he would make it up to Moira, big time.

Like all plausible lies, his held a grain of truth. 'Robbie's been down since Stella left with the baby. She's gone to live with her parents in Cape Town. They say the pain of separation or divorce is like grieving for a loved one's death. Robbie needs company.' But a lie is a lie with elements of deception and manipulation. 'I'm worried that he might do something silly. He was the best man at our wedding and my best friend since primary school. I should support him through this tough time.'

Robbie focussed on trying to make something out of his fledgling engineering business. But he also enjoyed his newfound freedom, and in this light, suggested to Mark a trip back to Zimbabwe.

Mark found the idea irresistible, but for one problem. He and Moira moved from Bulawayo to Johannesburg, the big city, less than a month earlier. Now he planned to leave her all alone in their apartment in that strange city while he visited Zimbabwe for a bit of fun. They'd looked forward to moving to Johannesburg and reconnecting with Robbie and Stella, who moved 'down south' a year earlier. But when they arrived in Johannesburg, they found their friends' marriage in tatters, and nothing seemed the same. With Stella gone, Moira knew no one.

For good reason, Mark held back the news of his camping trip until just two days before his departure. Moira wouldn't be happy with the news, but with such short notice, he'd limited the time he would suffer any negative consequences. Since his disclosure of the camping trip, Moira, silent and sulky, put him under pressure. On the eve of his departure, he tried to make things better. 'It's just a few days. I'll be back before you know I've gone.'

Moira was not swayed, and when he left for the trip, she bade him a rather cool farewell, giving him a light peck on his lips. 'Take care. I worry about you in Zimbabwe. Bad things can happen there.'

'Don't worry, I'll be careful, and I won't do anything stupid. We'll camp under the stars with a few beers around a fire, and we'll fish during the day.'

'Watch out for crocodiles.'

'Yeah, I will.'

* * *

It was a long, hot drive from Johannesburg, through Botswana, to Zimbabwe. For much of the trip, Mark was a million miles away, thinking of Moira. The mesmerising throb of the engine and the hum of the tyres on the tarred road surface aided his daydreaming. The bonnet of Robbie's four-wheel drive seemed to swallow the highway at one hundred and twenty kilometres per hour.

Robbie tried to make conversation with little success. 'Are you still with me or what? Am I talking to myself?'

His words jarred Mark back to consciousness.

'I was just enjoying the scenery.'

'You've been quiet ever since we left Joburg. Moira didn't mind you coming away for a few days, did she?'

'Well, she was OK with it, but it's the first time we've been apart since our wedding.'

'So, she wasn't that happy then?'

'Well, I feel selfish leaving her alone in Joburg while I'm away on a week's holiday.'

'I didn't plan to drive for eleven hours and waste time in customs and immigration at two border crossings for you to be a bore, worrying about Moira. She'll be fine. It's time for you to switch into camping and fishing mode.'

Typical of Robbie, thought Mark. Nothing ever bothered him. He told Moira how cut up Robbie was over his marriage break-up, but in truth, it seemed he didn't give a damn. 'Robbie, is this mate of yours aware we're coming to camp on his property?'

'No, but he said I could camp there anytime, and didn't need to give him advance notice. He said he'd lend me fishing rods and perhaps even a rifle to shoot a buck or two.'

'Well, you never mentioned that, so I've brought my own rods.'

* * *

Robbie wanted to arrive at the campsite by mid-afternoon to give themselves time to get organised and explore the surrounding area.

The drive to the turnoff at Marula was an hour from the border post near Plumtree. Then, it was a further one-and-a-half-hour drive on a dirt road to the campsite. Robbie planned to go straight to John Boyd's house to announce their arrival and pick up the fishing rods and rifle. 'We'll be there around half-past three.'

The main road in Zimbabwe was in poor condition, and the dirt road was even worse. The four-wheel drive bumped and rattled and jarred in the large potholes. Robbie took out the hand-drawn map his friend John gave him and followed the detailed written instructions. 'Thank God for the Land Cruiser. I hope John hasn't been optimistic in his estimate of the time on this road.'

'Well, I suppose he's familiar with how long the drive takes.'

'He's got a monstrous amphibious truck that would sail over these potholes and corrugations. If he's basing his estimate on that, it might take us much longer.'

After an hour on the dirt road, they turned onto a narrow dirt track just wide enough for one vehicle. The tall grass on either side gave them a lost-at-sea sensation. 'Are you sure we're on course?'

'Yep, I'm just following John's map.'

As they rounded a bend, they saw a black Toyota Land Cruiser approaching them. 'Snap!' said Mark, patting the dashboard of Robbie's white four-wheel drive.

The vehicles stopped nose to nose, and a tall African man got out and approached them. 'What are you doing here? This is private property.'

'We're heading to John Boyd's campsite,' said Robbie.

'John Boyd isn't here anymore. This is now my property.'

'Who are you?'

'I'm Jackson Mpofu.'

The friends recognised the name of the governing party bigwig.

'You bought his property?'

Mpofu frowned. 'I don't have to buy what's already mine.'

'Do you know where John Boyd is?'

Mpofu shrugged. 'Maybe, Bulawayo.'

'He said we could camp at his campsite.'

'You can camp there, but part of the security fence is missing. The villagers steal the wire. You know what we blacks are like.'

Robbie laughed, and Mark was about to say something, but stopped himself. It was fine for Mpofu to make fun of his fellow blacks, but he might not welcome similar comments from a white. That didn't stop Robbie.

'Yeah, don't I know it!'

Mpofu's face darkened. 'Keep away from the house. My guards don't welcome visitors.'

'Is the campsite safe if part of the security fence is missing?' said Mark.

Mpofu nodded. 'I don't think you'll have any problems.'

As the two four-wheel drives edged past each other with their offside wheels in the tall grass, Mpofu looked across at them with an amused smile.

'I don't trust that slimy bugger,' said Robbie. 'He might have been lying about John. Let's check the house to see if he's still there.' Soon they arrived at a fork in the dirt road and turned right. Only two kilometres down the track, a boom gate blocked their path. Three scruffy looking young black men with machetes emerged from the long grass. A fourth sat on a log, looking sullen, with one calf dressed in bandages.

'Go back. This is private property,' one of them said.

'We're here to see Mr Boyd,' said Robbie.

'He's not here.'

'Where is he?'

'The young African shrugged. He's gone away. Mr Mpofu owns this property now.'

Robbie reversed fifty yards to a clearing where he turned the Land Cruiser. 'Well, Mpofu said it's OK to use the campsite.'

'It's lucky I brought my rods. We won't be using John Boyd's rods or rifle on this trip.'

They returned to the main track and turned right. Soon, they entered a heavily wooded area and drove about four kilometres. A sign indicated the campsite lay down an overgrown track on their right. Before long, they left the forest, and a kilometre farther on, they reached their destination. A faded campsite sign hung from a tall gate post.

The gate, and part of the mesh fencing, was missing. The site comprised hard, trodden earth with scattered tufts of grass. Tall trees shaded the western edge of the campsite, and the ground sloped down to the river about a hundred metres to the south. Seventy metres to the east ran a low ridge covered by small, scrubby trees.

'That's a good spot for the tent,' said Robbie, pointing to a bare, flat area of earth on a slight rise. 'If there's any rain, it will flow away from the tent.'

They placed a tarpaulin on the ground and took the tent out of its bag and unravelled it. Robbie, a seasoned camper, assembled the tent in record time with minimal help from Mark. It was early January and well into the rainy season. He attached a rain fly over the tent, extending the wings to keep the raindrops as far away as possible. From the front, it looked like a pterodactyl, stretching its wings in readiness for flight. The entrance to the tent faced the river.

The camp came alive with the noise of shouted instructions and laughter and the unloading of the kettle, pots and pans and cooking utensils. 'Have you noticed there're no birds and not a breath of wind?' said Robbie. 'It's a hot afternoon, and nothing stirs until the cool of the evening. Would you like a beer?'

Mark laughed. 'Let's collect wood for the fire and put the kettle on for tea. The beers can wait for sundown.' In their chitter-chatter, neither noticed the slight movement in the small scrubby trees on the ridge.

'Did you see that lightning?' said Robbie. Soon, dark clouds gathered on the horizon beyond the river. More flashes of lightning and the distant sound of thunder threatened the evening. 'Looks like a wet night. If we're lucky, it might by-pass us, but we'd better cook an early supper, just in case.'

'And what delicacy are you cooking up tonight?' Mark asked.

'Sausage supreme, fried eggs and beans.'

The clouds grew dark and angry, but the rain held off, and the friends enjoyed their meal, sipping their cans of lager as they watched the daylight snuffed out over the tall trees.

'This is the life,' said Robbie. 'It's what I miss most about Zimbabwe. Joburg is too big and crowded, and miles from the bush.'

Mark sipped on his beer and wondered what Moira was doing at that moment. He wished she were there to share his sleeping bag, even though he loved camping with his best friend. Back in high school in

Bulawayo, he, Robbie, and the gang went camping on the holiday long weekends. Now, most of the gang were scattered throughout the globe, building their lives in countries they'd read about in geography lessons.

The fire crackled and spat and threw a light over a small area of their campsite. Eight o'clock seemed like midnight, and dark clouds raced past the moon. After downing their fourth round of beers, it was time for bed. Mark walked towards the dark perimeter of the campfire's dancing light. 'If you're going for a pee, stay in the light. Anything might lurk out there. With half the fencing wire gone, we better not take any chances.'

A strange sound, like a cough or gurgle, came from the ridge. 'Did you hear that?' said Mark.

'Oh, just an animal or bird, I expect.'

Mark shivered, suddenly noticing the cool breeze that sprung up while they talked and enjoyed their beers. Now he looked forward to the warmth of his sleeping bag.

The narrow tent was a tight squeeze for the two of them. When they zipped up the entrance flap, the interior plunged into total darkness. Within moments, Mark heard Robbie's deep breathing, but he was not yet ready to sleep. In the darkness, his thoughts slipped back to Moira and the last four days. The thoughts swirled in his head, and as hard as he tried, he couldn't clear his mind.

For Mark, a perk of married life was cuddling Moira in bed each night. They slept on their sides, close together, like two spoons in a close-packed cutlery canteen. They'd turn over in their sleep, yet they always woke cuddled up in the same position. In winter, it was like sleeping with a giant hot water bottle. Tonight, he struggled to switch off, but as his body warmed, he became drowsy. The rain that threatened all evening arrived in a steady, soporific patter, rather than a drumming downpour. Soon he was asleep.

In the early hours, with the rain a little heavier now, Mark stirred; still half-asleep and sweaty, with Moira cuddled up so close to him. He put his arm behind him and patted her on the backside. 'Move up, Luv, you're making me hot.' She grunted and moved a little away from him.

'Who are you talking to?'

Robbie's gruff voice, in the confines of the dark tent, jolted Mark awake. I'm talking to Moira.

'You're dreaming. Go back to sleep.'

'I swear, it seemed she was here, right next to me.'

'Yeah, dreams can seem real.'

'No, I'd have sworn she was here. I felt her weight against me, and the tent here is warm, almost hot.'

'You've been lying up against the tent, so it would be warm, wouldn't it?'

Mark lay awake for a long time, thinking about his realistic dream. He'd tell Moira about it when he got back to Joburg. Did she have a similar dream? Close in so many ways, it often seemed a telepathic force bound them. His dream of Moira cuddling up to him was so real, making indistinguishable the moments of sleep and wakefulness. The belief she was with him telepathically comforted him, and he drifted off again.

* * *

After the rainy night, they woke to a bright morning with a fresh breeze. Both Mark and Robbie were hungry. 'See if you can find dry wood under the trees,' said Robbie. 'I'll boil water for tea and get the fried eggs and bacon going.'

Mark busied himself collecting wood for the fire, rejecting anything too damp. Robbie filled the camp kettle and clattered the pans, preparing for breakfast. 'Come here,' shouted Robbie. Something in his tone suggested urgency. Mark glanced up to see him standing beyond the tent, inspecting the ground. Still carrying the firewood he'd collected, Mark walked up to Robbie.

'What's the problem?'

'See these paw prints? I'd say this was a big one.'

Mark stared at the sodden ground and the unmistakable prints of a large lion.

'It looks like it sheltered from the rain under the tent fly,' said Robbie. 'So, you didn't dream it. You said Moira felt heavy cuddled up next to you. See the crushed tufts of grass? I reckon we forget about breakfast and move out of here.'

Mark needed no second invitation. The two friends pulled down the tent in minutes and packed everything into the Land Cruiser. For Mark, it seemed they moved at too slow a pace. Robbie appeared unhurried, lacking the urgency he considered necessary. Typical Robbie, he thought, trying to look macho and unconcerned even when their lives could be at risk. They'd almost finished packing, and Mark looked around to make sure they'd not forgotten anything when he noticed a young African woman approaching them. 'Where does she come from? Is there a village near here?'

'Please, Sir, are you going to the main road? Can you give me a lift?'

'Yes, OK,' said Robbie. 'Squeeze in the back seat with the junk. Where are you going?'

'To the police station, Sir.'

The young woman was a simple village girl with little English, so no further discussion followed.

'What's the plan for today?' said Mark.

'We'll drop her off and go find a safe campsite, maybe in Botswana. First, let's stop somewhere for a decent breakfast.'

The return trip to the main road seemed shorter, now that they knew the way, and with the morning's events focussing their minds elsewhere. At the junction with the main road, they turned right and headed for Figtree, thirty kilometres towards Bulawayo. 'There's the police station,' said Robbie. 'Perhaps we should tell the police about the lion.'

In the police station, the young African woman spoke excitedly with the police officer at the front desk. 'What did she want?' Robbie asked the sergeant in charge.

'Her name is Mary. She is the village head's wife. She says a woman is missing from her village.'

Mark and Robbie related their story to the surprised police sergeant. 'It's dangerous to camp in that place. Didn't anyone tell you?'

'We met Jackson Mpofu on the way to the campsite. He said it was OK for us to camp there,' said Robbie.

The sergeant chuckled. 'The Lady's been in the area for three weeks, and she's already killed two villagers.'

'What lady?'

'That's what the villagers call her. She's an outcast from her pride, a cub killer, so now she's attacking villagers. Without the support of her pride, they're easier for her to catch than her natural prey.'

'Hell!' said Mark, suddenly aware of the risk they'd taken. 'We sat around our campfire past eight o'clock!'

'Perhaps the fire protected you.'

'Ha,' said Robbie, 'In bed with The Lady! Wait till Moira hears about that. And not just any lady, but the district's most notorious man-eater!'

'The district's only man-eater, I'd hope,' said Mark.

'We'll search for the missing woman near the campsite and the village,' said the sergeant. 'You can show us where you camped.'

'Surely, you don't need us,' said Robbie. 'You know where the campsite is. The lioness must have taken her.'

'How do we know you're not responsible for the missing woman? Perhaps, The Lady didn't take her. Perhaps you did.'

'For heaven's sake! You can't believe that?'

The African police sergeant raised himself to his full height. 'Leave your four-wheel-drive here and come with me and my constable and Mary. Now we must hurry before it rains and removes the evidence of what's happened.'

'We haven't had breakfast.'

'No time for that. We must go now!'

CHAPTER 4

Sergeant Dube Investigates

CONSTABLE Sibanda drove, with Sergeant Dube next to him in the passenger seat. Mary Moyo sat between Mark and Robbie in the back seat of the four-door Toyota Hilux bakkie. As they set off, the sergeant spoke in Ndebele to the constable, and they both laughed. Mark wondered what they found so amusing.

'So,' said Dube, 'Jackson Mpofu tried to feed you to The Lady? You were lucky. Perhaps, she does not like white meat. They say it tastes like chicken.'

'Maybe she's got a taste for black pudding,' said Robbie.

'Shush!' said Mark in a hushed voice. 'The sergeant may not appreciate your sense of humour.' Mark's forced smile betrayed his thoughts. This wasn't the time for Robbie's big mouth.

'I heard your comment,' said Dube. 'My English girlfriend's mother introduced me to black pudding. It was delicious.'

'You have an English girlfriend?' said Mark.

'I had an English girlfriend when I was studying for my MBA at Loughborough University. Now I'm married to a good Ndebele woman.'

Oh, yeah! Pull the other one. English girlfriend, MBA, sure! 'If you're an MBA, what are you doing here in a country police station?'

'The call of my homeland was too strong. I had to come back. Then I met my wife and got caught in her spider's web.'

'Why aren't you working in business for a big company or the government?'

'Most companies in Matabeleland have closed. The government has made it difficult for business in Zimbabwe. And I am Ndebele. What chance do I have of a business career or in government service?'

'Yes, I had to move my engineering business from Bulawayo to Johannesburg and start over again,' said Robbie.

'You have your own business? Perhaps you can give me a job?'

'You suspect us of taking the missing woman, and now you want me to give you a job?'

'When you get out of jail, you can give me a job.' Everyone burst out laughing.

'Yes, OK, you can be my sales manager.' Office cleaner, more likely, thought Robbie.

At least Dube and Sibanda possessed a sense of humour. Mark and Robbie settled back in their seats to enjoy the passing landscape and exchange reminiscences with the two police officers. Only Mary sat impassively, with much of the conversation beyond her.

'Turn right here,' said Dube. 'We'll warn Jackson Mpofu about The Lady. He might not know she's so close to his property.' Turning to Mark and Robbie, he said, 'This Mary is very brave. The villagers discovered the woman was missing, but only Mary had the courage to search for her. The village piccanins told her you camped nearby, so she thought the missing woman might be with you.'

'Yes, very brave.' Or idiotic, thought Mark. She put herself in real danger.

The police bakkie bumped and rattled along, shaking everyone inside so that their voices sometimes quivered as they spoke. Soon they arrived at the boom gate, where Mark and Robbie had stopped the day before. Three armed, surly young men surrounded the bakkie. A fourth with an injured leg remained seated on a nearby log.

'The boss is not yet back from Bulawayo,' one of them informed Sergeant Dube.

The sudden shriek hit Mark like an electric shock, deafening him with the ringing in his ears. His heart raced as he tried to make sense of what had happened. Mary was sitting forward in her seat, her back straight, eyes wide and blazing, and her eyebrows arched. She seemed enraged, shouting in Ndebele at the police officers and then at the youths surrounding the vehicle. Constable Sibanda hurriedly reversed the police bakkie before turning in a small clearing and sped from the scene. Only brief pauses to catch her breath interrupted Mary's outbursts of vitriolic diatribe, each louder than the last.

The sudden verbal assault caught Sergeant Dube off guard, and at first, he tried to calm the hysterical woman. As the commotion continued, Dube's eyes narrowed, and his moustache bristled. The fingers of his right hand drummed the dashboard.

'Enough!' Dube shouted, but that seemed to energise Mary, who only grew louder.

When, at last, Mary seemed to exhaust herself and grew silent, she sat with her arms folded and her eyes fixed on the floor in front of her. Robbie asked Dube about the cause of the fuss.

'She says those are the men who came to her village yesterday to harm her husband. She asks why they are free when her husband is still in jail? I wasn't on duty yesterday, so I don't know the circumstances. Sibanda, you were on duty yesterday. Why are we still holding her husband when the other suspects are free?' The constable shifted in his seat, with the unexpected question, and kept his eyes straight ahead. In a low voice, he mumbled something in Ndebele.

Dube turned towards the back seat. 'He says Jackson Mpofu phoned to say his men were innocent, so the police on duty let them go. No one will argue with a government bigwig. Their jobs are too precious for that.'

'What about her husband?'

'I will investigate the circumstances when we get back to the police station. Sergeant Mutasa was in charge yesterday. I will have a word with him.'

Soon, back at the fork in the road, they turned towards the campsite. They drove in silence for the rest of the trip. Even Robbie, never short of a word, was quiet.

* * *

This time, upon arrival at the campsite, Mark didn't find it as welcoming as the previous afternoon. Their brush with disaster made the campsite look cold and eerie. The unknown fate of the missing woman added to the sombre atmosphere.

They all tumbled out of the police bakkie and scoured the area where Mark and Robbie pitched their tent a day earlier. The paw prints of the man-eater lay visible in the sun-hardened earth, with the dry ground showing no sign of last night's downpour. 'Hmm, she's a big one,' said Dube. He and Sibanda returned to the bakkie and pulled out two rifles from the cargo tray.

'At least we're well protected,' said Robbie. Under his breath, he whispered. 'These buggers probably couldn't hit the side of a barn from ten paces. It would be better if they handed us the rifles.'

'Sibanda, you look under the tall trees, and I'll check the ridge,' said Sergeant Dube. Robbie opted to go with Sibanda, and Mark and Mary followed Dube.

The low ridge was not steep, but a generous sprinkling of thorn bushes covered it. By the time the small group mounted it, they all sweated in the bright mid-morning sun. The overweight sergeant's face glistened a shiny black. Almost at once, the loud buzzing of flies struck Mark. There lay the body of the missing woman, with her dress shredded. Huge scratch marks raked her back. A sizeable bite on her upper thigh suggested it was The Lady's doing.

Dube whistled across to Sibanda and Robbie to join them. The group stood gathered around the grisly scene, and for several minutes, no one spoke. As usual, Robbie broke the silence 'One bite from the thigh will not satisfy an adult lion. Something must have disturbed her. Perhaps we did. We better keep an eye out for her. I don't want to be next on her menu.'

Sibanda needed no second invitation as he swung his head from side to side. If they'd disturbed The Lady, where was she now? She could not have crossed the open ground towards the campsite without being seen. The village lay beyond the ridge, so it was unlikely she moved in that direction. Perhaps she was still somewhere on the ridge? The vegetation wasn't too thick, but looking along the length of the ridge, it gave the lioness plenty of cover to stay concealed from the cautious group. Mark could feel the hair stand up on the back of his neck.

Dube sent a rather pale Sibanda back to the Hilux to fetch a black plastic body bag. 'We'll take her to her family in the village. It's obvious what has happened here. There's nothing more we can do.'

The sergeant and Sibanda lifted the woman and placed her in the plastic body bag and closed the zip. The four men each took one corner of the bag and carried it down the ridge towards the village, with Mary following in silence.

In the village, the women wailed when they heard the news. Dube did his best to get details of the dead woman from her distraught husband, but the task proved more difficult than the sergeant expected. A woman hovered in the background, trying to get Dube's attention. 'What is it, Woman? Can't you see I'm busy? Are you a relative of the victim?'

'No, Sir. My name is Nancy, and I can tell you things.'

'What things? What are you telling me?'

'I must warn you, Sir. You should be careful.'

'Warn me? Warn me about what?'

'That one, Mary, speaks to the spirits. She is the village head's wife, and evil things have happened since she arrived.'

'What things?'

'She was number two wife, but she was jealous and talked up a crocodile in the river to take number one wife. No crocodiles live in this river.'

'Hah! Is that all?'

'No, Sir. When the men came for their white cupboard, they planned to beat the village head and Mary for stealing it. Just before they started, your police came and saved them.'

'They didn't call us.'

'No, Sir. The spirits did. Last evening, Mary and Ethel, the dead woman, argued while collecting water from the river. Later that night, when Ethel woke, she went outside to the toilet. It was then she must have met The Lady.'

'What's that to do with Mary?'

'Anyone who goes against her is in danger. Yesterday, the police arrested her husband and took her white cupboard with all her things inside it. I am just warning you, Sir. You must be careful.'

'Well, I wasn't with those police yesterday when—'

Loud cracks, the unmistakable sound of gunfire rang out. Several shots, then silence. Sergeant Dube cocked his head. 'That shooting is near Jackson Mpofu's property. Sibanda, come with me.'

'What about us?' shouted Mark.

'You wait here. We'll come back for you two.' The police officers ran towards the ridge and their Hilux parked on the other side.

CHAPTER 5

A Night to Remember

MARK and Robbie sat on a log at one edge of the village. What was taking Sergeant Dube so long? They walked in the immediate surrounds, but no further, for fear of bumping into The Lady. The villagers were friendly enough, particularly the curious children, but no one offered them something to eat. Mark and Robbie were starving, as they'd not eaten since last night's dinner. The villagers also did not appear to be eating. A small patch of stunted mealies promised a meagre meal in a few weeks. Perhaps the women saved their food resources for the evening meal, but Mark hoped to hell they wouldn't still be waiting for Dube by that time.

The women and children spoke little English. Only Mechanic, the village handyman, had a reasonable grasp of the language. Tired of inquisitive eyes staring at them, Mark and Robbie walked to the river with a trail of children in tow. A blistering sun beat down, with the little group sweating in the humidity caused by the recent rains. Three of the children splashed on the river's edge, running on the shelf that preceded the deeper water.

'Pleasant spot for a swim,' said Robbie.

'Yeah, with bilharzia and maybe a crocodile.'

'The children wouldn't play in the water with crocodiles here.'

'I wouldn't trust any waterway in Zimbabwe as far as crocodiles go.'

Suddenly, a young girl lost her balance and fell off the edge of the shelf into the deeper water. The children screamed, their eyes wide in panic. The men watched for an instant, before it became clear the child couldn't swim. Robbie threw off his shoes and socks and ran into the water. The girl was out of reach, so he jumped into the deep water to save her. In two powerful strokes, he reached her and grabbed the girl before she disappeared under the muddy, fast flowing water. Returning to the shelf proved more difficult as he fought against the flow, swollen by the recent rain. He passed the girl to Mark before clambering back onto the shelf.

The entire episode took less than a minute. The young girl and the other excited children ran back to the village, shouting at the top of their voices.

'Jeez, with the sun shining on the surface, you wouldn't know deep water was there, and how fast it's flowing,' said Robbie, brushing his wet hair with his hands. He took off his shirt and squeezed the water out of it. 'Lucky it's so damn hot. My clothes will dry in no time.'

Mechanic came to the river with an anxious woman who, in her limited English, struggled to thank Robbie and Mark for saving her daughter. As the four walked back up the slope towards the village, Robbie said under his breath, 'If they want to thank us, they can give us something to eat.'

'It's mid-afternoon. Lunch is long gone.'

'I don't care. I just want something to eat.'

But just as they approached the huts, Sergeant Dube and Constable Sibanda pulled up in their vehicle in a cloud of dust. 'Oh great! Just what I needed; wet clothes and covered in dust.'

'At least we can head home now,' said Mark.

* * *

The African police officers were in a hurry, and Mark and Robbie piled into the rear seat of the Hilux, relieved to be leaving the village. It had been a long day.

'What was the shooting about?' Robbie asked.

'The Lady attacked a man at the boom gate,' said Sergeant Dube. 'She must have been hungry, because she already started eating him by the time we arrived, but we must have scared her away. The boom gate lay open, so we took the body to Jackson Mpofu's house. His men will get the poor fellow back to his village for burial.'

'Be careful, Sergeant,' said Robbie. 'Earlier this morning, you frightened the man-eater from last night's kill, and now you've chased her off again. She'll be hungry and may have marked you for special attention.'

Sergeant Dube gave a thin smile. 'The villagers will have to be careful. Man-eaters are cunning. They're difficult to shoot, and no one in this district is keen to hunt her. Perhaps someone from Bulawayo can help.'

The police vehicle bumped along the dirt road. It seemed as if Sibanda aimed for the potholes. Mark was sleepy, so he closed his eyes and lay back against the headrest. The thought of a clean motel room with a hot shower and comfortable bed replaced the hunger pangs that gnawed at his stomach all afternoon. A loud bang and a screeching, whirring sound woke him with a start. 'What the hell was that?'

Constable Sibanda jumped out of the vehicle and opened the bonnet. Soon, Sergeant Dube and Robbie got out to help find the problem. A few minutes later, Mark clambered out of the rear seat to join the puzzled trio staring into the silent engine.

'It's buggered,' said Sibanda. 'We'll get a mechanic to fix it tomorrow.'

'Tomorrow?' said Robbie. 'You mean we must spend the night here in the bush?'

'No, we'll go on the motorbike back to the police station.'

'What motorbike?'

'We always carry a motorbike in case of a breakdown,' said Dube.

'All four of us on a motorbike?' said Mark.

'No, go back to the village. It's only three or four kilometres. We'll come back for you tomorrow.'

'Oh, great!' said Robbie.

Dube and Sibanda dragged an ancient-looking motorbike from under a tarpaulin in the bakkie's tray. It started the first time with the motor idling in a contented purr. The Africans retrieved their rifles from the Hilux and prepared to leave.

'Can we sleep here in the bakkie?' said Mark.

'No, it's against regulations for members of the public to be in control of police property,' Sergeant Dube replied. 'Ask the villagers if you can stay the night in a hut.'

'Hang on,' said Robbie, his voice rising in irritation. 'You expect us to walk back four kilometres on this bush road with a man-eater on the loose?'

'Sibanda, give them your rifle!' Dube ordered.

A reluctant Sibanda handed his rifle to Robbie. 'You must keep it clean and give it back to me tomorrow.'

With that, the two police officers rode off with Sibanda riding pillion, holding Dube's rifle.

'We've got Sibanda's rifle, said Robbie. Didn't Dube say, "it's against regulations for members of the public to be in control of police prop-erty"?'

'Let's move,' said Mark. It's getting late, and the sun's getting low. I don't want to bump into The Lady.

The sting of the afternoon sun lessened, and a comfortable evening light painted the sky. The two men kept up a steady pace to reach the village before dark.

'I reckon we've covered over three kilometres and we're still some way from the village,' said Robbie.

'Yes, but we better be careful. The grass is tall all along this track, and The Lady could be anywhere. Have you noticed how quiet it is? Listen, can you hear?'

'I can't hear anything.'

'That's right! Birds go silent when a predator is on the prowl.'

'Who told you that?'

'I read it in a book about hunting man-eaters in India.'

'I think it's an old wives' tale, but the quicker we're back at the—'

'Did you see that? Look up there! The grass by the bend moved. There's something big in the grass.'

'It's probably just a gust of wind. Don't let your imagination run wild.' Robbie slipped off the rifle's safety catch.

'If it was a gust of wind, I didn't feel it.'

The men edged closer to the bend. Robbie raised the rifle, ready to shoot if the man-eater charged. The grass moved again. There was no doubting it this time. And then, a large crashing sound betrayed the fast approach of the beast coming through the long grass. The two held their breath, and their hearts raced. Robbie aimed the rifle towards the sound, and the grass parted with a fearsome braying. The donkey brushed past him, knocking him to the ground as it raced across the road into the bush.

Robbie and Mark's hearts pounded in their chests, and they both burst out laughing.

'That's the village donkey,' said Mark. 'We must be closer than we thought.'

'It's just as well I didn't fire. We wouldn't have been too popular asking for lodging after shooting their means of transport.'

'Something must have spooked it.'

'Yes, perhaps we did.'

The two friends chuckled as they walked, the threat from the man-eater forgotten. Soon, the village was in sight.

* * *

It surprised the villagers to see the dirty, tired white men back. Now it was dusk, and everybody hurried into their huts before nightfall. Robbie explained to Mechanic they needed a hut for the night. After much loud debate between the villagers, Mechanic showed them to a vacant hut. 'It's all we have,' he said, eager to get to his hut in the gathering gloom.

'Thank you, it's better than nothing,' said Mark.

The two men looked around the hut. It was empty, save for three cooking pots lined up against the wall. 'Damn!' said Robbie. 'We forgot to ask them for something to eat.'

'Didn't you see their nervousness? They wouldn't hang around to feed us. Who can blame them? They're scared the man-eater will return.'

'I don't know who is hungrier, the man-eater or us. If it dares to come back, I'll eat it.'

In all the excitement, Robbie forgot about his wet clothes and didn't notice when they dried. Dry clothes were a necessity now because when the two men sat on the hard earth floor, they found it ice cold. 'How will we sleep in here? It's pitch black with the door closed, the floor is cold, there're no sleeping mats and no blankets to cover us.'

'What's the time?' asked Mark. 'My watch doesn't have luminous hands.'

'Mine neither. I reckon we've been in here for about half an hour, though it seems much longer.'

Exhaustion cut the men's chatter short, and soon they slept.

* * *

Something woke Mark. He wasn't sure what. He opened his eyes, but he might as well have kept his eyelids shut. The windowless hut was pitch black. Mark felt uneasy. He sat in the blackness, hoping his eyes would get used to the dark. But it was hopeless. He could see nothing.

Then he heard a creaking sound. But from which direction did it come? It seemed close, almost surrounding him. Something was in the room! But as he tried to focus on the sound, the creaking stopped. Mark strained his ears. Total silence. Was he dreaming? Did he imagine it? No, he was sure he was awake before the noise fell silent. He sat there, barely breathing, wondering if the noise would return. Tempted to close his eyes, but too nervous to sleep, He waited and listened. Silence, apart from the occasional brief creaking sound. The more he tried to focus his hearing, the harder it became to judge any noise.

Just when Mark's eyelids got heavy and closing, there, the sound again. This time, he was sure he wasn't dreaming. It sounded like slow steps making a creaking sound, but now it stopped again.

'Robbie, Robbie, are you awake?'

'Yeah, man. Did you hear that noise? I think it's coming from the roof.'

'Oh hell! I hope it's not The Lady on our thatched roof.'

A faint scratching sound started. Tentative, slow at first, but then becoming faster, louder, more urgent.

'Hell, Robbie! She's trying to come in through the roof! Can you smell the dust?'

'Wait, I'll get the rifle and try to work out where she is. A bullet in the stomach will be a nice surprise for her.'

The rifle leant against the wall, a metre to Robbie's right. He reached out and grabbed it and slipped off the safety catch. The rifle was an old bolt-action military 303. It packed a punch and would solve the district's man-eating problem if he could figure out where the lioness's chest or stomach lay on the thatched roof. Earlier, when he took the rifle from Constable Sibanda, he checked there was a bullet in the chamber. One in the chamber and more in the magazine, according to Sibanda. That should be enough.

From the frantic scratching, Robbie estimated the distance from the front paws to the body of the lioness as she tore at the thatch. But which way did the beast's body lie? From the scratching sounds, he judged the lioness lay parallel to the edge of the thatched roof with its tail to his right. He estimated the probable location of her chest, took aim, and squeezed the trigger.

Nothing! Only the loud click of the firing pin, the sound of the lioness's scratching, and the smell of dust falling from the roof. He quickly worked the bolt and pointed the rifle up once more and squeezed the trigger. Again, nothing. 'Bloody hell! Two duds in a row!' He worked the bolt again and again, but every squeeze of the trigger failed. Nothing!

Mark's alarm grew with each ejected round that hit the hard earth floor.

Soon the magazine was empty, and Robbie fancied he saw twinkling stars through the fast-thinning thatch. 'That idiot Sibanda gave us dud bullets or a faulty rifle. Maybe the firing pin is missing.'

'Hold on!' said Mark. 'Where are those cooking pots?' He stood up and edged across the hut towards the point he remembered seeing them. In the blackness, he held his arms out in front of him to avoid walking into the hut's wall. He found the pots when he knocked against one with his foot. He groped for the two largest and hurried to the sound of the scratching. A gaping hole was forming, and soon the lioness would break through the thatched roof.

With a pot in each hand, Mark swung them together above his head with all his strength and screamed his loudest. One pot broke free of its handle and smashed into the hut's wooden door with an almighty crash, adding to the cacophony of his loud scream and the clang of the pots.

Mark hoped to continue bashing the pots together, but now he held only one. He turned to get the other pot but realised the scratching sound had stopped. Complete silence.

'Do you think it's gone?' said Mark.

'I don't know. Lions are persistent buggers, and man-eaters even more so. You better get the other pot and stay awake, just in case. We won't be getting any more sleep tonight.'

'What do you mean, "any more?" I don't believe we got any sleep. I was still half awake when I first noticed the noise.'

'You snore when you're awake, do you?'

'The hole in the roof lets in light. I can just about see you now.'

'You notice, despite all the racket, no one came to see if we're OK?'

'The villagers aren't stupid. They won't check on us until the sun's up.'

'Well, what about that brave woman, Mary? She'd have no trouble scaring away the man-eater. Ask Sergeant Dube.' The two friends laughed at the thought.

* * *

As dawn broke and the light increased, Robbie picked up all the bullets that lay scattered in the hut. 'Look at these! They aren't bullets; they're dummies. See, they are wooden bullets stuffed into empty cartridge cases. School cadets sometimes used them to practise loading magazines. Fancy Sibanda hunting for a man-eater with these? I wonder if Dube's rifle has live rounds. It wouldn't surprise me if it didn't. And imagine, when we came here with them yesterday, we put our lives in their hands.'

'Yeah, and we might've met the man-eater on our walk back to the village last evening.'

The dawn light grew brighter, and the two weary men emerged from the hut.

'Keep your eyes open,' said Mark. 'The man-eater may still be here somewhere.'

'Don't these buggers ever eat anything? There's no sign of anyone cooking breakfast.'

'Eggs and bacon and a hot cup of tea would be nice. But you know, these villagers have little. I'd feel guilty if they offered me food and I ate it.'

'OK, but a cup of tea would be nice.'

'This evening, we'll be sitting in a motel somewhere, enjoying a decent meal, but these poor people will still be hungry.'

'This evening? You reckon? You're putting a lot of faith in Sergeant Dube.'

'Speak of the devil! Here he comes.'

A beaming Sergeant Dube jumped out of the police van.

'So, you got it started,' said Robbie.

'No, this one is different, not as reliable as yesterday's van. A breakdown truck is towing the other vehicle back to Figtree.'

'Tell me, do you have live rounds in your rifle?'

'Of course. Why do you ask?'

'I'll tell you on the way back to the police station.'

Constable Sibanda and a third man in civilian clothes got out of the van. 'This is Mary's husband, Josiah, the village head,' said Dube, introducing him to Mark and Robbie. 'We have released him. His arrest was all a big mistake.'

Just then, Mary rushed out of the hut and grabbed her husband's arm. Her joy soon turned to annoyance. 'Why didn't you tell me the white cupboard was for storing food and not clothes? You made a fool of me in front of the village and the visitors.'

As Mary led a stuttering Josiah into her hut, Dube turned to Mark and Robbie. 'Perhaps releasing him was an even bigger mistake.' The men smiled, and Sergeant Dube roared with laughter at his own joke.

On the way back to the police station, Dube showed his rifle magazine to Robbie to prove it held live bullets. He replaced the magazine and tried to steady the rifle's butt on the car floor, but a sudden jolt through a pothole caused his finger to slip onto the trigger. A deafening bang made everyone jump.

'Sergeant Dube, don't tell me you walk around with a live round in the rifle's chamber?' said Robbie.

'No, it was because I showed you my rifle was loaded with real bullets.'

'That hole in the roof is real enough,' said Mark 'Oh look! There's another one.'

'What do you do if it rains?' said Robbie.

'If it rains, I drive and Sibanda puts his finger in the hole.' Everyone laughed.

'It's lucky the two holes are close together,' said Robbie. 'Sibanda can use two fingers from the same hand.' More laughter.

'Sibanda, where did you get those dummy bullets?' Dube asked.

'From the counter at the station. I grabbed them on the way out. I thought they were mine, but this morning, I found my magazine in my desk drawer.'

'Hah, that explains it. A member of the public handed in that magazine with dummy bullets. They found it lying on the road. I didn't have the chance to inspect it because that's when you two came with Mary into the police station yesterday and interrupted me.'

'So, Sergeant Dube, it's our fault then that The Lady almost ate us?' said Robbie.

'Yes, perhaps you're right.'

'I hope no one is planning to sleep in that hut tonight,' said Mark. 'With that hole in the roof, they wouldn't stand a chance.'

'Yeah,' said Robbie, 'but the man-eater may try breaking into another hut's roof tonight.'

'Ah,' said Dube, 'these man-eaters are very cunning and learn fast, but the villagers have also learnt from your experience.'

CHAPTER 6

A Modern Woman

Six months later. The sweltering sun kept the village quiet, with the listless villagers confined to the shade of their huts. Only the children ventured out, seeking relief under the trees overlooking the river. It hadn't rained for months. The occasional hot gusts of wind raised small dust clouds where they brushed the parched earth. Sunday afternoons were often quiet in the village, with the men gone in search of a drink at the nearest beer hall. But that was several miles distant, and today, no one could muster the energy for the hot trek. It was late October, and the relentless summer sapped the body and mind of the long-suffering villagers.

Mary sat in the shade in the open doorway of her hut, darning a tear in one of her husband's shirts. Josiah was away in Bulawayo, visiting a sick relative, and Mary took the opportunity of the greater freedom it afforded her to catch up on long overdue chores. It was a dreary afternoon, but it soon passed for the industrious wife of the village head. Mary's hut allowed her a long view across the shallow valley that the road to the village dissected.

At first, it looked like a transient heat haze in the distance. But then a trail of dust showed the approach of a speeding vehicle. This was both exciting and worrying. The chance of another confrontation with Jackson Mpofu's band of hoodlums concerned Mary. But a visit by the police was welcome, especially if it was the affable Sergeant Dube. Who else would visit the village on such an inhospitable Sunday? It was doubtful it would be a social call, so it must be important. A troubling thought flashed across Mary's mind. Perhaps something had happened to Josiah? He was the only person absent from the village. What else might it be?

Soon the vehicle was close enough to see it wasn't a police van. The vehicle's glossy black paint sparkled in the sunlight, and the new-looking four-wheel drive suggested someone important was visiting.

The Range Rover pulled up in a cloud of dust in the bare space between the huts. Everyone stared at the arrivals, but no one came out to greet them in the energy-sapping heat.

Like the rest of the village, Mary sat staring at the stationary vehicle. The engine grew silent, and for a time nothing happened. Then, the passenger door opened, and a long shapely female leg emerged, followed by the second one. The lady wore high heels that disappeared into the dust of the desiccated earth. A short, canary yellow dress, huge sunglasses and a broad-brimmed straw hat completed an elegant picture of the glamourous woman who stood surveying the village.

'Mary, are you here?' the visitor called.

Was it possible? No, surely not! 'Is that you, Lulu?' said Mary, rising from her chair.

Yes, it was her sister, her parent's second daughter, the next one promised in exchange for a lobola—bride price. Mary didn't recognise her younger sister, but the voice was familiar. It was two years since Mary last saw her. Over that time, Lulu transformed from a gangling teenager into a beautiful young woman.

'Aiee, look at you.' said Mary. 'I'm not our father's prettiest daughter anymore.'

'Well, you might be if you had my clothes.' The sisters hugged each other, laughing. The driver's door swung open, interrupting the two women. 'This is my boyfriend, Joller Ngwenya. Joller owns a clothing store in Francistown and is about to open a branch in Gaborone.'

The slight, dapper figure wore pinstripe trousers, a waistcoat, and shiny black shoes. The jacket of his three-piece suit lay on the back seat of the Range Rover, a sign of surrender to the unrelenting heat. Joller nodded to Mary with the faintest of smiles. His pencil slim moustache suited his aloof manner.

'Come! Come into my hut. Have a drink. There's water or tea.'

Joller muttered something to Lulu, who turned to Mary. 'He wants to stay outside and smoke, but I'd like water.'

Lulu followed Mary into her hut.

'How are Mama and Papa? Do they know you're visiting me?'

Lulu frowned. 'I'm sorry to tell you, Mary, Mama died over six months ago.'

Mary recoiled in shock. 'Poor Mama! What happened?'

'She just got sick and died. We were all surprised. It was so sudden. Papa wanted to bury her straight away. We wanted to call you home, but there was no time to collect you.'

'Poor Mama!'

'Papa has taken a new wife. That is why I left home. I won't let Papa marry me off for lobola. His new wife has money. She can pay our sisters' school fees.' Lulu's defiant attitude shocked Mary. She would never have dreamed of disobeying her father.

'Joller is suspicious about how Mama died and how soon Papa buried her and brought a new woman into our home,' said Lulu.

'And what about Joller?'

'He's a generous man, and rich.'

'Are you going to get married?'

'He already has a wife, and I've told him I won't be a second wife to anybody. He says he will get divorced after he has opened his new shop in Gaborone. His wife doesn't treat him well, and for a long time he's planned to divorce her, so it's not because of me.'

'And our three sisters, are they well?'

'Yes, they are fine. I am not sure about Meredith, our middle sister, but the two young ones have accepted our father's new wife. But I don't like her. I think she wanted me gone, so I left and caught the bus to Bulawayo.'

'Bulawayo! Where did you stay?'

'I went to a cafe to buy food. That's where I met Joller. He wouldn't let me pay for my dinner, and he also paid for a room for me to stay. I've been with him for six months now.' 'You've been living with Joller for six months?'

'No, Joller lives in Francistown, but he has visited me as often as possible.'

'You drove from Bulawayo just to see me?'

'No, we're going to Francistown. I will work there in Joller's menswear shop.'

'Menswear?'

'Clothing for men.'

'Aiee, be careful of the number one wife! There might be trouble if she finds out about you.'

'Joller will look after me.'

'I hope so.'

When Mary and Lulu emerged from the hut, Joller was wiping down the Range Rover with a microfiber cloth. A fine layer of dust covered the vehicle, giving it a faint golden tint.

'This is a beautiful new car we have,' said Lulu. 'It cost us a lot of money.'

Joller looked at Lulu's feet with mild disapproval, noting she'd taken off her high heels and walked barefoot in the dust. 'Are you bringing that dust into the car?'

'I didn't want to spoil my shoes,' said Lulu.

'If your shoes get dusty, you can wipe them, and if you ruin them, I will buy you another pair.'

The arrogant tone in Joller's voice underlined Mary's first fleeting impression of him. She suspected his wish to smoke outside was an excuse to avoid entering her simple dwelling. Perhaps he feared dirtying his clothes on one of her chairs. Mary was house-proud and kept her hut spotless, but he was not to know that.

While Joller busied himself dusting his vehicle, Mary lowered her voice to speak to Lulu. 'Come to me if you need help. Josiah and I would both welcome you.'

'Sister, I wouldn't wish to live as a village woman when I can be a city wife. You live a simple life in the bush and not experienced the comforts and pleasures of modern living.'

'Yes, but if the comforts and pleasures disappear, you are welcome here.'

'No, I'd never return to such a squalid, dull life.'

'Squalid?'

'Dirty and rundown. Joller says village people live in squalid conditions. He wasn't keen to come here today.'

'Sister, we are poor and live a simple life, but our village is not dirty. You saw how clean my hut is. All the others are the same.'

'Yes, but you have no electricity and modern comforts. I could never live like this again.'

Joller looked at his gold watch and signalled to Lulu.

'We must go now. Joller doesn't like driving after dark. Cows on the road at night destroyed his last car.'

'But you've been here only fifteen minutes. Can't you stay a little longer?'

Lulu shook her head. 'Perhaps we can come again sometime. Francistown isn't too far away.'

'Can you drive here to visit me?'

Joller gave a derisive snort.

'I can't drive. Perhaps Joller will teach me one day.'

Somehow, Mary doubted that would happen. She'd assessed the man in less than a quarter hour and already had concerns. But the ostentatious Joller and his wealth impressed her naïve younger sister. Mary hoped she'd misjudged him, but a niggle worried at the back of her mind.

'If you had electricity and a cell phone, I would call you, but in this desolate place, you have nothing but nosy neighbours. Let me take a photo of you with my phone.' Lulu took a rectangular piece of black shiny plastic from her bag and held it up to Mary, saying, 'Smile now.' Then she stood next to Mary with her arm around her shoulder, and they both smiled at the shiny black plastic.

The images on Lulu's phone stunned Mary. It was magic. Before now, she'd never seen a telephone, let alone a cell phone.

'But you said you needed electricity to make it work? Josiah said the same thing about the white cupboard that keeps food cold.'

'One day, when we have more time, I will explain it to you, Mary. You see why I couldn't live here, now that I'm a modern, city-woman.'

'Perhaps I can visit you in Francistown?'

'You will need a passport to visit me. Otherwise, they won't let you into Botswana.'

'A passport?'

'Yes, get your husband to explain it to you.'

Curious villagers gathered around the impressive vehicle, and both Joller and Lulu preened themselves in front of the admiring group. The excited chatter did little to diminish Mary's concerns. The couple relished the attention they received, and it reminded Mary of the pride she'd felt as the owner of the white cupboard. She remembered the embarrassment she experienced when the police took it away. Once again, she recalled her mother's words, 'Pride comes before a fall.'

Mary didn't want her sister to go through what she'd suffered. As she waved her goodbye, she worried Lulu was going into an unpredictable situation that might end in tears. Joller hadn't made a good impression on her, and she feared for her sister's future.

The Range Rover drove along the dirt road, layering another tint of golden dust on its shiny black body. As Mary watched it growing smaller in the distance, she wondered about this magic thing called electricity. Josiah said it replaced batteries, but Lulu told her it made batteries new again. She claimed the battery in her cell phone only worked if there was electricity. Josiah must have forgotten to tell her about the battery in the white cupboard.

Engineer's fifteen-year-old daughter, Agnes, came up to Mary's side. 'That nice man said he'd give me a job in Francistown.'

'In his menswear shop? What would you do in his shop? Is he looking for a cleaner?'

'I don't know, but he said I was pretty, and his customers would like me.'

'Have you told your father?'

'No, the man said it was a secret between him and me. But if your sister is with him, I'm sure he won't mind me telling you.'

Mary frowned as she studied the small scrap of paper on which Lulu wrote the address of Joller's shop in Francistown. Perhaps, one day, she'd be able to visit her sister there. She carefully folded it and put it in the old Player's cigarette tin, where she kept all her important things. The years removed most of the paint, and the tin showed signs of rust around its hinges, but like its contents, it was one of her treasures.

Lulu's visit was a most exciting event for her. What a pity Josiah wasn't there to share it with her. It caused a stir in the village. Mary possessed a talent for that. The villagers talked for days about the important visitors in the beautiful car that purred like a kitten.

The village women acted a little more friendly towards Mary, and the children became her greatest admirers. They knew nothing about her background, but she certainly made their lives more interesting.

Mary's gossipy, fair-weather friend, Nancy, was losing her poisonous influence over the other women. As her hold over them slipped, and her status waned, Nancy resolved to get rid of Mary once and for all.

CHAPTER 7

The Value of Books

SERGEANT Dube leant back in his chair with his feet on the desk, mulling over recent happenings in the area. He pondered the warning he'd received from Nancy, the village woman. He scoffed at the idea when he repeated her words to his colleagues, but his own brief dealings with Mary Moyo seemed to confirm the woman was different. Was it possible she might have supernatural powers?

Did she not taken revenge on Jackson Mpofu's thugs, directing The Lady to attack them? The lioness satisfied her hunger by killing and eating part of the most aggressive one. He was the gang leader who addressed the village, accusing Mary and her husband, Josiah, of stealing Jackson Mpofu's refrigerator. He threatened to burn down their hut, and who knew what he planned to do to Josiah with the knife he held aloft? His bandaged leg, wounded by the police bullet, made him slow. His companions raced off, leaving him at the mercy of the ravenous beast.

And once Mary finished with the thugs, she used two small village boys to remove the man-eater. No one would forget how she managed that.

* * *

There are certain things best avoided. Antagonising the neighbours is one of them. The nine-year-old rascals, Zenzo and Zamani, were yet to learn that lesson. They caused most of the mischief in the village. It was they who stole the missing chicken and killed and cooked it over a fire behind the ridge. They never imagined a passing villager would discover them eating it.

Then there was the time they rode Mechanic's oversized bicycle. They rolled down the hill, moving faster and faster. They couldn't stop or get off the bicycle as Zenzo's little legs struggled to reach the peddles, and they ended up in the river with a tremendous splash. Fortunately, there was no sign of the infamous crocodile that ate the village head's number one wife, but the bicycle sunk to the bottom. The villagers all stood around arguing about the best way to recover it. In the end, one brave soul agreed to dive to the bottom and bring up the cycle.

One hot afternoon, the boys accompanied two adults going to fetch honey from a wild bees' nest. They watched in fascination as one man climbed the tree and used a small smouldering log to smoke the nest hidden in a hollow of the trunk. The men raided the nest the previous year and didn't need a honeyguide bird to show them the location. The youngsters came back excited and full of chatter about the venture.

Mary had noticed bees buzzing around the old tree behind her hut. 'One day,' she said to the boys, 'you might smoke those bees yourself and get honey.'

But waiting for 'one day' to arrive seems like a lifetime to the youngsters. Soon they hatched a plan, and on a quiet afternoon with the adults otherwise engaged, they pinched a box of matches and prepared a smouldering branch. While Zenzo climbed the tree, Zamani stood guard at the bottom.

Neither of the boys noticed the amber eyes watching their every move. The Lady licked her lips and flattened herself to the ground in the nearby yellow grass.

Zenzo's presence with his ill-prepared smouldering log disturbed the bees. There was insufficient smoke to calm them, and a few bees stung Zenzo. This, together with his youthful impatience and inexperience, sped up the boy's efforts. Zamani stood at the bottom of the tree, calling out encouragement. Nothing stood between him and the man-eater.

The Lady raised herself a little off the ground and moved towards the unaware Zamani. Just as she quickened her pace and readied herself to launch her charge, Zenzo slipped and grabbed at the bees' nest to keep his balance. In doing so, he dislodged a part of the nest and it fell to the ground.

The enraged bees came out of the nest en masse and, attracted by the moving form of the man-eater, launched their attack. The Lady stopped, startled by the stings on her lips, nose, and eyelids, and a moment later she fled with the swarm in pursuit. It was the last reported sighting of The Lady in the area. The villagers claimed she crossed back to Botswana after her brief foray into Zimbabwe.

When their parents admonished the two young rascals for disturbing the bees, they protested their innocence and claimed Mary told them to do it. The villagers interpreted it as her means of ridding the area of the man-eater, and the legend of Mary Moyo grew.

* * *

All this, on top of what Nancy told him, convinced Sergeant Dube that it was dangerous to upset Mary. He released her husband, Josiah, from the jail as a precaution against earning the woman's wrath. But he'd never admit that to anybody. Was he, Sergeant Dube, not an educated man? As an MBA graduate from Loughborough University, he'd lived in England for a time and adopted English ways. He didn't hold with the traditional superstitious beliefs, but then, why tempt fate? How could Mary have the powers attributed to her by the jealous villagers? But he'd known of stranger things. No, he was pragmatic, that's all. Why risk provoking the spirits? Not that any such beings existed.

While Sergeant Dube tried to justify his actions to himself, his release of Josiah only increased Mary's reputation as a witch doctor. The villagers believed she took control of Sergeant Dube's mind and commanded him to release her husband. Many now feared her, but others came to her for help. Mary herself didn't know of her growing reputation because the villagers and others who spoke to her were too afraid to discuss such matters. Even Josiah did not talk to her about it.

Mary found it odd so many people sought her advice. What did she know? She was only a young married woman with little worldly experience. In due course, she realised people saw her as a person with special powers. The thought frightened her. She possessed no powers, but her visitors sat in awed silence when she spoke. Her popularity grew because she gave her advice freely, not expecting payment, though she accepted money or gifts from those she knew could afford it.

A worrying thought gnawed at her. When would the villagers in the area realise her services did not provide any meaningful benefit? Mary didn't yet understand human nature, and she would have worried less if she did. Things have a way of working out. The villagers credited her with the positive results. These included the return of the errant husband; a worker who lost his job, but soon found a better one; the wife who became pregnant after years of trying; a school child who did unexpectedly well in their exams; the mother-in-law trampled by an elephant; and so forth.

Those who didn't get a positive outcome continued in hope, like someone who buys a lottery ticket each week. The reward, like a ripening fruit, required patience. But it would surely come, for had not Mary cast her spell? No one thought to blame her for the delay in achieving their wish.

From the time Mary arrived in the village, a pile of four books stood as a doorstop in her hut. She often dusted off the white ants they attracted. Each season, the books looked older and more worn, even though their covers remained shut. A bulldog clip held together the spine of the most damaged book. Mary could not read or write, and in the village, only her husband, Josiah, boasted that skill. Despite that, Josiah failed in his efforts to read or make sense of those four books. He claimed they contained magic spells that only the spirits or the wisest of the witch doctors might decipher.

One morning, when Josiah was out and no one else was around, Mary wondered if she might possess the power to interpret the books' meaning.

She cautiously opened the cover of the top one in the pile, taking care not to open it too wide in case an evil spirit escaped from between its pages. The small black print was unintelligible to her, and she quickly put the book down, fearing the consequences of her illicit peek under the cover.

Nothing untoward happened after Mary's investigation of the book, and soon she summoned the courage to look at the others, but they were similar. She couldn't make sense of them. But an idea occurred to her; an idea she would come to regret. Mary worked out the power of positive thinking might resolve many of her clients' ills. If they weren't afraid or depressed or angry or jealous, their problems would improve, if not disappear. Perhaps, if she pretended to understand the words in those pages and uttered incomprehensible sounds, her clients' belief in her counsel might strengthen further, and even more people might achieve positive results.

Mary meant well, for she loved helping people. She'd already saved one man who seemed determined to kill himself. But her plan was riddled with hidden dangers not yet plain to her. She'd been inadvertently drawn into the role of a witch doctor, but now she would play a more active part in the charade.

The plan worked like a dream, and her reputation grew. It attracted clients from far and wide, all seeking help with their various problems. Mary would sit on the ground cross-legged with the client seated opposite her. She'd open the book and appear to enter a trans-like state. After a silence of five to ten minutes, she'd utter any strange words that came into her head. It was an impressive, unrehearsed act. In the closing stages of the consultation, Mary would tell the client she'd interceded on their behalf but had no power over the spirits' decision whether to grant their wish. This last step was insurance; an attempt to avoid any blame if her spell did not work.

Soon, news spread about the female witch doctor with magical powers. Mary's clients now included two police officers, a senior civil servant, and an opposition politician. Clients travelled from as far afield as Bulawayo and Plumtree, and one businessman even crossed the border from Francistown in Botswana. Other witch doctors also heard about her, and jealousies festered.

Mary's spreading fame alarmed Josiah, and it caused a few arguments between them. He worried that a disgruntled, powerful client might cause trouble for them. But Mary's confidence grew, and she felt she could handle the problem if it ever arose. After one of their arguments, Josiah walked out into the bush to calm his jangled nerves. When he stubbed his toe on a jagged rock, he cursed, and it did little to improve his mood.

As he ambled along, he thought about things. He admired his wife's initiative and strength of character. Her success in the new venture both frightened and amused him, but he prayed no one would discover she was an ordinary woman; a simple village woman at that.

Josiah smiled at the prospect of his wife helping the villagers in the region. And when he saw important men beating a path to their door, he laughed out loud. He'd forgotten all about their silly argument. He'd go back and tell Mary his love made him cautious for her safety, but he'd always support her. Then, as always, she'd make tea, and they'd sit in front of their hut and watch the sunset, content in each other's company.

A happy and relaxed Josiah turned for home. It was a beautiful balmy evening with a cooling breeze blowing over the veld. The large trees on the edge of Jackson Mpofu's derelict camping site swayed as if bowing to Josiah as he passed. He had his health and a lovely young wife, full of spirit and ideas for their future. Josiah breathed in the fresh air. He felt blessed with a wonderful life. Tomorrow promised so much. As he walked along, admiring the autumn leaves of the trees painted gold by the lowering sun, he didn't notice the puff adder lying in his path.

CHAPTER 8

One Rotten Apple

As Mary prepared dinner, she reflected on how she was happier now than any time since leaving her parent's home. Her loving husband encouraged her enthusiasm and ambition. Though much older and wiser than Mary, he spoke to her as an equal and considered her sometimes naïve comments without derision. But life has a nasty habit of throwing up unexpected challenges.

Mary's husband, Josiah, stumbled into the hut, wide-eyed and ashen. Between bouts of vomiting, in a trembling voice, he related what happened. The villagers gathered in disbelief in front of the hut. Soon, Mechanic raced off on his bicycle to get help in Figtree, a four-hour ride, perhaps more on a dark, rutted, dirt road.

The villagers milled around in a panic. One woman suggested someone bitten by a puff adder should stay still and sit in an upright position. If the victim lay down, the poison would reach the heart much quicker. She also said they needed to put a tight bandage on the lower leg to slow the blood flow. Everyone scattered to find pieces of cloth or rope; anything to help bandage Josiah's lower leg. The intense pain and the effort it took to walk home after the puff adder's bite drained Josiah's strength. The area around the ankle wound swelled, and watery blood oozed from the puncture marks.

Around midnight, Josiah fell asleep in his chair, but Mary stayed awake, dreading what might happen. In the early hours, a shiver ran through her as the eerie cackle of nearby hyenas reached her ears. On most nights, she would be fast asleep and miss the sounds of those evil creatures on their nightly forays hunting some poor animal. Tonight, their whoops, hoots, and cackles seemed to carry a portent of disaster.

Mary's thoughts drifted back to Alias. Everyone knew the story of the unfortunate, disfigured man from a neighbouring village. With his nose and one cheek missing, he terrified the children when he visited Mary's village several weeks earlier. On a hot, drunken night, he slept outside to escape the stifling October heat. Other men joined him. But for Alias, it was a disastrous decision when a passing hyena needed a midnight snack.

In the early morning, just before the first rays of dawn spread its tentacles across the shallow valley, the police Land Rover came into view. Sergeant Dube was at the wheel, accompanied by the anxious Mechanic and his bicycle. When Mechanic arrived at Figtree, the police station was closed, and he spent much of the night trying to track down where Sergeant Dube lived. The frantic Mechanic found Dube's house at almost four in the morning. 'Puff adder bite,' was all Dube needed to hear to get him moving. Speed was of the essence. Dube and Mechanic raced to the police station to collect the Land Rover for the mercy dash to the village.

Mary and the sickening Josiah swapped places with Mechanic and his bicycle, and the loaded vehicle raced off into the brightening dawn. Sergeant Dube determined the nearest help would be in Bulawayo, a two-and-a-half-hour drive from the village. Before heading off, they made a quick stop at the police station to pick up Constable Sibanda. It was pedal to the floor, with Sergeant Dube at the wheel.

Josiah was in extreme pain, and Mary's heart thumped in her chest, making her breaths short and laboured. She willed the old vehicle to move faster, watching the odometer tick over at a glacial rate. The road signs showing the distance to Bulawayo seemed so far apart, and they teased her when they appeared. Fifty kilometres! But didn't the last one show fifty? Mary's state of mind made it difficult for her to keep track, and the closer they got to their destination, the slower their progress seemed.

The streets of Bulawayo were already busy at seven-thirty in the morning. And when the Land Rover pulled into the grounds of Mpilo Hospital, it was almost eight. The medical staff rushed to help Josiah while a doctor hurried to search for the antivenom for a puff adder bite. Several minutes later, he returned with the news that nothing was available other than three vials eighteen months past their use-by date. 'There's no money for medicines these days. We'll use these vials,' he said, 'but try to find a vet in the wealthier eastern suburbs. One of them might have a few current doses, though I doubt it.'

The hospital admitted Josiah while Sergeant Dube and Constable Sibanda sped off in search of a vet. Mary sat next to Josiah's chair in the emergency ward, talking to her husband and afraid to leave his side.

Half an hour later, Sergeant Dube raced in with four vials of antivenom, and the doctor inserted a fresh intravenous drip into Josiah's arm. It would be an anxious wait for Mary and the two police officers. Josiah appeared brighter, but at other times he looked defeated. Mary hoped and prayed, but at five o'clock that evening, the doctor pronounced Josiah dead.

A slow, creeping horror flooded Mary, together with a hollow loneliness she'd never known. Her eyes filled with tears, and her temples felt crushed in a vice. Her throat felt raw, and her speech was little more than a hoarse whisper. The hospital brought in a body bag for Josiah's trip home to the village. Mary wanted to ask questions. How did they know he was dead? Perhaps he was just unconscious. Could they try to revive him? The busy, understaffed medics didn't have time to discuss the situation. A constant stream of injured and sick people came into the hospital, and Mary and her party needed to leave.

Mary long dreamed of visiting the wonderful city of Bulawayo, but though she drove through the city streets twice on that fateful day, she paid scant notice to her surroundings. She completed the return trip in a trans-like state; not noticing the passing scenery or the setting sun. All too soon, she was home. Mary walked into her empty cold hut, and a wave of loneliness washed over her. She asked the two police officers to put Josiah's body on his bed, where she found his presence somehow comforting.

The villagers greeted her with sympathy. Not only had she lost her husband, but they had lost their village head. As Mary was Josiah's only close relative present, the villagers took over the preparations for his funeral. Josiah often said he wanted a simple Christian funeral, free from the traditional tribal rituals.

The men wasted no time the next morning, digging a deep grave for Josiah at the foot of the ridge that ran between the village and Jackson Mpofu's camping site. In better times, the village women would prepare food for the mourners at the funeral, but they struggled to feed themselves, so they'd forgo that luxury. The multi-talented Mechanic made a coffin for Josiah from old timber boards he scraped together, and the old men of the village volunteered to act as pallbearers.

Two days later was Saturday, and Sergeant Dube and Constable Sibanda brought the local priest for the burial service, which all the villagers attended. Mary's reputation was widespread, and people from neighbouring villages came to pay their respects. Josiah's sons from his first marriage did not attend, as nobody knew how to contact them in South Africa. Josiah's uncle, his only other close relative, died earlier in the year, and none of the distant relatives or guests at Mary's wedding came.

That afternoon, after the funeral, the skies darkened, and huge thunderclouds formed. The first heavy rain of the season arrived, reflecting Mary's sombre mood. From her open doorway, she watched the lashing rain. Fast-flowing rivulets carved narrow channels into the dry earth in front of her hut. It seemed to Mary those rivulets washed away the cosy life she'd shared with her husband. She walked through her front door and stood in the pouring rain, letting her tears join the flow.

How would her life change? In normal circumstances, a deceased husband's family would support the widowed wife, but Josiah's only immediate family were his progressive sons who didn't hold with the old ways and customs. Mary needed time to think. She'd try to carry on as normal, but she realised nothing would be the same.

* * *

Mary wiped the tears from the corners of her eyes. It was three months since she buried her husband, but the pain of his passing was still raw. Josiah was her rock. He was caring and tolerant of his young wife's mistakes and shortcomings. Josiah encouraged her youthful enthusiasm and provided gentle guidance whenever he saw that her eagerness took her down the wrong path. Perhaps, if he'd not been so indulgent, she'd be more independent and less in need of his validation.

Each day dragged, and Mary struggled for the motivation to keep going. It was odd then, looking back, how the months following her husband's death seemed to have passed so fast. Whenever her thoughts dwelt on Josiah, a lump rose in her throat, and the pressure built in her temples and behind her eyes. But that happened less and less often now.

Mary was ready to restart her business, and soon, the constant demand of her clients from the neighbouring villages, and from further afield, kept her busy. Her reputation as a woman with magical powers grew in the area, and her fellow villagers at last accepted and admired her. Even the jealous Nancy came around, though Mary did not forget how quickly the woman's friendship evaporated when the police confiscated her white cupboard.

* * *

Everyone knew of Mary's magic book, the one only she could read. If no others could read the book, who would question her interpretation of it?

Today, an important visitor was coming to visit Mary to seek her help. Dennis Nyathi was a popular figure in the area and planned to stand in the next election. He described himself as an Mthwakazian; a person who favoured separating Matabeleland and the western Midlands from

Zimbabwe. Unlike many other Mthwakazian political aspirants, his ambitions were not for personal gain or power, but for the people he hoped to serve. Nyathi possessed a charismatic personality and a powerful oratory that excited the people.

Word of Nyathi's visit got around, and singing and dancing villagers greeted his arrival. They jostled each other, trying to touch him as he walked from his Toyota Prado to Mary's hut. There was no doubt where their support lay. The elections weren't due for over three years, but political tensions in the country rose as the Lacoste and G40 factions in Mashonaland struggled for ascendancy in the governing ZANU-PF party. Together with the MDC opposition party, it was looking like a three-way contest. Until Dennis Nyathi's emergence, none of the splintered Mthwakazi hopefuls looked like presenting any political threat.

Nyathi was a tall, handsome man with an athletic build. The pleasant timbre in his voice kept his audiences mesmerised, and his bright intelligent eyes drew people to him.

Mary welcomed Nyathi and offered him a glass of calming water before she began her routine of humming and muttering incomprehensible words over the book that lay open in front of her. Then, after several minutes of silence, she asked Nyathi about the purpose of his visit.

'I am hoping to contest the next parliamentary election, three years from now. I'm pleased with my progress and the support I receive, but I have powerful enemies, and between now and the election, much can go wrong. Can you make the bones point me on a favourable path to the next election?'

'I hear you want to serve the people. If that's true, I'll ask the spirits to guide you to the election. They will help you if they believe you are true to your word. But if you fail them and betray your promises, your dreams will turn to dust and blow in the wind. I cannot guarantee their support. Only you know your heart, so you, more than anyone, will determine the success or failure of your request to the spirits.'

Mary turned to another page in her book and spoke to the spirits in her incomprehensible tongue. A few minutes later, she said, 'It is done. The spirits have received your request and will consider it. They will watch your actions and listen to your words.'

'Thank you, Mary. Your answers please me. Can I pay you for your services?'

'There is no need. Serve the people! That will be payment enough.'

As Nyathi walked to the door of her hut to leave, he put down two hundred US dollars on the nearby table. Mary had never seen so much money in her entire life. Apart from losing Josiah, everything was going so well.

* * *

Early the next afternoon, as Mary sat mending a tear in her dress, a black four-wheel drive skidded to a halt in a cloud of dust in front of her hut. The driver jumped out and strode to her door. It was Jackson Mpofu. Three of his thugs made a theatrical display of standing guard beside the vehicle.

Mpofu walked into Mary's hut without knocking. He stood in front of her with his clenched fists on his hips. 'I'm told you are helping Dennis Nyathi with his election plans?'

'How can I help him with his election plans?'

'You have interceded on his behalf with the spirits.'

Mary didn't understand the big word, but guessed its meaning. 'The spirits will decide whether to help Nyathi.'

Mpofu's eyes blazed, and the gap between his eyebrows narrowed. 'Don't give me that mumbo jumbo! It's not the spirits who are helping him; it's you.'

'If you don't believe in the spirits, why are you so angry?'

'You have two days to withdraw your help from Nyathi. Call him back here and ask the spirits to cancel his request. If you don't, it'll be you who needs the help of the spirits.'

'How did you hear Dennis Nyathi came to see me?'

'I have eyes everywhere. Do you think you can work against me in my district?'

'Did someone from this village tell you?'

Mpofu's angry face turned into a smirk. 'I have eyes everywhere. Of course, someone from this village told me. The villagers love me and tell me everything that happens. Remember, you have just two days.' Mpofu stormed out of the hut, slamming the door behind him.

The tyres of the four-wheel drive spun, creating an enormous cloud of dust as Mpofu sped away, careless of any villagers or children in the immediate area.

Mary knew the villagers did not love Jackson Mpofu, but one rotten apple can spoil a barrel, and it wasn't difficult to guess who that jealous, rotten apple might be.

CHAPTER 9

A Fork on the Road

AFTER Jackson Mpofu's visit, Mary spent a sleepless night. Mpofu's threats were seldom idle. Mary had every reason to fear the ruthless, manipulating bully and his violent reputation.

What could she do? She'd no means of contacting Dennis Nyathi in time, even if she wanted. She needed to do something, but what?

There was only one thing for it. Next morning, she tidied her hut and gathered a few of her most precious possessions, including her magic book, and put them into a small suitcase.

The day passed slowly as she waited for the opportunity to speak to Mechanic alone. In the late afternoon, she found him washing his bicycle by the river. 'Mechanic, I want to talk to you about something most important. You must promise me you'll tell no one what I'm about to tell you until after I've gone.'

'Gone, Mary! Gone where?'

'The spirits have summoned me, and I must go to them. Tomorrow morning, while it's still dark, I will be on my way.'

'But where are you going to, Mary? Will you be back tomorrow night?'

'I don't know where I'm going or how I'll travel. The spirits will guide me once I start my journey, and they'll tell me when I can return.'

'Can I give you a lift on my bicycle?'

'Give me a lift to where, Mechanic? If you are with me, the spirits will not guide me. You must stay here and explain to the others the spirits have called me. Now listen carefully…'

* * *

Mary faced a second sleepless night, tossing and turning. Was she doing the right thing? Now, she would be all alone without family, friends, or neighbours. She needed to get beyond Jackson Mpofu's reach, but she was leaving her village where many admired her. Soon she'd be an anonymous face in the outside world.

At four in the morning, Mary rose, ate a cold mealie cob, and drank a little water. Outside, the darkness greeted her with a chilling breeze blowing across the shallow valley. She locked the door to her hut, remembering the day twelve months ago when Mechanic installed the Yale lock Josiah brought back from Bulawayo. Mary dropped the key into her purse, took a deep breath, and turned to gaze into the darkness that concealed both the valley and her future.

As Mary set out on her journey, she noticed Mechanic standing in the doorway of his hut. Neither spoke, though Mechanic raised his hand to shoulder-level in a single wave of recognition.

Mary's eyes soon adjusted to the dark as she walked down the slope leading into the shallow valley where the road swung left and disappeared into the forest. The distant whoop of hyenas on the hunt focussed her attention. She'd not considered the risk of walking at night through the African bush. But the hyenas called behind her, and she took comfort that she walked in the opposite direction.

Now alert to the potential dangers she faced, she imagined every knock, crackle or thump in the bush presented a threat to her safety. Perhaps it would have been wiser to wait until daybreak before setting out. But then, she would have left under the gaze of her neighbours, some of whom would no doubt link her departure with Jackson Mpofu's angry visit.

The adrenalin flowing through Mary's body helped her keep up a good pace, and before long, she entered the dark wooded area on the southern edge of the shallow valley. It was still an hour until sunrise.

Mary realised the walk to Figtree might mean two nights on the road. She hoped to spend one night in a village on the road to Marula. But she'd not planned where she'd spend the second night.

The walk through the forest passed quicker than Mary expected, and bright sunlight greeted her as she emerged from the gloom. Soon, she saw the turnoff to Jackson Mpofu's farm on the left. Now she entered the extensive area of long grass and scrubby thorn bushes that bordered the road for miles. The road's rough surface made walking harder, and the ruts made from tyre tracks in the rain presented a tripping obstacle that slowed her progress.

So far, despite her nervousness, the walk was pleasant. But as the sun rose higher in the sky, the late morning heat took its toll. Mary glistened with sweat, and she slowed her pace so as not to soak her clothes any further.

To her relief, no cars passed in either direction. She didn't want to run into Jackson Mpofu and his men. She intended to dash into the long grass if she heard an approaching vehicle. Any vehicle approaching from behind would come from Jackson's farm. A car coming from her front could be anybody, but likely a visitor to the farm.

Buzzing flies troubled Mary in the intense early afternoon heat. She'd never liked those creatures near her face, though many piccanins didn't seem to mind flies sitting on their lips or the corners of their eyes.

The long, lonely walk sent Mary into a dwaal (daze), a mindless lack of concentration where she became oblivious to the distance she'd travelled and even to the heat of the day. As the early evening took the sting out of the sun, Mary's thoughts flooded back into consciousness. Now, where were those villages? Had she passed them on her walk, or did they still lie ahead? Josiah told her where the villages were, but she'd never visited them. She needed to rely on landmarks, but she'd not been concentrating through the scorching afternoon. Now she was confused as the evening shadows lengthened. She remembered Josiah telling her you could not see the villages from the road.

Darkness falls early in this part of Africa, and Mary struggled with the road's potholes and ruts. An entire night in the open bush was a daunting prospect. A sudden rustle in the grass to her right startled her. Was it her imagination? Perhaps a gust of wind? She stopped to listen. Total silence. When she walked on, the rustle in the grass seemed to move with her. She stopped again to listen, but apart from the distant calls of hyenas, there was silence.

Mary stepped out a little faster, hoping not to trip in the darkness. Again, that rustle moved with her. A rising sense of panic set her heart pounding in her chest. The hairs on the back of her neck bristled. Any creature following her must be a predator. Mary's pre-dawn fears returned with a vengeance. This wasn't how her story was supposed to end. She held hopes and ambitions and never imagined herself ending up as a meal for a hungry beast. She pictured hyenas and ants cleaning up her remains. It was too much to contemplate.

A blinding beam of light pierced the dark night, stopping Mary in her tracks. 'Mary, is that you? What on earth are you doing here?' Sergeant Dube's voice boomed in the darkness.

Relief flooded Mary like the warmth of the rising sun. The welcome blaze of the police van's floodlight once more brightened her prospects of survival.

'Mary, you shouldn't be out alone at night, especially here.'

'Why are you here, Sergeant Dube?'

'A man in a village near here attacked his wife with a hoe. After he killed her, he started attacking others. The villagers chased him into the bush but lost him. So now we are looking for him before he kills someone else. They say he has gone mad.'

'When I walked along the road, something followed me.'

'That might have been him. It's lucky we're here, or you might have been his next victim.'

Sergeant Dube swung the Land Rover's searchlight over the swaying grass and thorn bushes, casting ghostly dancing shadows across the dark bush. Constable Sibanda stood on the roof of the vehicle's cab, straining his eyes for any sign of movement in the bush.

'We won't find him tonight, Sibanda. Warn the village men to be alert. We'll return in the morning and find him then.' Sergeant Dube turned to Mary. 'Can we give you a lift back to your village? It's a long way to walk.'

'No, I must go to Figtree to catch the bus to Bulawayo.'

'Where are you spending the night, Mary?'

'I don't know. I'll wait near the bus stop.'

'You can sleep at the police station tonight. The Plumtree to Bulawayo bus passes through Figtree at about eight in the morning.'

At the police station, Sergeant Dube said, 'Mary, we must lock you in a spare cell for the night. Sibanda will be in early to release you in time for your bus. Sibanda, don't forget to let her out by seven o'clock before the others arrive.'

Mary remained alone in the darkened police station after Sergeant Dube and Constable Sibanda left. She wondered how many others had slept in the cell, awaiting their uncertain future in the eerie environment. Whilst not a prisoner, Mary worried fate might pass judgement and sentence her the next day.

* * *

It was almost a week before Jackson Mpofu and his thugs returned to Mary's village. As before, the sound of the black four-wheel drive skidding to a halt, and the slamming of doors, announced their arrival. Mpofu strode to the door of Mary's hut and rattled it. 'It's locked! Where is the damned woman?'

'She's gone, Sir.'

Mpofu swung around to glare at the speaker.

Mechanic stepped out of the shadow of his hut's doorway. 'The spirits have called her to meet with them.'

'Rubbish! The spirits wouldn't waste their time with her.' Mpofu turned to his thugs. 'Break down the door! We'll see what this false witch keeps in there?'

'Wait!' Mechanic shouted. 'Mary has left a spirit in there. She said it would be dangerous for the person who released it.'

'Nonsense! How could she lock a spirit inside her hut?'

'It's true, Sir. She said if we listened, we would hear it moving around in there. We have all heard it and moaning sounds too. Ask anyone here.'

'Then we'll burn down her hut.'

'The thatch will burn, and the spirit will escape. Do you want to risk that, Sir?'

'When will she return?'

'She said the spirits will decide.'

'I'll put an end to this false prophet. I'll go to Plumtree to see the Great Sangoma (witch doctor) and ask him to expose this pretender who has you under her spell.'

Jackson Mpofu jumped back into his car, giving little time for his henchmen to board. He revved the engine and jammed his foot on the accelerator, almost losing control at the bottom of the slope that marked the edge of the village.

The village dogs barked in alarm, and the piccanins shouted with excitement. It was always a tense time when the local member visited the village. Mechanic thought it well Mary was not present, though he believed she would have handled the angry politician. But Jackson Mpofu was a terrifying prospect when he gave in to his notorious temper.

* * *

Word soon spread that Jackson Mpofu was to meet the Great Sangoma on the following Sunday. Any audience with the Great Sangoma was big news. The population from the surrounding area would flock to the Great Sangoma's village to watch the happenings and gossip about the meeting's purpose and speculate on the outcome.

Jackson Mpofu, dressed in his best three-piece suit and driving his shiny black Land Cruiser, watched the people heading towards the Great Sangoma's village. What surprised him were the huge numbers, forcing him to drive at a crawl. He thought it unusual so many people congregated. But then, it wasn't often an important member of parliament met the Great Sangoma. Jackson thought it was a sign of his importance and the high regard people held for him.

'I shall speak to the people after my meeting with the Great Sangoma,' said Mpofu to his accompanying henchman. 'They will expect me to make a speech. I'll tell them of my plans for a new school and medical clinic at my farm. And I'll also tell them about the government's plans to secure a reliable water supply from the Zambezi. They'll also be interested in my efforts, on their behalf, to access food aid donated by overseas countries.'

'Isn't that what you told them before the last election, Sir?'

Mpofu scowled into the rear-view mirror at the speaker in the back seat. The man shrank back, trying to make himself inconspicuous; too late, now that he'd blurted out his thoughts. The man prayed Mpofu's audience with the Great Sangoma went well. Then he'd be in a good mood and might overlook the careless comment.

As they drove past a group, Mpofu couldn't resist the opportunity to take political advantage of the situation. He rolled down the window and called out to a group of walkers dressed in their Sunday best. 'I never expected so many would celebrate my visit to the Great Sangoma.'

'We are walking to the funeral, Sir.' said a member of the group.

'Funeral! What funeral?'

'The Great Sangoma has died, Sir.'

Jackson Mpofu slammed on the brakes of his Land Cruiser. 'What! When? No one told me.'

'He died during the week, Sir. He went to sleep one night and didn't wake up the next morning.'

Mpofu did a three-point turn on the dusty road and threaded his way through the oncoming throng.

'Shouldn't we attend the funeral, Sir?' said a voice from the back seat.

'I'm a member of parliament. I don't have time to waste on trivial matters.'

'Perhaps Mary's magic was more powerful than his. She'll be the new Great Sangoma.' The man who spoke sat directly behind Mpofu, and that spared him the scowl that intimidated the last man who offered his unwelcome thoughts.

'Rubbish! Rubbish! Mary will never be the Great Sangoma. And don't you go spreading silly rumours about her magic powers!'

They made the rest of the trip back to Mpofu's farm in silence, but an uncomfortable feeling gnawed at Jackson's stomach. Mary's reputation would be even greater now.

CHAPTER 10

A New Dawn

ALTHOUGH late summer, it was a chilly night, with only a single blanket in the bare cell at Figtree's police station. Mary stirred and stretched her stiff joints after a night on the hard, unforgiving bed.

Back in her village, she would wake to the early morning chirrups, tweets, and whistles of the feathered chorus. The fire's crackle and spit, and the sound of water boiling in the communal kitchen, would add timpani to the morning orchestra, while the squeaking of the neighbours' door hinges filled in for the string section. The otherwise all-pervasive silence of the bushveld amplified the morning sounds, creating an effective wake-up alarm.

Muffled voices of the early risers would entice Mary from her bed to make her morning cup of tea. If sugar was available, the tea would be sweet and black, but that happened less often these days. Even the tea leaves needed frugal care and rationing.

But today was different. The jingling of keys in the cell door woke Mary. The unfamiliar sounds of a whistling kettle and a throbbing generator behind the building caught her attention. It was a sobering reminder of the significant step she was taking.

Constable Sibanda's appearance, with a steaming mug of hot, sweet, milky tea and two thick slices of bread covered with jam, cheered her. Perhaps this strange world mightn't be too bad. There was even a bathroom where she could shower with warm water.

As she emerged from the bathroom, Sergeant Dube greeted her with his cheerful smile.

'The bus will arrive in half an hour, Mary. Get your things together. Are you ready to go?'

'You said you wouldn't be in today, Sergeant Dube?'

'I couldn't let you leave without saying goodbye. When will you return?'

'I don't know. The spirits will guide me.'

Though an educated man, Sergeant Dube did not doubt the spirits guided her. Everyone knew of her magical powers.

The pair chatted at the bus stop as they waited for the bus. In the distance, the large vehicle appeared, looking somewhat crab-like, approaching at an angle that proclaimed the state of the chassis. The enormous load of the passengers' possession on the roof made the bus appear wider and half as tall again.

Mary wrinkled her nose at the pungent smell of diesel as the bus stopped in front of them, with a cloud of black smoke enveloping her and the Sergeant. The sight of the bus alarmed Mary. The monstrous machine rattled and shook like an angry buffalo, and she hesitated to board it.

'Don't worry,' said Sergeant Dube. 'The bus will get you safely to Bulawayo. It has always looked a wreck. Don't forget, if you need anything, just phone the police station and ask for me.'

Mary thanked the Sergeant and heaved herself up the steps to face the bus driver. She paid the fare and looked down the aisle for a vacant seat. The bus was full. A woman sitting near the front whispered to a little boy next to her. The boy rose and motioned towards his vacated seat. Mary thanked him and sat down, placing her small suitcase in front of her legs. The little boy sat down in the aisle next to her.

'Your first bus trip?' the woman asked.

'Yes, how did you know?'

'Your face told me. You looked worried.'

'Yes, I've only been to Bulawayo in a police van. Not on the bus.'

'You don't look like a policewoman. Were they taking you to the court?'

'No, they took my husband and me to Mpilo Hospital to treat my husband's snake bite, but he died.'

'Oh, sorry! Do you have family or friends in Bulawayo?'

'No.'

'What will you do there?'

Mary shrugged.

'Will you look for work?'

'Work?'

'Yes, my daughter works as a housemaid in Bulawayo. It's a good job but hard to find. She has her own room and bathroom on the property, gets free food and money.'

'What work must she do for that?'

'She cleans the house, looks after the children, and sometimes cooks. When I last spoke to her, she said the neighbour needed a new servant. Can you cook and clean?'

'Oh, yes.'

'I will give you her address. If you go to see her, she might help you. But you better be quick. Everybody wants such work.'

Mary settled back in silence, watching the scenery race past the window. To her, the ponderous old bus seemed to move at an incredible speed, rattling or shuddering, depending on the incline or condition of the road surface. A woman sitting across the aisle from her held two frightened chickens in a crude basket on her lap. Further back on the bus, a goat bleated, and one passenger coughed incessantly.

Mary found the crowded bus an uncomfortable experience. Accustomed to the open spaces of a remote country life, she took an instant dislike of the stuffy confines. At least she was near the open door of the bus. She pitied those stuffed in the back. Josiah made this trip often, but never once complained about it.

The friendly woman next to Mary must have guessed her thoughts. 'Many passengers are returning from Botswana with goods they have bought to resell in Zimbabwe. That's how the unemployed survive the shortages. The government does not encourage it because they say this way of trading is causing our supply of US dollars to leave the country. They want to keep the US dollars for themselves so the bigwigs can get their regular supply of luxury cars.'

Mary understood this. Jackson Mpofu always seemed to have a brand-new car, alternating between black and silver.

As the bus neared Bulawayo, an occasional house appeared, and then another and another. The open country transformed first into outer suburbs and then abandoned factories and more impressive suburbs closer to the city. Mary didn't recall them from the trip to Mpilo Hospital with Josiah. That traumatic experience, and her concern for her husband, made that visit to Bulawayo a blur.

Mary's fellow passenger interrupted her thoughts again. 'This bus will stop at the station. Many passengers will catch a train to their home, and others will stay on the bus. You should get off at the station and walk back along Thirteenth Avenue and turn right onto Robert Mugabe Way. Make sure you keep left and go down Hillside Road until you see the big Mater Dei Hospital. My daughter lives near the hospital. Her name is Frida. She won't be there today, so go tomorrow as soon as you can.'

When the bus stopped in the station carpark, the passengers scrambled to alight and retrieve their belongings from the roof before someone else did. Mary thanked her travelling companion for her advice, grabbed her small suitcase, and climbed down from the bus. She stood overawed by the milling crowd and the surrounding buildings.

After taking in the scene, Mary walked the short distance to Thirteenth Avenue and turned right. She marvelled at the shops along the first block, more for their numbers than their decrepit state. Not even Figtree could match this. On the opposite side of the road stood half a dozen tall, grey, circular buildings that didn't appear to have windows or entrances. She was unaware these were the cooling towers of the power station that supplied that magic called electricity.

Further along Thirteenth Avenue, the newer buildings and surroundings entranced her. She needed to watch out for scurrying pedestrians, bicycles, and cars on the busy streets. Mary needed all her concentration to dodge the fast-moving traffic and found the hooting of impatient drivers intimidating.

Soon, she was thirsty and looked for somewhere to get a drink. She was reluctant to stop someone to ask for help, but what else could she do? A pleasant-looking old African man directed her to a nearby cafe where he said she could buy a cup of tea. Mary hesitated to enter the premises and watched what others did. She summoned the courage to walk up to the counter and ask for tea. The woman behind the counter wanted money, and Mary offered her a note.

The woman frowned with impatience. 'Haven't you got change?' Mary remembered the coins she received from the bus driver in return for her paper money. She offered them to the woman, who took what she needed, leaving several coins in Mary's palm. Mary carried her tea to a vacant table near the cafe entrance. She sat down in a chair and placed her suitcase at her feet.

Everything fascinated Mary. In her village, Mechanic's bicycle gave him status, but here, so many people rode them. And so many cars! People everywhere, but none of them greeted or acknowledged her. How strange!

Just as she finished her tea, a man leant through the doorway and grabbed the handle of her suitcase. In a flash, Mary jumped up, struggling to gain a grip on the case. The man tugged hard, trying to free it from her grasp. Mary felt her grip slipping, but suddenly the handle broke loose. The man dropped it in disgust and fled along the pavement before turning into an alleyway. Nobody reacted or seemed to notice what happened.

This was Mary's lesson number one of life in the city. It took her a few minutes to steady her shaking hands. She retrieved the handle and put it inside the case. But now, carrying the case was awkward, and soon it felt twice as heavy.

Frequent stops to rest and enjoy the passing scene ate away the day, and Mary made little progress. When she arrived at Robert Mugabe Way, she turned right, but after only two blocks, the city buildings ended. Already mid-afternoon, Mary stayed in the city to explore the immediate area. Tomorrow, she'd find the house near the hospital. She needn't hurry, as Frida's mother said her daughter wouldn't be back from leave until the next day.

Mary made a slow reconnoitre of the area between Fifteenth and Twelfth avenues and bounded by Robert Mugabe Way (Grey Street) and Samuel Parirenyatwa Street (Borrow Street). By early evening, she'd identified somewhere to spend the night. This was a relatively quiet part of the city matrix and ideal for sleeping rough. The evening rush hour provided her with much entertainment, watching the folk all heading home after a day in the city. Soon dusk fell, but she would bide her time before settling in for the night at her chosen refuge.

Earlier, on her reconnoitre, Mary observed a staircase in the entrance to an apartment block. The alcove below the staircase was an ideal spot for her to spend the night, hidden from view of the building's residents or passers-by. In the alcove stood a low wooden door, which aroused her curiosity. She turned the doorknob. It was unlocked. When she opened it, she saw several small, black, metal boxes with glass fronts and rows of complicated looking white, bone-like items on the wall. She'd no idea it was the apartments' power board. There was insufficient room for her to enter, but enough space for her suitcase. To protect her possessions, she would sleep, propped against the door.

In the excitement, Mary didn't think of food. She'd not eaten lunch or dinner, and now her stomach rumbled. Confident her suitcase was safe in the cupboard below the staircase, she went in search of food. She remembered the cafe nearby on Thirteenth Avenue and headed off to find it.

The poorly lit avenues made her wonder if any danger lurked in the city at night. The area comprised houses in darkness and unlit apartments. As she walked along the street, she saw four or five women standing on the pavement in the block ahead of her. Mary took it as a sign it was safe for her to walk in the area. But as she came nearer to the women, they started shouting, 'Go away! There are too many of us here! Find somewhere else!' Mary slowed her approach, then one woman hurled a rock in her direction, and the others followed her lead. Mary hurried to retrace her steps, spurred on by the shouted insults of the women. What odd behaviour, she thought. Dinner tonight looked like a forlorn hope.

When she reached the apartment block, she found the wrought iron doors to the entrance locked. She'd not even noticed them before now. The bars extended from floor to ceiling, with no obvious way into the premises. After hanging about the apartment block entrance for over an hour, hoping someone would pass through the wrought iron doors, Mary retreated to her second choice for a place to spend the night. It was behind the ground floor staircase of a large apartment block around the corner on Robert Mugabe Way.

Sleep eluded her as she struggled to relax. She worried about her suitcase and when she might get it back. What if someone else found it? What if the wrought iron doors stayed shut? She needed to find Frida as soon as possible to ask about the job. Frida's mother told her to be quick. 'Everybody wants such work.'

Mary stirred at the sound of early morning traffic. It created a hum that, at first, she struggled to identify. How strange this place, with its unfamiliar sounds and smells. Mary took a deep breath. The air wasn't as sweet as in her village, even with its smoke from the communal kitchen's fire. Her suitcase! Mary jumped up and hurried around the corner to the apartment block with the large wrought iron doors. They were open.

No one was around. When did the doors open? Mary held her breath as she opened the low door beneath the staircase. There it stood. The spirits looked after her once more. Mary tucked the suitcase under her arm and turned to leave the building. She jumped when a firm hand seized her arm.

'Did you steal that suitcase?' the gruff voice asked.

The big security guard towered over her.

'It's mine, my suitcase. You're hurting my arm.'

'What's this?' The man snatched the case from Mary's grasp and turned the contents onto the floor. He searched through her few belongings and studied the book for a moment. 'What have you got in your bag?' He snatched her bag from her shoulder and opened it, going straight to the small purse. 'Aha! You have a lot of money.'

'I need that. It's all I have.'

'I'm not a greedy man. Fifty dollars is a fair price to let you go.'

'No, I don't have a job. I need the money.'

'Well, you can give me fifty dollars for trespassing on these premises or I'll call the police, who will fine you double. Which do you prefer?'

Mary had no choice. 'OK, take fifty. I must go to find a job.'

'Hah! Village women like you have no chance of finding a job in the city. Even skilled people are unemployed. But if you come back to see me tonight, I'll have a special job waiting for you.'

'No, you'll not see me tonight,' said Mary, hurrying down the steps to the pavement.

'We'll see.'

As she increased her pace to get away from the man, he called after her, 'Good luck. See you tonight.'

Mary didn't turn to look back.

CHAPTER 11

A Strange New World

THE helpful woman on the bus told Mary to contact her daughter early because jobs were scarce. Mary thought about breakfast. Perhaps she could buy it on the way. So she set out to find Frida before someone else took the job.

Mary struggled to remember the woman's words. Oh, yes! Walk south along Robert Mugabe Way. The road forks near the garage (service station) on the right. Stay left and walk along Hillside Road as far as the big Mater Dei Hospital. You'll see it on the left. It all sounded simple enough, and it was a beautiful morning for a walk.

After a short distance, Mary transferred the suitcase from under her right arm to her left. She wished the handle was back on the suitcase. When she married Josiah and left home, her parents gave her the old cardboard suitcase, lined with an imitation leather veneer, peeling in patches. She treasured it, ensuring it never sat on the ground where the white ants could attack it. That was one valuable lesson she learnt from the mysterious, disintegrating books in her hut.

'Can I carry that case for you, Sister?' a young man walking behind her asked.

'No, thank you.' Mary was cautious after her experience the previous day when the man at the cafe tried to snatch it.

'Where are you going?'

'To the Mater Dei Hospital.'

'You are on the wrong path. This goes to the Matopos Road. Cross over to the Hillside Road at the zebra crossing just before the garage. I will show you.'

At the crossing, she thanked the young man before he went on his way. The rush hour traffic worried her, and despite what the young man told her, she didn't believe the vehicles would stop when she stepped out onto the road.

Mary stood, waiting for a gap in the traffic, but none seemed wide enough to risk a crossing. But then, a car stopped, and the driver waved her through with short impatient gestures. She passed in front of the car, but another car in the inside lane whizzed past, missing her by a few inches. Mary scurried back to the roadside. The driver in the stationary car hooted and threw up his hands in disgust and drove off, revving the car engine and shaking his head.

As she reached the side of the road, two men passed her and walked across it, chatting and paying scant attention to the cars that stopped for them. Mary made to follow, but the traffic moved again. This wasn't proving as simple as her travelling companion on the bus suggested.

After several failed attempts to cross, Mary moved from the road's edge and stood in the shade of a small tree. Life in the city was complicated. What should she do now? How long would the traffic continue? A small group of women came walking down the road and slowed as they approached the zebra crossing. It looked like they intended to cross. Mary didn't want to miss this opportunity and attached herself to the group. Within a minute, they reached the other side.

At last, on Hillside Road, Mary headed out of the town centre. She walked past The Academy of Music and the Trade Fair grounds. Hunger pangs gnawed at her. She'd missed dinner the night before, and breakfast. An elderly woman walked in her direction, and Mary took a deep breath before stopping her to ask where she could buy something to eat.

'Just across the road in the Food Lover's Market. You can buy anything you want there at Pick n Pay.'

Mary looked across at the small shopping complex in a garden setting. She was tempted, but although the traffic thinned, she couldn't face crossing the road again. She thanked the elderly lady, who then added, 'You might also try the Bradfield shops a little farther down on the left.'

A row of vendors' stalls stood in front of the Bradfield shops. Most sold items of clothing, but one woman sat behind an enamel bowl filled with bananas. Mary bought one and ate it on the spot, in case she wanted another. The vendor asked her where she was headed.

'I'm going to the hospital.'

'Are you sick?'

'No, I'm visiting someone who lives near there.'

'Oh, visiting a friend?'

'No, someone who will help me find a job.'

'A job! Hah! There are no jobs in Zimbabwe.'

The vendor shouted to the others. 'This girl is looking for a job.' All the women burst out laughing. 'I tell you, my child, the best thing you can do is become a vendor like us. I was an experienced housemaid, and my madam even bought me a car to do the grocery shopping. When my madam left for South Africa, she gave me good references. I knocked on every door in Bulawayo, but no one wanted me. So, now I do this. If you can't find a job, come back and I'll help you set up a stand like mine.'

'Wouldn't I need money for that?'

'Oh, yes. My madam gave me one thousand US dollars when she left.'

'I only have one hundred and thirty dollars.'

'Ah, that is unfortunate. It will not be enough. Visit me and let me know what you are doing. My son runs a business that is always looking for pretty young girls like you. If you are desperate, maybe he can help.'

Mary walked on, and soon the large grey building with a white cross came into view. That was the building and sign the lady on the bus mentioned. Still only mid-morning, Mary pressed on to look for Frida. She turned left into Burns Drive and walked four blocks before turning left again. This was the street, but which house?

The lovely old trees, edging the road, almost touched in the middle. As she walked down the road, the houses and gardens looked even more beautiful. Many properties didn't have numbers, and Mary walked around, searching for the house where Frida worked. It was puzzling. A few houses had numbers, and sometimes the neighbouring house skipped a number. She found one missing number across the road. How would she ever find Frida's address?

'Can I help you, Sister?'

Mary hadn't noticed the African woman standing amongst the trees bordering the garden of one house. 'Er, yes. I'm looking for Frida. She works as a maid in one of these houses.'

'I'm Frida. You must be Mary? My mother told me about you.' Frida was a pleasant-looking woman about ten years older than Mary. She had a reassuring air of confidence about her. 'I'm on my tea break, so I can take you next door to ask if the job is still available.'

Mary followed Frida through the gate of the neighbouring house with its neat garden and lovely big trees. Frida rang the brass doorbell with the bottle green sash. Mary was suddenly conscious of the sweat under her armpits. She wiped her glistening brow with her only handkerchief and waited breathlessly for someone to appear. A few moments later, a mature-looking white woman opened the door.

'Madam, I'm Frida from next door.'

'Yes, Frida, I recognise you.'

'You are looking for a maid, Madam?'

'Yes, but I'm busy. I'm in no hurry for a new maid.'

'Madam, my sister here is an excellent worker.'

'Oh, I've got so many other things to worry about, Frida. I don't have time just now.'

'True, Madam, she is one of the best. You can't find a better maid.'

'I don't know! Oh, all right, I'll try you,' said Julia Watson, looking at Mary. 'When can you start?'

'She can start straightaway, Madam,' Frida answered.

'Can't Mary speak for herself? Do you always speak for her?'

'Yes, Madam, she is my younger sister.'

'I can see that, but she looks too young to be an experienced house-maid.'

'Truly the best, Madam.'

Julia looked at Mary again. 'What's your name?'

'Mary, Madam.'

'Ah, so you can speak! How old are you, Mary?'

'Twenty-two years, Madam.'

Julia frowned. 'She might be a hard worker, Frida, but she can't be very experienced. And I hope she's honest. My last maid stole from me.'

'Oh, she's too honest, Madam.'

'We'll see about that.' Julia noticed the small suitcase on the ground next to Mary.

'There's a kia (detached servant's room) in the back garden. She can stay there, but she must clean it. I will give her blankets for tonight, and we'll have a closer look tomorrow or the next day.'

'Thank you, Madam,' said Frida.

'Thank you, Madam,' Mary repeated.

'Frida, why don't you take Mary to the back garden and help her settle her things?'

'My tea break is over, Madam. I can come back tonight.'

Julia sighed as Frida walked away. 'Come Mary, I'll show you your room.'

'Where did you work before now?'

'Yes, Madam.'

'No, Mary! Where are you from? Where, where?'

'My village is past Marula, Madam.'

'Village? What experience did you get as a maid if you lived in a village?'

'Yes, Madam.'

Julia rolled her eyes. This did not look promising.

The kia was bare apart from an old iron bed and a steel bedside cabinet. On top of the cabinet stood a burned-down candle, stuck on top of the tin lid of a long-lost marmalade jar. In the kia's passageway, a second door led to a shower and toilet. Mary gaped at this luxury. What a surprise!

'I'm afraid there's no hot water here, said Julia. If you want hot water, you must boil it on the grill.' In the short entrance passageway, the wall contained a built-in fireplace and grill. It lay open to the sky. 'If it rains, you can put that tin sheet across the brick sides to cover the grill. That will stop the fire going out.'

Mary didn't grasp what Julia said. She spoke so fast. 'Yes, Madam,' seemed the safest response.

'There's the broom to sweep your kia,' said Julia, pointing to a broom that stood behind the bathroom door. 'I'll find you blankets and a pillow which you can use tonight.'

Sweep! Mary understood that word. Did she not sweep her hut every morning to keep it clean and dust free? She took to the task with enthusiastic vigour. Soon, there was not a speck of dust anywhere on the smooth concrete floor. She couldn't reach the narrow windows that ran along the edge of the wall near the ceiling. They let in little light but were an improvement on her windowless village hut. There, she relied on an open door for light.

'My, that was quick!' said Julia when she returned to the kia. 'Tomorrow we'll see if we can find you a carpet. This floor will be cold in winter. There's firewood in the garage for your grill. Here's a box of matches, blankets, a pillow, and a tin of insect spray for the mosquitos.'

'Madam?'

'Mosquitos, Mary, mosquitos!' Julia missed the puzzled expression on Mary's face. 'Spray under your bed, in the corners, and in the bathroom and toilet.'

'Yes, Madam.'

'Come into the kitchen when you're done. You can cook the mash potato for me.'

Half an hour later, Julia found Mary hanging around the back door. 'Come in, Mary, come, come.' Must she repeat everything at least twice to Mary? 'Now, here are the potatoes. Peel them and boil them in the saucepan and use this masher when they're ready. I've already put the pot of water on the stove.' Julia left Mary in the kitchen and went to lay the dining table.

Mary looked around at the strange surroundings. She saw a white cupboard that seemed to hum. What made such an odd noise inside the cupboard? The grand white cupboard Josiah gave her was much bigger than this one, but it never occurred to her to keep a live animal in it. Mary thought she'd peek at the creature inside the white cupboard. Perhaps it contained bees, or a bird they planned to kill and eat. She opened the cupboard a chink, and a light came on. It surprised her to find the white cupboard filled with packets and bottles, but no animal making the noise.

Suddenly, the cupboard started beeping, giving her a fright. She slammed the door shut just as Julia returned to the kitchen. 'Mary, you haven't started the potatoes. What are you doing?'

'Sorry, Madam.'

'Get moving or dinner will be late.'

'Yes, Madam.'

Mary stood watching the potatoes boil. Everything was so confusing. When she judged the potatoes ready, she reached for the saucepan handle to remove it from the stove. But just as she did that, someone behind her grasped her breasts. Mary jumped in fright and sent the saucepan spinning across the stove top. Only luck prevented the water spilling or the saucepan flying off the stove.

Mary spun around to see a grey-haired man's grinning white face. 'No, Boss, you can't do that!' The man chuckled and walked out of the kitchen, leaving her flustered. She took the saucepan and emptied the water into the sink and mashed the potatoes with the implement Julia had earlier demonstrated with an energetic mime.

Soon Julia returned to the kitchen and laid out three plates. She took sausages from under the grill and green peas from another saucepan and added the mashed potato. 'This plate is for you, Mary. Eat here in the kitchen, if you like, or take it to your kia. Tomorrow, we'll buy cornmeal for you to make sadza. After we've finished dinner, clear the table, and wash the dishes, and then you can go.' Julia picked up two plates and walked through to the dining room.

'What's this brown stuff in the mash potato?' asked Gerald King, Julia's partner for the past two years.

'I believe Mary forgot to peel the potatoes before mashing them. She seemed distracted.'

'Well, she'll be your problem. I won't have to worry about it after tomorrow. It's a pity you couldn't find someone like Miriam. At least she knew what she was doing.'

'She would still be here if it wasn't for your nonsense.'

'Miriam didn't mind. She thought it was fun. It was a perk of the job.'

'Yes, and she took payment for it from my jewellery box.'

'You said they weren't valuable.'

'They had sentimental value.'

After dinner, when Mary finished washing the dishes, Julia accompanied her to the kia to check she had everything she needed. She gave Mary an alarm clock set for seven in the morning, a towel, a facecloth, and a bar of soap. 'Mary, did you use the insect spray I gave you?'

'Yes, Madam.'

'No, you didn't. I would smell it if you had. Where's the spray can?' Julia saw it on the cabinet beside the bed. She walked across, picked it up, and sprayed under the bed.

Mary recoiled and ran to the door. 'A snake, Madam!'

'No, it's not. The spray makes the noise.'

Mary stood wide eyed as Julia walked around the room with the spray and then sprayed the bathroom and toilet.

'Do this each night before bed, so the mosquitos and fleas won't bite.'

After Julia left, Mary washed her hands and face with the Sunlight soap Julia gave her. How strange white people are! They have such funny ways. She was worried about the boss. She didn't like him. Mary pulled her bed over to the locked door and jammed the foot up against it. She put the door key on the cabinet next to the insect spray can. Now she could relax.

Around midnight, a squeaking sound woke her. The round doorknob turned again and again. Someone was trying to enter the room. After several failed attempts, she heard a man's voice whispering her name. 'Mary, open the door, Mary.' It sounded like the white boss. Mary pulled the blanket over her head and curled up into a ball.

CHAPTER 12

Steal a Little Sugar

DESPITE the relative comfort of the kia, it proved to be a sleepless night for Mary. The city was full of surprises, and most of them were unpleasant. Must all housemaids spend their time avoiding the boss? Everyone said jobs were hard to find. She needed to work. She saw how fast money disappeared in the city. Perhaps the boss would leave her alone after she told him he mustn't touch her.

Mary dragged her bed back to its original position in the room. She took the soap and towel the madam gave her, and checking nobody was around, nipped into the shower. The key was missing, so she'd have to be quick. She worried the boss might come in and see her naked. What would she do? It was still late summer, and she was used to bathing in cold water, so the prickle of the cool jet of water on her skin proved a welcome novelty. But there was no time to waste. The unwelcome prospect of the boss turning up speeded her ablutions.

Through the open kitchen door, she glimpsed Julia standing at the stove. The smell of fried eggs and bacon wafted across the back garden. Until then, she hadn't considered breakfast. Her mind was elsewhere. She hung back, hesitating to ascend the two steps to the kitchen door.

'Come in, Mary,' Julia called. 'There's no point hanging around in the garden.'

Mary understood the first part of Julia's sentence, but the rest just sounded like the rattle of the generator at the Figtree police station. She stepped up into the kitchen doorway and stopped.

'Come on, Mary! Snap to it! Nothing will get done if you don't move faster. Boil the water for tea and bring it to the table when it's ready.'

Mary saw Julia make the tea after dinner the previous evening and noted where everything was kept. She knew how to make tea: three tea bags in the teapot, milk, and sugar. Strange, the milk jug and sugar bowl were missing! Mary couldn't find another milk jug. From a carton in the fridge, she poured a little milk into a tumbler. There was no sign of sugar anywhere. She'd have to ask the madam.

Last night, the amazing electric kettle boiled the water in no time. Why wasn't it boiling now? The water just sat there. No hissing or bubbling. Nothing!

'Mary, what's happened to the tea?' Julia called.

'The kettle is broken, Madam.'

'Oh no, not another power cut!'

'I pressed the button, Madam, but it doesn't work.'

Julia came into the kitchen to check the situation. 'Mary, you haven't switched on the electricity.'

'I pushed the button, Madam.'

'Yes, but you must also switch it on at the wall over here, Mary!'

Another embarrassing mistake. Mary's face flushed, and she shook her head. 'Sorry, Madam.'

'All right, Mary, but you must listen carefully when I explain things to you. Now bring the tea in when it's ready.'

'There's no sugar, Madam.'

'The sugar is on the breakfast table, Mary. So is the milk,' said Julia, eyeing the tumbler full of milk, 'so you can drink that glass of milk.'

'Thank you, Madam.' It wasn't even eight o'clock and already she'd made three mistakes. What must the madam think? And she hadn't faced the boss as yet. Her body gave an involuntary shudder.

The boss's grinning face greeted her when she carried the tea tray through to the dining room.

'Good morning, Mary, said Gerald in an exaggerated cheerful voice.'

'Boss,' she responded in a quiet voice, lowering her eyes.

She was sure he must laugh at her silly mistakes. Mary swallowed hard and edged her way to the table to put the tray down next to Julia. She didn't make further eye contact with either of them. Without warning, her arms shook, and Julia jumped up and took the tray from her. 'What's the matter with you? You'll spill everything if you're not careful.'

'Sorry, Madam,' said Mary as she scurried from the room.

'You've landed yourself with a real lulu this time,' said Gerald. 'I don't know why you can't find a real housemaid.'

'She'll be fine. She just needs a little training.'

'You'll never train her. She's a real country bumpkin. She made no eye contact with us.'

'Mary seems more nervous than yesterday, but she was fine with me in the kitchen. You haven't been pestering her, have you?'

'Of course not! Do you imagine I'd pay attention to someone like her?'

'You paid attention to Miriam, didn't you?'

Julia left the table and walked into the kitchen. Mary stood silently by the pantry door with her arms crossed.

'Mary, we'll go out this afternoon and get you some supplies. In the meantime, there's only bacon and eggs in the frying pan. Get a plate and eat your breakfast. When you finish, come back and clear the table and wash the dishes.'

'Thank you, Madam.'

Julia watched her hurry to her kia with the plate of bacon and eggs. Why did she get the impression her new maid couldn't leave the house fast enough?

* * *

Back in her kia, Mary locked the door and ate her breakfast sitting on the bed. A jumble of thoughts raced through her mind. The madam seemed nice, but how long would she tolerate her silly mistakes? The boss was a problem. He laughed at her and enjoyed her discomfort.

In the village, Mary stood up for herself. But in the city, everything was complicated and different. If she stood up for herself now, she might lose her job. But what job was worth it if it made her so uncomfortable?

After eating, she returned to the house, cleared the breakfast table, and washed the dishes. Julia came into the kitchen, but Mary kept her eyes focussed on the sink.

'What's the problem, Mary? Something is troubling you.'

Mary shuffled her feet. 'Nothing, Madam.'

'Come on, Mary! You mustn't lie to me. What's wrong?'

'The work is too hard, Madam.'

'Nonsense! What work? All you've done is watch me work. You'll soon learn if you listen to what I say.'

Mary looked straight ahead, still not able to look Julia in the eye. 'And the boss, Madam.'

'I can't hear you if you're whispering, Mary. Speak up!'

'The boss, Madam.'

'The boss? What about the boss?'

'He touched me here, Madam,' said Mary, pointing to her breasts.

'Oh, did he now?' Julia's voice crackled as she stood with arms akimbo and drew herself up to her full height. With her eyes wide and her eyebrows arched, she stared at Mary, who shrivelled under her fearsome gaze. Then in a gentler voice, 'Don't worry, Mary. The boss is leaving today. He's going back home to England.'

'But when will he come back, Madam?'

'He's not coming back!' said Julia. 'Go to your kia and wait there! The taxi is coming straight after lunch. I'll call you when he's gone.'

Mary hurried out to the kia, worrying the boss might appear at any moment. She locked the door behind her. Now that she'd reported him, she might find herself in big trouble. What if he came back?

* * *

At two in the afternoon, Mary heard Julia calling her. 'You can come out now, Mary. The boss has gone. You're safe now. Remember, when you're in the house, you must keep your kia locked.'

Mary locked the kia door and followed Julia into the house. She breathed more freely now. Everything had changed in a moment. The house somehow looked and felt different. Perhaps she would like it here.

'Come, Mary, we're going to the supermarket for supplies.' Julia locked the back door and walked down the passage to fetch her handbag. Just as Julia disappeared into her bedroom, the front doorbell rang. Mary, alone in the front room, peeped through the window. A well-dressed African woman stood outside on the doorstep. She knocked again and then glimpsed Mary at the window. She gestured with sharp beckoning motions, and Mary hurried to open the door.

'Were you going to keep me standing here all day, you stupid girl?' The women's aggressive manner set Mary back on her heels. Julia loomed up behind Mary, and the woman turned her attention to her.

'Mrs. Watson, I'm Dorothy Mapfumo from next door. We've been neighbours for two years, so I thought I should introduce myself.'

'Oh! Please call me Julia.'

'And call me Dorothy. I'm happy to meet you after all this time. My maid Frida tells me you have hired a new housemaid. Is that who answered the door?'

'Yes, she's Frida's younger sister. She started yesterday.'

'Frida is lazy and a liar. Mary is not her sister.'

'I half guessed as much, Dorothy.'

'Frida has foisted this village woman on you. She's admitted to me that Mary has no experience as a housemaid. She comes from a remote village somewhere in the bush past Marula.'

'Yes, she's not familiar with everyday kitchen work. I've not let her loose anywhere else in the house so far.'

'Why don't you let me find you a proper, reliable housemaid? You can tell this one to go.'

'You mean a proper one like lazy, lying Frida?'

'No, no! We inherited her from the last owners of our house. I've considered getting rid of her. Perhaps we both need a fresh start.'

'Thank you for your kind offer, Dorothy, but I'll give this girl more time and see how she goes.'

'My Dear, it's impossible to train uneducated bush women. I've tried before, and they've never worked out. All you can say for them is they're cheap and won't pester you for more money.'

'Most important to me is honesty. If she doesn't steal, that'll be a good start.'

'Honesty? My Dear, have you ever known a maid who didn't steal? You better lock your things up before she makes herself at home.'

Mary stood by the kitchen door, trying to overhear the women's conversation. She caught mention of her name and Frida's, but couldn't make out much more.

Dorothy left, saying, 'If you change your mind, Julia, just call me. I must introduce you to my husband, Edward.' As she closed the front gate behind her, Dorothy noticed Mary standing in the drive beside the house. Mary couldn't miss the disdain on the woman's face.

Come, Mary, time to go shopping. Open the front gate. Mary hopped into the passenger seat next to Julia, and off they drove to the Food Lover's Market.

Julia turned the little Honda into one of the parking spaces under the trees. 'You can buy everything you need at the supermarket here. I'll get the vegetables while you get the mealie meal for your sadza, and anything else you need.'

The beautiful surroundings entranced Mary. Green lawns, ponds, and exciting new shops. Inside, the supermarket shelves displayed a bounty of goods in colourful packets and tins. Even the fresh vegetables lay in a neat, colourful display. The mealies (corn on the cob) were long, fat, and yellow, and nothing like the thin, dry, white, water-starved mealies in her village.

Before she had the time to satisfy her curiosity, Julia came up to her. 'Have you got everything you need, Mary?'

'Maybe mealies, Madam.'

'OK, but where's the mealie meal for your sadza?'

'I can't find any, Madam.'

'It's here, Mary, right next to you.'

Before now, Mary had never seen mealie meal in a colourful packet like this. In the village it came in large, reinforced, brown paper bags.

'Anything else, Mary?'

'I don't know, Madam.'

'We can come back if we've forgotten anything.' Julia realised there was no use asking her to find anything in packets or bottles because she couldn't read. Perhaps in time she'd recognise the colours and labels of the items in the pantry at home.

Back at the house, Mary helped Julia put their purchases into the pantry and kitchen cupboards. Julia explained the contents of each colourful packet and bottle.

'Now, Mary, I'll introduce you to everything in the kitchen you must use often. You've already used the electric kettle and hot plates on the stove, but there's also the oven and grill, the microwave oven, and toaster. You must learn where the salt, sugar, breakfast cereals, and other things are. I'll show you as we need them.'

Mary concentrated as Julia ran through all the essential kitchen equipment and ingredients. Soon her head spun with an overflow of information.

'You said you can cook, so tonight, Mary, you can make dinner. Be ready to serve at six o'clock.'

'Yes, Madam.'

'I'm going into my office now. Call me if you need anything.'

Julia disappeared down the passage leading to the mysterious rooms behind the closed doors.

* * *

Where was the madam? What should she do now? The madam said she must cook dinner. Mary went to the garage and found the firewood Julia mentioned. She carried it to her open grill and constructed a neat pile of twigs she collected from the garden and laid pieces of wood over the kindling. With the matches she used to light her candle, she set the small fire going. Soon it crackled and spat like the fires she made back in her village.

Mary returned to the house and set the dining table as close as possible to what she'd observed the previous evening. She took two cooking pots and the ingredients she needed for the meal. Last night, Julia blamed her for holding up dinner. Tonight, it wouldn't be late. When everything was ready, Mary picked up the silver dinner bell that sat on the dining table and shook it.

Julia came to the dining table and laughed. 'That bell is for me to call you, Mary. Not for you to call me. But perhaps it's not such a bad idea. It's only five o'clock. I said dinner at six. Tomorrow, we'll start with lessons on telling the time. It's lucky I set your alarm clock for you, or Heaven knows what time you might have turned up for breakfast. Well, seeing as you have everything ready, I might as well have dinner now. OK, Mary, I'm ready to see what you've made.'

A beaming Mary carried in a steaming plate.

'Stew? And mashed potatoes again.'

'No, Madam, sadza.'

Mary laid a plate with two mealies in front of Julia.

'Bring the salt, pepper, and butter please, Mary. How did you cook these mealies? They're crisp and brown.'

'On the fire, Madam.'

When Mary struggled to find the butter, Julia walked into the kitchen. Everything was tidy. Julia felt the stove. It was cold. 'Mary, where did you cook dinner?'

'On my grill, Madam.'

'What, on that dirty thing? Oh, all right! Tomorrow, I'll show you the braai. We'll also go over once again how you can use the stove.'

Julia tried the stew. The meat was edible, but where were the potatoes, carrots, onions, and spices? Sadza was not one of her favourite dishes, so Julia added salt to give it more taste. 'Hmm! This food is all right, Mary, but tomorrow I'll cook dinner, and you can help me.'

* * *

In her kia, after clearing the table and washing the dishes, Mary enjoyed her dinner. It was more food and tastier than the same meal in her village. This was one aspect of city life she would enjoy. She wasn't sure if the madam approved of her cooking, but she didn't get angry.

Mary barely finished eating when there was a knock on the door. Her eyes widened, and her stomach churned. Had she locked the door?

'Mary, it's me, Frida.'

Mary sighed with relief and unlocked the door to let Frida enter.

'I'm sorry I didn't come back again yesterday, but my madam kept me working late.'

'When you knocked, I worried the boss might be back.'

'The boss?'

'Yes, last night he knocked on my door and wanted me to open it.'

'Ag, that man! Sometimes, late at night when your madam slept, I'd see him going to Miriam's kia. She was your madam's maid until two weeks ago.'

'Is that why she left? Because he pestered her?'

'No, that Miriam was a big flirt. She encouraged him. Show me a man who could resist a shape like hers. Your madam told her to go, so now she's also kicked out the boss.'

'After he left today, an African woman came and spoke to my madam. Perhaps she asked about the job.'

'Did she wear a white dress with blue flowers on it?'

'Yes.'

'Ag, that's my madam. She's not nice. She wouldn't be asking about the job. All she does is dress up and paint her nails. She's only good for shouting at me.'

'She called me a stupid girl.'

'Don't worry. She calls me a lazy liar and worse. If you hadn't taken this job, I might have asked your madam about it. If I'd known she was going to kick the boss out, I would have spoken to her.'

'Are you looking for another job?'

'No, I like living here, but my madam often threatens to fire me.'

'I think my madam might also fire me. I made a lot of mistakes today, and she wasn't happy.'

'Oh, don't worry, you'll soon learn what to do.'

'I don't know if I can learn. There is so much to remember.'

'Knowing what to do is easy, but you must learn the politics.'

'Politics?'

'The one with power in the house. Your madam holds the power in your house, but in mine, it changes. On payday and two weeks after, the boss holds the power, so I'm extra nice to him. Then, until the next payday, my madam holds the power, and I must stay out of her way. If they fire me, it will be in the two weeks before payday.'

'Eish!'

'Do you know what you will steal?'

'I won't steal anything.'

'If you don't steal, how will your madam ever trust you?'

'I don't understand?'

'The madams always say we steal from them. If they catch you for small things, they are satisfied and won't dismiss you. Then, they won't notice when you take other things. But if they can't find anything you've stolen, they'll be suspicious. They might even accuse you of taking things you haven't stolen, things they've lost.'

'My madam said I can take what I need.'

'That is only because you're new, but soon, they will ration you. It happens to all of us.'

'My madam said she wants an honest maid.'

'Don't worry, I will help you.'

'How?'

'So far, you've only worked in the kitchen. If you take a cup of sugar, they'll notice and say you're using too much. But if you take half a bag of salt, they won't notice, and they'll look for what else you might have taken. It's better to steal a little sugar than a lot of salt. When they find the sugar missing, they'll warn you and tell you not to do it again. Then they'll watch the sugar and forget to check everything else. You must take sugar two or three times a year to keep them distracted.'

'Distracted?'

'Never mind. And remember, don't steal things they can count. Every maid must learn these lessons. Later, I'll tell you what you can take from the bedrooms, lounge, and laundry.'

After Frida left, Mary puzzled over her words. How can pinching sugar make her position more secure? The madam said she must take what she needed. Would that be stealing? Mary fell asleep, marvelling at the strange ways of the city.

CHAPTER 13

The Ladders to Heaven

Day three, Mary's second full day as Julia's maid. Today was different. The boss was gone, and Mary promised herself there'd be no mistakes today. There was nothing to distract her, and Julia said she'd show her once again the items and machines in the tricky kitchen area. Also, there was the rest of the house and related tasks to consider.

Mary loved the cool spray of the early morning shower as she soaped herself with the mottled blue Sunlight soap Julia gave her. She would also use it to wash her clothes in the large concrete sink in the kia's passageway. With no risk of interruption now, the shower was a luxury beyond imagination.

An early riser, Mary stood waiting at the kitchen door when Julia opened it at seven. She bubbled at the prospect of learning the skills needed by a housemaid. Her intelligence, coupled with an enquiring mind, always put her a step ahead of the others in her village. Why should it be any different now?

'You're early this morning, Mary. Couldn't you sleep? Put the kettle on for tea while I have a quick shower.'

Mary filled the electric kettle, turned on the wall switch, and pressed the kettle's start button. Nothing happened. While she waited for the kettle to boil, she got the milk jug and opened the fridge for the milk. The light didn't work. That's when she noticed the hum of the fridge was missing. Complete silence. What had she done this time? Perhaps she'd broken something, and now nothing worked.

Julia entered the kitchen to find Mary with her shoulders sagged, cupping her hands over her nose and mouth. 'What's the matter, Mary? Not another electricity outage!'

'Madam?'

'When there's no electricity, you must use the braai. Come, I'll show you!'

'But the electricity, Madam?'

'It'll be back when the authorities decide. This happens all the time.'

Mary was adept at building a fire, and soon the plate on the braai held a heating metal kettle, and the grill hosted the eggs and sizzling bacon.

'Have you eaten, Mary?'

'No, Madam.'

'Then, I'll also put eggs and bacon on for you. Use the braai fork to make the toast.'

As Mary stood, toasting the bread at a safe distance from the cheerful flames, she wondered why she'd ever bother to make her own breakfast if Julia kept providing it. She might soon get used to this breakfast, followed by tea and toast. The smell and sizzle of the eggs and bacon made her hungry.

'It's a lovely morning, Mary. We can eat breakfast out here in the garden.'

This time, Mary did not return to her kia to eat her breakfast. She sat on a log a little distance from Julia.

'You can sit here at the table, Mary.'

'It's OK, thank you, Madam.'

* * *

After breakfast, the tour of the house began. The lounge, dining room, passageway, and bedrooms boasted parquet flooring. 'You must only use this soft broom with the red handle in these rooms, Mary. Do you know why?'

'No, Madam?'

'Because of scratching, Mary. The broom you use in the kitchen and bathroom will scratch this floor.'

'Yes, Madam.'

'Use the carpet sweeper for the carpets and rugs, like this.' Julia demonstrated the contraption on the Persian carpet in the lounge and passed it to Mary to try. 'Every two or three weeks, you can use the vacuum cleaner. I'll show you how to use it when the electricity is back.'

The lounge furnishings comprised two plush, fabric-covered armchairs and a matching three-seater sofa. A glass-topped coffee table sat in front of the sofa, and two small side tables stood beside the armchairs. A tall, wide bookcase-come-cabinet covered the entire end wall, dominating the room. The bottom level comprised a row of six ornate wooden cupboard doors. Above the cupboard doors on each end, tall diamond-paned glass doors fronted shelves displaying glassware in one and a variety of bottles in the other. The top of the four middle cupboards provided a broad shelf, above which stood three bookshelves between the glass-door cabinets. Above those, two more bookshelves ran the entire width of the piece of furniture.

Mary gave a sigh of relief when the lounge presented no complicated equipment to challenge her. The bedrooms also presented no new challenge.

'This was the boss's bedroom,' said Julia, opening the door to show Mary. The small room contained a double bed, a bedside table, a table lamp, and a built-in wardrobe. 'Now it's the guest bedroom. My bedroom is the large one next door.'

Julia's room included a queen-size bed with bedside tables and lamps. A stylish dressing table stood at an angle in the far corner, past the large window overlooking the front garden. It also received more light through the long, narrow, horizontal window set high in the wall facing the side garden. In the corner, past the bed, a door led to an ensuite bathroom with a bath, shower, washbasin, and toilet.

'This room, overlooking the back garden, is my office. You can clean and dust my office, but you mustn't touch anything in here.'

Mary was relieved to hear that. Complicated equipment and screens filled the office, with a nest of wires leading everywhere. Cleaning that room would be difficult.

The second bathroom off the passageway only comprised a shower and toilet. Nothing to worry her there. The kitchen and office aside, Mary felt there was little she couldn't manage. But then they walked into the laundry. Two menacing looking white metal boxes stood silent and threatening.

'When the electricity is working, you can use the washing machine, and if it's a rainy day, you can also use the clothes dryer. I'll show you when we have electricity. Otherwise, do the washing in the bathtub and dry the clothes on the line.'

Mary felt more confident about the electric kettle, toaster, and hot-plates on the stove, following another kitchen run-through with Julia. She still held reservations about the oven and the grill, though she understood the concept. 'But, Madam, if you can't see the food, how do you know it's ready?'

'Don't worry, Mary, I'll show you when the time comes. Now it's time for morning tea. Please make me a cup of tea, and then you can have your tea break.'

* * *

Mary enjoyed two slices of bread and jam and stood at the front gate, admiring the large trees and lovely gardens. She could understand why Frida put up with her irascible madam to stay working in the area.

'Mary.' It was Frida, standing in the same spot where they first met. 'How are you going?'

'The madam showed me the other rooms today. They should be easy to keep clean. I must learn to use the vacuum cleaner, but the madam said I can use the soft broom or brush and pan if I want. The carpet sweeper is easy to use.'

'You know you must dust all those books each week.'

'Yes, the madam showed me the duster.'

'Did you notice the ladders to Heaven?'

'Ladders to Heaven?' Mary knew what a ladder was. Mechanic built one for the village from branches and rope.

'Yes, on those bottles in the bookcase.'

'I didn't get close to those bottles.'

'I'm talking about the ladders the boss put there. If you look at the labels on the alcohol bottles, you'll see they all have ink ladders.'

'Eish! What are you talking?'

'Every time a boss drinks, before he puts the bottle away, he marks the alcohol level on the bottle with a pen. That way, he knows if you steal any of his alcohol. It's the same with my boss. If you take alcohol, you must always remember to mark the new level. The lines on the bottle are a ladder to the heaven alcohol takes you.'

'I don't drink alcohol.'

'If you examine the labels, you'll see they don't trust us maids. Number nine fired Alice because they said she used a red pen instead of a blue one to mark the alcohol level. Then they took her back when they discovered it was their son who made that mistake. The boy was unused to drinking alcohol. He didn't know what he was doing. It ended well for Alice, but first they always blame the maid.'

'But you said Alice had left?'

'Yes, because the next time she stole alcohol from that bottle, she used a blue pen. She didn't notice they'd continued to mark that label with a red pen.'

'It won't be a problem for me.'

'But what if a boyfriend demands alcohol?'

'I'd never have such a man.'

'Have you seen the madam's dressing table?'

'Yes, it's beautiful.'

'Does she still have the tray full of earrings?'

'Yes. How do you know what's in my madam's house?'

'When your madam and the boss went out, Miriam sometimes invited me for drinks, and we used to try on the earrings.'

Mary gasped. Miriam's relationship with the boss must have led to her boldness. No wonder the madam told them both to leave. 'I would never do those things.'

'You can "borrow" your madam's earrings, but don't take the ones that stand out. Take the quieter ones. If your madam doesn't notice they are missing, you can keep them. But if she asks you if you've seen them, tell her no, but put them back, and she'll think she just missed them the last time she looked.'

Frida looked at her watch. 'I must go now. I'll come to you later.'

Mary remained at the gate, wondering about everything Frida said. Drinking the boss's alcohol and trying on the madam's earrings. It didn't seem right. Did all the maids do that? She would never do such things. The village wouldn't tolerate that behaviour. Why was it OK, even expected, in the city? Was everything Frida told her true, or was she trying to get her into trouble so she could take her job?

* * *

'Mary!' Julia's call interrupted her thoughts. Tea break was over.

'Yes, Madam.'

'Mary, I must go out, so I'm leaving you in charge of the house. First, I'm going to the Women's Centre to deliver these bottles and then I'm visiting a sick friend. The car is open. Please put these flowers and bottles on the back seat.'

Julia handed Mary a cardboard carton full of empty bottles with a bunch of flowers lying on top. The bottles were the tall, wide-mouth variety used for sauces and Mrs Ball's chutneys. Julia walked back into the house to get ready while Mary carried the carton with its precious load to the little Honda sitting in the driveway.

'OK, Mary, I'll be about two hours.' Julia jumped into the car and glanced over her shoulder to check the carton of bottles was secure. She stared in stunned disbelief. The bottle lids were removed, and a single flower sat in each one. Mary stood by, with her back straight, looking pleased with her work.

'Mary, what have you done?'

'Madam?' Mary frowned. 'Madam, you said I must put the flowers in bottles on the back seat.'

Julia rolled her eyes. 'No, Mary! I said, put the flowers and bottles on the back seat. And the bottles, Mary! Not in the bottles!'

Julia spent the next twenty minutes re-wrapping the flowers into a bunch and replacing the correct lid on each bottle. Mary stood there, her shoulders rounded, embarrassed, not knowing where to look.

Julia drove off, shaking her head. She was going to be late. Things progressed well in the morning with the attentive Mary listening to her instructions. But clearly, more work was needed.

* * *

Julia would be out for two hours. Mary wondered about the ladders to Heaven. She walked up to the cabinet, holding the bottles of alcohol. Was Frida telling her the truth, or was she making up a story? No harm in checking. The key sat in the lock of the diamond-paned door. Behind stood a treasure trove of fascinating bottles of alcohol in all shapes and sizes. It invited curious investigation. Mary's hand shook as she turned the key and picked up a bottle. She unscrewed the cap and smelled the contents. It was horrible, and as she pulled her face away from it, the bottle slipped from her grasp. It fell on the parquet floor but didn't break, splashing out liquid before she regained control. She rushed to the kitchen and grabbed a handful of kitchen paper to mop up the spilt Scotch.

Mary was sensible enough not to put the wet, foul-smelling kitchen paper in the kitchen bin. Instead, she took it outside and put it in the dustbin. When she returned to the lounge with her heart thumping in her chest, she looked at the bottle's label. There they were, the thin lines on the label, Frida's ladder to Heaven. Now, next to the lower level of liquid, there was no line. Mary hurried to the telephone, where she'd earlier seen a ballpoint pen. With great care, she drew a short blue horizontal line indistinguishable from the others. She took a tumbler from the kitchen and poured a tiny amount of the clear amber coloured liquid into it and took a sip. It was foul, tasting every bit as bad as it smelt.

Mary replaced the bottle and noted the ladders to Heaven on other bottles. She locked the diamond-paned door, washed the tumbler, and checked once again that the parquet floor showed no sign of the spill. Everything was in order.

Now her thoughts turned to the tray of earrings on Julia's dressing table. She would never pinch Julia's earrings, but wasn't it OK to just admire them? Several pairs of earrings in a variety of colours and styles lay there—all so pretty that none stood out. One white pair of dangling earrings, with light plastic pieces strung together, looked like feathers. Mary picked them up and held them to her ear. She thought they were beautiful. How would they look on her? To view them better, she slipped the hooks through her lobes, turning her head to the left and the right, admiring the white dangling earrings.

The jangle of the telephone in the front hallway startled her. Julia spent time that morning teaching her how to answer the phone, but now she hesitated to lift the handset. It was a lot easier when Julia was by her side. This would be her first test. Mary lifted the handset with great care, as if it was fine bone china. 'This is Julia Watson's residence. Mary speaking.'

'You must speak a little louder than that, Mary.' It was Julia. 'Mary, I will be later than I expected. Say around six o'clock. Please get the mashed potatoes and carrots ready, and we can cook the sausages and heat the green peas when I'm back.'

'Yes, Madam.' This time, Mary resolved to prepare the best mashed potatoes possible. She tried to remember Julia's instructions while she peeled the potatoes and carrots. She worked slowly and deliberately, determined not to make any mistakes. Just as she finished mashing the potatoes, she heard the squeak of the gate and Julia's car enter the driveway.

'You're looking very pretty tonight, Mary.'

'Thank you, Madam.'

'Those earrings suit you.'

'Thank y....' The realisation hit Mary like a thunderclap. She still wore Julia's white dangling earrings.

'Sorry, Madam, sorry.' Mary stumbled over the words as she struggled to remove the earrings from her earlobes.

'No, no, Mary, you can keep them. They look better on you than me. They're much too young for me these days.'

'Sorry, Madam. Thank you, Madam,' Mary stammered as she blushed with embarrassment.

'Now, let's see how you've done with the mashed potatoes and carrots.'

* * *

After Julia finished eating and Mary stood washing the dishes, there was a loud knock on the front door. Julia answered it, and Mary glimpsed an African woman standing on the doorstep.

'Madam, my name is Priscilla. I work at number eight. My boss and madam are moving to Australia, and the other maids tell me you're looking for an experienced maid. The other maids say your new maid has no training, so I'm available if you need me.'

Mary strained her ears to catch Julia's reply, but her madam spoke in a low voice, and Mary couldn't hear what she said. She saw Priscilla hand Julia a piece of paper and heard Julia thank her. After she finished the washing up, Mary took her dinner back to the kia, but her appetite deserted her.

CHAPTER 14

The Visitor

THREE weeks passed since Priscilla, from number eight, called to speak to Julia. Frida said Priscilla found another job in a neighbouring street, so Mary's job was secure for now. Mary didn't like those last two words when Frida explained their meaning. Still, she'd learnt a lot in three weeks, and each added week cemented her role, or so she thought. The madam hadn't said a word about Priscilla's visit. And didn't she say Mary's mashed potatoes were equal to the best she'd eaten?

Frida always offered Mary advice about the role and practices of a good housemaid. But Mary was her own person and didn't always follow the advice. Back in the village, she displayed her independent streak. At first, it made her enemies, but in time, she earned the respect and admiration of her fellow villagers. Would she achieve the same result in the city? She was aware she'd grown up in village life, and that gave her an advantage in the bush. The city was a different matter, and it undermined her confidence.

'Mary, I love your mashed potatoes, but must we have them every night?'

How could she answer a question like that, except with a sweet smile?

'I suppose you're smiling, Mary, because you didn't burn the sausages tonight?'

'Yes, Madam.'

'Soon, we can try you with cooking steaks.'

'Yes, Madam.'

'Hmm! On second thoughts, perhaps not just yet. Steaks are expensive.'

'I can't burn the steaks, Madam.'

'Are you sure?'

'Yes, Madam, I won't burn them.'

'I like my steaks marinaded and cooked medium-rare. I'll show you how to do it.'

Mary liked hearing those words. If the madam planned to train her, she must intend to keep her. She couldn't wait to tell Frida what the madam said.

Later that evening, when she relayed the news, Frida snorted in disgust. 'I've worked next door for two years and have cooked steaks for them many times. My madam always complains they're overdone or underdone or too tough. Employers are never satisfied. Don't be in a hurry to cook steaks for your madam, or you may find yourself with my problem. Tell her you are not confident with steaks and would rather wait to gain more experience with cooking before you try them. Also, it will mean more work for you.'

'But I want as much experience as possible, even if I fail. My mashed potatoes were not good when I started, but now my madam says they are the best.'

'Steaks are not like mashed potatoes. People who eat steak are fussy and always complain. Once they complain about one thing, they'll find other things to complain about.'

Mary lay in bed, thinking about Frida's advice. She'd not always followed it, but so far, she'd stayed out of trouble. The prospect of cooking something other than sausages, mashed potatoes, carrots, and peas excited her. Yes, she could cook sadza and stew, but the madam didn't seem too enthusiastic about her favourite dishes. The madam always took over preparing the stew, adding carrots, peas, and potatoes, and something she called herbs and spices. Mary realised she was yet to master the tricky art of cooking minced beef. The madam said it was lumpy and clumped together, but then she'd only shown her three or four times how to cook it. Mary was sure she'd soon get the knack. No, she would ignore Frida's advice and accept every challenge the madam threw at her.

* * *

Two months on, Mary had learnt things and was more comfortable in her role. Late summer passed into early winter with its lovely sunny days and chilly nights.

Today was another beautiful, sunny morning. The madam's good mood pleased Mary, who benefited from extra perks on such occasions. Yes, it meant a garden breakfast of bacon and eggs with the madam. Mary fired up the braai and cooked what the madam called an English breakfast—the madam said she did it well.

'Next weekend, my daughter, Vera, will visit us. She'll arrive on Friday evening and stay until Monday morning. We must go to the Food Lover's Market and buy some things.'

'Yes, Madam.'

'I think I'll get beef rump and make a nice roast. That's her favourite dish. And, Mary, please give the spare bedroom a good dusting, and sweep the floors with the soft mop and clean the windows.'

'Yes, Madam.'

Friday evening was only two days away, and Mary worked harder than ever. Julia also worked hard, rubbing and scrubbing the imaginary dirt on the various surfaces. The house was always clean and tidy; Mary made sure of that. After all the cleaning, their joint efforts didn't produce any visible difference. Well, perhaps the front driveway displayed a few less leaves, but everything else looked the same. The madam's daughter must be important to warrant such strenuous preparations.

Frida later warned Mary, 'Be careful of that one, the madam's daughter. She is very demanding and expects a high standard. Miriam never liked her visiting.'

* * *

Late Friday afternoon, a large white van pulled up at the gate and hooted. Julia hurried out to open the gate for her daughter.

'Welcome back, Dear. I see you've got your campervan out of storage.'

'Yes, I'm driving up to Mana Pools on Monday. A French travel magazine wants photos and a story about a driving holiday in Zimbabwe, ending with a visit to Mana Pools.'

'Goodness! You're so busy. You only arrived back from your Thailand trip this afternoon, and already, you're on to another assignment.'

'The life of a travel journalist is hectic, but I love it.'

'Are you taking your regular photography assistant? Zachariah, wasn't it?'

'Yes, Zak is a great help. He's not just someone to carry the equipment. He understands photography.'

'I'm glad you're not out there alone, but how do you manage in the campervan?'

'I sleep inside, and Zak sleeps on the roof. So, I must contend with the heat, and Zak with the mosquitoes. But we both need mosquito nets, so I reckon he's got the better deal out in the fresh air.'

'Ah, here is Mary, my new maid.'

'Hello, Madam, can I take your suitcase?'

'No, thank you. I'm not helpless.' The tone of Vera's voice and her penetrating look suggested an impatient personality, quick to judge.

'I must check the vegetables aren't burning,' said Mary as she hurried back to the kitchen. Vera walked into the spare bedroom to unpack her things, and Julia joined Mary in the kitchen. 'I'll cook tonight, Mary. We're having tofu and stir-fried vegetables, which I haven't yet shown you. There's also enough dinner for you, so you'll learn how it should taste. After you've finished serving and washed the dishes, you can go.'

'Thank you, Madam.'

Mary enjoyed the strange new dinner but thought the leftover sadza from lunch improved it. She got through the evening without making mistakes and did nothing to upset the madam's daughter.

* * *

For breakfast the next morning, Mary added milk and sugar to the last of the sadza. Most days, she'd have breakfast cereal from the kitchen pantry, but she didn't want to test Vera's tolerance by being around her any more than necessary.

The day passed without incident until Julia asked Mary to cook her signature dish for dinner that night: sausages, mashed potatoes, carrots, and peas. Under normal circumstances, Mary loved to prepare the one meal she did well. But on this occasion, it felt like a test, and her thinking and actions seemed sluggish, requiring an extra effort to concentrate.

At dinner, Julia, as usual, sat with her back to the kitchen, and Vera sat opposite her. Mary fancied every time she approached the stove; Vera's eyes followed her. So apart from one or two fleeting trips to the stove, she stayed unseen near the kitchen sink.

After she finished serving, she stood at the kitchen sink, washing the dishes.

'Mary, is there—'

Mary jumped at the sudden booming voice close behind her. The side plate slipped from her grasp and smashed on the kitchen floor. 'Madam!'

'Tch! Never mind! I'll do it myself,' said Vera, checking the electric kettle for more hot water for the coffee.

Mary cleared up the splintered pieces with the brush and pan. It was the first mistake she'd made since Vera's arrival. The incident replayed continuously in her mind.

'That silly girl of yours has broken one of your side plates.'

'Never mind, Dear, accidents will happen. She's not a silly girl. She just seems a little nervous around you. I expect it's because you are the first visitor we've had since she started.'

Julia came into the kitchen. 'Mary, take tomorrow off. But please come in the evening to serve dinner and wash the dishes?'

'Yes, Madam.'

* * *

Sunday morning; the last full day of Vera's visit. Mary spent most of the day in her kia or on the secluded sunny patch of ground next to the washing lines behind it. She turned down the volume on the battery-operated transistor radio Julia gave her, so as not to attract unwelcome attention. Sunday was the day for washing her clothes and sweeping her hut. Frida would turn up if she got away from her demanding employer.

Sure enough, Frida's smiling face found Mary sitting in the sun behind her kia. 'So, how's the visit going?'

The two maids chatted all afternoon until Mary said she needed to get ready to help Julia in the kitchen. Fresh and eager, she arrived at the kitchen door to find the beef roast already in the oven.

'Don't worry, Mary, next time I'll get you to help from the beginning, and you'll see how it's done. In the meantime, please lay the table.'

Today differed from normal. Julia took a large dark brown bottle from the pantry and two glasses from the cabinet in the lounge and placed them on the round raffia coasters at the table settings. If the fridge was working, Mary would put a tumbler and a chilled bottle of sparkling water on the table. This was something different. She watched as Julia cut several thin slices from the roast.

Vera walked into the kitchen and noticed three plates on the counter. 'Oh! Is someone else coming to dinner? The table is set for two.'

'No, Dear, one plate is for Mary.' She'll eat her dinner here in the kitchen.

Vera didn't comment until she and Julia were seated, sipping their wine, and enjoying dinner. 'Does Mary share your food every night?'

'No, she likes her sadza and vegetables or stew. When I cook something new, I let her try it to see how it tastes.'

'I notice you do all the cooking, Mum. You said you wanted a maid who could cook?'

'I only cook the special dinners that Mary hasn't learnt yet. Most nights she cooks dinner, or part of it at least.'

'You mean the least part of it!'

'No, no, she's coming on well. I'm teaching her.'

'Her dinner last night was OK, but what else can she cook?'

'Well, not a lot. Fried eggs and bacon for breakfast. But she'll soon learn.'

'I don't know why you bother with all these waifs and strays. Why can't you get proper, qualified servants?'

'She'll be fine, you'll see.'

'Yes, like Henry the gardener, and that awful thieving Miriam.'

'They have so little. What they steal means a lot to them, but nothing to me.'

'Yes, I noticed how Mary is wearing a pair of your earrings. You loved those earrings, and now she's got them.'

'I haven't worn them in years, and they look so good on her.'

'When I get back from Mana Pools, I'll find you a proper maid.'

'No need for that.'

'No, it's settled; you need proper servants to take the load off you. What's the point of getting servants if you end up working for them?'

'Mary keeps the house nice and clean and does all the laundry.'

'That's not enough to keep her busy in this small house.'

'That's why I'm teaching her how to cook.'

'No, Mum, I'll take you in hand. I'll find a capable cook when I'm back from the bush.'

Julia laughed. 'Really, Vera, I'm not decrepit just yet. I can do most things for myself. If I leave behind a good cook when I'm gone, that will be part of my legacy.'

'Nonsense! You need free time to work on your blog. It's settled then; I'll find you someone who's properly qualified. Someone who can introduce you to new dishes.'

Mary ate her dinner in the kitchen while the two women chatted over their meal. At first, her thoughts were far away, but then she heard her name mentioned. With Vera's loud voice, it was difficult not to overhear, though Mary realised she was trying to speak in hushed tones.

Why did everybody want her job or to find someone else to take it? She and Julia got along well. The madam never got angry or uttered any cross words. Yes, sometimes she spoke emphatically, in a manner that suggested there was no use arguing the point. But Mary understood that and obliged. She liked the madam, and the madam seemed to like her. Now the madam's daughter planned to replace her. How could the daughter overrule the madam's wishes? Eish! It would be another sleepless night.

* * *

In the morning, Mary cooked breakfast on the braai for the madam and her daughter to eat in the garden. She'd already eaten and was careful not to include anything for herself, conscious of Vera's penetrating gaze.

After breakfast, Vera went to pack, with Julia keeping her company. Mary cleared the breakfast items and washed the dishes. She'd just finished when Julia and Vera came out of the bedroom wing.

'Goodbye, Mary. Thank you for dinner on Saturday night. Please make sure the madam doesn't overwork.'

'Yes, Madam. Thank you.' She missed the criticism buried in Vera's farewell.

Mary watched from the front doorway as Vera waved her mother goodbye and reversed the large vehicle out of the drive. 'Goodbye, Mum. See you in two weeks.' The madam's daughter was gone, but for Mary, the pressure remained.

Later, she relayed the details of the dinner conversation to Frida.

'Eish! Don't worry about that one. When daughters grow up, they think they know everything. They try to tell their mothers what to do. Most mothers don't listen to them. They are still their children. What do they know?'

Mary hoped the madam wasn't influenced by her daughter's visit. But the overheard conversation troubled her.

CHAPTER 15

Mana Pools

A T the end of the road, Vera eased the large white campervan left onto Burns Drive. Soon she passed the long yellow grass edging the Bulawayo Golf Course on the left and Townsend High School on the right. A little farther on, the road took her between Milton High School and the Holiday Inn and onto George Avenue. A short distance on, at the junction opposite the defunct old Bulawayo Airport, she turned right onto the Harare Road.

Apart from keeping a close eye on the eroded road surface and significant potholes, she could relax into her long drive to Harare. Once a comfortable four-hour drive, but now a six-and-a-half-hour trip, if she was lucky. The last thing she needed was a damaged wheel or busted shock absorbers. She looked at her watch; ten o'clock. She'd arrive in Harare during the five o'clock rush hour.

The uneventful drive to Gweru soon passed. Vera looked for a place to buy tea and eat the sandwiches Julia gave her. She pulled up outside a half-decent looking cafe to get a cup of tea. An elderly white couple sat in one corner of the clean cafe. Otherwise, the place was empty.

The smartly dressed waitress took her order at the counter, and within a few minutes, placed the steaming cup in front of her. Vera sipped the hot tea while she watched the passers-by on the pavement. They were all black, and she reflected on her mother's memory of a time when they would have been mostly white. As a child, she paid little attention to them. She struggled to remember if they looked much different to now.

Perhaps the gradual change clouded her memory. If nothing else, it was a reminder of how fast a generation passes.

If Zimbabwe's problems continued, there would be even further change. Most whites were former Rhodesians; economic hostages, getting on in years. Soon they would all be gone. Julia grew up in a white Rhodesia, while Vera's earlier memories were more of a coffee shaded Zimbabwe. After the farm invasions and consequent inflation, the whites left in droves. The country took on a charcoal look. When the remaining former Rhodesians died out, the country would be black Africa like states to the north.

Vera paid the bill and thanked the waitress. The cafe was a good choice, and she made a mental note to add it to her list of suitable stops. She opened the heavy door of the campervan and heaved herself up into the driver's seat. It seemed harder than it used to be. Perhaps the recent assignments made her soft. In Thailand and India before it, she'd been chauffeur driven, and before that, she drove herself in a luxury limo in the USA. It was months since she'd driven this old lady.

Back on the road, she unwrapped Julia's sandwiches. Lettuce and cheese, and curried egg; two of her favourites. It felt good being back in Zimbabwe. She enjoyed the overseas assignments, but six months away was too long. Nothing compared with the yellow and light green bush of this country. And the animals; oh, the animals! She laughed. It was exhilarating being back home.

The lure of international travel faded. She still loved travel and adventure, but to travel for work differed from holiday travel. Constant travel was isolating, and she'd not developed any serious relationships. If you meet someone, that's fine, she'd tell herself, but looking for love did not appeal. Some of her friends looked desperate in their search for the perfect partner. No, she liked her independence, but if she continued to travel the world on her own, nothing would ever change.

Perhaps it was time to move back in with her mother. Julia, now in her early seventies, could do with a little company. Then she'd choose her assignments with care and only travel when it suited her. Perhaps she'd start an adventure tour company based in Bulawayo. She'd built a name for herself in the travel magazines, and that might give her an advantage with the prospective customer base.

With her thoughts a thousand miles away, the small towns flicked past: Kwekwe, Kadoma, Chegutu. Soon she'd be approaching Lake Chivero, the former Lake Mcllwaine. Crocodiles inhabited the lake now; something unthinkable only fifteen years ago. A quarter past four. She'd made good progress, avoiding the worst potholes and driving instinctively as her thoughts wandered.

Tonight, she'd have a comfortable room at the Bronte Hotel, her last luxury before a week of roughing it. It would have been difficult if she'd not phoned from Bulawayo and booked ahead. Soon, the city loomed up ahead. The traffic looked heavy, and the pedestrian traffic was even worse. Vera knew Harare well and headed for the Bronte. Samora Michell Avenue looked slow, so she turned left into Prince Edward Street and drove for three blocks before turning right into Baines Avenue and driving eight blocks to the hotel.

She drove into the beautiful hotel grounds that resembled botanical gardens and parked her campervan next to a row of luxury vehicles. It seemed incongruous in this food challenged country.

The efficient receptionist welcomed her with a warm smile. 'Was your drive OK, Madam? Not too many police roadblocks?'

'Just a few.'

Once settled into her comfortable hotel room, Vera punched a number into her cell phone. She recognised the deep voice on the other end. 'Zak, howzit?'

'Good, Vera, welcome back.'

'Are you all set for tomorrow?'

'Ja, ready to go.'

'How's Minnie and the kids?'

'Good, thanks.'

'OK then, I'll meet you opposite the Meikles Hotel at half-past eight. Same as last time.'

After a hot shower and an early dinner in the cosy hotel dining room, Vera returned to her room and got ready for bed. The long drive tired her more than she realised. Tomorrow would also be a tough day behind the steering wheel. But at least she'd have Zak for company. It was eighteen months since their last assignment together, so they would have a lot of catching up to do.

* * *

A hearty breakfast of cereal, eggs, and bacon, toast with marmalade and tea was Vera's preferred start to the day. She'd slept well and was raring to go. As always, Zak waited for her opposite the Meikles Hotel. His face split into a broad smile when he caught sight of the white campervan. Vera pulled up next to him, and Zak jumped into the passenger seat and dumped his rucksack by his feet on the spacious floorboard. They'd worked together over several years, and he was as excited as she about this assignment.

'You're looking fit as ever, Zak. How do you do it?'

'Hard work around the house. If I'm not painting the kitchen or re-pairing the roof or something, my wife keeps me busy in the garden. It gives her time to look after the kids.'

'Well, it keeps you in good shape.'

'And what about you, Vera? You're looking a little tired.'

She laughed. 'Thanks for that, Zak. You're as honest as ever. Remember, I'm ten years older than you. Time is taking its toll.'

'No, you're still a desirable woman. If I wasn't already married, I'd be interested.'

Vera laughed as she glimpsed Zak's mischievous grin. They'd been friends for years and soon relaxed into their usual banter. It was as if they'd last been on an assignment together only yesterday. Over the years, Vera fantasised about the big, handsome African, but she'd do nothing to hurt his wife and children. He probably wouldn't be interested, though one or two of his teasing comments made her wonder.

Might it be possible to have a sexual relationship with someone and stay just friends.? She doubted it. It would complicate things. Why risk a great friendship? She'd got along fine with no serious relationship, so why change things now? She was an attractive woman in her younger days, but she didn't mince words, and her forthright manner frightened off the young men around her.

'Which route are we taking?' said Zak.

'The usual; through Chinhoyi, Karoi, and Makuti.' It was a picturesque drive, and enjoyable, despite the deteriorating roads and signs of rural decay. The once beautiful farmlands, not so beautiful anymore, didn't detract from the lure of the lovely bush areas. They made a quick stop at Makuti for fuel, a cold beer, and a sandwich at the hotel. Then they resumed their tiring drive.

At Marongora, Vera pulled up at the Parks and Wildlife offices to sign in for an entry permit for Mana Pools. The fifteen US dollars per day per person park fee came to two hundred and ten dollars for the week for the two of them. No worries, she'd claim that back from the French magazine when she put in her fee. The distant views of the Zambezi Valley on the drive down the escarpment presented a spectacular welcome.

About eight kilometres past Marongora, Vera turned right onto the dirt road leading to Mana Pools. It was rough going, and she drove the big four-wheel-drive campervan at a leisurely pace to avoid the worst bits. About thirty-five kilometres down the corrugated dirt road, they came to a boom gate at the entrance to Mana Pools. Vera showed the entry permit to the guard, who opened the boom gate and waved them on with a cheerful smile. Only another forty kilometres to their destination.

On the road, they saw the occasional buck and a sole hyena. The ubiquitous baobab flourished in the thick bush in the immediate vicinity. Farther into the park in the forested areas of mahogany, wild fig, and the magnificent winter-thorn, the undergrowth in the shade of the majestic trees would thin out to almost nothing in parts, making it much easier for them to view the wildlife. The winter-thorn (ana tree) produced the apple-ring pods that entice the larger bull elephants to do their famous stunt, standing on their hind legs to reach the lofty branches.

No giraffe, wildebeest, or rhino roamed the park, but there were lions, buffalo, hippo, wild dogs, hyena, crocodiles, and cheetah. Warthogs and a variety of buck offered a steady diet to the predators. Vera and Zak visited most of Zimbabwe's national parks over the years, but they always loved seeing the wilderness with its magnificent animals.

A remote camping site near the river looked an attractive spot for the night. No other vehicles parked nearby, and the guide, who would usually attend a site, was absent. 'I wonder where he is,' said Vera. 'The guides normally point out where to park. Perhaps this site isn't manned anymore.'

'The park looks quiet. Maybe they're focussing on the main camp sites at present.'

Zak set about building a fire for their evening braai and boil water for tea. Vera prepared the steaks and cut the onions and egg plant they would have for their evening meal. The sinking sun provided the perfect light for photos, so she walked with Zak to the edge of the embankment to seek the best views.

Darkness was falling. 'Let's return to the fire,' said Zak. 'It's not safe, standing here in the open in this light. You don't know what's out there, watching us.'

After their meal, the pair sat by the fire, chatting, and solving all the country's problems. At half-past eight, Vera called a halt to the evening. 'We must rise at five-thirty in the morning and out on the road by half-past six. That's when we'll get the best photos.'

Zak needed to empty his bladder. He walked to the edge of the area, just beyond the point the light of the fire reached. Vera headed in the opposite direction for the same purpose. Then she handed Zak the heavy-duty sleeping bag she'd got from a friend whose father served with the army in the Malayan Emergency. A small tent formed the top half of the sleeping bag, and a thick padded canvas base made it ideal for sleeping on the campervan's hard roof, even in the rain.

Vera entered the campervan and locked the door while Zak climbed up onto the roof. With a tiring day and a comfortable temperature in the enclosed space of the campervan, Vera soon fell asleep.

Tat, tat, tat. Vera dreamt someone knocked at the window with a key or something similar. Again, tat, tat, tat. Suddenly awake, she wondered about the noise. Zak, is that you knocking? She called again, louder this time. Still no reply. She sat up and looked through the campervan window, but outside was pitch black. She was sure someone knocked on the window, but perhaps she was dreaming. Was it Zak, or an animal, perhaps? She thumped the roof of the campervan. Wake up, Zak! Did you hear that noise?

On earlier occasions, when she shouted out to Zak on the roof, he'd heard her and responded. This time, there was no reply. Perhaps he was deep in sleep and the knocks on the window, just part of her dream. She was not a nervous person, but a churning, slow chill worked its way down her spine and gnawed at her stomach.

They camped in a remote spot where dangerous animals abounded. Vera scanned the vicinity around the campervan. Nothing, as far as she could tell. It was a moonless night. But she couldn't relax without checking if Zak was OK. She wouldn't risk going outside in this area at night. She slid the door open an inch and called once more to him. The quiet amplified her voice. But still, there was no answer. If she slid the door open a fraction wider and stood on her toes on the edge of the doorway, she'd be able to take a quick peek onto the roof. It would only take a second. Vera eased the campervan door open a little wider, taking care not to make any noise. She stood in the doorway, and holding the edge of the roof, peered over the top.

CHAPTER 16

The World Upside Down

THURSDAY night, and Mary had not seen Frida since Monday evening. It was unlike her, and Mary wondered about her absence. It wasn't long before she discovered the reason. On Friday morning, loud voices next door disturbed the customary peace of the neighbourhood. Mary couldn't make out the words, but she recognised Frida's voice and the louder voice of Mrs Mapfumo, Frida's madam. Mary didn't need to understand the words to realise a heated exchange was in progress.

The confrontation continued for about thirty minutes before peace returned. Julia noticed the row next door and opted for breakfast indoors. Mary returned to her kia to eat her breakfast. As she ate, she heard Frida's periodic mutterings and the slamming of doors. Frida's kia stood near the high wall that separated the back gardens of the two properties.

Mary returned to the house to clear the breakfast table and wash the dishes. Julia came into the kitchen carrying her handbag in one hand and her car keys in the other. 'I'll be back around eleven, Mary.'

'Yes, Madam.' Mary hurried to open the front gate to see Julia off.

Mary took immense pride in keeping the kitchen in a sparkling condition. House-proud when in her village, she was no different here. She wiped down the sink and draining board, and as she turned her attention to the other surfaces, a whispered voice called her name.

'Mary, it's me, Frida.'

'Frida, you and your madam argued. Is everything all right?'

'No, that woman has fired me.'

'Oh, no! Why?'

'She always complains about my work, so I got fed up and told her she should find someone else if she wasn't happy with me. I never expected the stupid woman to do it.'

'So where will you go?'

'Can I stay here in your kia with you until I find another job? All my things are in this suitcase.'

'Yes, I'm sure the madam won't mind.'

'Don't tell your madam. Madams are unpredictable. She may say no.'

'If you stay in my kia, I must tell her.'

'No! If she says I can't stay, imagine how bad you will feel when I'm homeless and begging on the street.'

'Homeless? Can't you stay with your mother?'

'No, my mother's new husband doesn't like me being around her. He says I'm a bad influence.'

'But if I don't tell my madam you're staying here, she will notice I'm taking more food and other supplies. She will find out.'

'I won't be here that long. By the time she gets suspicious, I'll be gone.'

'If I don't get my madam's permission, it makes me feel dishonest.'

'Don't worry about that. We maids must stick together and help each other.'

'But—'

'We can talk later. In the meantime, say nothing. I need time to plan.'

'OK, but no playing the radio too loud.'

'Don't worry. No one will suspect I'm here.'

* * *

Frida, as persuasive as ever, relaxed into the comfort of Julia's unwitting hospitality. She even visited other maids in the street. On one occasion, Frida bumped into Julia on her way back to the kia. Julia assumed Frida came to see Mary, though she wondered what was behind her furtive manner.

Mary worried about Frida's presence over the weekend, but three nights passed without incident. She worried how much longer her guest would be staying. If at the beginning she got the madam's permission, it wouldn't be a problem. Perhaps it wasn't too late to talk to the madam about Frida.

Mary polished the small stoep at the front door with the red Cobra wax polish, her thoughts a thousand miles away. She didn't notice Dorothy Mapfumo's approach until the woman almost stood over her.

'Tell your madam I want to see her.'

'Yes, Madam.'

Julia came to the front door. The look on Dorothy's face told her it wasn't a social visit.

'Mrs Watson, the maids in this street tell me you are harbouring Frida. I won't let you steal her away from me, just so you can replace your stupid maid.'

'I can assure you, Dorothy, I am not harbouring Frida, and I wouldn't dream of replacing my maid.'

'Oh, really! Everyone in the street is aware of it, except you. Check what your dishonest maid is doing behind your back. That's the trouble with you bleeding heart whites; you let them get away with murder.'

'Dorothy, that's enough!'

'Tell Frida she must return at once. She's been AWOL since Friday morning. Only today, I found out about your involvement.'

Dorothy Mapfumo turned and strode off down the drive, her short sharp steps showing her indignation and suggesting she'd satisfied her need to have her say.

Julia turned to see an open-mouthed Mary standing behind her. 'Well, Mary. Is that true?'

Mary's mouth went dry, and her English language skills deserted her. 'Madam, I, I, I—'

'Let's have a look at your kia, Mary. It's time for an inspection, anyway.'

A crestfallen Mary followed Julia to her kia. Julia opened the kia door and entered the room. 'Mary, where is your mattress?'

Mary pointed to the corner, where the mattress lay under two crumpled blankets.

'You're sleeping on your bed springs? There're three blankets on your bed, Mary, so you've helped yourself to another two from the linen cupboard. Has Frida been sleeping there, in the corner, since Friday?'

'Yes, Madam.'

'Your guest is not as tidy as you, Mary.' The pair stood in silence, surveying the room. The sound of soft African music wafted on the morning breeze.

Julia walked towards the back of the kia. There sat Frida, warming herself in the early winter sun. 'Frida, your madam wants you back at work this instant. She's angry, so you better hurry.'

'Yes, Madam. Thank you, Madam.' Frida raced around, collecting her possessions and stuffing them into her suitcase.

Julia turned to Mary. 'When Frida's gone, come into the house. I want to talk to you.'

'Yes, Madam.'

* * *

Ten minutes later, Mary walked with trepidation to the house, hesitating before ascending the two steps to the back door. She walked through the kitchen to the dining room, where Julia sat at the dining table, her face serious.

'I'm sorry, Madam.'

'Mary, I'm disappointed in you. If you'd asked me if Frida could stay in your kia, I wouldn't have minded, and if I'd known, I would have lent her my camp bed.'

'Sorry, Madam. I was going to tell you.'

'When, Mary, when? Frida spent three nights in your kia. You'd tell me in three weeks, or perhaps three months?'

'I was going to tell you today, Madam.'

'Today! Are you sure?'

'Yes, Madam.'

'When you first came here, I told you I wanted an honest maid.'

'Yes, Madam. I am honest.'

'How can I trust you, Mary?'

'You can, Madam. You can. I promise.'

'Now Mrs Mapfumo, next door, believes I am a liar. She thinks I tried to pinch Frida to work for me. Your actions have embarrassed me and made me look like a fool.'

'Sorry, Madam.'

After a long silence, Julia sighed and spoke again. 'I realise Frida must have influenced you, so I will give you another chance. All I can say is, I'm disappointed in you.'

'Sorry, Madam. Thank you, Madam.'

Mary hurried back to the kitchen, flushed but relieved. She had kept her job for now. But then she remembered Vera's words and worried all over again. From now on, she'd be more careful about following Frida's advice.

* * *

Since Vera's visit, Mary tried even harder to absorb Julia's lessons. Her English was much improved since her arrival, and the need for Julia's repeated instructions grew less. It was over a week since Vera left for Mana Pools. Mary swept the parquet floor in the lounge with the soft mop while Julia worked in her office. The phone rang with its loud, persistent jangle. Mary picked up the handset. 'This is Julia Watson's residence. Mary speaking.'

'Is the madam home?' The African man's voice sounded formal and urgent.

Mary walked to the office and knocked on the open door. 'Phone call, Madam.'

Julia hurried to the phone. She treated each of the infrequent calls as a matter of urgency. Mary listened as Julia's cheerful voice trailed off and then became serious and quiet. Following the call, Julia walked into the kitchen, and Mary looked up expectantly.

'Mary, please make tea.'

Mary realised something troubled the madam, but it wasn't her place to enquire. Julia spent the day in her office and didn't come into the kitchen when Mary prepared dinner. Mary missed the madam's chatty company, and even when she served dinner, the madam remained silent. Perhaps the madam's daughter found a replacement maid. And now Julia couldn't face telling her she was no longer needed? The unfortunate incident with Frida made that possibility ever more likely. When she discussed the matter with Frida, her friend offered no advice on what might be wrong.

Frida only wanted to discuss the situation with her madam. 'She told me to leave and never return. But when I saw my madam on Monday, she was sweet, like honey. She said she never meant it, and I was a silly girl to think she was serious about firing me. I soon saw the reason she was so nice. The place was in a terrible mess. It took me ages to get it tidy.'

Mary's mind was elsewhere, and she heard little of Frida's prattle. Perhaps tomorrow, things would be better. And hadn't the madam said she'd give her another chance? But the madam was still quiet at breakfast and answered Mary's comments with grunts or one-word answers. Soon, Julia retreated to her office, and Mary heard her tapping away on the keyboard. The morning dragged, when just before tea, the doorbell rang. Mary hurried to open the front door. A mature, distinguished-looking African man and a young police constable stood there.

'I am Inspector Kutumela. Is Mrs Watson here?' She recognised the formal voice from the previous day's phone call. When she knocked on Julia's closed office door, it opened almost at once. The madam must have been expecting a visit or a phone call.

'Mary, please put the kettle on for tea,' said Julia, as she hurried to greet the visitors.

The hum of the electric kettle obscured the hushed conversation in the lounge. Mary stood by the kitchen door, but couldn't overhear what they said. The visitors left before the kettle boiled. Julia took the cup of tea from Mary and disappeared into her bedroom, closing the door behind her. A moment later, the door opened, and Julia called out to Mary. Don't worry about dinner tonight, Mary. I'm not hungry.

Mary ate her dinner in the kia, listening to Frida go on and on about her ungrateful, demanding madam. She didn't take in a word Frida spoke. Her thoughts dwelt on her own madam and what troubled her.

When Julia didn't come out of her room for breakfast the next morning, Mary knocked on her bedroom door. Tea and breakfast, Madam!

'Just leave it at the door, please, Mary.'

When she checked later, Mary found the teacup empty, but the breakfast untouched. She tried to interest Julia in lunch, and later, in dinner. Julia said she wasn't hungry, and although Mary left meals at the bedroom door, she only took the tea.

The next two days were the same. Mary now changed tack. 'You must eat, Madam. You can't go on without food.' Friday evening, and Julia had eaten nothing since Tuesday breakfast. It perplexed Mary, and Frida was no help.

'Stop fussing. She'll come out when she's hungry.'

'But she would have been hungry by Wednesday morning.'

'Well, there's no understanding the whites. They have their strange ways. Especially the older ones.'

'The madam is not so old.'

'Maybe her daughter has driven her mad.'

'You said mothers didn't listen to their daughters.'

* * *

On Saturday morning, a rather subdued Julia emerged from her bedroom. Mary tried in her absence to keep busy, cleaning the house, cooking the meals, and sweeping the driveway, but it was hard going. Now, as she cooked breakfast, she felt as light as air.

'You seem happy this morning, Mary.'

'Because you are eating again, Madam.'

'Goodness! Does your happiness depend on me eating?'

'Yes, Madam. I was too worried about you.'

'Well, I'm sorry if I upset you.'

'It's OK, Madam.'

'I must tell you why I have stayed in my room since Tuesday.'

'It's OK, Madam.'

'On Monday, the police phoned to say park guides found my daughter's van abandoned, and she and her assistant were missing. Then on Tuesday, the police came to tell me the guides at Mana Pools said poachers must have killed them, and wild animals removed all traces of their bodies. Someone stripped the van of valuables, so the police believe the guides are right.'

'Sorry, Madam, I didn't know.'

'The police said drag marks led to the river, so crocodiles may have eaten them. But poachers could have made the drag marks, taking the bodies to the water. The ground was disturbed, so the police think the poachers may have tried to remove any trace of their footprints.'

'That is terrible news, Madam.'

'I must stay strong, Mary. That is what Vera would have wanted.'

'Yes, Madam. Sorry, Madam.'

* * *

In bed that night, Mary's thoughts whirled. She couldn't believe what had happened.

Most disturbing of her thoughts were the parallels between her marriage to Josiah and her job with the madam. Josiah's number one wife wanted to get rid of her, just as the madam's daughter wanted to get rid of her. Both met with unfortunate ends. In the village, Nancy proved to be a false friend. Would Frida turn out the same?

What other parallels might develop? Was she cursed? Would she have to flee the city? But to where?

CHAPTER 17

The Scarecrow

THE tragic circumstances of Vera's disappearance foreshadowed a bleak winter. Despite her determination to stay strong, Julia often retreated into lengthy periods of silence. During these times, she missed dinner and retired early. Mary would find herself alone, wondering how she might cheer up Julia and help her through her pain.

One thing Julia did to keep herself busy and occupy her mind was to launch into an ambitious upgrade of Mary's kia. She hired a painter to transform the dull grey walls into a fresh white, making the interior so much brighter, both day and night. Julia replaced the round coir mat with a large wool carpet that almost reached the walls on all four sides. A clean-burning, odourless lamp fuel replaced the kerosene that Mary used in her lamp to light her kia each night.

Electricity outages were common, so Julia organised a man to build a wood-burning hot water system, using a forty-four-gallon drum installed over a brick fireplace at the back of the kia. It used a generator to serve both the house and the kia, and saved on electricity charges.

A light brown wooden cupboard with drawers and hanging space for Mary's clothes made an unexpected appearance one morning, and Julia gave Mary items of clothing she no longer needed. Jumpers and dresses found their way from Julia's cupboard into their new home in Mary's kia.

The upgrade in her living conditions provided luxury beyond Mary's dreams, and it made Julia feel she did something worthwhile. But soon, that project was complete, and Julia was at a loose end again. She'd lost interest in her blog, for the time being at least, and sank back into her periods of quiet.

Mary noted the signs and struggled over how to help Julia. She'd lie awake at night, worrying about it. Then, she had a brilliant idea that kept her mind active, and sleep eluded her that night. But would Julia agree to her plan? Julia tackled the upgrade of the kia with gusto. From this, Mary perceived her to be energetic and open to new projects.

The idea seemed clever, lying in bed at night. But in daylight, it appeared more problematic. A beautiful morning, and Julia opted for a breakfast outdoors at the braai. Mary loved these occasions when she cooked the fried eggs, bacon, and tomatoes on the hotplate. She was proficient at preparing the perfect toast over the flames as the whistling kettle joined in the fun.

The whole breakfast came together to form one of her favourite meals, and through it, Mary gained a confidence in her growing list of skills. But her newfound confidence didn't settle the nerves jumping in her stomach. As the two women sat sipping their tea, admiring their surroundings, Mary wondered how to broach her brilliant idea.

'Madam, this garden is beautiful.'

'Uh-huh.'

'The front garden is beautiful. The side garden, with the trees, is also beautiful.'

'Uh-huh.'

'But this large back garden is empty.'

'Um? Why do you say that?'

'The grass here is too dry. It is just a big open space.'

'Yes?' Julia drew out the word. 'It's because of the water shortage. If the rains aren't good, we don't water this back part.'

'Vegetables are expensive, Madam.'

'Yes, they are.'

'Maybe if we grew vegetables here—'

'Vegetables need a lot of attention and lots of water.'

'I can do that, Madam.'

'Well, I'd also help, but let me think about it. What vegetables would you suggest?'

'Mealies and gem squash, Madam. Also, lettuce, carrots, potatoes, tomatoes, and other things.'

'Goodness! That sounds ambitious. How much space would it need?'

'A lot, Madam. We must leave a wide path next to the house and around the edge of the vegetable garden, and between the rows.'

'Water is still a problem.'

* * *

Mary's argument must have been persuasive because by mid-afternoon both she and Julia worked in the back garden, pulling up the grass and turning the soil with garden forks Julia retrieved from the garage.

The next day, Monday, Julia bought a big compost bin and arranged for a large rainwater tank to be installed near the corner of the house, separating the side garden from the back. 'The man said we'd have our rainwater tank before the start of the wet season. In the meantime, he's plumbing in an underground drip system which he says will save us water if we only use it when conditions are dry. He will connect it to the rainwater tank and to the mains water.'

Over the next two weeks, Julia took Mary to buy manure, chemical fertiliser, and mulch. Mary was not familiar with the last two items, or the modern technology Julia ordered, but she learnt fast. She was pleased to see Julia's enthusiasm for the task helped her to become her old self again.

The rainwater tank, which sat just below the eaves of the roof, arrived three weeks later. The man from the shop connected the underground drip system to the water supply. Early October, and the relentless sun beat down on the dry earth. Now they needed to wait for the rains. Julia didn't want to use the mains water as the city's dams were low. The radio was full of talk about when the rains would arrive. Impatient to start their vegetable garden, the women found that time dragged. The dark clouds teased them, looking promising one day and then racing away to leave empty blue skies the next.

Still, the rains didn't come. November arrived, and the empty blue skies persisted. Gradually, the storm clouds gathered, but as the old saying goes, 'a watched kettle never boils,' and the stubborn clouds looked like it would never rain. Each day, the dark clouds threatened, but nothing happened.

'It looks like the rains are late this year, Mary.'

'Soon, Madam. Soon it will rain.'

And then it did. The smell of ozone before the downpour, and afterwards, the rain on the dusty dry earth, petrichor, was the fragrance of Heaven. When the rain stopped, Mary and Julia got to work preparing the soil. After the next rain, they would plant the seedlings. Only two days later, the rain returned.

Mary planted the entire first bed, next to the braai, with mealies. Julia planted the second bed with gem squash, zucchinis, and potatoes. Between them, they planted the third bed with carrots, radishes, lettuce, tomatoes, and basil. The fourth bed they left empty for rotation or other vegetables. With the planting done, they spread a generous amount of mulch over the beds. Now, they needed to wait for the results of their labour and keep the beds watered on hot, rainless days.

Most mornings saw a garden breakfast under the shady trees that grew along the fence. Julia and Mary sat looking for any sign of a green shoot peeping from the mulch. The first one to emerge, the sign of new life, delighted them. Then other shoots sprang up everywhere. But now, the birds pecked and pulled at the shoots and scattered the mulch. When Mary observed them from the kitchen window, she'd call out to shoo them back into the trees. At first, the birds flew off when Mary shouted out of the kitchen window. But soon they realised there was no danger, and they became bolder.

'We must make a scarecrow,' said Julia.

Mary stood by and watched as Julia nailed two pieces of timber into the shape of a tall cross. She put it on the edge of the path between the two inner beds. With chicken wire, she fashioned the body, arms, and head, and tied different coloured pieces of wool to the end of each arm. Next, she placed a long, loose white nightdress on the scarecrow and a floppy hat on its head. Everything flapped in the breeze, acting as a noisy mobile to scare the birds.

'Madam, this nightdress it too good to be outside on the scarecrow. My nightdress is old. Can I exchange this one for mine?'

'Yes, if your nightdress is suitable.'

Mary brought out her old nightdress, also long, loose, and white, but tattered, so that the bottom edge flapped in the wind.

'Oh, yes, Mary. Your nightdress is better for the scarecrow. It flaps more in the breeze. Now, you both have new nightdresses.'

'Thank you, Madam.'

Every morning there was more growth, with a few shoots developing faster than others. Soon, the backyard looked like a real vegetable garden. Julia often made minor adjustments to the scarecrow, and the constant changes worked well, keeping the birds guessing. Her finishing touch was a hoe placed in the scarecrow's hand to make it look like it worked in the vegetable garden. The scarecrow looked more realistic with each change, developing a personality of its own.

Mary became obsessed with the garden's progress. In her village, the mealies seldom achieved the rate of growth she saw in Julia's garden. While she thought of it as Julia's vegetable garden, Julia often corrected her, saying it was their vegetable garden.

On moonlit nights, when Julia when to bed, Mary would often sit near the braai in the evening's cool breeze, looking at what they'd achieved. On one such occasion, she sat in her white nightdress, admiring the vegetable garden, when she noticed a movement at the far corner of the house. At first, she assumed it was Frida coming to visit, but soon realised it was a man.

His manner was furtive, stopping every few steps to glance around. He started at the sight of the scarecrow, ducking low to study the apparition. Satisfied it was harmless, he grunted and moved to the back door. He tried the handle, but the door was locked. He then tried the door leading into the garage. It swung open. Julia's car always stood in the driveway, and the garage housed gardening equipment and other odds and ends.

The thief had not noticed Mary sitting deep in the shadows underneath the trees. She stood up and crept towards the scarecrow, and grabbed the hoe. The man's boldness incensed her. He was a thief. The villagers would not accept such behaviour. They would have chased and beaten him, giving him reason to fear for his life. Why should the city be any different?

A short while later, the man emerged from the garage, pushing the wheelbarrow filled with an assortment of garden tools. He looked around, as if searching for what else he might steal. The man glanced at the scarecrow dressed in a flowing white robe and carrying a hoe. He almost tipped the wheelbarrow over, when suddenly, it seemed to move towards him.

With an almighty, blood-curdling scream, Mary ran at the man with the hoe raised high. The thief tripped in his hurry to escape and crashed to the ground. Still, the creature in the white robe raced towards him, waving the hoe. He jumped up and raced through the front gate and down the road.

The light flicked on in Julia's bedroom, and she got up to investigate the commotion. 'It's lucky you were in the garden, Mary, and brave enough to confront that man. You don't know how he might have reacted. Goodness knows what else he might have stolen if you'd not been here. We must lock the garage each evening.'

While Julia went to search for the key to lock the garage, Mary returned everything to their rightful place. She placed the garden hoe in the scarecrow's hand and headed for bed in her kia. She'd smudged her white nightdress with dirt from the garden tools that she returned to the garage. No worries, she could wash it tomorrow.

* * *

The next morning, the two women sat at breakfast by the braai, admiring their fast-developing vegetable garden.

At morning tea, Mary saw Frida standing near the garden gate and walked across to say hello.

'All the maids are talking, Mary.'

'What do you mean?'

'They say a thief tried to steal your garden tools last night.'

'How do you know that?'

'The thief must've told someone in the street. The maids say your house has a spirit that protects the garden.'

'A spirit?'

'Yes, they say your scarecrow chased the thief and tried to kill him.'

Mary could tell Frida was uncomfortable about the prospect of a spirit next door. 'I've never seen a spirit here, Frida. I'm sure you'll not face harm if you visit me in my kia at night.'

Despite Mary's assurances, Frida's night visits abruptly ended, but the rumours didn't. The maids didn't believe that Julia, a white woman, could conjure up spirits. Mary must be responsible. Before now, no spirits roamed the area. Only since Mary arrived in the street did such a thing happen. What if one of them somehow offended her? Would she take revenge by turning the spirit on them? They argued about what they should do. What if this woman brought evil upon them? All the women spoke at once.

'Mary said that her madam built the scarecrow.'

'But Mary could've taken advantage of that. The white madam wouldn't have knowledge of spirits in our culture. Mary must have brought in the spirit.'

'Perhaps we should consult a sangoma?'

'No, the government bigwigs have the power. Where is her village? We must see which member of parliament looks after the area. We can ask him about her.'

'Where is her village?'

'My mother said she got on the bus at Figtree,' said Frida.

'What's wrong with you all? There are no such things as spirits. There must be some other explanation.'

'You are wrong, Clara. Abigail's boyfriend said it was a scarecrow that became a demon when it saw him. There is bad medicine here.'

'You say you have seen this thing, Frida?'

'Yes, it looks like a scarecrow in daytime, but its eyes always follow you.'

'You've seen its eyes?'

'Yes, they are red like the colour of blood. Mary says they are just buttons that her madam sewed onto its face, but I'm sure they're more than that.'

'Should we call Mary to explain our worry about the spirit?'

'No, she says, she's never seen it.'

'If she's a witch, she might put a spell on us.'

'Stop sisters, you are all imagining the worst and talking nonsense.'

'If you don't want to believe it, Clara, that's your problem. But don't come crying to us if she turns her demon on you.'

The overactive imaginations of the women worked them into an excitable state, with their raised voices resembling a flock of cockatoos welcoming the dawn. The group resolved not to upset Mary, but to avoid her where possible. In the meantime, they designated one of their group to find out which member of parliament represented the Figtree area.

'Frida, where are you?' a voice bellowed. 'Why is your tea taking so long today?'

It was Dorothy Mapfumo calling her maid. The excited chatter ended, and the gathering broke up as the maids returned to their respective households.

Mary was unaware of the gathering. Her thoughts dwelt on the vegetable garden.

CHAPTER 18

Two Steps Forward…

THE coming of the rains always signified Christmas was close. Thunderous downpours kept the garden well-watered, and the gutters directed much of the rain from the roof to the rainwater tank, which soon overflowed. The remaining downpipes filled the forty-four-gallon drums parked at the bottom of each one. In Zimbabwe, water was a precious commodity, and when it rained, people collected it in any suitable container.

The rainwater tank incorporated a mesh system that prevented access to mosquitoes, but the drums attracted them in numbers. Julia kept small fish in each of the drums, and the mosquitoes and their larvae provided a nourishing meal for the occupants. The advantage of the tank and drums was they didn't rely on electricity. Boreholes, a common source of water, often didn't work because of electricity outages—an all too frequent occurrence with the ageing infrastructure.

It was a time of plenty, and the vegetable garden thrived. Julia and Mary agreed they needed to schedule their planting of vegetables with a little more care. Waiting for the rains to plant the seedlings meant much of their planting was early or late. But a shortage of water before the rains gave them little choice. It was also plain there would be a surplus of some vegetables, way beyond their needs. Still, they might swap certain vegetables for others they did not plant. Many people converted their lawns and flower beds to vegetable gardens, so there was an opportunity to trade.

With low or non-existent supplies, getting seeds or seedlings was a problem. It meant they needed to select from what was available. Fortunately, Julia's good connections got her supplies and equipment unavailable to others.

'Madam, why don't we get chickens and have our own eggs?'

'Goodness, Mary, it's hard to keep up with you and your projects. Our chicken coop hasn't been in use for years. I'm sure it will need repairs. There is chicken wire netting in the garage if needed.'

* * *

Mary puzzled why Frida didn't visit her in the evenings anymore. Perhaps, she realised Mary didn't always follow her advice. From time to time, she saw Frida near the gate, and they chatted as normal, but gone was the closeness that developed early in their relationship. Mary found it hard to imagine the scarecrow incident would frighten off a confident, modern maid like Frida. But then, many intelligent and educated Africans, like Sergeant Dube and Jackson Mpofu, kept their instinctive superstitions and had not outgrown their traditional beliefs. Despite her lack of education, Mary always maintained a scepticism in such matters, though she was not above using them in her consultations with those who sought her advice.

After their gathering, the maids in the street all kept a polite distance from Mary. Clara, the one exception, appeared even friendlier than ever. Mary wasn't close to the other maids in the street, so didn't notice their absence; though she often wondered why Frida didn't include her on her frequent visits to them.

Agnes, the maid whom the group assigned to find out which bigwig represented the Figtree area, reported back to the other maids on her findings. 'The chef's name is Jackson Mpofu. When I said the name, Mary Moyo, he put down the phone. So, I called him back, but he said he didn't want to talk about her—she was trouble.'

It wasn't welcome news, and only confirmed the maids' suspicions, but they were stuck with the situation. Apart from the occasional chat at the gate with Frida and a cheerful passing greeting with Clara, Mary's only companionship was with Julia. Working in the vegetable garden together made her and Julia's situation more akin to a friendship than one of mistress and servant.

One sunny morning, sitting in the shade of the trees near the braai, a thought crossed Julia's mind. 'Mary, you haven't asked me about taking time off at Christmas.'

'Christmas, Madam?'

'Yes, don't you want to go home to your village?'

'No, Madam.'

'But what about your family? Don't you want to visit them?'

'No, Madam. My mother is dead, and my father has a new wife, and has no interest in seeing me. My sister lives in Francistown, in Botswana. I have a house in my husband's village, but he is dead, and I have no relatives there.'

'So, what will you do for Christmas?'

'Nothing, Madam. I'll stay here.'

'Oh! In that case, we must make it a happy time.'

'Can you be happy without your daughter at Christmas, Madam?' Mary had spoken without thinking and at once regretted the boldness of her question.

'Vera was overseas the last two Christmases. Yes, she did phone, but I spent those two Christmases here with the boss, and I visited my friend who recently died in hospital. I won't miss the boss, but I will miss my friend a little.'

'Yes, Madam, I remember when you took the flowers to her.'

Julia laughed. 'Yes, the flowers in the bottles. I'll never forget it. To-morrow, we'll go to the city and look around the shops. I don't like our chances of finding too many Christmas things to buy.'

* * *

The next morning, Mary wore the earrings and a dress Julia gave her. It was her first visit to the city centre since she passed through it on the way to Mpilo Hospital with her sick husband and Sergeant Dube.

'My, you look smart today, Mary! Dressed like that, we must stop for coffee somewhere, or perhaps even lunch.'

After breakfast, the two women jumped into Julia's little blue Honda and set off for the city. Rush hour was over, so the traffic wasn't too heavy, but in the CBD, cars filled the parking spaces and people walked everywhere. Julia found parking outside the Bata shoe shop, opposite the Haddon and Sly supermarket in Fife Street. As they got out of the car, a young African teen hailed them.

'Look after your car for you, Madam? Keep it safe?'

'I'll pay you when we get back,' said Julia. She wouldn't fall for that old trick.

The two women crossed the road towards Haddon and Sly and then crossed over to the city hall, where the African curio sellers lined the pavement. Soon, a group of vendors surrounded Julia, inviting her to buy their works of art and other items. But Julia was neither a tourist nor a buyer. Such an array of arts and crafts was something new to Mary, and she stood there wide-eyed, but the vendors ignored her, preferring to concentrate their efforts on the white madam. After rejecting multiple offers of trinkets thrust at her, and invitations to view various ranges of handmade goods, Julia purchased a colourful wooden key ring in a flame lily design.

When they extricated themselves from the enthusiastic curio vendors, Julia and Mary made their way to Jason Moyo Street (formerly Abercorn Street), where many of the larger stores stood. They browsed in Edgars and Truworths, and the neighbouring shops. Julia bought one or two small items, and soon it was time for lunch. The teen wasn't around when they returned to the car—no surprise there.

Julia drove down Eighth Avenue to Josiah Tongogara Street (formerly Wilson Street) and parked next to the Indaba Book Cafe where they ate a curry lunch. Mary felt she was in a dream. The street shared her dead husband's first name, and here she shared a table in a cafe with the madam. Somehow, it differed from sitting on bench seats at the large outdoor breakfast table by the braai at home. For Mary, the closeness to Julia in the intimate quiet of the cafe was the best part of their city visit.

After lunch, Julia took Mary to show her the Ascot Centre shops, which were a little like the Food Lover's Market. Both centres boasted Pick n Pay supermarkets, overflowing with goods and delicacies.

Back in the car, an idea crossed Mary's mind. She asked Julia if they could drive home along Josiah Tongogara Street so she could show her where she spent her first night in Bulawayo. It disappointed her there was no sign of the security guard. She wanted to show him how wrong he'd been. Near the old Bradfield shops, Mary asked Julia to stop. She emerged from the car and walked to the last vendor. 'Two bananas please.'

The woman's jaw fell open when she saw the well-dressed Mary standing in front of her. 'You, I recognise you! You're the country girl who looked for a job.'

'Yes, and I found one.'

'Dressed so smart, I thought you were a businesswoman.'

'I'm just a housemaid with a good madam. We came to the city today for shopping and lunch.'

'Eish! How can that be? Nobody is that lucky.'

Mary smiled and thanked the vendor. 'Take care, Sister. I will come again sometime.'

'Did you get what you wanted, Mary?' Julia asked.

'Yes, I bought two bananas from that vendor. One for you and one for me. I bought two bananas from her when I came to ask you for the job.'

Julia smiled. She understood how proud Mary felt when she saw the woman again today.

After dinner that evening, Julia handed her a small package wrapped in coloured tissue paper. 'Open it, Mary. It's not really a present, but it's something you'll need.'

'Oh! Thank you, Madam.' Mary unwrapped the package, taking care not to tear the delicate paper. Slowly it unfolded, and she saw the colourful key ring with the flame lily pattern. Attached was a bright silver Yale key.

'It's the key to the back door, Mary. Now you won't have to wait for me to open in the morning.'

Mary was delighted to receive her own key to the house's back door. She lay in bed that night thinking about how the day unfolded and how it signalled a significant change in her situation. Lunch with the madam was a highlight. But getting a house key was even a bigger thrill. It meant she'd earned the madam's trust. At last, she felt secure. The madam always said she wanted a trustworthy maid. Mary worried the business with Frida eroded the madam's confidence in her, but the key showed her the indiscretion was forgiven, if not forgotten.

* * *

Julia awoke to the sound of hammering. Only seven a.m.? Mary wasn't due in until seven-thirty. Julia opened the upper half of the kitchen's stable door. 'Mary, what's that racket you're making so early in the morning? The neighbours will complain.'

'I'm fixing the chicken coop, Madam. It doesn't need much more work.'

'Well, leave that for later. Now that you're up, let's have an early breakfast at the braai. Please make a start, and I'll join you after my shower. Henry is coming to cut the grass today, so we must finish in the garden before he arrives.'

Soon after morning tea, Henry arrived. Julia introduced him to Mary and left the two chatting in Ndebele, and returned to her office.

It was the first mowing of the season, and Henry went through his routine of checking the hand lawn mower and removing the accumulated winter dust. He oiled the axle, which held the wheels and cutting blades. Once satisfied, he carried the mower to the front lawn, which he always cut before tackling the side.

Julia sat at her computer, which stood in front of the window over-looking the back garden. A little before lunch, she noticed Henry must have finished cutting the grass because he helped Mary with the chicken coop. Soon, Mary came to the office door to tell Julia that Henry was leaving.

'Here, please give Henry this money, Mary, and ask him to come again in three weeks.'

* * *

The next morning, Julia found a bright-eyed Mary in the kitchen, pre-paring a tray for breakfast at the braai.

'The braai again, Mary! I didn't think we had any eggs left.'

'Two eggs, Madam, enough for you.'

'No, one egg each, then.'

'OK, Madam.'

The two women sat eating their breakfast under the trees, admiring the mealies that grew taller by the day. Out of the corner of her eye, Julia noticed movement in the chicken coop.

'Mary, what's that in the chicken coop?'

'Chicken's, Madam,' said Mary, beaming. 'I bought them from Henry. There're two chickens. That's where our eggs came from this morning.'

'I didn't know Henry kept chickens.'

Julia walked over to the chicken run. 'Oh, Black Australorps! Good egg-laying hens. When did you get them?'

'Henry brought them last night, Madam.'

'Well, we better buy poultry food and a proper nesting box for them, or they'll stop laying.'

* * *

In the mid-afternoon, Mary noticed Frida standing in the corner of her garden next door and hurried over for a chat. Even though Frida's vis-its ceased, Mary did not take exception and chatted to her when the opportunity arose. Mary was keen to talk about the vegetable garden's progress and the two hens, but Frida spoke first. 'Priscilla came around here today.'

'Oh, how is her new job?'

'OK, but she said two hens are missing from her employer's chicken run. Her boss said they either escaped or someone stole them last night, so he sent Priscilla to ask if anyone had seen them.'

'You told me Priscilla's new employers have a big dog that growls at her. How could anyone steal them without it barking?'

'Priscilla's boss says it might be someone the dog knows. They questioned her, but agreed any deliveryman or maid in the area might be responsible.'

'What is Priscilla's house number? If I hear anything, I'll let her know.'

'Number five. The modern house with a big garden. But be careful of the dog.'

Half an hour later, Mary took a walk around the block. She'd not visited the neighbouring streets before now. She'd learnt the art of questioning everything, and now Frida's words hung heavy on her mind. Mary turned left at Burns Drive and left into the next street. She searched the garden walls and fences for the house numbers. Then, her heart fell when she saw number five's expanse of freshly mowed lawn. Too much of a coincidence?

Henry would return in three weeks. She didn't know how she'd wait so long to question him about the hens. What should she do? Should she talk to Julia about her suspicions? She'd only just won Julia's full trust, and now this. Mary tossed and turned all night. By morning, she decided she must tell Julia of her concerns. The madam might think her stupid, buying the chickens without her approval.

The hens laid another two eggs, which Mary put in the refrigerator to wait until they'd accumulated four. Julia ate her breakfast of cereal and toast in the dining room, and Mary returned to her kia to eat her toast and jam, together with a little leftover sadza from dinner. The madam was chattier at the braai. It would've been easier to discuss the issue there. Mary took a deep breath. She needed to return to the kitchen to make tea and tell Julia the troublesome news.

'I admire your initiative, buying those chickens, Mary. You've done the right thing, telling me. We could wait to ask Henry about it, but what if someone finds out about our hens in the meantime? It would be very embarrassing if they were the stolen chickens. It would be best if we go to number five in the next street and ask them if they are missing two Black Australorps. That'll show we've nothing to hide. But I can't believe Henry would steal hens from his clients.'

'Clients, Madam?'

'Customers, Mary, customers. Come, let's visit number five right now.'

CHAPTER 19

The Devil at the Gate

JULIA and Mary stood at the front gate of number five in the neighbouring street where the two hens went missing. They didn't enter the garden, and the householder didn't need a doorbell to tell him visitors awaited. The huge, short-haired, white dog with pale blue eyes and long yellow teeth snarled and frothed, threatening to leap over the gate, which suddenly looked way too low.

'Easy, Raja, easy. These two ladies won't harm us.' The tall, slim Indian man introduced himself. 'I'm Sanjeev Patel. How can I help you ladies?'

Julia introduced herself and Mary. 'We wanted to talk to you about your two missing hens.'

The loud, rumbling growls from Raja made hearing difficult. 'You ladies better come in, otherwise he won't stop making a noise.'

'What! Into your garden?' asked Julia, placing a protective hand over her throat.

'Yes, he won't harm you. He's just a pussycat. Raja is scared. That's why he's kicking up a fuss. If I invite you in, he'll understand you are not a threat, and in future you'll be able to walk through the gate with no trouble. He's quick on the uptake, and next time, he'll lick you in greeting.'

Julia hesitated, and Mary's eyes grew wide and round, emphasising the whites.

The two women entered the property, taking small steps, and loathe to shut the gate behind them. But sure enough, Raja stopped growling, though he bared his teeth once or twice at Mary, who was doing her best to keep Julia between them.

'Mr Patel, we wanted to ask you about your two missing hens. Were they, by any chance, Black Australorps?'

'No, no, they were Rhode Island Reds.'

'Ah! Well, that's a relief. We bought two Black Australorps, and when we heard you'd lost two hens, you can guess what we imagined. We use the same lawn man as you, so when he offered us the two hens, we thought we better check with you.'

'Ah yes, Henry, he's a fine chap. I'm sure he wouldn't steal my hens, but I wondered how the thief got past Raja. At first, we accused our maid, but then we realised it could be any delivery man that Raja had met. As I say, the next time you two visit, you can walk straight in, and you won't get a peep out of Raja.'

'Henry has cut my grass for years, and I do trust him, but it seemed such a coincidence.'

'Thank you for enquiring, Mrs Watson. I appreciate it. You must meet my wife sometime. Rani is out at present, but perhaps we can arrange a dinner. She is a wonderful cook if you like curry.'

'Oh, yes, thank you, Mr Patel. I'd like that.'

As the two women walked home, Julia said, 'I thought Henry wouldn't have stolen those hens. He's always been most trustworthy. Still, it wasn't a wasted visit. We've met a neighbour, and it's a beautiful morning for a walk.'

'Yes, Madam. A beautiful morning.'

* * *

Christmas was a fortnight away, and Julia rummaged in the hall cupboard, dragging out the cardboard cartons that surfaced once a year. Mary stood by, waiting to help.

'You can observe how I do it, Mary.'

'Observe, Madam?'

'It means watch.'

'That's how I learn, Madam.'

It was true. Mary hadn't seen Christmas preparations like this before now. In her village, Christmas meant one of the infrequent visits by family members, returning from their places of work in the city. They would bring chickens and other food items with them, and the occasional small gift. But here, Julia assembled an artificial Christmas tree, and decorated it with baubles and small wooden figures and stars. She put up colourful paper streamers, stretching from the pelmet over the lounge window to the bookcase, and from the bookcase to the wooden picture rails that ran high along the walls surrounding the room.

None of the tree decorations lit up because, with the frequent power outages, there was little point in adorning the tree with electric lights. More in hope than with any confidence, Julia plugged in a small electric glass tree that changed colour through a cycle of red, orange, yellow, green, blue, and purple.

Mary was thrilled when Julia gave her a small Christmas tree for her bedside table. She marvelled at the simple decorations. Somehow, they built up an anticipation in her she found thrilling. The warm days cooled by the summer rains added to the atmosphere and a pervading sense of expectancy.

As Christmas approached, Julia busied herself in the kitchen accumulating ingredients and other items to prepare for the big day.

* * *

Two days before Christmas, Henry turned up to cut the grass. He was all smiles and full of Christmas cheer. Soon the lawn, refreshed by the rains, looked like a green carpet. When he finished, Mary gave Henry a mug of tea, and they sat chatting in the shade near the chicken run.

'We want another two black hens.'

'The Australorps are all sold.'

'What hens do you have?'

'I can get you two Rhode Island Reds. They are good layers.'

'How many do you have?'

'Only two.'

'I must ask the madam. She said she wanted Australorps.'

Mary trotted up the steps into the kitchen and moments later, returned with Julia.

'Henry, didn't you tell Mary you only sold Australorps? If you said you also sold Rhode Island Reds, we may've taken those instead.'

'They're a new consignment, Madam, but I only have two Reds left. I never know what my suppliers will offer me.'

'We'll leave them for now, Henry.'

'Do you want me to put in an order for Australorps, Madam?'

'No, thank you, Henry. We'll see how these two do. They might meet our needs. If we change our minds, we'll let you know.'

As he was about to leave, Henry said, 'Christmas box please, Madam.'

Julia smiled and handed him an envelope. 'I haven't forgotten, Henry. It's in the envelope.'

When Henry left, Mary said, 'Madam, do you think his two hens might be Mr Patel's missing hens?'

'They might be his missing hens, Mary. I would have liked the Rhode Island Reds, but I thought it a risk. If word got around, we'd be suspect even if they weren't Mr Patel's chickens.'

* * *

Christmas Eve, with the smell of rain in the air. Yesterday's puddles evaporated, and the hollows that helped in their making waited in ambush for the next downpour. Julia was ready for Christmas Day lunch. 'In the garden if it doesn't rain. Otherwise indoors,' said Julia. Somehow, she'd obtained a small turkey. She bought the vegetables from Pick n Pay at the Food Lover's Market because the potatoes and carrots in the vegetable garden were not doing as well as hoped.

'Mary, taste this, and tell me what you think.'

'Madam?'

'I think you'll like this,' said Julia, handing her a small glass of sherry. 'Don't gulp it. Take little sips.'

Mary put the glass to her mouth and let the sherry touch her lips. She didn't swallow any but licked her lips to get the flavour.

'Sip more than that, Mary. You barely touched it.'

Mary tried again, and this time, a trickle of the sweet liquid rolled down her tongue and into her throat. 'Oh! Very nice, Madam.'

'It's called sherry. Don't drink too much because it makes you tipsy, like drinking too much Chibuku.'

'Women make beer in the village, Madam, and I've seen the men get drunk.'

'If you like the sherry, we can have more before lunch tomorrow.'

'It's nice, Madam.'

'Yes. Last year I drank it on my own because the boss didn't like sherry. All he wanted was beer. Perhaps you've more sophisticated tastes than the boss.'

'Yes, Madam.'

Julia smiled. Mary mightn't understand the word *sophisticated*, but the thought of her maid proving a more suitable drinking companion than her former partner amused her.

'Mary, can you tell the time on the alarm clock I gave you?'

'Oh yes, Madam, sometimes.'

'Sometimes? What do you mean, sometimes?'

'Sometimes it's difficult, Madam. I can tell the hours, but minutes are hard.'

'Why are the minutes hard?'

'They are big numbers, Madam.'

'Can you count to ten?'

'Yes, Madam.'

'So, what comes after ten?'

'A lot, Madam.'

'What about eleven and twelve?'

'Yes, Madam, eleven and twelve.'

'And after twelve?'

'I don't know, Madam.'

'Mary, when you go to the shops, how do you know they give you back the correct change?'

'They take the money and give me back some, Madam.'

'How do you know it's the right amount? They might give you back too little.'

'No, Madam. They must give me the right money back.'

'Good grief, Mary! After Christmas, I'm going to teach you numbers and reading.'

'Thank you, Madam.'

'I've seen you can't read, but I never realised you didn't understand numbers.'

* * *

Christmas morning dawned, and Mary was up earlier than usual. The madam said she needn't come in early because she'd make her own light breakfast. But Mary couldn't lie in bed with the prospect of the madam cooking Christmas lunch on her own. Today, there'd be no cleaning or washing, other than the dishes.

After her shower, Mary dressed in a summer frock the madam gave her and put on her treasured pair of dangling earrings. She admired herself in the wall mirror Julia conjured up from somewhere. Mary guessed that her appearance required a little more care on such a day. She was ready —A lady of fashion.

Now, she'd surprise the madam with an early breakfast. She hurried to the backdoor and opened it with her key and stepped into the kitchen. The surprise was for Mary. Julia was already there, having her tea and toast. The oven was on amid other signs of kitchen activity.

'They are forecasting rain this afternoon, Mary. Let's aim for lunch around half-past twelve. When you finish your tea, come into the lounge.'

Mary was puzzled. Yesterday, the madam said there'd be no work on Christmas Day. She only invited her into a room when she needed to explain a task or point out an overlooked dusty corner. But that seldom happened these days. Mary was fastidious, with an eye for the smallest detail.

* * *

'Yes, Madam.?'

'Come in, Mary. Sit on the sofa.'

Sit on the sofa! She hadn't dared before now. Well, not while the madam was home. But here she was, sitting on the sofa by invitation from the madam herself. The room always looked nice, but with the colourful Christmas decorations, it seemed special.

'Oh! Look, Mary, there's a small parcel here with your name on it. Father Christmas hasn't forgotten you.'

Mary wasn't sure about Father Christmas. Some people said he didn't exist, but then, if he'd brought her a present, who knows? She unwrapped the present with care, and inside, she found a thin leather box. 'What is it, Madam?'

'If you open the box, Mary, you'll find out.'

Mary cautiously lifted the hinged lid as if something dangerous might jump out. A scorpion or a spider. Her jaw dropped. There lay a sparkling silver wristwatch with a black face.

'Vera needed a new watch, so I ordered it for her. But now, it's yours.'

'Oh, thank you, Madam. It's beautiful.'

'That's not just for decoration, Mary. It's for telling the time. It's why I asked you yesterday if you could tell the time. Here, let me put it on your wrist.'

'So, Madam, now you will teach me.'

'Yes, I will.'

'But, Madam, I didn't get a present for you.'

'Yes, you did. My present was the two hens you bought from Henry.'

* * *

Mary walked to the chicken coop and soon returned with two eggs. 'See, Madam, the hens also give us a Christmas present.'

'Yes, it looks like there're many Father Christmases.'

'One hen didn't want me taking the eggs. She pecked my thumb.'

Throughout the morning, Julia made frequent trips to the kitchen to see that nothing burned. Mary set two places at the long table by the braai, and Julia brought table decorations and colourful Christmas serviettes. At a little past twelve noon, lunch was ready. Julia poured two more sherries and introduced Mary to the tradition of toasting Christmas.

First came the avocado and smoked salmon. Mary was familiar with avocado, but the cold smoked salmon was something new. Then, the main course followed. Julia carved the turkey and served the roast potatoes, carrots, and broccoli. Gravy and cranberry sauce added moisture to the tender young bird. Mary mistook the turkey for a chicken but agreed with Julia the flavour was different, especially with the stuffing. The feast ended with Christmas pudding and custard, followed by coffee. So many new flavours, but she enjoyed them all. Julia loved cooking, and the pleasure for her was the appreciative Mary. It was so different from the past two years, cooking Christmas dinner for the judgemental Gerald.

After lunch and with all the dishes washed, Mary returned to her kia in a half-daze. Not only did the madam cook and serve her a memorable meal, but the silver watch on her left wrist demanded attention.

Julia reflected on how much fun it was, introducing Mary to new experiences.

Both women rested in the afternoon as the clouds opened and shed a thunderous downpour. It was common this time of year. At six o'clock,

Mary returned to the house and sat with Julia at the dining table, eating a smaller version of their lunch. With the dishes done, they enjoyed a coffee and one more sherry in the lounge.

Following the eventful day, both women struggled with heavy eyelids. Julia went to bed, and Mary headed for her kia. She felt a strange unsteadiness as the compacted sandy drive swayed. She'd not noticed it do that before now. It was fortunate her kia was close to the house. She decided she loved Christmas. Tomorrow she'd ask the madam when the next one was due.

It wasn't long after getting dressed in her white nightgown, Mary heard the shouting.

'Julia, open the door!' The shout caught Mary's attention. She turned her head to listen. There it was again. But she couldn't make out the drunken, slurred shouts. The third time, she caught the words *Julia* and *the door*.

'Come on, open the door!' A cold shudder ran down Mary's spine. She could hear now. That voice! Might it be the boss? The madam said he'd returned to the UK.

'Julia, you silly old cow, open the door!' That last shout was too much, and a burning anger coursed through her veins. No one spoke to her madam like that. She pulled on her slippers and hurried to the scarecrow. Mary grabbed the hoe and raced around the house, through the side garden, past Julia's bedroom window. She didn't want to come between the drunken man and the open gate. She raised the hoe and ran towards the figure, yelling at the top of her voice.

CHAPTER 20

Strike Two

Boxing Day presented its usual quiet face following the Christmas Day activities. It seemed the entire city slumbered after a day of over-excitement; and over-eating for a lucky few. For Mary, there was no work. She and Julia washed the dishes after the Christmas dinner, and the house was tidy.

The two women relaxed under the trees by the braai, sheltered from the mid-morning sun. The surrounding air felt comfortable, tempered by the heavy afternoon rain that fell on Christmas Day.

'Last night, I dreamt someone was shouting in the street. It was so real, it woke me,' said Julia.

'There was a drunk man in our garden, Madam. He banged on the front door. I tried to chase him off before he disturbed you.'

'Oh, thank you, Mary. What would I do without you?'

Mary's smooth brown skin emphasised her sparkling white teeth as she beamed with pleasure at Julia's comment.

'Life has got more interesting since you arrived.'

'Thank you, Madam, but Christmas helped to do that.'

'Yes, this year it has. The last two Christmases were less enjoyable.'

'When is the next Christmas, Madam?'

'One year from now, Mary. If you follow the seasons, you'll see the next Christmas comes soon after the start of next year's rains.'

'Oh! So long!'

'You sound disappointed. Never mind, next week is New Year. On New Year's Eve, we'll have another special dinner.'

'New Year's Eve?'

'Yes, the last day of the year. The first of January always arrives one week after Christmas every year.'

'Then I can get you a present, Madam.'

'No, we don't give presents for the New Year. You must wait for my birthday. We only give presents on birthdays and at Christmas.'

'When is your birthday, Madam?'

'In May. Four months from now. When is yours?'

'August, Madam.'

'When in August?'

'I can't remember, Madam.'

'Do you have a birth certificate?'

'Yes, in my kia.'

'Well, you must look at your birth certificate and see what date it says.'

'Yes, Madam. Can you read it and tell me?'

'Yes, if you get it, I will.'

* * *

The next morning, after breakfast, Mary stood at the kitchen sink washing the dishes, and Julia was in her bedroom. A loud knock at the door signalled a visitor. By the time Mary dried her hands, Julia had answered the door.

'Oh! Inspector Kutumela, it's you again. Any more news of my daughter?'

'Good morning, Mrs Watson. No, I'm sorry, there's no news of your daughter, but I've come about another matter.'

'Oh?'

'A gentleman, Mr Gerald King, came to visit you on Christmas night, but he complains your maid tried to kill him, and drove him away with a garden hoe.'

'Goodness! I'll call Mary and see what she has to say.'

Mary needed no invitation, as she already stood in the kitchen door-way, listening to the discussion.

'Mary, you said a drunk man banged at the front door?'

'A rude drunk man, shouting for you, so I told him to leave.'

'Mr King said you tried to kill him with the hoe.'

'I carried the hoe because bad people can sometimes come, and I must protect myself.'

'Did you try to hit him with the hoe?' Inspector Kutumela asked.

'I waved it to show him it protected me.'

'Is Mr King injured, Inspector?' Julia enquired.

'No, but he says she would have killed him if he didn't run for his life.'

'Inspector, that man has always exaggerated things. He lived with me for three years, so I know his character. And why is he in Bulawayo? He said he was returning to the UK.'

'Mr King lives in Cape Town now and had business to attend to in Bulawayo.'

'Well, I don't want him coming around here and worrying us, Inspec-tor. As you can see, he's already caused us trouble.'

'All right, Mrs Watson, I'll tell him not to return here. He's flying back to Cape Town tonight, so that should be that.'

'Thank you, Inspector, goodbye.' As the inspector walked down the drive, Julia asked, 'Did you try to hit him with the hoe, Mary?'

'A little, Madam, to scare him away.'

* * *

The inspector closed the gate behind him and called to his constable, leaning on the fence, talking to Frida.

'Sir, what did the maid say?'

'She denies attacking him.'

'Sir, this woman says the maid keeps an evil spirit in the garden, and it's almost certain it was the spirit that attacked the man.'

'Nonsense, the maid says she asked the man to leave, and he did.'

'Yes, Sir, but not before the spirit attacked him.'

'It's true, Sir,' said Frida. 'The spirit is a scarecrow by day and roams the garden as a spirit after dark. Mary may have told you she asked the man to leave, but she is trying to protect the spirit by keeping it a secret.'

'You should not be spreading such gossip,' said Inspector Kutumela.

'There was another attack here, Sir,' said Frida. 'We have witnesses.'

Kutumela walked to the police car. 'Come on, Constable, we must go.'

While driving back to the police station, Constable Shima asked, 'Why didn't we inspect the scarecrow, Sir?'

'Those things are best left alone, Shima.'

'What do you mean, Sir?'

'If someone goes into that garden or causes trouble at that house, they shouldn't complain if the spirit confronts them. If the spirit doesn't trouble people outside the property, it's not our problem.'

'Do you believe in the spirits, Sir?'

Kutumela hesitated before answering. 'I've seen enough strange incidents to know it's dangerous to ignore them. That scarecrow may not be a spirit, but unless we must, why risk disturbing it?'

* * *

Back in the street, Frida was busy telling the other maids about the inspector's reluctance to investigate the scarecrow. 'If he's afraid of the scarecrow, he must also suspect it's a spirit.'

The women all nodded in agreement. 'That Mary must have a special connection to the spirits,' said one maid.

'Sangoma's can't be so young,' said another.

Someone else suggested her parents might have been witches, so she was born into it.

Only Clara remained aloof from the hushed whispers that fuelled the women's imaginations. 'If you are all so worried, why don't you ask Mary about it?'

'We can't do that,' said one maid. 'If she knows we suspect her, she might send the spirit to deal with all of us.'

Then the excited women all started talking at once. 'Frida, what is the inspector's name?'

'Did you get his telephone number?'

'We may need to call him if something else happens.'

'Have you seen that expensive watch Mary's wearing?'

'Her madam bought it for her.'

'Yes, and her madam cooked the Christmas lunch and ate with Mary in the garden.'

'And she invited Mary to eat dinner with her at the dining table on Christmas night.'

'She's put a spell on her madam.'

'Is the inspector aware of that?'

'We should tell him.'

With tea break over, the agitated maids returned to their respective households. Like their last meeting, they couldn't agree on how to handle the situation. They realised they must learn to live with Mary and her spirit guardian, at least for now. They didn't like it, but what choice did they have?

* * *

'Madam, can I cook the dinner for New Year's Eve?'

'Yes, Mary, if you wish. What are you planning to cook?'

'The same as Christmas, Madam, but with chicken instead of turkey.'

'All right. Any special reason you want to cook the New Year's Eve dinner?'

'Yes, Madam, I watched everything you did for the Christmas dinner, so I want to copy it before I forget.'

Julia was impressed by Mary's capacity to absorb everything she showed her. Not only matters related to cooking but also her ability to learn unfamiliar words and their meaning after only one or two mentions. It was only eight months since Mary's arrival, but the change in her was remarkable. No longer the ignorant village girl, Mary understood almost everything Julia said. She learnt many words through their context rather than needing one of Julia's explanations. It seemed inconceivable she couldn't read and write or count above twelve. Julia resolved to change that.

'Madam, you said your sister rang you every Christmas, but she didn't ring yesterday.'

'Yes, she did. She rang just after I went to bed. It was a WhatsApp call on my cell phone.'

Mary furrowed her brow. She thought she knew almost everything, but Julia's reply reminded her there was more to learn. She recalled her sister, Lulu, the modern, city woman, possessed a shiny black plastic which she said was a cell phone. But what was a WhatsApp call? Mary realised at that moment, she'd never be a modern, city woman until she also was the proud owner of a shiny black plastic cell phone.

In the afternoon, she saw Frida standing in her usual place in the corner of Dorothy Mapfumo's front garden, close to Julia's front gate.

'Frida, do you know anyone who owns a cell phone?' Mary asked.

Frida guffawed, spraying a mouthful of tea through her nose onto the leaves of the surrounding bushes. 'You mean, do I know anyone who doesn't own a cell phone?'

'Oh!'

'Yes, there's one, and that's you. Every maid in this street has a cell phone, except you. You can't be in the city without a cell phone.'

'Why?'

'Well, how else can you make a phone call?'

'So, you own a cell phone?'

'Yes. If your madam hasn't given you a cell phone, she can't have much confidence in you.'

Frida's comments puzzled Mary. She'd talk to the madam about it. If every maid possessed one, shouldn't she also? Without a cell phone, how could she do her job as a housemaid?

* * *

As she peeled the potatoes for dinner that night, Mary raised the matter. Julia was de-frosting the fridge; a task she'd not yet shown her.

'Madam, Frida says every maid should have a cell phone. Her madam gave her one.'

'Somehow, I can't imagine Mrs Mpofu giving Frida something like a cell phone, Mary. Are you sure it's what she said?'

'Yes, she said all the madams in the street have given their maids cell phones.'

'I think she's making it up, Mary.'

'Making it up, Madam?'

'She's teasing you or trying to make you jealous. What would you do with a cell phone, Mary?'

'I'd make phone calls, Madam.'

'Who would you call? I thought you said you had no one.'

'I'd call you, Madam.'

'But Mary, you're always with me. If I go out alone, you can always use the house phone to call me. I'll give you my cell phone number in case you ever need to do that.'

'All right, Madam, It's OK.'

'And, Mary, if you want to phone your sister in Botswana, you can also use the house phone for that.'

'I don't have her number, Madam.'

'I tell you what, Mary. If you learn to read and write and understand numbers, I'll teach you how to drive. Then, if you take the car to the shops to buy groceries, I'll get you a cell phone so you can call me if something goes wrong. There're not too many maids in the street who drive their madam's cars to the shops. How would you like that?'

'Oh! Thank you, Madam. I'd like that very much.'

* * *

Mary couldn't wait to tell Frida the exciting news. But when she saw her the next day in the corner of her garden near the gate, Frida was dismissive.

'Hah! You'd be silly to believe that. That's what madams tell you when they want you to stop pestering them. You'll be waiting forever before that happens if you can't already read and write. It takes years to learn.'

'No, I'll learn quickly. My madam says I'm a fast learner.'

'You'll need to be,' said Frida as she walked away.

Mary returned to the house, but Frida left her garden and walked over to the group of maids congregating in the shade of a large tree, four houses down from Julia's. Peals of laughter rang out as Frida told the other maids what Mary said.

The laughter was too distant for Mary to hear, but Frida's tale drew conflicting responses from the other maids. One said it proved that Mary cast a spell over her madam, but another claimed, if she was that gullible, she couldn't be a witch communicating with the spirits.

The debate over Mary's powers had a sobering effect on the gathering. Tea break ended, and the maids returned in silence to their respective households, pondering on the latest news.

CHAPTER 21

Learning to Read

MARY stood near the front gate, chatting over the fence to Frida next door. 'We drank sherry over Christmas. I know the madam trusts me because she hasn't marked the ladder to heaven on the bottle's label.'

'That is not a good sign. If she hasn't marked the ladder to heaven, there's no evidence, and she can accuse you of drinking her sherry. She's preparing to get rid of you.'

'My madam won't get rid of me. She says life is more interesting since I arrived.'

'That can soon change. A hot coffee mug ring on a side table is all the excuse she'll need.'

'I always put down coasters for cups or glasses.'

'Yes, but you can forget. We all make mistakes. Sometimes, one mistake is all it takes for them to dismiss you.'

'The madam says you learn from mistakes.'

'All the maids know how easy your madam is. They are waiting for you to make a mistake and get fired. Then you'll see how fast they come to enquire about your job. They're more experienced than you and your madam will be happy with any of them.'

'My madam is happy with me. She says I can even cook the New Year's Eve dinner.'

'Can't you see she is giving you a chance to fail so she can get rid of you?'

'I don't believe that.'

'All the maids know what's happening. Only you are blind to the ways of madams.'

Mary cut off her conversation with Frida and returned to the house. All her discussions with Frida ended with her having doubts and feeling insecure. The madam gave her no cause for concern about her job, but Frida's comments always gnawed at the back of her mind.

'You're quiet this morning, Mary,' said Julia. 'I saw you talking to Frida near the gate.'

'Yes, Madam. I'm sorry I was back late from tea.'

'You weren't back late. But what difference does it make? We're not going anywhere. In fact, I thought we could start your reading lessons this morning.'

'Oh, yes, Madam!'

Julia handed her a sheet of paper. 'Here are the letters of the alphabet. There are twenty-six letters you must memorise. Letters make up words. If you want to read, you must learn which letters make up each word. Do you understand?'

Mary's knitted brow told Julia she did not.

'I know it's difficult, so we won't go too fast. You must learn the letters of the alphabet, and I'll tell you how each one sounds. Now, repeat after me: *ay, bee, cee, dee, ee, ef, gee.*'

By lunchtime, Mary realised learning to read and write wasn't as much fun as she first imagined. But Julia, a former English teacher, enjoyed being back in her old role. 'Now come on, Mary, one more time after me: *ay, bee, cee, dee, ee, ef.*'

'Madam, I must do the ironing.'

'No hurry for that, Mary.'

'Madam, I must also start preparing the dinner.'

'OK, Mary, all right. We'll do more tomorrow.'

'Yes, Madam, but we must go tomorrow to buy more vegetables for New Year's Eve dinner.'

'Plenty of time for that, Mary. I can always help you if we run short of time. But you must practise the alphabet every day, so you don't forget.'

'Yes, Madam.'

* * *

Each day, the furrows on Mary's brow grew deeper. She'd learnt the alphabet, but now the madam spoke of consonants and vowels, and in the latter's case, she spoke of long vowels and short vowels. Mary pleaded with Julia to give her two days' rest so she could focus on preparing the New Year's Eve dinner. Much to her relief, Julia agreed to postpone further lessons until the second of January.

Julia hovered in the kitchen as Mary dried the white bread and prepared the sage and onion stuffing, not forgetting to include the celery. It was the way Julia prepared it for Christmas. The cranberry jelly was the easy part, as it came from a jar. Everything was going to plan, and Julia's help was not needed.

New Year's Eve, only two days away. The prospect of serving Julia a traditional roast excited Mary. Dessert would be left-over Christmas pudding with brandy custard.

Although the madam gave her time off from her English study, Mary practised reciting the alphabet every night before bed, and in her mind even separated the vowels from the consonants. She was determined to be ready for the madam's next flood of English lessons.

The preparations for the dinner ran smoothly, but the weather looked threatening. Dinner would be indoors, safe from the rain and mosquitoes. Julia laid the table while Mary busied herself in the kitchen.

When dinner was ready, Julia lit a candle in the middle of the table. The first course was a half avocado with a squeeze of lemon. Julia brought the bottle of sherry to the table and poured a glass for Mary and one for herself. It was fortuitous she'd lit the candle because, as Mary brought in the main course, a flash of lightning and a crack of thunder extinguished the electric lights.

Julia lit another candle in the kitchen and a second one on the sideboard, and the dinner proceeded without further interruption. Julia smiled. Mary's dinner was a triumph. 'Mary, your cooking improves every day. It's just like I would have cooked it.'

'Thank you, Madam, but I still need to improve my minced beef.'

'You will, Mary. I'm sure you will.'

When the electric lights came back on, Julia switched them off. The candlelight provided a much cosier ambience. Mary brought in the Christmas pudding and the brandy custard. She poured more brandy over the Christmas pudding and lit it with a match—just as Julia did on Christmas Day. The pudding flared for a few seconds before the flames died.

Mary's effort in producing the dinner impressed Julia. 'You will go a long way, Mary. If you're as quick to pick up reading and writing, there'll be no holding you back.'

'Thank you, Madam.'

Neither Mary nor Julia kept late nights, but with their chatter about the dinner and comparisons between chicken and turkey, the time soon passed.

Midnight arrived, and Julia showed Mary how to toast in the New Year with another glass of sherry. It was a strange ritual to Mary, but she was developing a taste for the lifestyle.

The romantic candlelight made an odd scene, with the madam and her maid chatting about food and the best time of year to plant various vegetables.

* * *

Julia promised Mary that New Year's Day would be free from study. But after Julia's compliments the night before, on the progress of her cooking, Mary was keen to transfer those compliments to her progress in reading and writing. So, at Mary's request, they sat in the front room near the bookshelf, practising the alphabet.

Julia scanned the bookshelf, muttering, 'We must find you a suitable book to read. Unfortunately, Mary, I gave away most of my school reading books when I retired from teaching. I never thought I'd need them again. But I may have kept one or two of Vera's from her early childhood. They'll be old-fashioned, but they'll do for now.'

'Madam, I have a book. Can you teach me to read from that?'

'Well, if you get it, I'll see if it's suitable.'

Mary hurried to her kia to get her book. She returned a moment later with her eyes gleaming. At last, someone who'd know how to read her book—what magic it contained. She laid the book on the coffee table in front of Julia. It was a hardcover with faded gold embossed writing on the red worn fabric.

'This looks old,' said Julia, carefully turning the pages. Then she laughed. 'You can't learn to read from this book, Mary. It's not written in English.'

Mary frowned, puzzled by the instant dismissal of her book.

Julia turned to the front pages of the book. 'What language is this? Aha! It says here, Budapest. This must be Hungarian.'

'You can't read it, Madam?'

'No, I don't speak Hungarian.'

'You were a teacher, Madam.'

'Yes, an English teacher.' Julia saw the disbelief on Mary's face. 'Mary, you speak Ndebele and English, right?'

'Yes, Madam.'

'You don't speak Shona.'

'No, Madam.'

'Well, I don't speak Ndebele, Shona or Hungarian. I only speak English. Only someone who speaks Hungarian can read this book. Do you understand?'

'Yes, Madam.'

But Julia knew from Mary's face, she didn't.

'Now Mary, recite the alphabet once more, and explain the difference between long and short vowels. Then we can read about the cat that sat on the mat.'

* * *

Mary was more than pleased when the English lesson finished early. She returned to the kitchen to prepare a light lunch while Julia rummaged through cardboard boxes stored in the garage, looking for Vera's old early learning books.

So, school is like this, thought Mary. Perhaps she hadn't missed much after all. She learnt by watching, copying, and doing. Learning from squiggles marked on paper was exhausting.

But Mary had two significant advantages. She possessed a phenomenal memory and had developed reasonable speaking skills in the short time she'd worked for Julia. Within a few days, she mastered the first two of Vera's early learning English books. They emphasised short vowels such as the letter *a*, in the words: *cat, sat, mat, fat, rat, and hat*. Mary marvelled at how a different letter in front of *at* spelt so many words familiar to her.

When Julia showed her how to convert short vowels into long vowels by adding one or two more letters, learning English became a game for Mary. She took every opportunity to read things and pestered Julia to explain unfamiliar words. Soon, it was Julia who sighed with relief when each English lesson ended. The problem was they didn't ever really end because Mary hounded Julia for explanations of words throughout the day.

Compared to reading, Mary found numbers easy, at least the counting part. Addition, subtraction, multiplication, and division became progressively harder, though she grasped the concepts without too much difficulty.

Julia now looked for a suitable book for Mary to read. Mary's voracious appetite for learning soon consumed all of Vera's early learning books. Julia scanned the bookshelves for something appropriate. She found it strange how books could disappear in plain view on a bookshelf. They were often thinner, or the covers were a different shade from what she remembered. Julia passed over the books she searched for several times. But when she found what she wanted, she decided they wouldn't be suitable. She would check with the bookshop in town.

Two fresh-faced, earnest looking, young white men walking up the driveway interrupted Julia's search. 'Good morning, Madam. We bring you good news.'

'Has the government got hold of more petrol supplies?'

'No, we mean you can get answers to your prayers.'

'I prayed for more petrol.'

'Would you like a copy of our pamphlet? There's no charge. If you have questions, you will be welcome at our church. The service times are in the pamphlet.'

'All right, thank you.'

'We'll drop in again the next time we're passing.'

'OK, bye for now.' Julia glanced at the pamphlet, wondering what Mary might make of it. Perhaps a little too difficult with the added complexity of religious teaching. It would make a change from reading the boxes, tins, and packets in the grocery cupboard. Mary was a little too easily swayed by the promotional words on certain items. Words like *goodness*, *healthy* and *nutritional* led to those items finding their way into almost every meal. The search for a suitable book for Mary to read was becoming a matter of urgency.

* * *

Reading was one thing, but writing was an altogether different matter. Mary didn't appreciate the need for both print and cursive writing. She laboriously copied the letters from sheets Julia downloaded from the internet and printed. Uppercase cursive letters created one problem for Mary, and another was writing from her imagination. She found reading easier by the day. But when she tried to write, her mind went blank.

'Just write one message a day to me, Mary. For example, "We need milk" or, "Today is sunny".'

'Yes, Madam.'

The next morning, a message for Julia lay on the breakfast table. The tidy print read, 'We need milk.' And the following morning, the message read, 'Today is sunny.'

'Mary, you can't just repeat what I told you to write. You must think of something yourself.'

'Yes, Madam.'

On the third morning, the message read, 'The cat ate the rat on the mat.'

'I think we are past the cat sat on the mat stage, Mary. Try to think of something more practical.'

'Yes, Madam.'

Each day, Julia would put Mary's messages in a file, just as she'd done for Vera years earlier. Tears welled in her eyes two months later, when the message on the breakfast table read, 'Madam, thank you for teaching me to read and write. Love from Mary.' The note, written in a neat cursive hand, thrilled Julia.

'Tonight, Mary, we will celebrate. I will cook dinner and open another bottle of sherry. You've worked hard and made good progress. Your reading and writing will continue to improve. You'll see.'

'Thank you, Madam. It took too long to write that.'

'Well, it's a beautiful message, and I'm proud of you.'

CHAPTER 22

Home Alone

MARY stood at the kitchen sink, washing the cups after morning tea, and admiring the beautiful sunny day with its blue sky. There was little sign of the previous afternoon's downpour. The vegetable garden flourished, and she smiled with satisfaction. She and Julia were addicted to self-sufficiency, a necessity in a country of shortages and high inflation. These days, they seldom needed to go to the supermarket for fresh vegetables and eggs. When they went, milk, bread, and other packaged products made up the shopping list. Julia often commented that Mary's initiative not only saved money, but also made life so much more interesting.

The phone rang and Mary heard Julia answering it from the bedroom extension. A phone call was an infrequent occurrence, and Julia would often talk to her about them. No surprise then that Julia appeared at the kitchen door a short time later. But on this occasion, she wore a serious expression.

'I've just had bad news. My sister in England has suffered a heartattack and died. Her solicitors in London say I should go to the funeral and afterwards, sort out legal matters.'

Mary only understood the first part of Julia's news. 'I'm sorry about your sister, Madam.'

'Thank you, Mary. I must make travel arrangements straight away. You must look after the house while I'm gone. Please make sure you have everything you might need in my absence.'

'Yes, Madam.'

Mary disappeared into the pantry, and afterwards, she checked the refrigerator. When, an hour later, she handed Julia a neat handwritten list of items running low, Julia barely registered the significance. Only a few weeks earlier, Mary couldn't have done that, but now, following her reading and writing lessons, she had proved capable.

'We'll shop for these items this afternoon,' said Julia, 'and then I'll pack my bags. My flight leaves for Johannesburg tomorrow, just after lunch. I'll have a taxi pick me up after morning tea and take me to the airport.'

'How long will you be away, Madam?'

'Oh, at least two weeks, I imagine. I'll phone you from London and let you know what's happening.'

From that moment, everything seemed rushed. Mary's mind whirled, searching for questions she should ask Julia, but couldn't think of anything. Somehow, she didn't seem able to focus on any line of thought. She knew as soon as Julia left, there'd be many questions. The solution seemed to lie in cleaning. She polished the kitchen sink, made sure all the glassware sparkled, and dusted the bookshelves.

'There's plenty of time for that, Mary, after I've gone. You can finish early this evening, and we'll make an early start tomorrow.'

* * *

Mary woke at six in the morning feeling apprehensive. Only now, she realised how accustomed she'd become to Julia's company. Two weeks on her own in charge of the house was a daunting prospect.

'Now, Mary, here's the front door key. Put it in your keyring with the backdoor key.'

'Yes, Madam.'

'On this sheet of paper, I've written my cell phone number in case you need to call me. This other number is the phone number of the solicitors in London. I'm sure you won't need to use it, but you never know. If I lose my phone or it gets flat or stolen, at least you have a number where you can leave me a message. I'll put the paper under the phone, so you don't lose it.'

'Thank you, Madam.'

'I think I've taken care of everything, Mary, so you don't have to worry. Just look after the house. I'm sure you'll be fine. Anything else you need to know?'

'No, Madam. Thank you, Madam.'

As the taxi pulled out of the driveway and Julia waved goodbye, she noticed a worried frown on Mary's brow. There was no one she'd rather have looking after the house. And she was confident Mary would take good care of it.

Mary watched the taxi drive to the end of the road and turn left onto Burns Drive, and disappear around the corner. Most servants would love to see their employer leave for a fortnight. No one to stand over them, giving them orders. But a creeping loneliness swept over her. Two weeks! Such a long time. Perhaps, if her friendship with Frida hadn't cooled, things might be different. But as it stood, she was all alone.

On most days, the hours raced by, but today, every minute dragged. Following afternoon tea, Mary would prepare the vegetables for the evening meal, but she'd no inclination to cook on this occasion. She looked at her watch. Oh! Not yet mid-afternoon. Not even lunchtime. The madam left only forty-five minutes ago.

Ever since she started working for Julia, a transistor radio stood on the kitchen windowsill. Until now, she'd never thought to turn it on because her work preoccupied her, or she'd be chatting with Julia. Mary turned the knob, and the radio came alive.

Mary patrolled the house to see what needed doing: a forgotten dusty surface, unwashed laundry, anything. With everything clean and put away, nothing suggested itself. Now, she regretted the cleaning she'd done yesterday while Julia was still there. She'd busied herself dusting clean surfaces and polishing sparkling glassware.

What about outdoors? She must have neglected something. No, she'd weeded the garden, watered the vegetables, cleaned the henhouse, and swept the front driveway. Perhaps she might mow the lawn? But Henry mowed it the week before, and she wouldn't want to take his job. He'd come again soon after the madam's expected return.

Mary yawned and looked at her watch. Lunchtime, but she wasn't hungry. Besides, it would just make a mess of her beautiful kitchen. The kia was also tidy and clean. She'd used the old carpet sweeper and then the brush and pan around the edges.

The madam would say, read something. But when she was called away at short notice, she didn't get around to finding her a suitable book. Perhaps they could've visited a city bookshop, but in the rush to prepare for the London trip, they didn't give it a thought.

The phone rang. At last, something to do! Mary picked up the handset. 'This is Julia Watson's residence. Mary speaking.'

'Mary, it's Julia. How is everything?'

'Hello, Madam. Everything is fine.'

'What are you doing?'

'Nothing, Madam.'

'Nothing? Why don't you practise your reading? It might not be easy, but it's better than doing nothing.'

'Yes, Madam, I will look for something.'

'I just phoned to make sure everything was OK.'

'Yes, Madam, everything is OK.'

'Good. My flight leaves tonight, so it's a long wait. I'll call you again when I get to London and am settled.'

'OK, Madam.'

'OK, Mary, bye for now.'

That call made all the difference. Mary felt much better. The madam hadn't disappeared from the earth. She checked under the phone to make sure Julia's number was still there.

Perhaps she would start preparing dinner. Maybe something different that she'd perfect while the madam was away. New dishes always took longer. She looked in the pantry for Julia's cookbook. She was competent with numbers, so times and temperatures weren't a problem, but the ingredients proved challenging. Hmm! What's this one? *spag hetty bo log nessy?* Mary tried to sound out the words in the way the madam taught her. The jumble of letters made it hard to pronounce. The dish sounded complicated.

Go u lash. That one sounded easier. The recipe looked straightforward until she came to *pap rika.* She recognised pap, another word for sadza, but when she studied the recipe, there was no mention of corn flour or mealie meal. It remained a puzzle until she realised sadza must be a side dish. While searching the pantry for the ingredients, she found a small jar filled with red powder. On the homemade label in the madam's writing were the words *hot paprika.* Hmm! OK, she'd also add that to the concoction in the pot.

Mary followed the recipe as best she could. She understood the numbers, but some words next to them, she didn't recognise—words like *ounces* and *pints.* When unsure, she used her judgement to decide how much of each ingredient to include in the mix. Before she was satisfied with the flavour, the serving for two quadrupled in size. How would she eat all that food? She opted against cooking the sadza side dish. Bread would do.

The finished dish looked like a stew but smelt different. The cookbook recommended eating the goulash with a glass of red wine. Mary recognised those words because she'd served it to the madam and the boss the night she first arrived at the house. Now, where's the red wine? Oh, yes, that open bottle the madam used for cooking. She'd seen the madam pour herself a glass and sip it while cooking dinner. The madam said she wouldn't like it, as it wasn't sweet and might make her sick. It was time to test that assumption.

The meat was tender, and the potatoes were perfect. The gravy, perhaps a little too spicy, but the madam liked it that way. Now the time flew. Already five o'clock. Mary ladled the goulash into a soup plate and carried it to the dining table and set it down on the table mat she'd placed opposite Julia's seat. She took a wineglass from the cabinet in the front room and poured the cabernet sauvignon from the open bottle she brought from the pantry. 'Cheers, said Mary, raising her glass to Julia's empty seat.'

Mary enjoyed her meal. The red wine countered the spicy gravy. Each mouthful of her goulash needed a sip of wine to soothe her burning tongue. Soon, she poured herself a second glass, and then a third. What tasted fine when she sampled it from the pot while cooking now proved a challenge.

After the meal, Mary washed the dishes and stared in trepidation at the large pot of goulash in front of her. Her full soup bowl did little to diminish the contents of the pot. She sipped from her fourth glass of wine. How would she eat all that food? She'd cooked way too much, and the wine bottle was almost empty. Once that was gone, what would douse the fire that burned her mouth?

Without warning, the room began a slow spin. Mary slumped onto the sofa in the front room, and as she looked at the ceiling, it spun faster and faster. She gripped the sofa as the spinning threatened to throw her to the floor. That was the last thing she remembered.

The phone near the front door rang, but somehow, she couldn't reach it. Every time she approached the phone, she discovered she remained several feet away from it. The ringing stopped before she got there. Then it rang again. This time, Mary woke and opened her eyes. She jumped off the sofa and tripped on the rug in front of it. She leapt up and raced to the phone.

'Thithit Julia Wathon's residenth. Mary shpeaking.'

'Mary, it's Julia. What's wrong?'

'Nothing, Madam. Hello, Madam,' said Mary, as she struggled to unglue her lips and separate her tongue from her dry palate.

'You sound funny.'

'I'm OK, Madam.'

'All right. Well, I'm in London now and checked into my hotel. Is everything fine?'

'Yes, Madam. Everything is fine.'

'You still have my number safe under the phone?'

'Yes, Madam.'

'OK, I'll call you again in the next couple of days to see how you are getting on.'

'Thank you, Madam. Bye, Madam.'

When Mary put the phone down, she noticed her thumping headache and… she was about to vomit. She raced to the toilet and brought up a burgundy red liquid and undigested remnants of last night's meal. It was a good time to vow she'd never again drink red wine, even if the madam offered it. And she couldn't face another helping of goulash.

Mary looked at her watch. Twelve noon! She'd slept throughout the night and morning. She shuffled to the kitchen and saw the large pot of goulash sitting on the counter. Oh, no! What to do with it? Then a brilliant idea. Soon it would be Frida's lunch break. Perhaps she could offload a generous serve to Frida and the other maids.

The madam kept several disposable plastic containers under the kitchen sink. Mary selected four and filled them to the brink. The tops clipped over the containers, and they were ready for delivery.

Half an hour later, she saw Frida standing in the corner of her garden by the gate. She grabbed a container and hurried to the gate. 'Frida, before the madam left on her trip, she cooked me food, but it's too much for me. Would you like some? I have three other containers. I'll also ask the other maids.'

'Oh, don't worry, I'll give it to them and tell them it's from you.'

'Thank you. I'll bring them now.' Mary hurried to the kitchen and soon returned with the three containers and handed them to Frida.

'Tell me if you and the others like it.'

'Yes, I will. I'm sure they will be pleased.'

'You're supposed to eat it with sadza, but I didn't cook any.'

'I'll tell them.'

* * *

The maids gathered for their afternoon tea break, and Frida appeared, carrying three of the containers. The fourth one she kept for herself. 'I cooked this food last night and thought of my sisters, so I've brought some for you.'

The excited women gathered around, inspecting the contents. It looked and smelt good. 'Did your madam give you all this beef?' asked one.

'Shh! No, I pinched it. Don't tell anyone.'

The maids all laughed. Frida, as devious as ever! It made her popular with the women. They all hurried back to their respective households to fetch containers to take their share of the feast.

Frida was missing for the next two days, and Mary wondered where she might have gone. Perhaps she was visiting her mother. Did she and the other maids enjoy her new dish? The street seemed quieter than usual. Where was everyone?

* * *

It was four days since Julia left, and Mary polished and dusted, keeping the house in sparkling condition. She didn't have enough work to keep herself entertained.

Mary always admired Julia's bathroom. It smelled fresh and gleamed with the lights on, or in the sunlight through the narrow strip window near the ceiling. She examined the bottles balanced on the small table next to the bathtub. One showed a picture of a lady cloaked in a bed of bubbles. Mary twisted off the cap and inhaled the scent. It was like a perfume.

While she was not one to take advantage of her employer's absence, she couldn't help wondering what it would feel like to have a bath. She'd only bathed in a river and never sat in a bathtub. What harm would it do if she tried it? She'd only ever used the bathtub to wash items too large for the basin in the laundry.

The temptation was too much. It was three o'clock in the afternoon. Plenty of time for a bath before preparing dinner. Mary turned on the taps and poured a generous amount of the perfumed liquid into the bath. In an instant, the bubbles rose, and rose, and rose. Eish! A little too much magic liquid, perhaps? She put her hand in the water to test the temperature. It was perfect, and the bath was nice and deep.

Mary stripped off her clothes and stepped into the bath. When she sat down, water splashed onto the floor. It was lucky the bathroom was a step down from Julia's bedroom, or the water may have flowed onto the parquet floor. The water soaked the bathmat, but the tile floor would be easy to mop. It was fortunate she'd put her clothes on the chair in the corner.

It was a pleasurable, relaxing experience. A sensation she'd never known. She brushed the rising bubbles off her face, but more rose at an alarming rate. Next, she tried to push the bubbles to the bottom end of the bath, but with little success. Eventually, the bubbles got the message and stayed away from her face. The effect of the bath was soporific. Mary closed her eyes, thinking of the shallow ledge on the river's edge where the crocodile took Miriam, Josiah's first wife. She often washed on that shallow ledge, and the thought she might have met the same fate made her skin crawl.

The ringing doorbell and banging on the front door didn't at first register. But then Mary's thoughts crashed back to the present. Who banged on the front door and rang the bell so persistently? She jumped out of the bath and put her clothes on without drying herself. She hurried to the front door and pulled it open. 'Yes!' she said, irritated by the intrusion.

Two stern-looking uniformed police officers stood there. Surprised, Mary stepped back.

CHAPTER 23

The Companion

THE taxi rolled down the road and slowed to a stop outside the front gate. After a brief delay, the taxi driver jumped out and opened the kerbside rear door. A slim figure stepped out. The driver then opened the boot and took out the passenger's travel bag. Julia thanked the driver and waved goodbye as the taxi drove off.

She turned and looked at the house. She'd only been away a fortnight, but it seemed much longer. The garden looked neat, but a stillness about the property concerned her.

Where was Mary? Since she last spoke to her ten days ago, Mary answered none of her calls. Julia walked up the driveway, conscious of the crunch each of her footsteps made on the compacted sandy surface.

Perhaps she was ill? Julia walked past the house to the back door to find it locked. She put down her travel bag by the door and walked to the kia. The doors were locked, and there was no answer to her knocking. Mary wasn't there. Julia returned to the house and opened the back door with her key.

The kitchen looked tidy, with everything in order. She walked past the dining and front rooms and down the passage to her bedroom. Again, everything looked fine. Might have Mary returned to her village to deal with an unforeseen emergency? But then, why didn't she phone before leaving the house?

Julia unpacked her travel bag and hung up her clothes in the bedroom's built-in cupboard. She picked up her toothbrush and toiletries and walked into the bathroom. She stopped in the bathroom doorway as her eyes fell on the uncharacteristic scene.

A crumpled bathmat lay on the floor and the bathtub filled with soapy water, almost to overflowing. Water stains on the linoleum floor showed a water spill left to dry. Now Julia was even more concerned. Mary must have departed in an unexpected rush.

Perhaps Dorothy Mapfumo might know something? Julia locked the house and walked next door to talk to her neighbour. She rang the doorbell, and a moment later, Dorothy opened the front door. Before Julia got a word out, Dorothy launched into a tirade.

'Mrs Watson, that awful maid of yours, tried to poison Frida. For an entire week, my stupid maid lay shivering sick in bed, and I had to cook and do the housework. Mary also tried to poison other maids in the street, so I called the police to come and deal with her.'

'What do you mean, deal with her? Where is she? Do you know where she is?'

'I don't know! Talk to the police!'

'And is Frida all right now?'

'She was lucky to survive.'

'So, she's fine? Are you sure you didn't overreact?'

Dorothy Mapfumo gave Julia a withering look and closed the door.

Julia walked back to her house and looked at the card Inspector Kutumela gave her on his last visit. She picked up the handset and dialled the number. 'Inspector Kutumela, it's Julia Watson speaking.'

'Hello, Mrs Watson. What appears to be the problem?'

'I believe the police have taken my maid, Mary, into custody. I was overseas, so I'm not aware of all the details, but I can assure you, she wouldn't set out to poison anyone.'

'Hang on, Mrs Watson. Let me check our charge sheets. I didn't arrest your maid. I need to investigate what's happened.'

Julia hung on, pacing up and down by the telephone near the front door.

'Mrs Watson, your maid is still in the cells here at the police station. She's on tomorrow's prison transfer list. The duty officer showed me the charge sheet. It states she has twice tried to kill someone with a hoe and now attempted a mass poisoning of the other maids in your street.'

'Inspector Kutumela, you're already familiar with that business with the hoe, and I'm certain she would not have tried to poison the maids in the street. There must be a misunderstanding. Is there anything you can do? Please speak to her and get her side of the story.'

'I'll have a word with her, Mrs Watson, and call you back with any news.'

'All right. Thank you, Inspector. Bye.'

Julia put down the phone and sat in a chair at the dining table. This wasn't the homecoming she expected. She wasn't hungry, but Mary would have prepared a nice dinner for her and brought her up to date with gossip and neighbourhood news. Sitting there alone, the house felt so quiet and empty.

Perhaps a glass of wine would help to cheer her. She remembered the bottle of cabernet sauvignon in the pantry she opened the night before she left. With the screw top, it should still be drinkable. Julia walked to the pantry and grabbed the bottle. Almost empty! 'Goodness, Mary, you have been busy!' Julia poured the remnants into a glass she fetched from the bookcase cabinet in the front room. Only a trickle, it filled less than half a glass.

What to do? She took a mop from the laundry and walked through to her bathroom. She took out the bath plug to drain the bath and used fresh water to mop the floor. Then she dried the floor with the crumpled bathmat and tossed it into the laundry basket. She'd wash it and her travel clothes first thing in the morning. With a clean facecloth, she wiped the bathtub until it sparkled like new.

After a tiring flight, she needed an early night. If Inspector Kutumela didn't ring her first thing in the morning, she'd call him. She didn't bother with a bath and showered instead. She was in bed by nine and asleep in an instant.

The phone rang. Groggy from sleep, Julia picked up the handset next to her bed.

The voice on the phone sounded distant. 'Mrs Watson, Inspector Kutumela here. I spoke to both Mary and the inspector in charge of her case. Mary explained the circumstances of the meal she gave to the neighbour's maid, Frida. Perhaps her arrest was an overreaction. The inspector isn't happy about dropping the charges because it goes against his arrest record. But he says he can make the charge sheet disappear for one hundred US dollars. If you're happy with that, you can pick her up in the morning.'

'Yes, that's fine, Inspector Kutumela. Thank you.'

'Good night, Mrs Watson.'

* * *

Julia overslept. It was ten o'clock. Almost time for morning tea. She must've been more tired than she realised after her long flight from London. She dreamt she received a telephone call from Inspector Kutumela, telling her she could collect Mary from the police station if she paid a hundred US dollars. It seemed like a dream, but so realistic, she was uncertain.

Inspector Kutumela did not ring through the morning, so at twelve noon, Julia picked up the phone to call him. She was in luck. The inspector answered the phone.

'Yes, Mrs Watson, you can come and pick her up. Don't forget the one hundred US for the arresting officer.'

'All right, I'll be there soon. I thought I dreamt the whole thing.'

'You sounded sleepy. I'm sorry to have woken you, but I thought you'd like to know as soon as possible.'

'Yes, thank you. I'm sure it helped me to sleep better, and that's why I overslept.'

Inspector Kutumela laughed. 'We're seeing a lot of each other, Mrs Watson. You can thank Mary for playing a large part in that.'

'Yes, you're right, Inspector. I'll be down in half an hour to fetch her.'

Julia put down the handset and shut the windows and locked the back-door. She picked up her car keys, grabbed her handbag, and slammed the front door behind her. The old Honda started first time. Two weeks sitting idle in the driveway did not drain the battery, as she feared. But then, she took good care of her car and never missed a service.

The little blue Honda turned onto Burns Drive and right again onto Hillside Road. It buzzed along with the windows open, blowing out the warm air that accumulated over two weeks of blistering sun on the driveway. Julia was eager to hear Mary's side of the story. She couldn't imagine the earnest, hard-working maid trying to harm anyone. But the near empty wine bottle and the overfilled bath suggested she might be a little more adventurous than she'd first imagined.

Julia parked her car near the police station. She took her handbag from the passenger seat and jumped out, locking the door behind her. One advantage of parking so close to the police station was no youths lingered, offering to protect the car while the driver shopped or went about their business.

Inspector Kutumela saw Julia enter the police station and walked over to talk to her. 'Good morning, Mrs Watson. I hope you are well. Did you bring the release fee?'

'Yes, Inspector, it's in this envelope.'

'Good! The paperwork is complete. I'll bring your package out to you.'

Inspector Kutumela walked down the corridor and out of sight. Two minutes later, he returned with a downcast Mary, dressed in crumpled clothes and barefoot.

'Come, Mary, I'm taking you home.' Mary's response was inaudible. Julia turned to the inspector and thanked him for arranging her release.

'Mrs Watson, please try to control your maid. I can't always be around to help resolve her scrapes with the law. The arresting officer was reluc-tant to let her go. Now that he knows he can get money for her, he could arrest her under any pretext.' Kutumela tapped his chin with the envelope containing the hundred dollars. It was a message both Julia and Mary couldn't misinterpret.

'Thank you, Inspector, we'll be careful.'

Julia bundled Mary into the car and drove off down Leopold Takawira Avenue before turning right onto Robert Mugabe Way, and heading for the Hillside Road.

'I'm sorry for all the trouble, Madam.'

'Don't worry, Mary.'

'I made too spicy food and needed the wine to stop my mouth burning.'

'It's OK.'

'Then, the wine made me sick, like you said it would.'

'Well, now you see why I told you not to drink red wine.'

'And I wanted to have a bath, Madam, but I spilled water, and the doorbell rang. The police wouldn't let me finish dressing or put on my shoes. They only let me lock the house and my kia. I didn't know those police officers. They were not nice, like Inspector Kutumela. I'm sorry I did all those bad things.'

'It's all right, Mary. In your position, I would have done the same. But why did they say you tried to poison Frida and the other maids?'

'It wasn't poison, Madam. The food was too spicy. That's all.'

'Mary, why are you shivering? Are you cold?'

'No, Madam, the police cells were cold at night and no blankets. Other prisoners were also sick and coughing.'

'When we get home, you must go straight to bed. I'll make you tea and something to eat.'

'Yes, thank you, Madam.'

By the time they arrived at the house, uncontrollable shivers racked Mary.

'Right, straight to bed, Mary.'

Julia toasted four thick slices of bread and buttered them. On two she spread peanut butter, and on the other two she spread strawberry jam. She made a mug of sweet milky tea and carried the food to the kia.

Mary tried to drink the tea, but found it difficult to hold the mug to her lips. Because of the violent shaking, she could only snatch gulps of tea between the shivering and the coughing.

'I'm going to call the doctor, Mary. I'll be back soon. In the meantime, try to eat and drink.'

The doctor arrived in the late afternoon. 'There're several early season cases of influenza going around. I'll give you something that should help. She must take the cough mixture every four hours, day, and night. There's a repeat prescription for the tablets.'

After the doctor left, Julia drove to the chemist to pick up the medication and returned home to give Mary her first dose. 'Hmm! Now let's see. It's almost six o'clock now, so your next dose is at ten tonight, then two in the morning and six in the morning. Mary, I can't come traipsing out here at all hours. You must come into the house. Put on your slippers and dressing gown. You can sleep in the boss's old room. I'd already made up the bed for when Vera returned, but she won't be needing it now.'

Julia locked the kia and helped Mary walk to the house. 'Now get into bed. The house is warmer than your kia, so you should be nice and cosy. You can use the bathroom and toilet across the hall.'

'Thank you, Madam.'

* * *

The next two weeks kept Julia busy, making soup and other meals for Mary and doing the housework. She set her alarms for two o'clock and six in the morning to get up and give Mary her medicine. It reminded her of the times when, as a child, Vera was sick, and she'd get up at night to dispense the medicine to her reluctant daughter. Mary was an adult, but young enough to be her granddaughter, and Julia couldn't help her maternal feelings.

She followed the strict medication regime the doctor ordered, and bit by bit, Mary's condition improved. The rains had gone, and the days cooled. On chillier evenings, Julia lit the fireplace set into the front room wall opposite the windows. In no time, the warmth spread through the house, creating a cosy atmosphere.

Mary was recovering. She showered and dressed each day, sitting close to the window in the front room to warm herself in the early shaft of morning sun.

On the morning Julia gave her the last dose of cough mixture, Mary suggested she was now well enough to resume her work duties.

'All right, Mary, after you've made morning tea, bring it to the dining table. I want to talk to you.'

Tea at the dining table sounded important. On most days, Julia drank her morning tea in the front room. After all the trouble she'd caused, trying to cook an unfamiliar dish, drinking almost all the red wine, and making a mess in the bathroom, the madam might dismiss her. Yes, tea at the dining room table was a bad sign. The madam worked so hard over the past ten days, getting up in the middle of the night to give her medicine, cooking her meals and doing all the washing and cleaning. It wouldn't surprise her if the madam wanted to replace her with a proper maid.

The thoughts played upon Mary's imagination, and downcast, she carried the tea tray through from the kitchen. When the madam collected her from the police station, she said, *'When the cat's away, the mice will play.'* She'd explained the meaning to Mary and laughed, but now Mary feared the madam would dismiss her. She'd heard Frida and one or two others talk about it.

'Mary, I thought you'd recovered, but you're shivering again.'

'I am better, Madam.'

'All right, sit down, Mary.'

Another bad sign. Mary hesitated before taking a seat at the table.

'The nights are getting quite cold, and your kia is not as warm as this house. We don't want you getting sick again, so you can continue sleeping in the second bedroom, at least until the end of winter. Would you like that?'

'Oh, yes, Madam, but what if one of your relatives wants to visit you?'

'Vera's father, my husband, died in the Bush War when his truck drove over a landmine.'

'Oh! Sorry, Madam.'

'Then, as you know, Vera disappeared at Mana Pools.'

'Yes, Madam.'

'Now my sister in England has died from a heart attack, and my only remaining close friend in Bulawayo died in hospital last year.'

'Yes, Madam, I remember. Sorry.'

'I have no more relatives, Mary, so I'm all alone.'

'No family, Madam?'

'No family.'

'Sorry, Madam.'

'It's quiet here in the house by myself at night. We can chat in the evenings and keep each other company. I notice Frida doesn't visit these days.'

'Yes, Madam.'

'So, do you want to do that?'

'Yes, Madam. Thank you, Madam.'

'One more thing, Mary. Call me Julia. Madam sounds so old-fashioned.'

'Oh, I almost forgot. While in London, I picked up this book for you to read. I think it will stretch your reading ability, but I believe it's about the right level for you.'

'Thank you, Madam.' Mary hadn't been up to reading in the past week, and she eyed the book with trepidation. 'So thick, Madam!'

'This is what they call a young adult book.'

Mary studied the cover. '… Train to….'

'Ghost Train to Devil's Siding.'

'Oh! Thank you, Madam.'

'Now don't forget, you must say thank you, Julia, not thank you, Madam.'

'Oh, yes! Thank you, Madam.'

'And bring your things into the house. It will save you going back and forth the whole time.'

'Yes, Madam, Julia.'

* * *

Despite Julia's invitation, Mary worried that moving all her clothes and other possessions into the house might look like she was taking advantage of Julia's kindness. Her solution was to smuggle the items in when Julia wasn't looking.

Over the next few days, she brought in an item or two when Julia was busy in her office or her bedroom. The furniture remained in the kia because her bedroom in the house was already furnished. The last item to come into the house was her magic book. Mary studied the bookshelves and found a suitable place next to *Shakespeare's Sonnets*, a hardback book with embossed decoration. *Ghost Train to Devil's Siding* lay on her bedside table, inviting a taxing half hour each night before she switched off the bedside table lamp.

Mary's clandestine relocation did not go unnoticed. Julia smiled when she saw Mary's old Hungarian book on the bookshelf. She guessed what might be on Mary's mind as she made her protracted move from the servant's quarters to the house.

CHAPTER 24

A Moment of Madness

MARY worked in the front room, dusting the furniture and book-shelves when she glimpsed Frida next door, smoking in the cor-ner near the gate. It was almost a month since she'd last seen her. Apart from a few words with Clara, who passed by on the road one morning, she'd not seen the other maids, either. Mary put down the duster and hurried to the gate to catch Frida.

'How are you, Frida? My madam tells me you were sick.'

Mary's sudden appearance appeared to startle Frida, who seemed pre-occupied.

'Fine, now, but I was sick after eating the food you gave me. I shivered for a week, and my madam wouldn't let me in the house. She cut my wages for the days I didn't work.'

'Did your bones also ache?'

'Yes, and my head ached. One week later, I was still sick, but my madam said I must return to work, or she'd find another maid.'

'The same illness came to me. The doctor said it was flu.'

'No, your food poisoned me.'

'I'm sure my madam doesn't keep poison in her kitchen.'

'Mrs Watson told my madam you cooked the food. Why did you pretend she cooked it?'

'I thought you may not want to try the food if you knew it was me.'

'You lied to me. Nothing is worse than a liar.'

'But Frida, Clara said you told the other maids you cooked it.'

'Don't listen to what Clara says. She's also a liar.'

'Why would Clara lie? You thought the food would be good if my madam cooked it, so you pretended you did. Now the other maids think you lied. That's why I haven't seen you passing by to visit the other maids down the road.'

'Eish! I can't waste my time arguing with a stupid country girl.'

Frida turned and walked back to the house, leaving Mary watching her retreat. She could tell from Frida's reaction she'd judged her motives correctly. She was sure Frida's illness was flu and not a poisoning. That must also be the reason one or two other maids imagined they'd been poisoned.

Suddenly, Mary remembered she put the remnants of the suspect dish in the freezer. She hurried back to the house to throw the food away, just in case. She didn't want to risk poisoning the madam.

'Mary, what are you searching for in the freezer?'

'Madam, I put a bowl of food here before the police took me. Now I can't find it.'

'Oh, you mean the goulash? I ate it with bread the night I returned from London.'

'Didn't it make you sick, Madam?'

'No, it was quite tasty. Perhaps, a little hot.'

'You liked it?'

'Yes, of course, or I wouldn't have eaten it. And how many times must I tell you to call me Julia, not *Madam*? You make me sound like an old maid.'

* * *

After dinner, they sat in the front room drinking coffee and chatting. The wood crackled and spat in the fireplace, creating a cosy glow that made it unnecessary to switch on the electric lights.

'Mary, did your parents ever talk to you about the Gukurahundi?'

'Oh, yes, they often spoke about it.'

'And what memories did they have?'

'Everyone lived in fear. Often, they heard news of what happened in nearby villages. Terrible stories! In their village, they organised a warning system. If it was rumoured the Fifth Brigade was coming, they'd run into the bush. One person would go to warn the next village, and someone from that village would run and warn the next one.'

'Goodness, what a way to live!'

'If the soldiers surprised a village, they'd kill the men and bury them in ditches. They'd smash babies against the walls of the huts, and rape and sometimes kill the mothers.'

'Thank goodness your parents survived, otherwise you wouldn't be here.'

'My parents' village was lucky because it was further away from the road than the others. In the village next to ours, the Fifth Brigade killed my uncle and aunty and all their children. Someone told my father they hacked my uncle with pangas. Then, they put my aunty and cousins in a hut with other women and children and set it alight and burned them.'

'It's too horrible! Beyond imagining!'

'I was a little girl, but I remember when, at Joshua Nkomo's funeral, President Mugabe said Gukurahundi was "a moment of madness". People listened on the radio, and everyone talked about it. Mugabe never apologised, even though the Fifth Brigade reported to his office, and he knew what they did.'

'Yes, I also remember that day. I was working on my computer when I saw the news. Fancy dismissing the slaughter of twenty thousand innocent people as "a moment of madness". It's hard to imagine such a thing happening in our beautiful country. Worse still, the British High Commissioner in Zimbabwe, along with other senior officials in Britain, downplayed the massacres. They put Britain's economic and political interests ahead of the lives of the people in Matabeleland.' Julia realised Mary may not follow everything she said, so she finished with, 'What a terrible time!'

'Yes, Julia, a terrible time.'

'Ah, at last! You've remembered my name.'

'I never forgot your name, Madam.'

'Oh dear!'

'I mean, Julia.'

'Mary, now that you've learnt my name, it's time we made a start on your driving lessons. Before you drive a car, you must learn the rules of the road and get a provisional licence. That's what they call a learner's licence. I will print all the rules for you to learn. When you read them, it will also help with your English. So be ready. Tomorrow, you will have a lot of reading and learning to do. If you can't understand a word, I will explain it to you.'

Before turning off the bedside lamp, Mary read *Ghost Train to Devil's Siding* for half an hour. As usual, she listed all the words she didn't understand, so Julia might explain them in the morning. Often, she could spell a word even before she understood what it meant.

Julia's promise of teaching her to drive made her even more determined to improve her English. But in the darkness, her mind raced, and sleep eluded her. Tomorrow she would start learning the rules of the road. Frida said it would never happen, but now she would show her.

* * *

Julia printed off the rules of the road and handed them to Mary. 'Read these rules and learn them. Ask me if you don't understand something.'

Mary was surprised. 'So many rules, and so many words!' She realised getting a provisional driving licence would not be as easy as she imagined. A quick flip through the printed pages told her there were many words she'd never seen. Somehow, she imagined learning the rules would take a few hours, and she'd be practising driving within a day or two.

'Anything worth having is worth a bit of effort, Mary.'

'Yes, but—'

'No, buts. Just settle down and start reading.'

'My work—'

'You did the laundry yesterday. There's nothing urgent right now. I'll make the morning tea. You focus on those rules.'

'But, Julia, so many new words.'

'Make a list, and we can go over them at morning tea. It's no good learning words off by heart. You must also understand their meaning.'

For Mary, it was as if she'd gone back to learning to read English from the beginning. There were many words new to her, but she tried to say them aloud, like Julia taught her. To her delight, she realised she could work out a few unfamiliar words, such as *petrol* and *corner*. She'd often heard Julia using those words and knew what they meant.

The words Julia never used were a puzzle, but by morning tea, the list for discussion was much shorter than Mary expected.

'Very good, Mary. You've made a lot of progress. After tea, you can read until lunchtime, but then take a break until tomorrow. If you try to learn too many unfamiliar words, you'll lose concentration.'

'*Concentration*, Madam?'

'Yes, that means you'll lose focus. Your brain will get tired.'

'Oh! And *unfamiliar* words?'

'Words you don't know.'

'Oh, so they're new words?'

'If you insist.'

'*Insist*, Madam?'

'Enough, Mary! Now listen. This afternoon, you can try to drive the car in the driveway. You are fortunate my car is a manual and not an automatic. That means you will learn to be a proper driver. Learners struggle to move off in first gear or reverse without jolting the car. So, you can start by practising moving forwards in first gear and backwards in reverse.'

With that exciting news, Mary tackled the rules of the road with renewed enthusiasm. Following a light lunch of tea and sandwiches, Julia led her to the little blue Honda in the driveway. She made Mary fasten her seatbelt, even though they didn't leave the property. She said it was a good habit to develop. Next, Julia showed her how to adjust the rear-view mirror.

'Make sure the car is in neutral.' Julia showed her the gear positions, though Mary was already familiar with these through watching Julia drive. 'Now turn the key to start the engine.' The engine started, but a loud squealing sound accompanied it. 'Let go of the key, Mary! You must let it go as soon as the engine starts.'

'Yes, Julia.' Mary was breathless, and her heart thumped against her chest wall.

'There are three pedals on the floor. The left pedal is the clutch which you press before you change gears, and the middle pedal is the brake for stopping. The right pedal is the accelerator, which makes the car to move. Those are all words you learnt today.'

'Yes.'

'Now, put your foot on the clutch and select first gear. Left foot on the clutch, Mary, left foot. Keep your foot on the clutch and release the handbrake. Now, gently release the clutch as you press the accelerator with your right foot. Remember, the brake is in the middle.'

The car lurched forward, jolted three times, and stalled. Mary slammed on the brake, but the car was already at a standstill.

'Hmm! You see why you must practise, Mary. You can't be thinking about everything you need to do. It must come as second nature.'

'Second nature?'

'Yes, it's like walking. You don't think about putting one foot in front of the other. You just do it without having to concentrate. It comes naturally.'

Mary wasn't too sure about Julia's words. How would she ever be able to move the car without concentrating? She read somewhere in the rules of the road, the driver must concentrate on their driving. They must watch the road ahead and look out for other vehicles and pedestrians. How would she drive without concentrating on the clutch, brake, and accelerator, and everything else she needed to keep in mind?

But Julia managed it. Mary felt safe in the car with her. Some drivers looked like a threat to themselves and everyone else around them. Julia said they won their driving licences in a raffle.

Mary tried several times to move the car without jerking. It was no good. The more she tried, the worse it got. What if Julia thought teaching her to drive was hopeless? She mightn't have another chance to learn.

After an hour, Mary noticed Julia looked a little frazzled.

'Sorry, Julia, it's harder than I thought.'

'Never mind, Mary. We'll try again tomorrow. It just takes practice. Try raising your left hand at the wrist as you lower your right. When you get the hang of it, sit in a chair with your legs stretched in front of you, and try doing the same thing with your feet. But you must be slow and gentle. I never, ever expected to feel seasick in my driveway. All that jerking has made me queasy.'

Mary wanted to ask Julia what *seasick* and *queasy* meant, but she sensed it wasn't the right time. 'A smooth start in the car is too difficult, Julia. It's like cooking beef mince with no clumps.'

'Well, we can't be good at everything, Mary.'

* * *

In the days that followed, Mary made marginal progress in moving the car backwards and forwards in the driveway. Her study of the rules of the road proved more helpful to her reading than to her driving skills.

Julia's explanation of how prefixes reversed what certain words meant fascinated Mary—words such as *unzip, undress, unintended* and *unfamiliar*. She considered it a clever device to reduce the number of words she needed to learn, but she didn't always get it right.

Mary worried about doing the laundry ever since she shrunk one of Julia's favourite wool dresses by washing it in hot water. On the positive side, she inherited the snug-fitting dress as she was a little slimmer than her employer, but the way the garment came into her possession embarrassed her.

From time to time, Julia passed down other garments from her crowded wardrobe.

'You give me so many clothes, Julia.'

'Well, some are too tight for me.'

'Did I shrink them as well?' said Mary, cupping her nose and mouth with her hands.

'No, you didn't shrink them.'

'Do you think you might have unshrunk, Julia?'

Julia laughed. 'Now, you're teaching me new words, but yes, I've put on a little weight.'

Mary's smile couldn't disguise her puzzlement.

'You can't just put a prefix in front of every word, Mary. You must learn the words where you can use a prefix, and those words where you can't.'

For Mary, that was bad news. It meant prefixes did not halve the number of verbs she must learn. Perhaps that might explain the mystery behind words that always used a prefix—words like *understand*, which she believed was the opposite of *derstand?*

It dawned on Mary that learning to read and learning to drive would be a lot more difficult than she first imagined. Yet Julia made them look so easy. Mary wondered if she should ask Julia if she could also win a driving licence in a raffle. She was sure Julia would help her improve her driving afterwards.

CHAPTER 25

Learning to Drive

OVER the next two weeks, Mary's driving improved, and her progress pleased Julia. Smooth starts and precise reversing were no longer a problem, so parking would not be a concern for her driving test. Her memory served her well, and she soon knew all the rules of the road. But she still needed to drive and steer the car in city traffic and on the open road.

Julia took Mary into the city to have her photo taken before going to the Vehicle Inspection Department (VID) to book a test for a provisional driver's licence. To Julia's relief, there was no sign of the rumoured crowds at the VID when they arrived. Horror stories of long queues and waiting times abounded. Mary produced her birth certificate as proof of identity, and Julia handed over the photos and paid the booking fee.

When Mary went in for her test, Julia returned to the car and waited. She worried Mary may succumb to the pressure of the test and stumble over the questions, which were all written in English. She needn't have worried. Mary approached the car with a beaming smile, her white teeth flashing in the late morning sun. She completed the test in the allotted eight minutes and answered all twenty-five questions correctly.

Now that she held a learner's licence, it was time for her to leave the driveway and go out onto the public roads. Julia searched the cardboard boxes in the garage to find the L plates from when Vera learnt to drive. Success! There they lay, in perfect condition, with their large red L against the white background. She attached one to the windscreen and another to the back window. 'Right, Mary! Time for a real driving lesson.'

Mary got into the driver's seat, with Julia in the passenger seat next to her. They put on their seat belts, and Mary adjusted the rear-view mirrors and started the engine. The car stood still, with the engine idling.

'Well, come on then! What are we waiting for, Mary? Let's get moving!'

'I must think about it, Julia.'

'What's there to think about? You've moved the car backwards and forwards dozens of times.'

'Yes, Julia, but there're cars on the road. I must be careful.'

Julia looked left and right. 'There're no cars on the road. Let's get moving!'

Mary took off the handbrake and gently pressed the accelerator as she released the clutch.

'Watch out! You'll hit the gatepost.'

Mary slammed on the brake.

'Relax, Mary. Driving on the road is no different from driving in the driveway. Just do what you've always done.'

Mary took a deep breath and edged the car onto the road and headed to the intersection, where she stopped and checked for traffic. All clear, so she eased the car left onto Burns Drive. She jumped from the sudden loud hoot as a car raced past.

'When I say do what you've always done, I don't mean for you to crawl along at five kilometres an hour. You must drive faster on the road than you do in the driveway. The cars behind you will get impatient.'

Mary picked up speed little by little. At Fairbridge Way she gave way to a car on her right.

'Good, Mary, now continue straight on Phillips Drive and turn left onto First Street. We'll drive around the blocks in The Suburbs. It's a quiet area for you to practise driving.'

Mary drove down half a dozen blocks before she came to a steep section where the road fell away in front of her. 'Eish!' She put her foot on the brake to slow the descent.

'Mary, you must change down to a low gear when you're descending a steep hill. You mustn't drive with your foot on the brake. Next time put it in third gear, or even second if the third gear doesn't slow you down enough. Go around the block and we'll try it again.'

Mary mastered it after a few attempts. But just as she was gaining confidence, Julia said, 'Now let's try hill starts. We must approach the steep section from the other direction.' Going up the hill was an unfamiliar sensation, and Mary's apprehension grew.

'Pull over by the kerb near that extra steep part. Don't forget to apply the hand brake.'

Mary stopped by the kerb and took deep breaths to steady her nerves.

'OK, Mary, now let's give it a go.'

Mary put the car into first gear. Each time she tried to move off, the car rolled back.

'We'll be at the bottom of the hill soon, Mary, if you're not careful. Press the accelerator a little harder before you release the handbrake.'

As Julia spoke, a black Mercedes pulled up behind them and parked. A well-dressed African man with sunglasses jumped out and locked the car door. 'Excuse me,' said Julia, 'we're practising hill starts. Do you mind moving your car?'

'Why should I move my car? Learn to drive somewhere else.'

'We don't want to damage your car if we roll back.'

'I've noted your registration number, so you better not roll back and damage my car. Anyway, women drivers shouldn't try to learn on this hill.'

'Will you move your car?'

'No.'

'Pompous idiot.'

The man laughed, waved his briefcase in a mock threatening fashion, and walked away.

'Alright, Mary, now remember, accelerate a little harder before you release the handbrake.'

Mary held her breath as she pressed the accelerator and released the handbrake.

'Stop!' Julia shouted.

Three feet was all the space the discourteous Mercedes driver left them. The gap was now only six inches. 'Should I take over, Mary? If you roll back this time, you'll have your first car crash.'

'No, Julia, I can do it. I won't roll back this time.'

It was Julia's turn to hold her breath as Mary revved the engine hard and released the handbrake. The Honda roared uphill faster than Mary intended, and a passing car hooted in alarm.

'Oh, yes! And don't forget to check the rear-view mirror for other vehicles before you enter the traffic lane.'

'Sorry, Julia.'

'It's alright. That was a good hill start except for the passing car. Vera and most other drivers in Bulawayo learnt their hill starts on First Street. I learnt here too, and we all experienced the same problem as you. I think that's enough for today, Mary. We'll try again tomorrow.'

Mary drove back to the house without further incident and sighed with relief when she pulled up in the driveway. Her first drive on the roads was an exhilarating experience, and she'd made significant strides with her driving. She was sure tomorrow she'd do much better.

Julia stepped out of the car and walked into the house. As she locked the car, Mary noticed Frida smoking in the corner of her garden and walked over to say hello.

'How are you, Frida? I don't see you much these days.'

'I suppose you've come over to tell me how clever you are, driving that car?'

'No, I just wanted to say hello.'

Frida snorted.

'We were friends, Frida, but you've changed. You seem to hate me. Why?'

'I got you that job, working for your madam.'

'Yes, and I thank you for that.'

'That job should have been mine.'

'Well, why didn't you talk to Julia about it before you helped me get the job?'

'Because of the boss. I didn't know your madam was going to get rid of him. If I'd known, I would have asked your madam for the job.'

'OK, but it's not my fault.'

'When the madam kicked the boss out, she should have dismissed you.'

'But I needed the job, and you said nothing.'

'Eish! You had never worked as a maid.' Frida walked away without looking back.

Mary felt sorry for her. Frida worked for an ungrateful madam, while she worked for Julia, the best madam one could have. But how could she help Frida? She no longer appeared to visit the other maids congregating down the road, and Mary knew Frida also blamed her for that.

Back in the house, Julia poured two glasses of sherry to celebrate Mary getting her learner's licence. They sipped at the liquid as they prepared the evening meal together.

'Mary, how much of Zimbabwe have you seen?'

'Only Figtree, Bulawayo, my village past Marula, and my parents' village.'

'It's time you saw more of the country. I'll think of somewhere.'

'Will we drive?'

'Perhaps, or maybe we'll go by train or aeroplane.'

'Train or aeroplane? I have never been on those things. Are they safe?'

'Yes, they are. I'll see what I can arrange.'

The exciting news kept Mary awake that night. Julia was introducing her to a whole new world. She felt bad each time she thought of Frida. But why should she worry about Frida? Her rude, erstwhile friend was jealous and undermining, but she couldn't help the nagging thought she robbed Frida of a chance for a better life.

Since her arrival, Mary's life improved beyond her wildest dreams, while Frida's circumstances remained unchanged. In her village, Mary helped many others with their troubles, but she didn't know what she might do to improve Frida's circumstances.

She worried she might have lost her touch. It had been so easy to help others when she mumbled incomprehensible words over her magic book. But she was not that woman anymore. The more she learnt from Julia, the harder it seemed to even imagine her former life as a pretend sangoma. Besides, Frida may be too sophisticated to benefit from that treatment. Or was she?

* * *

At breakfast, Julia seemed extra cheerful. 'I've decided where we are going on our trip, Mary.'

'Where?'

'Ah, that's a surprise. I'll book the trip and tell you what clothes you need to pack.'

'Is it far?'

'Quite far, so we won't go by car.'

'How long will we be away?'

'Four or five days.'

'What about my driving?'

Julia laughed. 'We can still go for driving lessons every day until we leave. But there's no hurry for your licence. We both need a break, and you can continue driving when we get back.'

Mary stood at the kitchen sink, washing the breakfast dishes, and thinking about the trip. Rat-a-tat—a knock at the kitchen door. A serious-looking Frida stood there.

'Frida, what's wrong?'

'You said you were my friend.'

'Yes?'

'My madam's family are coming for a visit from Harare. she says they need my kia because there's not enough room in the house for all of them.

She says I must find somewhere else to stay while they are here. Can I stay in your kia with you?'

'What about the evil spirit in the vegetable garden? You said you'd never visit again.'

'You said it wasn't an evil spirit.'

'I must ask Julia if it's OK for you to stay.'

'Please, Mary, ask her. I have nowhere else to stay. The family is arriving on Sunday, so I must move out by lunchtime.'

'Must you work while their family is visiting?'

'Yes, of course!'

'I'll see what Julia says, and I'll let you know.'

At morning tea, Mary told Julia about Frida's request.

'That girl has a cheek, Mary, after the way she's behaved towards you.'

'Yes, Julia, but she has nowhere else to go. The other maids aren't talking to her.'

'Well, Mary, it's your kia, so it's your decision. I have no objection if you don't.'

'Thank you, Julia.'

'If she comes on Sunday, she'll be on her own all week. I've booked our trip and we're leaving on Tuesday.'

Mary passed the good news to Frida that she could stay in the kia. She also told her she and Julia would be away.

'But if you're not here, I'll be alone with the evil spirit?'

'Don't worry, I've told the evil spirit you have permission to stay, so it will protect you while we're away. You'll be safe if you care for the house and not have visitors.'

* * *

A little after lunch on Sunday, Frida turned up, carrying her suitcase and blankets. Mary opened the kia for her and told her she could sleep on the bed.

'But where will you sleep?'

'I sleep in the house in the boss's old room.'

'You sleep in the house? Your madam lets you sleep in the house?'

'Yes, I've been in the house since I was sick. Julia said she couldn't come to the kia late at night to give me my medicine, so I must move into the house.'

'Your madam got up at night to give you medicine?'

'Yes.'

'Aikona! But now you are better?'

'Yes, but I keep Julia company. She likes me in the house.'

'Ag, ag, ag! This is not right. No madams allow their maids to sleep in the house.'

'Julia says I am her friend, and not just her maid.'

Mary smiled at the puzzled expression on Frida's face. The news seemed too much for her. Perhaps she realised what she'd missed by not applying for the job when the opportunity was there.

The neighbours kept Frida busy from early morning to late, so Mary saw little of her over the next two days.

Early on Tuesday morning, Mary saw Frida leaving the kia on her way to work. Mary called out, 'Don't forget, Frida, we're leaving at half-past six this evening.'

Frida waved in reply.

CHAPTER 26

Ghost Train to Devil's Siding

MARY and Julia waited with their bags at the front door. Julia checked her watch. It was almost time. At a quarter-past six, the taxi arrived at the gate. It was already dark, and its welcome headlights lit the driveway. The driver put the bags in the car boot and closed the rear doors for them.

'Where to, Madam?'

'The station, please,' said Julia.

With over an hour to the train's scheduled departure, they were early. The little taxi bounced along Bulawayo's crumbling roads at a leisurely pace. Rush hour was over, and the evening streets were quiet. It was a short drive to the station, and within ten minutes, they arrived. The driver jumped out and retrieved the bags from the boot. Julia thanked him and paid the fare. Soon, the taxi drove out of sight, and the two women stood alone on the pavement with their bags.

'Well, come on, Mary, let's move.'

A shudder ran through Mary as she and Julia walked through the station entrance onto platform one. It was not because of the late-May winter breezes with their gentle caress of her cheeks one moment and a chilly gust the next. Rather, it was the dim platforms with their few working lights and dark shadows. The station's eerie appearance reminded her of *Ghost Train to Devil's Siding*, the scary book Julia was using to teach her to read.

Perhaps the choice of the book was an unfortunate coincidence, given that the overnight train to Victoria Falls would be their accommodation for the next fourteen hours. Julia insisted the language in the book was at the right level for Mary, as it was written for children approaching their teens. Mary wondered about that, because it had already given her sleepless nights. How might young children react to the story? Perhaps European children didn't believe in ghosts, but she knew better. People should never take evil spirits lightly.

Julia strode ahead in her usual confident manner. 'Come on Mary, stop dithering. We must get to platform four.'

'But Julia, the train leaves at half-past seven. We are early.'

'Better early than late and finding someone has moved into our compartment.'

Julia booked all four bunks in a first-class compartment, so they wouldn't have to share with strangers. But others warned that sometimes people occupied the apartment and could be hard to evict, despite not having first-class tickets.

The carriages standing on platform four did little to allay Mary's apprehension. Many of the compartments appeared full of junk. Back in her remote village, the huts may have had mud floors, but the villagers swept them clean and kept them tidy. The state of these carriages would shock those house-proud women.

'Don't worry, Mary, that's not our train. They store the derelict carriages here to use for spare parts. Our train will be further down the platform.'

Ahead, Mary noticed small groups of people waiting for the train to appear. Julia seemed unconcerned. She must have done many similar trips before now. But Mary experienced a strange mix of excitement and apprehension. This was her first train journey, and she bubbled with anticipation all week. Now she was not so sure. Another strong, chilly gust added to her disquiet. She and Julia dressed in warm clothing, but Bulawayo can freeze on winter nights. The open platforms, with only their narrow roofs for cover, invited the chill winds to torment the small, huddled groups of travellers.

At first, it sounded like rolling thunder, unlikely in the dry season. Then Mary saw it; a great black monster of a machine slowly rumbling down the platform towards them. Behind, the row of carriages looked like ducklings following their mother. There was nothing fluffy about this massive beast as the rails beneath it groaned with the weight they bore.

The huge Garratt locomotive eased to a stop with screeching brakes and a hiss of steam. Next came the clanking of carriages concertinaing to a halt behind it. Mary stepped back in alarm as another loud burst of hissing steam surprised her. She'd not expected the iron beast to come to a stop so close to where she and Julia stood.

The clanking and hissing of the locomotive sounded like the heavy breathing of an enormous dragon. High above the ground in a small open window, she glimpsed movement, as if the dragon's eye surveyed the scene. Dressed in a green shirt and matching cap, the tiny figure of the engine driver in the window looked like the iris of the huge beast's eye. The smell of burning coal in the firebox had a pleasant, mesmerising effect in the chilly winter night. The figure in the window glanced down at her with fiery red eyes. Mary froze; it must be the Devil, 'Or perhaps,' suggested Julia, 'the reflection of burning coal in the locomotive's firebox?' Transfixed, Mary only considered the former to be the likely explanation.

'Come along, Mary, we can't stand here all day, gawping at the engine. We must find our compartment and settle in before someone else does.'

Julia marched down the platform with her bag, and Mary scurried to catch up with her. Their compartment was the second one in the second carriage, so they didn't have far to walk.

Mary held up her bag as she boarded the train, taking care to not let it touch the dirty carriage floor. Her first sight of the compartment stopped her in her tracks. This didn't look first-class to her, and she wondered what Julia thought. Grey Formica laminate walls smeared with dirt, and the broken light covers with only one of the three lights working. The torn leatherette bench seats that converted into sleeping bunks; with one completely shredded.

The dim compartment promised a dreary start to their journey. Mary soon discovered that the latch to fold back one of the top bunks against the wall was missing, and the bottom bunk sloped at an awkward angle towards the wall. The wash basin lacked water, and one filthy window was jammed a little open. Worst of all, the missing door latch meant they couldn't lock the compartment door.

Julia made herself comfortable on the better bench seat, where the top bunk conveniently folded against the wall. But she'd have to contend with the jammed window.

'Julia, did you know about the train's condition?'

'I'd read about it, but it's worse than I expected. We must make the best of it. It's a pity the bedding was unavailable for this trip, but I brought along two sleeping bags, just in case. I've brought a box of tissues and wet wipes to clean our hands if the water wasn't working.'

At seven-thirty, a sudden jolt sent Mary sprawling onto Julia's bench seat. They were on their way. Mary walked to an open window in the corridor outside the compartment to watch the platform glide past the train. A few people waved off their friends or relatives. As her open window passed them, she fancied they gave her a knowing smile. Did they know something she didn't? Frida told her people died when the trains came off the railway tracks. She said it happened often, but the government kept quiet about it.

The platforms gave way to a web of railway lines heading in all directions. How did the engine driver know which railway tracks to follow? As Mary returned to the compartment, the train jolted and stopped, accompanied by the loud clanging of the carriages concertinaing once more.

The area was in darkness, and although she put her face close to the window glass and shaded her eyes, Mary saw nothing. 'Why have we stopped so soon?' she asked.

'I'd say the engine is moving to the other end of the train. When the train arrived, it surprised me our carriage was so close to the locomotive. First-class is always near the back.'

Mary didn't like the train standing still in a lonely, dark area. Anyone could climb on board, bad men, or evil spirits. After an interminable fifteen-minute delay and another powerful jolt, the train moved again. Mary soon learnt to keep her balance and hold on to any available supports in the compartment. She tried again to peer through the closed window next to her bunk, but with darkness outside, all she saw was her own reflection in the glass. Suddenly, she noticed the shape of a huge, menacing male figure looming up to the window. Mary screamed. Julia's heart skipped a beat at the blood-curdling yell.

'Tickets, please,' said the conductor, not reacting to Mary's fright.

After he'd left, Julia turned to her.

'What on earth is the matter with you, shouting like a mad creature? You almost gave me a heart attack.'

'I thought a spirit was coming for me. It just seemed to float outside my window. It was the conductor's reflection in the glass, but I didn't know he'd come into the compartment.'

'Well, he knocked before he opened the door. Instead of daydreaming, Mary, concentrate on what you're doing.'

'I wasn't doing anything, Julia, just trying to look through the window.'

'Time for tea,' said Julia, unscrewing the cap of the thermos flask.

Somehow, tea from the thermos tasted much better than normal, and Julia made it the way Mary liked her tea, with a dash of milk and the slightest hint of sugar.

Mary marvelled at the calm way Julia responded to their situation. She wouldn't be used to such dirty and uncomfortable surroundings, yet she didn't seem the least bit perturbed. Ever since she started working as Julia's housemaid, her employer stressed the need to maintain standards. Now that she'd adapted to Julia's cosy home, Mary found it difficult to accept the dirty condition of the train. Julia always spoke in glowing terms of the wonderful train trip from Bulawayo to the Victoria Falls, but this train did not fit the picture she'd formed in her mind.

Just as they finished their tea, the slow-moving train came to another jolting halt, followed by shouts and excited voices. Mary pulled down the window to check what was happening. It was only passengers boarding at a quiet siding a little distance outside Bulawayo. After a few minutes, the train began moving again.

Julia took out the two small sleeping bags from her holdall. One for Mary and one for herself. They both slept in their clothes as the surroundings were not conducive to changing into their nightwear. Mary switched off the single light and hopped into her sleeping bag. Soon, deep breaths indicated Julia was fast asleep, but Mary was too excited to sleep and a little concerned about the unlockable compartment door.

Her thoughts drifted back over the eighteen months she worked for Julia. She thought herself lucky to get the job as her housemaid. She wasn't qualified for the role, but Julia was distracted, thanks to a turning point in her life.

For Mary, each morning was the start of an exciting adventure. It was the first time she saw a refrigerator humming in action, and she smiled, remembering the 'white cupboard' that launched her on her new life's journey. And the dark wooden furniture in the lounge, so smooth, shiny, and cool that she thought it was glass. An understandable mistake. She loved dusting the cocktail cabinet and coffee tables, and later, Julia showed her how to polish them. So many wonderful things in Julia's house she loved to touch. She would close her eyes and run her fingers over the beautiful fabrics, glassware, and furniture.

From her perspective, Julia wouldn't understand the wonder Mary felt with each day's discoveries. Once Julia's life returned to normality, and she had the time to focus on Mary, she proved to be a patient employer, training her new maid, and dismissing her many mistakes, including the water ring she left on one of the coffee tables. She made it her business to educate Mary to the ways of the modern world, and Mary repaid her by being an excellent student.

Then came the day that changed everything. Julia called Mary to the dining room and invited her to sit down in a chair. Mary feared she was about to be dismissed, and her hands trembled. Julia looked so serious and formal in her manner.

'Mary, you have been with me for almost eighteen months now.'

'Yes, Madam.'

'You have learnt a lot in that time and become good at your job.'

'Yes, Madam, you can pay me less if you want.'

'What? Why would I pay you less?'

'I don't know, Madam, but if I'm too expensive.'

'No, stop, Mary. You don't understand.'

'Madam?'

'I want to change your situation.'

'No, Madam, I am happy with my situation.'

'Mary, you've been my housemaid, but to me, you're much more than that. You are more like a companion.'

'Madam?'

'A companion is a friend. You've got over your flu, so you can go back to your kia if you prefer, but I'd be pleased if you remained in the house. You are good company, and I enjoy our cosy chats in the evenings. So, you can stay on in the house if you wish. Would you like that?'

'Oh, yes, Madam.'

'I'll do my best to make up for your lost schooling. You must still do the same housework, but you can call me Julia and regard my house as your house. Do you understand?'

'Yes, Madam.'

'Julia.'

'Yes, Madam.'

'Julia.'

'Yes, Julia.'

It took Mary several weeks before she felt comfortable calling her employer by her first name, but after a while, it sounded natural.

The train stopped, and Mary hopped out of her sleeping bag to observe the activity. Another siding in the middle of nowhere. Slamming doors, excited voices, shouting and then silence before the train moved off once more. The compartment now seemed cosy compared with the chill of the night breezes outside, and Mary appreciated the charm of sleeper class on the overnight train. The occasional haunting whistle of the giant locomotive was a beautiful but lonely sound carried on the night air. She shivered as the whistle reminded her of *Ghost Train to Devil's Siding*.

Sometimes, she heard the locomotive's distant chugging, and at other times, only the carriage's squeak and rattle. It all depended on which direction the swirling night breezes blew, or when extra effort was needed for the engine to tackle an incline. The clickety-clack of the carriage bogies on the railway line made Mary drowsy, and despite her determination to view every siding on the line, she drifted off to sleep. Something caused her to wake. The door was a little ajar. She sat up, concerned that someone might have entered the compartment. Her heart skipped a beat when the door slid open. It was Julia.

'Where have you been? The door was open. I didn't know you'd gone out.'

'I went to the toilet. It's not very nice. No water to flush or wash. The latch is missing, so the door swings open and closed. The toilets are spacious, and you can't reach the door to keep it closed. It's fortunate it's the middle of the night and people aren't wandering around the train.'

'You shouldn't leave the compartment alone at night. Why didn't you wake me? You're the only white person on the train. It could be dangerous for you.'

'Well, if you go out, be careful. The doors of the carriage also swing open and closed. The way this train rocks and shakes, someone could fall out.'

Mary returned from her visit to the toilet, breathless with apprehension. 'Julia, two men floated along the corridor in front of me, and when they reached the end, they just disappeared. They might have been spirits.'

'Nonsense, Mary. None of the lights in the corridor work, and it's very dark. You must have imagined it. Why didn't you take the torch with you? How jumpy you are tonight! You must forget about the old superstitions. You're not in your village now.'

'No, I saw them just before they disappeared.'

'Well, they might have entered a compartment.'

'Maybe we should look, Julia. I won't be able to sleep otherwise.'

'All right, all right. Let me put my shoes on first.'

The women crept down the corridor, with Julia leading and Mary checking behind them to make sure no one followed. All the compartment doors stood ajar, and none of them seemed occupied.

'We're the only people on this train,' said Mary. 'Everyone else has left.'

'I'm sure there're plenty of people in economy class.'

'Do you think it's safe for us to continue on this train, Julia?'

'Of course. What's got into you, Mary? All this nonsense-talk about spirits. You know, the corridor turns at the end of the carriage. The two you saw moved to the next carriage. That's all.'

'What if they come back?'

'They didn't trouble us earlier. Why would they trouble us now?'

Back in the relative safety of the compartment, Mary said, 'This train is like *Ghost Train to Devil's Siding.*'

'Now go to sleep, Mary. If you keep us up all night, we'll be too tired to enjoy tomorrow.'

Mary zipped up her sleeping bag right to the top and covered her head with the bag's hood, leaving only her eyes and nose exposed. Soon she fell asleep.

In the early hours, the train slowed before coming to a stop. Mary woke to find an eerie orange glow flooding the compartment. Then reason prevailed. She'd seen a similar orange glow from the street lights in Bulawayo. It must be a big station, she thought. She slipped from the sleeping bag and stepped into the corridor and peered out the window. The station sign said Dete. A surprising number of people stood on the platform, waiting to board, while others disembarked. Departing passengers tossed bags out of the window into waiting outstretched arms, while other bags moved in the opposite direction. Dete was the largest station on the journey, and Mary didn't intend to miss a minute of it. A quarter of an hour later, the train jerked and moved again.

At seven o'clock, the bright winter morning woke Mary and Julia. For breakfast, they ate the ham sandwiches Mary prepared at home. While Julia relaxed in the compartment, Mary was up and down, taking photos with Julia's digital camera. There were no animals around, so she contented herself with photos of interesting trees with weaver bird nests hanging like Christmas decorations on the end of the branches.

With only an hour to go before their arrival at Victoria Falls, Mary's excitement grew. She'd heard stories of the great water, but she never imagined she'd ever see it. Julia found herself caught up in Mary's enthusiasm. It was so much more fun having a companion rather than a servant. Julia's friends all left Zimbabwe, but Mary, her new friend, was making up for that.

The train rolled into the quaint but ageing station. 'Oh!' said Julia. 'What a surprise! It's Victoria Falls, not Devil's Siding!' The passengers all hurried from the train. Most endured a long, chilly night in economy class.

Opposite the station, someone had made their home in derelict railway carriages parked in a siding. Baboons jumped onto the carriage roofs and entered the carriages through the open windows in search of food. The railway staff ran onto the train to chase out the determined pests. Mary wondered if the baboons accounted for the shredded bench seat in her compartment.

Victoria Falls at last. Warm and tropical in the middle of winter. What would the next few days bring on her holiday adventure with her best friend Julia? They'd already made an exciting start.

CHAPTER 27

Victoria Falls

To the right of the station building stood an arched gate saying Victoria Falls Hotel. But Julia and Mary weren't staying there. They picked up their bags and walked through the station entrance. The expanse of green lawn and huge shady trees between the station and the Victoria Falls and Kingdom hotels complemented the morning's warm tropical air. The two women breathed in the heady mix, filling their lungs to capacity. They felt energised by the cocktail of Zambezi Valley early morning oxygen and the smell of tropical vegetation.

In front of the Kingdom Hotel, the cshuk, cshuk, cshuk of a garden sprinkler accompanied a high, oscillating, fan-shaped spray, watering a row of large-leaved, tropical plants growing against the hotel wall. The water droplets hung in the air, creating a small rainbow. Julia and Mary laughed with delight at the scene. Mary took a photograph of the sun shining through the mist the sprinkler generated.

The women ambled across the lawn and walked up to the stone towers at the Kingdom Hotel entrance, and crossed the bridged moat leading to the hotel reception. On the left, a long reception counter accommodated half a dozen busy receptionists. A young African woman hurried over to welcome the couple, and Julia filled out the check-in form. It was quick and efficient, and the receptionist hailed a porter to carry the cases and show the guests to their room.

They walked through the spacious foyer lounge with its grand piano and past the enormous open dining area on the floor below them. Gigantic stone pillars around the dining area's perimeter supported the tower-ing ceiling, providing a spectacular backdrop to the entrance foyer. The women followed the porter along the corridor to their room, halfway down the second passage.

When the porter opened the door, Mary gasped in amazement. She'd never seen such a luxurious room. At the far end, beyond large sliding wooden shutters, the balcony looked onto the lush green canopy of the hotel's inner garden, giving the room complete privacy. The balcony ac-commodated two slatted wooden chairs and a low table. That, together with the bedroom's wicker furniture, gave the space a tropical island feel-ing. Near the door, on the left, stood the cupboards, room safe, refriger-ator, and tea-making facilities. Opposite was the bathroom with a bath, shower, and toilet.

Julia selected the queen-size bed, and Mary took the lower bunk of the bunk bed. She was agog. Such luxury; even better than Julia's bedroom at her house in Bulawayo. She walked onto the balcony and sat in one of the slatted chairs, so comfy and relaxing after the sleepless night on the dirty train.

'Don't make yourself too comfortable, Mary. I'll make tea, and then we must go out and explore the area.'

'I could sit here all day, Julia.'

While Mary sat enjoying the peace of the green canopy, Julia went for a shower to freshen up and remove the travel grime. Then it was Mary's turn. Soon, ready and eager, they stepped out to see the sights. They'd seen the spray of the falls from the train. It was time for a closer look.

They passed the reception desk where the friendly receptionist waved to check all was in order. 'Yes, thank you.' They walked on over the bridged moat at the hotel entrance. At the gate, the guard stood talking to a tall, well-built, bare-chested young African man wearing an animal skin loincloth with headband and matching armbands resting above his biceps.

'You want a photo of me, Madam?'

'Not just now, thank you.' said Julia. 'Perhaps when we get back.'

'I'll be waiting, Madam,' said the young warrior, a practised salesperson, accustomed to dealing with tourists.

Mary and Julia walked to the hotel corner and turned towards the bridge. The afternoon heat set in as they crossed the road towards the Ilala Lodge Hotel. In the bush next to the hotel, a group of elephants grazed. Two young bulls jousted with widespread ears, pushing and shoving each other in a display of dominance.

On the way to the bridge, a scattering of African men walking in ones and twos offered Julia small curios or Zimbabwe dollar notes of astronomical denominations. Julia resisted all offers.

'All the African men ignore me, Julia.'

'That's because they think I have the money.'

'But if I'm a tourist walking with you, I might also have money.'

'They think white tourists are more likely to buy.'

'Even the young man at the hotel gate ignored me.'

'Yes, for the same reason, I expect. Don't tell me you're jealous, Mary?'

'No, no, not jealous.'

'Consider yourself lucky they are not pestering you. I'm sure the young man at the gate didn't talk to me because he thought me attractive. If you like, I'll tell him to talk to you because you also have money.'

'No, Julia, you mustn't say that!'

Julia laughed. 'I'm just teasing you, Mary. But he was a handsome young man, don't you think?'

'I didn't notice.'

'Oh, is that so? This walk is longer than I remember, and it's getting hot.'

Soon, they walked past the entrance to the rainforest on the left. Opposite stood the curio stalls and parking area. At the border post, they entered the building to get the re-entry permits that would allow them to walk onto the Victoria Falls Bridge to see the views, and then return to Zimbabwe. They showed the re-entry permit to the guard before passing through the gate.

The roar of the falls was constant now, though the tumbling, frothing water lay hidden from view by the thick vegetation of the rainforest. Deep in the gorge, the racing, olive-coloured water churned white from the impetus of the flow. The spray carried on the breeze resembled a heavy mist that covered the distant views and created a rainbow close to the bridge. The cooling droplets flowed over the two women in gentle clouds, interspersed with short dry spells when the breezes died down.

As they moved across the bridge, the white raging water of the falls came into view, a heavenly, spellbinding sight. Julia never tired of seeing the falls, but this was Mary's first visit, and she was enthralled. The two stood in silence, resting their arms on the yellow railings of the bridge. Words couldn't do justice to the scene before them. The periodic bursts of spray cooled their arms and faces in the hot sun. It was the perfect complement to the vision they beheld.

Further along the bridge, they saw the elevated Knife Edge walkway built from the Zambian side to the wooded outcrop in front of the falls. The two women walked on past the sign warning them they'd entered Zambia. They walked only a metre or two past the sign, but it thrilled Mary to think she'd visited another country.

On the way back across the bridge, they paused near the bungee jump. A tiny figure, far below, dangled on the elastic rope like a spider riding a loose thread hanging from its web. In the distance, on the Zimbabwean side of the gorge, the Victoria Falls Hotel with its beautiful gardens stood like an isolated mirage in the wilderness. After surrendering their re-entry permits at the Zimbabwean border post, they returned to the Kingdom Hotel to freshen up before going out to explore Victoria Falls village.

It was years since Julia last visited the falls. In the interim, the village developed into an interesting little centre with restaurants, bars, tourist shops, and essential services, catering to locals and tourists alike. On Livingstone Way, across the railway line, they came upon the Landela Complex with its small shop fronts. In the middle of the row of shops, a shallow, open-sided arcade contained a tapas restaurant. Behind the complex, they stopped for a cooling drink at the Mama Africa Eating House. The open-sided dining veranda, opposite a roofless stage decorated with paintings of band musicians, gave the garden setting a relaxed atmosphere in the shade of a large tree.

Julia and Mary crossed the road and investigated the shops and restaurants along Parkway Drive and the arcade in the Victoria Falls Centre. It took them on a circular route back to the corner on Livingstone Way, where the Shearwater Restaurant boasted an inviting open air dining space. It was still early evening, but the advertised discount for early diners was too tempting to ignore. The cool of the evening replaced the sting of the hot Zambezi Valley afternoon. They enjoyed a super-tender steak with salad and chips, followed by a bowl of ice cream.

Mary was learning how some others lived. The concept of a holiday eluded her till now. She wondered how they could ever return to normal everyday life.

'You know, Mary, holidays go by fast. After a week back in Bulawayo, it will seem ages since we visited here.'

Mary smiled. Julia must be wrong. For her, the trip was a turning point that would always seem like yesterday. 'Can we come here again, Julia?'

'Of course. As often as we want.'

'But isn't it expensive?'

'Yes, but if we don't enjoy ourselves while we can, one day we may wish we'd spent more time having fun. You can't take the money with you when you die.'

'Don't talk like that, Julia, it's bad luck.'

'You're funny, Mary.'

'No, you shouldn't invite fate to the table. The last time I spoke to my husband before his snake bite, we argued. I wish I could change that, but I can't.'

It was getting dark by the time the women walked back to the hotel. Out of curiosity, they dropped into the hotel's Makasa Casino, but it was early, and the dimly lit, empty gaming floor gave them nothing to see.

They walked into the hotel foyer, where a pianist played the grand piano for the benefit of the guests dining in the hotel restaurant on the floor below them. Although several diners sat at the tables, the enormous space looked empty.

'I'm glad we ate at the restaurant in the village, Julia.'

'Yes, it was cosy. Perhaps we can go there again tomorrow evening.'

* * *

Breakfast was a surprise. The dining room was almost full.

'All these people, Julia! Where were they last night?'

'I suppose they must have dined out like we did.'

After a welcoming pot of tea, an enormous choice of foods faced the women.

'Even a bigger choice than we have at home,' said Julia.

It was more food than Mary could have imagined. She didn't know where to start, so she followed Julia's example.

'You must choose your own food, Mary. You don't have to copy me.'

'But you know the best things to choose, Julia.'

'I wish I did. I'm having the same difficulty choosing as you.'

They ended up eating a breakfast much like the one at home.

'So much lovely food,' said Julia, 'but we are creatures of habit.'

After returning to the room and brushing their teeth, they collected their hats and sunglasses and headed out to visit the rainforest. The warm, mid-morning winter sun was not yet at its zenith. Julia paid the entrance fee but declined the offer of umbrellas and raincoats.

'Julia, those other people are taking raincoats. Is it wet, out there?'

'If we don't get wet in the spray, we'll miss half the fun of visiting the rainforest. Don't worry, we'll soon get dry, but don't let the camera get wet. It's not weather protected.'

The women visited Dr Livingstone's statue and the Devil's Cataract, where an endless stream of water cascaded seventy metres—two hundred and thirty-three feet—into the gorge. Then they walked along the path to the Rainbow Falls, where the water plunged one hundred and eight metres—three hundred and sixty feet—in a deafening celebration of the raw power of nature.

Mary was in awe of the stirring sight. She tried her best to take photos and keep the camera dry. As on the bridge, the breeze carried the spray in waves. But the heaviest spray at Danger Point was like a constant downpour of rain. Mary and Julia were soaked, but most of the other tourists wore raincoats. Mary thought Julia should have accepted the offer of raincoats at the entrance. But after the short walk to view the bridge, they'd almost dried.

Julia noted with satisfaction how tourists who elected to wear raincoats tried to dry their clothes soaked with sweat. The wisdom behind Julia's decision to refuse the raincoats did not escape Mary's notice.

On the return trip along the rainforest walk, a small group of tourists waited while a man tried to shoo off a large male baboon. He made threatening gestures towards the baboon, which responded in kind. 'He won't leave if you challenge him,' said Mary. 'If you ignore him, he will ignore you. Then it will be safe to pass.' The tourist frowned at her interference before backing away from the baboon. Soon, the creature wandered off into the thick vegetation, allowing the tourists on their way.

At the rainforest entrance, on their way out, Julia and Mary stopped to read all the posters, giving information about Victoria Falls and the surrounding area. The history, geology, fauna, and flora were all covered. It was an informative and educational half hour for both.

'It's almost lunchtime, Mary. Let's go back. I want to show you some-where special.'

CHAPTER 28

Paradise Not Perfect

Julia and Mary walked back towards the hotel. But they passed the Kingdom on their left and walked on to the Victoria Falls Hotel—the grand old lady of the tourist industry at Victoria Falls. Unlike the Kingdom's stone facade resembling the Zimbabwe Ruins, the Victoria Falls Hotel presented a luxurious picture of yesteryear. Small-paned windows and colonial era decor welcomed visitors. The Residents Only signs were gone, and non-residents could now walk in the hotel's attractive grounds.

Mary followed Julia to the back veranda with its sweeping views towards the bridge. Julia flagged down one of the busy waiters and secured a table for two. They both ordered a light dish of crocodile and salad and sat back, enjoying glasses of tomato juice. The expanse of green lawn and large shady trees gave a welcome cooling effect in the middle of the day. Also enjoying the surroundings, a family of warthogs nibbled on the green grass, ignoring the gaggle of tourists walking past them.

'When Vera was a child, we always stayed here when we visited the falls. It makes me feel sad because everywhere I see reminders of her. I'm glad you're with me, Mary. It helps me take my mind off those sad thoughts.'

'Oh, I'm sorry, Julia.'

'The visits to Victoria Falls and the Wankie Game Reserve set her on the path to becoming a travel writer. At school, most of her essays would be about our trips to various places. She loved hearing from people she inspired to visit places about which she'd written.'

Although there appeared to be an abundance of waiters, the service was slow. Mary glanced at the diners at the other tables, and suddenly, she stiffened. Four or five tables down sat her nemesis, Jackson Mpofu. What was he doing here? He promised she'd be sorry if she didn't withdraw her support for Dennis Nyathi and his election ambitions. She did not follow Mpofu's demands, and that was why she left her home village and moved to Bulawayo.

Mary froze as the man returned her glance before looking away. Did he recognise her, smartly dressed in a short-sleeve white blouse and khaki trousers she got from Julia? Just before the trip, she visited a hairdresser to weave intricate patterns into her hair. Would Mpofu expect the elegant young woman sitting opposite Julia to be the village woman who dressed in tattered old clothes?

Mary tried her hardest to not look at Mpofu, but she found it difficult to avoid checking from time to time whether he'd spotted her. Then, when she sneaked a quick glance at him, he looked straight back at her. She quickly averted her eyes. Did he notice? She cursed herself for not resisting the almost overwhelming urge to keep a watch on him. What should she do now? He got up from his chair, and his male companion also rose. Too late to warn Julia about what might happen.

But then, a porter called to Mpofu in a loud voice, 'Mr Mpofu, your airport taxi is here.' Jackson Mpofu and his companion followed the porter, who picked up the suitcase standing beside their table before heading towards the hotel entrance. To Mary's relief, he didn't look at her as he left the veranda restaurant. It looked like he'd not recognised her after all. As she related her concerns to Julia, a waiter came up and handed her a business card. 'Mr Mpofu asked me to give you his card, Madam. He always gives me his card to pass to young ladies. He said you can phone him if you want. Mr Mpofu is an important man in the government. His room number is on the back.'

'Hasn't he left for the airport?' Mary asked. 'The porter carried his suitcase.'

'No, that's his assistant's suitcase. Mr Mpofu is seeing him off at the airport.'

'When is Mr Mpofu leaving?'

'He's flying to Bulawayo tomorrow, so you better phone him tonight or you'll miss him.'

Julia sensed Mary's unease. 'Let's make ourselves scarce around the village this afternoon.' After lunch, in the foyer of the Kingdom Hotel, Julia stopped at the excursion counter and booked a two-hour sunset cruise on the Zambezi. The tour bus would pick them up at the hotel entrance a little before four o'clock, with the scheduled cruise departure time at four-thirty.

Julia and Mary arrived early at the hotel entrance to make sure they didn't delay the bus's scheduled departure. They found seats near the front and made themselves comfortable. The minibus left the hotel with a small group of eight tourists. The bus drove into the village and turned at the Shearwater Restaurant, where they ate the previous evening. Soon it left the village behind and rolled along the narrow undulating road past the Elephant Hills Resort. Two kilometres past the resort, the minibus turned right and headed for the cruise boat terminal.

Three other minibuses already waited at the terminal, where half a dozen boats were moored. The minibus driver directed his eight passengers to the last boat on the jetty. Nearby, a group of African men dressed in traditional skins leapt into action, beating their drums and kicking their legs. Julia and Mary passed the dancers and boarded the boat to find good seats at a table near the front. One or two tourists stopped to take photos of the dancers and paid a couple of US dollars for the energetic entertainment.

When all the tourists boarded, a jovial cruise boat captain welcomed the visitors with information about the two-hour trip. Following her sighting of Jackson Mpofu, Mary studied the faces of everyone. She didn't want to run into him again.

The cruise boat eased into the river as a welcome evening breeze on the water cooled the occupants. Julia and Mary applied mosquito repellent on their faces and arms. When the boat reached the centre of the river, it turned its nose upstream. A small flock of swift birds skimmed the surface of the water as they raced past the boat. The attendants served snacks and drinks to the passengers, who settled back to enjoy the comfortable ride.

Other cruise boats passed by on the river, and the boat captain spoke to them on the radio. They passed messages about hippo and elephant sightings, making the game viewing a team effort. Thick vegetation on the banks came down to the water and in many places covered it, providing hiding places for birds, fish, and anything else the river supported. Crocodiles that basked in the hot sun slipped into the water as evening approached. The choppy river made it impossible to see what lurked below the surface.

The boat headed to the Zimbabwe riverbank, where a family of hippos relaxed in the shallows. Two showed the top of their heads before sinking back under the surface. A little further upstream, a herd of about fifteen elephants took turns to drink and bathe, and afterwards, enjoy a dust-bath. An elephant on the edge of the group stood knee deep in water, pulling up reeds for an evening snack. A white egret walked in attendance close to an elephant's enormous feet. Elephants and cruise passengers alike enjoyed their sundowners.

Further upriver, the setting sun turned the horizon a gentle yellow, before transitioning the sky from peach to burnt orange to blood red. The horizon became a deep black in the west, while to the south, a salmon-coloured Zimbabwe sky silhouetted tall palm trees.

It was dusk when the returning cruise boat approached the jetty. The group of African dancers sprung to life. Their energetic moves kept them in trim, but older members of the troupe must have breathed a sigh of relief when the tourists drifted off to the minibuses.

Mary experienced innumerable beautiful African sunsets, but sundown on the Zambezi was something she'd always remember. She'd momentarily forgotten about seeing Jackson Mpofu at lunchtime until Julia spoke.

'We'd better skip the cafe tonight if Mpofu is still in the area. We'll go tomorrow night after he's left Victoria Falls. Tonight, we can stay in and order room service.' In the hotel, the women freshened up, and Julia studied the menu before placing the order. This was an unaccustomed luxury for Mary to experience. After another application of mosquito repellent, they sat eating their dinner on the veranda and relaxing in the peaceful evening air. In winter, few mosquitoes remained, so they stayed on the veranda until bedtime at ten o'clock.

* * *

Julia and Mary enjoyed a leisurely breakfast in the room and spent a lazy morning on their veranda. Both feared the prospect of bumping into Jackson Mpofu. They didn't know the reason behind his visit to Victoria Falls, but if it was a leisure break, they risked bumping into him in the small village or at one of the tourist spots.

'We'll book a game viewing tour to the Zambezi National Park this afternoon. Mpofu will have gone by the time we return to the hotel,' said Julia.

At two o'clock, the minibus picked up Julia and Mary and four other tourists. It was a short drive to the private game reserve, and soon they bounced along the dirt track in an open vehicle, keeping an eye out for the wildlife. For the best views of the animals, they sat behind the driver. The abundance of game surprised Mary. She was used to seeing animals in the bush near her village, but here, the wildlife was more plentiful. The tour guide knew where the animals congregated and took them to see elephants, buffalo, lions, giraffes, and lots of antelope.

Part way through the tour, the guide stopped the vehicle and served the tourists snacks and drinks. The sun held its customary bite, so Mary was glad Julia insisted they both wore hats and sunglasses and applied sunscreen. The animals were used to the vehicles and allowed them to get close. Mary clicked away with Julia's camera. She viewed the wildlife differently, no longer as food or a threat, but a source of entertainment.

Three hours is a short time when you're having fun, and soon, once again, they sat in the open air for an early dinner at the Shearwater Cafe.

'You don't have to worry, Mary. Mpofu will be at the airport by now, waiting for his flight.'

Back at the hotel, the African dancers entertained the diners. Julia shook her head. 'I don't know how they keep up all that jumping and kicking. They must be exhausted.'

'No Julia, they all looked too strong.'

* * *

The next morning, Julia and Mary ate their usual breakfast, despite their stated intention to try something different. After breakfast, they packed their bags and walked down to the hotel reception to check out and pay the bill. The Bulawayo flight departed at six -thirty, so there was all day to spare. They left their bags with the hotel concierge and walked out to revisit the bridge and admire the views.

They returned to the rainforest and again explored the length of the falls. Mary stood entranced, glued to the spectacle of the raging curtain of water in front of her. The roar of the falls, the smell of the rainforest, the soaking spray, and the vibration in her chest all emphasised the irresistible force of nature.

Mary was less chatty than usual, and Julia put it down to the overwhelming experience of seeing the falls. She understood, for some, it could be like a religious experience. The scenic beauty was only part of the reason for Mary's quietness. She also suffered from end of trip blues. Although their evening flight to Bulawayo would be another new experience for her, she didn't want to leave this wondrous place.

After a light hotel lunch, they walked to the village to explore the shops. Julia bought a white cotton blouse for herself and a souvenir Victoria Falls T-shirt for Mary. At five o'clock their taxi to the airport arrived, and they said goodbye to the Kingdom, for now at least.

CHAPTER 29

Winter Worries

THE taxi pulled up at the airport terminal, and Julia and Mary jumped out and waited for the driver to fetch their luggage from the boot. Julia paid the driver, and the taxi sped off, leaving the two women standing on the pavement. Nearby, the glittering new Chinese-funded international terminal was close to completion. The women picked up their bags and walked into the old terminal building.

They travelled light with only carry-on luggage, so check-in was quick and easy. Mary eyed the passengers to see the types who flew in aeroplanes. Many dressed in casual clothing, and a few looked scruffy—most likely tourists. Four men dressed in dark suits with white shirts and ties sat around a table, chatting and laughing. Politicians perhaps, or businessmen. The passengers checking in dried to a trickle, so it was clear the plane wouldn't be full. Soon Julia tapped Mary on the arm, telling her it was time to board.

They presented their boarding cards to the hostesses at the gate and followed other passengers walking across the tarmac to the waiting plane. Mary's heart thumped in her chest as they climbed the stairs to the open doorway. She'd seen planes race across the sky many times. And often, she wondered about the helpless passengers and their precarious situation in the silver tubes moving so high above, with no visible means of support. She never dreamt that one day she'd be in one of those things. The open doorway of the plane reminded her of the open mouth of a predatory creature, and she worried they may never get out again. The overpowering smell of aviation fuel added to her apprehension.

At the top of the stairs, a cheerful air hostess checked their boarding cards and pointed towards their seats. The narrow aisle and confined space made Mary claustrophobic, and the stuffy atmosphere didn't help. Suddenly, the dirty overnight train trip didn't seem so bad after all.

They found their seats and put their hand luggage in the overhead lockers. Julia let Mary sit by the window and showed her how to use the seat belt.

'Read the safety card, Mary, and make sure you understand it.'

'What is the card for, Julia?'

'It's in case something goes wrong and the plane crashes.'

Mary gulped. Did they think the plane might crash? The other passengers seemed quite relaxed about the fact they may all soon die.

'Julia, why are we travelling on such a dangerous aeroplane?'

'It's not dangerous, Mary. It's just a safety precaution.'

Somehow, Julia's words didn't reassure her. She'd always relied upon Julia and trusted her judgement, but this time she seemed to tempt fate. And now, the cheerful air hostess stood near them, explaining what to do if the plane crashed. Mary sat in her seat far above the ground in the stationary plane. To go even higher seemed like madness, and the Fasten Seatbelt sign did nothing to ease her concern.

The whisper of the air-conditioning started as the air hostess concluded her safety instructions, but Mary was too nervous to notice. The plane taxied to the runway and along it for a time. It made slow and gentle progress, but as it reached the end of the runway and turned, Mary tensed.

The gentle throb of the engine got louder and louder until it screamed like a demented demon. The plane moved forward slowly at first, but then it picked up speed. In seconds, it hurtled down the runway. Mary gripped the armrest and her knuckles turned white. Julia put her hand over Mary's and smiled at her and said, 'I'll... side.' The scream of the engine drowned out Julia's words. But the moment distracted Mary from their impending doom, and in a minute, they floated high above the ground with the engines now a peaceful hum.

The air hostess jumped up, and moments later, returned with the drinks trolley rattling down the aisle. Julia and Mary asked for coffee, while many other passengers selected alcoholic beverages. A premature death was now the furthest thing from Mary's mind.

It was black outside the window, but near Bulawayo, a few scattered lights appeared, and then the glow of the city on the horizon. The flight was a short forty-five-minute trip, and soon the air hostess announced the landing preparations. Mary's consternation returned with the sound of the engines easing back.

'Next time, if we travel during the day, you'll see a lot more,' said Julia.

Mary smiled. She wasn't yet sure if she'd look forward to that experience. She saw the airport building on her left and dug her heels into the floor as the plane got lower and lower, but didn't feel the touchdown. The sudden sound of the tyres on the tarmac startled her, but as the plane slowed, she relaxed again.

When the plane stopped and the Fasten Seatbelt sign switched off, Julia and Mary took down their bags from the overhead locker and stood waiting for the plane's door to open. They said goodbye and thanked the cheerful air hostess. As they emerged from the plane's doorway, the chill of the Bulawayo winter night hit them. It was such a contrast to the tropical warmth of the Zambezi Valley. They descended the stairs to the tarmac. In the distance, the lights of Bulawayo twinkled. And though Mary didn't want to leave Victoria Falls, she was glad to be home.

Many of the passengers hurried to pick up their checked-in luggage. Julia and Mary walked through the terminal building and out onto the pavement. Two taxis waited there, and the women jumped into the first one. It was pure luck because taxis weren't always available, and in that case, they would have needed to use the less than reliable shuttle bus. As they drove out of the parking area, Mary noticed the four men dressed in suits climbing into a black Mercedes. The sight reminded her of Jackson

Mpofu on the veranda of the Victoria Falls Hotel, and a worrying niggle started at the back of her mind.

The smooth, pot-hole free road from the airport to the city resembled the airport road in Victoria Falls. But as the taxi neared the city centre, its headlights brought the crumbling road surface into focus. Mary studied the streets and pedestrians as if searching for a familiar sight. The towering street lights in the city fascinated her. But once on the Hillside Road, she was back in familiar territory. Near the Mater Dei Hospital, the taxi turned left into Malindela, the suburb where they lived.

The taxi pulled up in front of the house, and Julia and Mary scrambled out and retrieved their bags from the boot. The house and kia were in darkness, with no sign of Frida. 'She may be asleep or still at work next door,' said Julia.

The women unpacked their bags straight away and put their dirty clothes into the wash basket. It felt good to be home, and while Mary made tea, Julia prepared a quick supper of fried eggs on toast. They'd only been away four nights, but it seemed much longer.

'In a week or two,' Mary, 'it'll seem like ages since our trip.'

'Thank you for the holiday, Julia. Now I understand what that word means.'

'Well, now that you understand, we'll do more trips soon.'

A hectic four days and the flight home tired the women, so they needed an early night. After a second cup of tea, it was time for bed.

* * *

Saturday morning was back to routine. In the cooler weather, they ate breakfast indoors. Julia laid the table while Mary cooked scrambled eggs and made the toast. They chatted about the highlights of the trip and all the wonderful sights they'd seen. Breakfast took longer than usual, and when they left the table to wash the dishes, it was already time for morning tea.

Outside, it was a blustery day with grey skies. The chilly gusts of wind carried the dry winter dust that blew into people's eyes and ruffled their hair. Sudden, extra powerful blasts thudded the windows, rattling and threatening to shatter them. These uncomfortable days didn't come around too often. Usually, sunny winter days followed the icy mornings. The real chill came at night, and sometimes ponds could freeze, particularly on their shallow edges. The cold, grey, windy days would visit now and then to remind everyone it was still winter.

Late morning, Mary saw Frida standing in the corner of her garden, smoking in the blustery conditions. Mary wrapped a shawl around her shoulders and hurried out to speak to her.

'Frida, how are you? The kia was dark last night. I thought you might be sleeping.'

'No, I only stayed in your kia one night and then returned to mine.'

'But what about the visitors?'

'After you left, my madam and the visitors fought, so next morning they left, and I got my kia back.'

'So, you are OK now?'

'Yes, thank you, and here's your key. I've had it in my pocket to give to you.'

'Did you find everything OK in my kia?'

'Yes, but I always finish work after dark, so I needed to pass your evil spirit at night. I saw its eyes following me when I walked to your kia. It scared me.'

'Remember, I told the spirit you would stay in the kia? It watched to make sure it was you who passed, and not someone else. So, how are things?'

'Not good. Eveline's madam is leaving Zimbabwe, so she'll be out of a job. Monica's madam said they don't need a housemaid anymore. They can't afford her. And Cathy says, she thinks her madam might also leave. She heard her madam and boss talking, and they spoke about moving to Cape Town.'

The news shocked Mary. 'Oh! So many going! That is bad. What will they do?'

'Those maids may come looking for your job, or mine. My madam is always threatening to get someone new.'

Back in the house, Mary pondered the news. Too many jobs under threat. Those maids worked for their madams for years. What if Julia left? The thought consumed her, as she too now worried about the future. The holiday in Victoria Falls, already a distant memory.

As they prepared dinner together, Julia said, 'Mary, you seem quiet. It's not like you. Most times, you can't stop talking. Is something wrong?'

Mary took a deep breath and told Julia all about the news Frida gave her.

'Goodness, that is a lot of changes in the week we've been away. I know Monica's boss has retired, so they will have to watch their expenses. But people's plans often come to nothing. Perhaps Cathy's employers won't go to Cape Town. They're well off, so they can afford to stay here. Most people leave Zimbabwe if they can't afford to stay, or they are forced to, for health reasons.'

'It is too sad, Julia.'

'Yes, it is sad. Are Eveline and Monica good housemaids?'

'I think so.'

'Our other neighbour, old Mr Benson, is all alone. He's getting on now, so I'll speak to him and suggest it's time he needed a little help.'

'You're very kind, Julia.'

'Well, I can't promise. I can only try. When men reach his age, they can be stubborn. With them, it can be a matter of pride that they don't need anyone's help. He's a nice old man. I'll talk to him tomorrow, and I'll also introduce you. It's time you met him.'

'It would be wonderful if he took on Eveline or Monica. Frida says they're both worried about their future.'

'You are also a kind person, Mary. When you were so quiet, I knew something troubled you. You like to help people with their problems, and that's good.'

'I don't only worry about others, Julia. I thought, what if you left Zimbabwe? What would I do?'

'I would never leave Zimbabwe, Mary. But if I had to leave, I'd want you to come with me.'

'Go with you, Julia?'

'Yes, Mary, if you wanted.'

'Oh, I would. I was so worried you might also leave.'

'You needn't worry, Mary, I'll never leave, but if I did, I wouldn't leave you here.'

'Oh, I'm so happy.'

'And you make me happy, Mary. As happy as I can remember.'

'But what about your daughter, Julia? Didn't she make you happy?'

'Yes, of course. When she left school, she went to the university in Cape Town. After university, she was always off somewhere or another with her travel writing. I looked forward to her visits, but they were infrequent and often short, and I saw little of her in her adult years. But you are always with me, Mary, and that's what makes me happy.'

CHAPTER 30

The Fruits of Labour

AFTER breakfast the next morning, Julia took Mary to meet old Mr Benson next door. There was a thick hedge growing between Julia and Mr Benson's properties, so Mary paid no attention to the neighbour on that side. Mr Benson's thick hedge ran down to the front fence. It afforded complete privacy, unlike Frida's side, where they could chat over the low fence that separated their front gardens.

As they walked past the thick hedge, Julia spotted Mr Benson working in his garden and called out to him. The cheerful, grey-haired old man waved and came over to the front fence. He was a big, kindly looking man with twinkling blue eyes.

'Mrs Watson, how are you? Although you live next door, it's been a long time.'

'Well, you might see us if you trimmed your hedge, Mr Benson.'

'What, spoil this beautiful hedge?'

'I've brought Mary here to meet you. I've told her you'll help her if ever I'm away and something goes wrong.'

'Is Mary your housemaid?'

'My companion.'

'Oh! Pleased to meet you, Mary.'

'Pleased to meet you, Sir.'

'Are you a part of the morning tea group that gathers over the road?'

'No, Sir, I have morning tea with Mrs Watson.'

'Oh!'

'Mr Benson,' said Julia, 'your garden looks lovely.'

'Thank you, Mrs Watson. It is hard work. Some days I feel so stiff I struggle to get out of my armchair in the evening.'

'Please, call me Julia.'

'Yes, and please call me George.'

'It must be difficult for you, George, with all the gardening and house-work?'

'Yes, too difficult, sometimes.'

'You could do with help, George.'

'It's difficult to get reliable help, Julia.'

'Well, you're in luck. Mary here can get you an excellent maid. You can choose from two and even ask their employers about their work.'

'If they're excellent, Julia, why would they be leaving their employers?'

'Well, you know how it is, George; people leaving Zimbabwe for South Africa, the UK or elsewhere.'

'Both maids are hardworking and trustworthy, Sir.'

'Are they your relatives, Mary?'

'No, Sir.'

'Well, I'm not sure. I'll think about it.'

'It is better to decide now, Sir. They won't be here for long. They'd prefer to work in Malindela, but lots of employers would take them.'

George Benson looked at Mary for several seconds as if assessing her truthfulness. 'What do you say, Julia?'

'I say if Mary recommends them, it's worth looking to see if one suits you.'

'To be honest, I've been thinking about getting help in the house. What about you, Mary? Are you available?'

Mary laughed. 'No, Sir, I am already taken.'

'All right then, all right. If you recommend them, I will interview them and then we'll see.'

'I will try to bring them here this afternoon, Sir.'

Mary caught up with Frida when she saw her standing in the garden, smoking during her morning tea break.

'Mr Benson is thinking of hiring a housemaid. I told him about Eveline and Monica. He will interview them if they go to see him this afternoon. I don't know them well. Perhaps you could tell them about the job.'

Frida jumped at the opportunity to repair her reputation, following the food poisoning scare. Yes, she would talk to them.

Later that afternoon, Eveline and Monica went together to see Mr Benson. It turned out Monica's madam did not mean to end her employment. She'd suggested the possibility, to head off any request for a wage increase. Monica accompanied Eveline to the interview to support her. None of the maids knew George Benson, and Eveline was nervous to meet him. Mr Benson offered the same wage as Monica now earned, so there was no advantage for her to move to his employment.

'Well, Eveline,' said Mr Benson, 'as soon as your madam leaves Zimbabwe, you can come and work for me.'

'Thank you, Boss. I must thank Frida for finding me this job.'

'Who's Frida?'

'The girl who spoke to you about me.'

'No, no, I've never met Frida. It was Mary next door who told me about you.'

Eveline and Monica looked at each other.

'OK, Sir, I will thank Mary then.'

Eveline and Monica walked next door and stood by the gate, wondering if they should enter. They feared the evil spirit in the back garden.

Julia looked through the lounge window and noticed them. 'Mary, who are those girls standing at our gate? Please find out what they want.'

Mary came out of the kitchen and joined her at the window. 'I think that's Eveline and Monica. I'll speak to them.'

It turned into a ten-minute chat with the three women, laughing and gossiping.

When Mary returned to the house, she explained to Julia the women came to thank them both for getting Eveline the job. What Mary didn't say was she'd given Julia all the credit for finding Eveline's job.

* * *

Julia was right. Already the Victoria Falls trip was a distant memory. Yet, it was only six weeks since their trip. The pleasant memories remained, but foremost in Mary's mind was the encounter with Jackson Mpofu on the veranda of the Victoria Falls Hotel. It was unfortunate their visits coincided, but such things happen, and Mary realised it was not always possible to run away from one's problems.

Did Mpofu recognise her? It seemed unlikely, given how much she'd changed since leaving the village. Her overall appearance and manner differed from her village days. But the business card he sent with the waiter remained a concern. What if she bumped into him again? Would he recognise her then? She could never visit her village while he and his thugs controlled the area. Somehow, she'd have to resolve the matter, but she was not sure how.

'Come, Mary, it's time for your driving practice. You're going for your test next week, and you must try to get your licence on your first go.'

Julia's voice interrupted Mary's thoughts. Her driving improved beyond recognition. She followed the rules of the road and always drove when she and Julia visited the shops. Hill starts were no longer a problem, and with all her practice in the driveway, parking came easily to her. Mary was already a confident driver, but Julia left nothing to chance. Mary's driving practice was in effect a drive around Bulawayo while they chatted, but it gave her the chance to familiarise herself with Bulawayo and its surrounds.

'Your passport should arrive soon, Mary. It's been six weeks since you applied.'

'But they said it might be longer because of high demand.'

'Ah, yes, but I paid a priority fee, remember? The officer told me it should come through in six weeks and we could bypass the queue when we collect it.'

'People shouldn't have to pay to get proper service, Julia. What if they can't afford a priority fee?'

'You're right, it's not fair.'

'Why do I need my passport so soon? Would it matter if it took longer?'

'I must go to Johannesburg for my annual medical check next month. You'll need a passport if you want to come with me.'

'To South Africa?'

'Yes, we'll make a holiday out of it.'

'If you go to *chuch*, do you still need doctors, Julia?'

'Yes, Mary. And the word is church, not chuch. Remember what I told you about long and short vowels? And besides, I don't go to church.'

'But wouldn't it be easier if you did, Julia?'

Julia gave Mary a long, silent look and then added, 'You don't go to church either.'

'My mother said we should, but my father didn't agree.'

'Did you have a church near your village?'

'No, but sometimes the African church would hold prayer meetings in the bush a few kilometres from our village. Sometimes on a Sunday, people would dress in their best clothes and walk to the church meeting.'

'What about your husband?'

'No, my husband's village was too far. When my husband died, the police from Figtree brought a priest to hold a funeral service for him.'

* * *

The next month brought several developments for Mary. First, her passport arrived. She wasn't too happy with the photo, but loved the status the formal green document gave her. She put her passport in the small tin where she kept her birth registration certificate and the scrap of paper with her sister's Francistown address.

Julia heard rumours of counterfeiters working in the passport office, sometimes issuing fake passports. They sold the genuine passports for an exorbitant fee to criminals. Before leaving the passport office, Julia asked the officer to verify its authenticity. All was clear.

Next came Mary's driving licence. She was confident and relaxed during her driving test. The examiner commented she drove like an experienced driver; not like someone taking their first test. Later, the examiner spoke to Julia, who waited for Mary while she took her test. 'You should be a driving school instructor, Madam. You prepared her well for the test.'

Best of all, Mary broke through with her reading and writing skills. Suddenly, everything seemed to make sense, and she became obsessed with improving her vocabulary, grammar, and pronunciation. It was fun, and she made a game of surprising Julia with her fast-increasing knowledge.

'Goodness, Mary, I wish more of my students over the years were as keen as you to learn and improve their English.'

Julia set up a small desk and notebook computer for Mary in the study. She showed her how to search the internet to find answers to her questions about the English language. For Mary, it was slow, painstaking work, but practice improved her use of the computer.

* * *

Now, Mary was to accompany Julia to Johannesburg. Bulawayo airport in the daytime looked different from the airport at night. Although nerves jumped in Mary's stomach, she wasn't as nervous as the last time she flew. She again sat next to the window, high above the ground. As the plane taxied to the end of the runway, the air hostess explained the safety instructions. The plane turned and paused, giving Mary the opportunity for a quick glance at the terminal building in the distance.

The gentle throb of the engines became a high-pitched whine as the plane moved forward, followed by what sounded like an irreversible scream as the plane charged down the runway. As before, the alarming sound dropped almost instantly to a pleasant hum as the plane became airborne. The ground fell away as the plane climbed into the sky.

An astonishing view of Bulawayo presented itself to Mary as she picked out the Mater Dei Hospital, Julia's house close by, and the Hillside Dams in the distance. Soon, the houses and suburbs faded into the distance. The rattle of the drinks trolly interrupted her fascination with the view.

She and Julia both ordered tomato juice, and a relaxed feeling swept through the plane. The prospect of a light lunch excited Mary. Below, the land was dry and brown, with no distinguishing features on the landscape stretching to the horizon. Mary was determined to enjoy every minute of the one-and-a-half-hour flight. She flipped through the flight magazine she'd keep as a memento.

All too soon, the pilot announced the landing preparations. Passengers secured their tray tables and fastened seatbelts, while the air hostesses hurried down the aisle, checking on the passengers and making sure armrests were down. Within minutes, the passengers felt the unmistakable sensation of the engines throttling back, as the plane turned and reduced altitude on its approach to the runway. Mary looked at the city's buildings that ran into the distance. Was there no end to them?

After a gentle landing, the plane showed no sign of stopping. Eventually, it slowed and turned off the runway. The plane's taxi to the terminal seemed to go on forever. But at last, it pulled up near one of the air gates. The Fasten Seatbelt sign turned off, and the passengers scrambled for their hand luggage in the overhead lockers. After an inexplicable delay, the queue moved down the aisle, past the smiling hostess, and out through the plane's exit. A few passengers hurried, almost ran along the corridor connecting the plane to the terminal.

In the terminal, everyone seemed to be in a hurry, irrespective of their destination. The scene reminded Mary of a disturbed ants' nest. It was a long walk to customs. Julia seemed to know the way, and Mary stuck close to her. Through immigration, they passed by the baggage carousels where other passengers gathered. They travelled only with carry-on luggage, but it needed to pass through the x-ray machines. Soon they walked out past the terminal shops to the car-hire kiosks.

Julia completed all the formalities before an attendant showed them to the car parked nearby. They tossed their bags into the boot and drove out of the parking area. Only a short distance farther on, Julia stopped behind a white BMW at a red traffic light.

Mary jumped as a man wearing a khaki jumper tugged at her door handle. He looked like a police officer as he waved his handgun in front of her. He stood at the locked car door, tapping on the window with the muzzle of his gun.

'Get out of the car!' he shouted.

Another man in a khaki jumper stood next to Julia's window, waving a handgun. Following a moment's indecision, the men ran to the BMW in front, but its doors were also locked. The driver in the BMW sped onto the main road with tyres squealing. Cars braked, hooted, and flashed their lights, but somehow the driver avoided an accident.

Julia wanted to follow, but the red light and heavy traffic on the main road blocked her path. The two men raced back towards them with their guns raised. In the next instant, the traffic lights turned green.

CHAPTER 31

Johannesburg

JULIA put her foot on the accelerator a little too hard. As it picked up speed, the car slewed from left to right, brushing aside one man. The other man jumped clear, with centimetres to spare. For a second, it seemed Julia wouldn't make the turn as the car swung wide. But it steadied and raced off down the road.

Julia spoke in a breathless voice. 'It's lucky we locked our car doors, Mary. Especially here in Joburg. I was about to ask you if you'd locked your door when that man tried to wrench it open.'

Mary was too shocked to reply. She found it hard to believe such a thing would happen.

This, a sobering first experience of the big city she'd yet to see.

When at last she spoke, she said, 'I'm glad we live in Bulawayo, Julia.'

By this time, it was late afternoon, and Julia drove as the rush hour built. Mary was glad it was not her driving in the heavy traffic. She gasped in amazement at the large buildings on the skyline.

'That's Ponte City Apartments,' said Julia. 'If we have time, we'll do a tour of the building. I believe it has the best views of Johannesburg.'

The elevated road circling the city centre fascinated Mary.

'So many tall buildings, Julia.'

'Yes, and that's Johannesburg Station there. And now, we're coming up to Wits University where we turn off for Rosebank, where our hotel is.'

Soon, the city centre gave way to residential suburbs. 'The houses here are nice, Julia.'

'Yes, and there's the zoo. We're almost there.'

A few minutes later, Julia turned off Jan Smuts Avenue. Two blocks further on, they came to the Crowne Plaza Hotel, where she always stayed on her annual visits to Johannesburg. 'It's convenient here because of the shopping centre opposite, and my doctors are also nearby. When I've finished with them, we can go shopping.'

The comfortable twin-share room didn't match the luxury of the Kingdom Hotel at Victoria Falls. The canopy of trees stretched to the horizon, with a distant view of the Johannesburg skyline.

After settling in and freshening up, Julia and Mary looked for a nearby restaurant. The concierge recommended The Grillhouse, a steakhouse in The Firs shopping centre, only two blocks from the hotel. The restaurant sent a shuttle bus to pick them up for the less than three-minute drive. It was within walking distance, but perhaps not wise for two unaccompanied women walking at night in Johannesburg.

The cosy atmosphere, attentive service, and tender steaks made for a wonderful evening. Julia and Mary shared a bottle of Merlot, which was more than their usual intake. Mary was living a dream from which she never wanted to wake. Since she worked for Julia, it was one wonderful experience after another. She couldn't get over how her life changed since she moved to Bulawayo.

For Julia's part, she relished Mary's companionship. Not since her daughter, Vera, left school many years past, did she have a constant, agreeable presence in the house. The demanding and unreliable Gerald King proved to be poor company. Julia also enjoyed introducing Mary to new experiences and teaching her life skills. She found it fascinating to see the young woman blossom.

'Goodness! I hope this wine doesn't affect my medical tests tomorrow,' Julia joked. 'While I'm with my doctors, Mary, you can look around the shopping mall in Rosebank.'

'I'd rather wait for you, Julia.'

'You'll be bored, sitting in the hotel room, waiting for me.'

'No, I'll wait for you at the doctor's rooms.'

'You'll be even more bored there. I'll take you to Woolworths before my appointment tomorrow morning. If you stay in that shop or close by, you'll find a lot to keep you busy.'

Mary smiled, but the picture of the car hijackers stuck in her mind. She worried that Johannesburg, even a nice centre like Rosebank, wasn't safe.

* * *

After breakfast, Julia walked with Mary to the Rosebank Mall.

'I should be finished by lunchtime. If you stay around this area, I'll find you. Start here in Woolworths. There's lots of interesting things. I'll be back as soon as I can. And buy yourself a coffee at eleven o'clock.'

Mary watched Julia walk away until she disappeared around the corner of a building. All the passers-by walked with purpose. Someone jostled her, bringing back memories of the first time she tried to cross Hillside Road on her way to find Frida for the job interview with Julia. It seemed like she stood in the middle of a road, so Mary nipped between two groups and stood against a shop window. She stared at the passing parade for a few minutes before slipping into Woolworths.

The atmosphere in the department store was one of calm. A few un-hurried people browsing among the displays seemed less threatening. None of the staff approached her to sell her something, and that suited her. Although Julia gave her money to spend, Mary valued her opinion and wouldn't buy any item of clothing without her approval.

After walking around the store several times, Mary looked at her watch. Ten to eleven. Time for a coffee. As she passed the cosmetics counter, a girl called out to her. 'Would you like your face done? We have a free promotion.'

Mary hesitated.

'Come on, you'll be even more beautiful when I'm finished.'

Beautiful? Although an attractive young woman, Mary never thought of herself as beautiful. But she dressed well and possessed a smooth coffee complexion. Africans fell into many shades of black, from dark-skinned to lighter-skinned and all shades in-between. She was lighter, like Frida, and other maids commented on how lucky she was. Ironically, Africans discriminated against their darker skinned fellows.

'Come on then! It won't take long. Only fifteen minutes.'

Mary thought refusing the offer might be more difficult than accepting it, so she ambled over to the beautician, herself, a glamorous young woman. She sat on the stool and relaxed as the young woman pampered and fussed about her. The procedure took longer than the beautician suggested, but it filled in time, waiting for Julia.

When Mary looked in the mirror, she adjusted it, thinking someone else stood next to her. She couldn't believe the result. The makeup accentuated her almond eyes, and the pale red lipstick suited her coffee-coloured skin. She looked a lot like the girls in the large glossy promotional photographs and couldn't help the flush of pride that coursed through her.

Two women stood watching the proceedings. 'Any product would look good on your beautiful model,' said one woman.

'This lady is not a model, Madam. She's a customer.'

Lady! No one called her that before, but she now looked the part. She thanked the beautician and rose from the stool just as Julia arrived. She gave Mary a brief glance and walked straight past her.

'Julia, Julia, it's me!'

'Mary? Goodness! You look... beautiful. You're always lovely, of course, but I didn't expect to see you in makeup. That lipstick looks made for you. Have you bought it?'

'Er, no. I waited for you.'

'We'll have that lipstick for my friend here,' said Julia, addressing the beautician.

'Yes, Madam. And how about the other items I used to do your friend's face?'

Julia bought the makeup together with a white long-sleeved shirt and tight, tan-coloured long pants that would show off Mary's slim figure. The pair then walked out of Woolworths to find a coffee shop.

The rest of the afternoon, they explored the shops. Julia bought Mary two lovely knee-length dresses that she claimed would give her an air of sophistication. 'No one will argue with you when you wear those, Mary.'

'Julia, have you seen the clothes in the men's shop? They are so colourful.'

'Yes, they are rather gaudy, aren't they?'

They so enjoyed their dinner at The Grillhouse the previous night, they went again. Mary wore a dress Julia bought her that morning. The attentive waiters proved even more attentive, flitting around them as if they were celebrities. Now, she felt like a companion to Julia, rather than an attachment.

* * *

Julia booked a tour of the Ponte City Apartments, combined with a walk around Hillbrow, once Johannesburg's premier night entertainment area. They drove up to the tall-barred gate manned by several security guards. An uneasy sensation gnawed at Mary. The huge round building's forbidding appearance was overpowering. It didn't help that Julia referred to it as Johannesburg's version of Dracula's castle. Mary had only just finished reading that book, and it kept her awake at night.

One of the security guards showed them where to park. Their car was alone in the parking area that spiralled up the building's lower floors. Perhaps they were the first ones to arrive for the tour. The guard led them to a large ground floor office that appeared to double as a childcare centre, though no children were there now. They paid for the tour and signed an indemnity form, releasing the tour operators from any liability for injury or damage.

The group grew to twelve tourists and four guards by the time the tour started. At the barred entrance to the lifts, a large sign advised visitors that the building's owners were not liable for any incidents, including murder, assault, mugging, robbery, or theft. Visitors entered at their own risk.

'Julia, should we go on this tour? It looks dangerous.'

'Of course, Mary. Nothing will happen.'

'Then why do they have that sign? And why did we sign those forms?'

'It's just a precaution to protect themselves.'

'So, something could happen?'

'Yes, but most unlikely.'

The group waited for the lift to take them to the building's fifty-fourth floor.

'Why not the fifty-fifth floor?' someone enquired.

'The top floor was servants' quarters. There's nothing to see,' said the tour guide.

The fast lift took them to the fifty-fourth level in no time. They stepped from the lift into an internal passageway that ran around the entire floor. The windows looked into the hollow core of the round building. Welded shut, there was no easy means of cleaning the filthy glass. From their vantage point, the sealed windows made it impossible to see lower than about the thirty-fifth floor. For Mary, it resembled the entrance to the underworld.

'When they built the building, they neglected to include a waste disposal system,' said the guide. 'That meant the residents needed to catch the lift to the ground floor to dump their rubbish. Before the building owners sealed the interior windows, the residents threw their rubbish into the centre where, over time, it reached the fourteenth floor. When the building's owners cleared it for the soccer World Cup in 2010, they found bodies and rats as big as cats. Up till then, you could buy anything you wanted in this building. Criminal gangs ran drugs, guns, fake passports, and prostitution. The authorities couldn't control the situation, so they cut off the electricity and water.'

Ponte once housed South Africa's premier residential apartments, but although the building's owners evicted the criminals, it still looked a mess.

The tour group sipped tea and coffee while they enjoyed the spectacular views of Johannesburg. Mary feared heights, and her stomach twisted in a series of uncomfortable tingles.

After refreshments, the tour party caught the lift to the ground floor. They walked past tired looking shops that appeared closed or abandoned, and out to the spiral parking area. A narrow, dark doorway led to several flights of unlit stairs descending to the building's centre. Missing wooden planks encasing the stairs let in a minimal amount of natural light. It was barely enough for the tourists to see their next step. The missing and loose planks presented a danger to any unwary tourist who slipped and fell against them.

The flights descended four floors to the bowels of the building, revealing the sloping, rocky outcrop on which it stood. A tiny circular patch of sky, fifty-five floors above, brought home the size of the building. The tour group ascended the flights of stairs back to the spiral parking area, and Mary breathed again. Litter from the apartments lay scattered on the ground surrounding the building's exterior. Ponte's 'adaptable' residents now used an alternate route to dispose of their rubbish.

The tour group reassembled in the courtyard near the exit to Ponte, and two more security guards joined the party for the walk through Hillbrow. The tour guide seemed nervous about anyone falling behind the group. When someone stopped to take a photo, two of the guards stayed with them.

To get to Hillbrow, the tour needed to walk through Berea. 'Many years ago, I lived in a flat in that building,' said Julia, pointing to a fifteen-storey block. Neither the security guards nor Mary could imagine Julia living in such an area. Berea was an odd assortment of derelict apartment blocks side by side with well-maintained blocks. Tree-lined streets hinted at the past prosperity of the suburb.

As the party walked into Hillbrow, the trees disappeared, and the buildings looked older and more commercially oriented. Apart from the sleazy-looking Summit Club, little sign remained of the nightlife that once identified the area. In Berea, on the way back to the Ponte, the party stopped at a cheap African style cafe serving large bottles of beer with a chicken and salad lunch.

It was the group's first opportunity to chat. It delighted Mary to discover two guides came from Bulawayo and spoke Ndebele. The food didn't meet the standard she and Julia maintained at home, but Julia seemed to enjoy it.

Piles of rubbish surrounded the residential apartment blocks in Berea. It seemed no one bothered to collect refuse, and garbage rotted everywhere. Hillbrow and Berea differed from Rosebank and other affluent suburbs to the north of the city. Bulawayo was not the cleanest of cities, but Mary had seen nothing like this. The unbelievable decline of the two suburbs made it a tourist attraction.

In the evening, Mary wore the second dress Julia bought her. The hotel shuttle took them to the Fishmonger Restaurant in the nearby Firs shopping centre. Julia ordered the Kingklip Coconut Curry, while Mary preferred to stick to a Beef Fillet Chilli Fry. A bottle of Backsberg Pinotage proved an excellent complement to the spicy dishes.

Julia booked the return flight to Bulawayo for mid-morning the next day. That meant an early rise, so they returned to the Crowne Plaza straight after dinner.

* * *

An early breakfast preceded the drive to the airport in heavy traffic. Though Bulawayo was quite close to the border with South Africa, the flight was an international one with all the attendant palaver and delays. The immigration process passed smoothly enough, and soon Julia and Mary browsed in the duty-free shops, buying two bottles of the best sherry.

Over her fear of flying, Mary now looked like just another seasoned traveller. She was fast developing a taste for seeing different places and eating in fine restaurants. Julia made life so exciting and already talked about a trip to London.

Because of the flight's timing, the hostesses only served sandwiches and packets of nuts or crisps, and an assortment of drinks, including tea and coffee. They would land at twelve-thirty in the early afternoon.

Bulawayo airport was so quiet compared to the hubbub of Johannesburg. The two women waited patiently in the sleepy environment of the queue for the immigration officers. But soon enough, they walked past the baggage carousel and car-hire offices out to the taxi rank.

'The advantage of carry-on luggage, Mary, is that you can beat the others to the taxi rank. Otherwise, if no taxis remain, you may wait a long time for another one. But we booked a taxi to meet us. It's essential in Bulawayo, where taxis aren't always available.'

'You think of everything, Julia. I don't know what I'd do without you. You make my life so interesting.'

'Well, I feel the same way about you, my dear.'

The taxi buzzed along and soon they entered the CBD with its busy pavements full of Africans walking, waiting, and shopping. Here, it was as busy as Rosebank.

'Julia, lots of white people shopped in Rosebank. Do you ever feel alone with so few white people in Bulawayo? We don't often see a white face walking in the centre of town.'

'I'm used to it, my dear. Lots of whites lived in Zimbabwe up till the farm invasions, then after that, the exodus began. Before 1980, this country was Rhodesia. Most faces in the town centre were white.'

'Like in Rosebank?'

'Yes, perhaps even more than Rosebank.'

'So, you're not lonely with all the whites leaving?'

'My dear, white faces wouldn't stop me from being lonely. Having someone close does that. You're as close to me as anyone has been. How could I be lonely when you're with me?'

After that, Mary remained silent. Julia's words filled her with a sense of security, pride, and happiness.

CHAPTER 32

The Jacarandas

FOLLOWING the Joburg trip, Julia pressed Mary harder and harder to improve her English. She focussed on grammar and pronunciation, reasoning that improvement in spelling and vocabulary would come to Mary over time, given her enquiring mind.

Julia also focussed on life skills, which she claimed was a natural complement to an educated, speaking voice.

'English, arithmetic, and basic science are important, and that's where you should concentrate most of your attention. Cookbooks have helped you in these areas, but if you also read other books, they will compensate for much of the formal education you missed, including history and geography. If you are an avid reader, you will gain a lot of knowledge.'

'Avid?'

'It means keen or enthusiastic.'

'So, my English will help me improve in all the other areas.'

'Yes.'

Mary needed no further encouragement to improve her literacy. She paid close attention to how Julia spoke, while Julia jumped on any grammatical error or mispronunciation she uttered. In a short period, Mary's speaking voice improved, and anyone listening to her talking would assume a level of sophistication far above the reality.

The outward change in Mary led to subtle changes in the way people responded to her. Frida became more distant, while Eveline, Monica, and Clara showed a growing deference towards her.

Julia and Mary often sat in the lounge in the evenings, talking until late. It was three months since their trip to Johannesburg. 'Let's open one of those bottles of sherry we bought in Joburg, Mary. I'd like a drink tonight.'

Mary got two sherry glasses and one of the sherry bottles from the bookcase cabinet. She used a small kitchen knife to break the seal and twisted off the top.

Julia raised her glass. 'Happy days, Mary!'

'Yes, happy days, Julia!'

'I love the jacarandas at this time of the year, with their lavender-coloured blossoms. Soon the blossoms will fall overnight, and the street will look like it's covered with snow. But to see it, we must rise early, before the cars squash them into a mess. One car driving over them is all right. It looks like tracks in the snow. But when more cars drive past, it soon becomes a purple, mushy mess.'

'I've never seen snow, Julia, but I have seen hailstones make the ground all white.'

'Last year we missed the blossoms' fall. All the things going on distracted me. This year we must watch out for it.' Julia finished her sherry and put the glass down on the coffee table. 'I'm tired. Time for my bed.'

Julia got up from her chair, walked over to Mary and, leaning over, kissed her on the forehead. 'Goodnight, my dear. I'll see you in the morning.' As she left the lounge, she turned to Mary. 'You must promise me, you'll never stop improving your English and learning new things.'

'Yes, Julia, I promise.'

Julia smiled and disappeared down the corridor to her bedroom.

Mary put the sherry bottle away and washed the glasses. She bubbled with happiness. She last saw her mother at her wedding to Josiah, when still in her teens. Since then, she'd not known the love and guidance of an older woman. Julia was like the grandmother she never knew, and her love and appreciation gave Mary a joy beyond anything she'd known. Josiah proved to be a kind husband, but somewhat remote. The closeness she felt with Julia was missing from that relationship. Now, her life was complete, and she fell asleep in bed with a warm, enveloping glow.

* * *

The first rays of dawn lit the room, and Mary stirred. A lifetime in the bush, waking with the dawn, was a habit she couldn't break. She stretched and smiled, refreshed after a good night's sleep. She bounced out of bed and put on her dressing gown. Her morning routine included a walk to the gate to peer up and down the road and assess the weather. As always, a beautiful early morning greeted her. A little past six o'clock, the air was still fresh from the cool night. By mid-morning, the dry air would be oppressive even in the shade. But soon the rains would refresh the land.

At the front gate, a magical scene greeted Mary. Did Julia have foreknowledge? Perhaps a coincidence? Fallen jacaranda blossoms carpeted the street. So that's what snow looked like! She must call Julia before a car drove over it. She hurried, almost ran back to the house to raise Julia.

Julia's bedroom door was ajar as usual, and Mary strode into her room. 'Julia, Julia, come quick, the jacaranda blossoms have fallen!' She touched Julia on the shoulder, but she didn't stir. 'Julia, wake up! The jacaranda blossoms are on the road.' She shook Julia a little harder. Julia? Julia's arm was cold to her touch. Mary put the back of her fingers against Julia's forehead. It was cold.

An icy panic welled up in Mary's chest. She couldn't rouse Julia. Mary rushed to the telephone stand to get the small notebook where Julia wrote all the important phone numbers. She flipped through the pages, and in her haste, missed some and needed to start again. Ah, there it was, Dr Andrew Jones. But this early in the morning, the surgery wouldn't be open. Then she saw two numbers for him. One marked surgery and the other marked home. She dialled the second number, and in an instant, a man's voice answered.

'Dr Jones, it's Mary, Mrs Watson's maid. The madam won't wake up, and she's cold. I've put an extra blanket on her, but she's still cold and won't wake up.'

'OK, Mary, I'll be with you in a few minutes.'

Mary returned to Julia and rubbed her hands, trying to warm them. The minutes dragged, and there was still no sign of Dr Jones. But within ten minutes, she heard the doctor's car pull up at the front gate. She rushed out to greet him, and they both hurried inside the house. While Mary stood by, Dr Jones felt Julia's wrist for a pulse. Then he listened to her chest through his stethoscope.

The doctor turned to Mary. 'I'm sorry, Mary, she's gone. There's nothing I can do. I'll call an ambulance.'

Mary's heart sank. A hollow sensation grew in her chest until it seemed it would burst. Then the tears rolled down her face as she tasted their saltiness on her lips. She held Julia's hand and stroked the soft skin of her arm. Dr Jones walked through to the phone by the front door. Mary could hear him talking, but her racing mind didn't take in his words.

Dr Jones remained in the house until the ambulance arrived. Mary held on to Julia's hand the whole time and kissed her forehead before the ambulance crew removed the body. Without further delay, the ambulance drove off and Julia was gone.

'I'll prepare the death certificate and arrange for the funeral, Mary, and keep you informed about what's happening.'

A bewildered Mary watched the doctor drive away. As she closed the gate, she noticed the tyre tracks in the road made by the doctor's car and the ambulance. The purple, mushy mess of the fallen jacaranda flowers looked a lot like the sudden turn in her life. Julia, her Julia, was now in the hands of others. She felt suddenly sidelined and alone.

Mary didn't bother with breakfast or lunch and spent the day sitting in her armchair in the lounge. Crestfallen and confused, she didn't move until the evening shadows lengthened on the floor in front of her. Dinner? No, she couldn't face dinner. Her mind cried out, Julia, Julia, where are you? Don't leave me!

In bed by six o'clock, Mary sobbed before crying herself to sleep.

* * *

The next morning, Mary woke at six. She'd slept for eleven hours and dreamt of the good times she and Julia shared. When she woke, reality came crashing back. But she needed to feed the chickens and water the vegetables. What then? Clean the house? It was already clean. Read or study English? No, she wasn't ready for that. Something physical, perhaps? Yes, that was it. Clean the clean house.

Mary missed breakfast but made herself a cup of tea mid-morning. And then it was clean, clean, clean. No lunch and no dinner. She ate two pieces of toast with jam and drank a cup of tea before going to bed at dusk. She did it again for the next two days.

Four days after Julia's death, there was a knock on the front door. Dr Jones stood there. 'Hello Mary, I'm sorry I didn't come earlier, but I've been sick. Julia's funeral service is tomorrow at the Anglican church in Leander Avenue in Hillside. After the service, her cremation will take place at the West Park Crematorium on Lady Stanley Avenue in Northend.'

Mary was worried about the cremation. Africans didn't believe in cremations and preferred to bury their loved ones. Dr Jones assured her that cremation was Julia's wish.

'I will pick you up for the funeral service tomorrow morning at half past ten.'

* * *

On the morning of the funeral, Mary dressed in her most conservative dress. It was one of the two Julia bought her in Johannesburg. Julia would have been proud of her appearance.

Henry, the gardener, came to cut the grass, but when he discovered what happened to Julia, he also wanted to attend the funeral. He wasn't dressed for the occasion, but that didn't matter. Mr Benson from next door also asked to get a lift. Dr Jones arrived to collect Mary, but was happy to take the two extra passengers. The church was a five-minute drive from the house, so the group arrived early and stood outside chatting.

Soon, another car pulled up at the church. Dr Jones did the introductions. 'Mary, let me introduce you to Winston Smith, Mrs Watson's lawyer.'

The Reverend Francis Ncube arrived two minutes later to conduct the service. After everyone introduced themselves, the small group entered the church. Reverend Ncube started with an emotional welcome to the mourners and followed it with the formal, though brief, funeral service. 'Who is the chief mourner here?' the reverend enquired. Dr Jones pointed to Mary, who stood up. 'Do you want to say some words for Mrs Watson, Mary?' said the reverend.

Mary walked to the front and placed her hand on the coffin lid. She turned to face the group. Her eyes glistened as she spoke. 'Julia here was my friend. My best friend. She will always be my best friend.'

As Mary returned to her seat, she noticed two men dressed in black standing at the back of the church. Through the doorway, she could see the waiting black hearse. The undertakers approached the coffin and rolled it on its trolley down the aisle to the church door. They, together with Dr Jones, Winston Smith, Henry, and Mr Benson, lifted the coffin and put it into the hearse. With no further formality, the undertakers drove through the gate and down the road.

Dr Jones arranged for tea and snacks at the nearby Cresta Churchill Hotel on the Matopos Road. The small group, including The Reverend Ncube, gathered in a private corner of the lounge where the attentive serving staff looked after them.

'Someone will deliver Mrs Watson's ashes to you within the next few days, Mary,' said Winston Smith. 'She requested you receive the ashes, as you'd know what to do with them.'

This took Mary by surprise. Julia never spoke about such things. What should she do with the ashes? She would have to think about it.

'You should think about joining our church,' said Reverend Ncube, 'especially now that your friend has gone to The Lord.' It was bad timing, given Mary's mind was still in turmoil.

Winston Smith needed to leave for another appointment. 'I will be in touch when we've sorted out everything, Mary.'

Reverend Ncube excused himself and left at the same time as Winston Smith.

Dr Jones took Mary, Henry, and Mr Benson back to Julia's house.

'What will happen now, Sir,' said Mary.

'Please, call me Andrew. Keep an eye on things here until Winston Smith gets back to you. Tomorrow I've got appointments all day and house calls in the evening. I'll visit the day after tomorrow to make sure you're OK and tell you what's happening.'

'I have plenty of food in the house, but not much money. There may be bills to pay.'

'Hold on to the bills, Mary, and we'll see to them later.'

Andrew Jones drove off down the road, leaving his three passengers standing at the gate.

Next to leave was George Benson. 'Well, I better be off, Mary. If you need anything, just call me.'

After Henry finished cutting the grass, Mary made tea and jam on bread for him and herself. They sat at the garden table talking about Julia and her kindness towards them. When Henry left, he wouldn't take payment for the grass cutting. He overheard what Mary said to Dr Jones and realised she had little money. 'No, the grass today is my gift to Mrs Watson. She was a nice lady, a good lady.'

Now Mary was all alone once more. But then a voice drew her attention. It was Frida. 'What will you do now your madam has gone? Will you be leaving soon?'

'I don't know, Frida. Julia's doctor and lawyer said I must wait until they tell me what to do.'

'They will tell you to look after the house until they sell it. Then they won't need you anymore. You should find another job somewhere else.'

'No, I'll wait until they tell me what to do.'

'They won't pay you for looking after the house.'

'I don't need payment to look after Julia's house.'

'My madam says it's funny how your madam died so suddenly.'

'What do you mean funny?' An edge crept into Mary's voice.

'Well, one day she was fine and the next, she's not here.' Frida plucked at the leaves of the bush next to her and wouldn't meet Mary's eyes.

'The doctor said her heart stopped. He said she suffered from a weak heart and her death was not a surprise.'

'They always say that. But then later they change their minds and find someone to blame.'

'People die all the time. Why should they want to blame anybody?'

'Well, your situation with your madam was unusual, so people might be suspicious.'

'Frida, I think you're trying to—'

'I have to go now, before my madam calls me.' Frida hurried away without waiting to listen to Mary's reply.

CHAPTER 33

A Time of Trial

TIME crawled for Mary, an agonising slow stretch from dawn to dusk. Each hour felt like two. Andrew Jones called in each day in the first fortnight to check on her. The distraction pleased her, but it did little to lift her depression. Life without Julia was unimaginable. The tricks life plays can be cruel. Everything was perfect. Her world came crashing down.

Now, she faced a practical problem that intruded on her grieving. Andrew Jones told her to hold any bills that came in, and they'd worry about them later. But what then? Julia and the house were Mary's world. How would she manage without Julia and money? Electricity and water outages were frequent, but what if the authorities made a permanent cut to her supply? She could revert to cooking over the kia's open fireplace and use the rainwater. But the house in darkness would just add to her misery.

In the third week after Julia's funeral, Mary was dusting the bookcase when a knock on the front door interrupted her. It sounded like Andrew Jones again. She hurried to open the door. Andrew Jones stood there with another man, Winston Smith, the lawyer. Andrew smiled. 'Mary, please put the kettle on for tea. Winston and I need to talk to you.'

That sounded ominous, and as she filled the kettle with water, she couldn't help but feel anxious. What did they want to talk about? Julia once said drinking tea was a gentle way to break bad news. Everything was already so bad; she might not even recognise bad news.

Mary carried the tea tray with three cups, teapot, milk, and sugar through to the lounge. Andrew and Winston both sat forward in their armchairs, speaking in hushed voices. It didn't look good, and despite her depression, her heart thumped in her chest. She placed the tea tray on the coffee table and poured the tea. No one took sugar, and while she added a little milk to her tea, Andrew and Winston drank theirs black.

Winston spoke. 'Mary, there's good news for you. Julia nominated you as her sole heir. That means the house and car, and everything here, is now yours. I must still complete the paperwork before it's all official, but all of Julia's property comes to you. There is only a little money, about one thousand dollars, in her bank accounts. I know that won't last too long, but if you don't have the means to keep the house, we can help you sell it if that's your wish.'

Mary's eyes opened wide with surprise. Julia, her best friend, did not forget her. It was a relief to inherit Julia's house and belongings. But a sense of panic rose in her chest as she worried how she would afford to keep the house. She didn't want to sell it, but she'd no means of funding its upkeep. How would she afford the rates, electricity, water, telephone, and internet? These expenses alone would soon eat into the thousand dollars she inherited, but she couldn't face the thought of selling the house. Now, a fresh worry compounded her misery.

'But how did Julia pay for the trips and the clothes she bought me?'

'If she knew she was about to die, perhaps she wanted to enjoy her money while she had the chance,' said Winston.

'No, if she knew she was dying, she would have told me. Only a few days before she died, she said we'd soon go to London.'

'I don't think she knew,' said Andrew. 'Julia's cardiologist in Johannesburg said she was doing well. It surprised him to hear of her death, but with a weak heart, you never can tell.'

Winston continued. 'As Julia's sole heir, Mary, perhaps you should go through all her private files. Julia only told me about the two bank accounts where she deposited the thousand dollars, but she may have money here in the house. Have you been through her cupboards and drawers to see if she has cash stored somewhere?'

'No, I will search her room.'

Winston and Andrew drove off, leaving Mary with a big 'headache'.

Now, she faced a difficult problem she needed to resolve, but it might help her take her mind off grieving for Julia.

A short time later, George Benson appeared. 'How are you doing, Mary? I see you're receiving visitors, so I thought it would be OK for me to visit you.'

Mary invited George in for a cup of tea and told him the news she received.

'Hmm. If I could, I would help with the money, but I'm afraid our president shredded my savings. I go to bed at dusk and rise at dawn. That way, my electricity bill is low. Also, I grow most of my food, and that's why I'm a vegetarian these days.'

'Yes, I'll do the same. Perhaps I can sell vegetables in the suburb. We have a lot growing in the back garden. That should bring in a little money.'

'Well, I wish you luck with that, Mary. There's no one I'd rather have as a neighbour. With you next door, it will seem a part of Julia is still here. She loved you very much, you know?'

* * *

Mary wasted no time putting her plan into action. As the various vegetables ripened, she put them into packets of a comparable size to those sold in supermarkets and offered them at a competitive price to the suburb's residents. It kept her busy but was hard work. She often walked to the shops to save the petrol in the car, but she needed to do the occasional run to keep the car battery going.

Despite all her cost-saving measures, it soon became obvious the income from the vegetable sales would not be enough for her to keep the house. She needed another plan. But what?

Mary's vegetable sales drew the other maids' attention and divided opinion between those who supported her and those who were quick to take up Frida's suggestion that something was wrong.

Eveline, Monica, and Clara championed Mary, but many other maids delighted in the idea she might have poisoned her madam to get possession of her property. George Benson let slip to Eveline that Mary now owned Julia's house. Eveline told Monica and Clara, and somehow, the word got out.

'Mary's been here less than two years and already she owns the house,' said Frida. The other maids grunted in agreement. 'She got rid of her boss, the madam's daughter, and now the madam. You can't say she hasn't used witchcraft to do that. How else would it be possible?'

One maid suggested they should tell the police.

'We told them before, and nothing happened,' said another.

'She even put a spell on Inspector Kutumela,' said a third.

'Well then, we should talk to another inspector,' said Frida. 'My madam knows another inspector, and she's not happy to have Mary next door. Perhaps she will raise the issue with the police. I will talk to her about it, but she is difficult, so I must be careful how I suggest it. She must think it's her idea, or she'll do nothing.'

'I wonder if Mary needs a maid,' said Betty. 'If my madam leaves, I might ask her for a job.'

All the other maids glared at Betty.

'She won't be here long,' said Frida.

When Frida returned to work, she set about peeling the potatoes for dinner and chatted with her madam, Dorothy Mapfumo. 'The maids say Mary next door will bring her three sisters from their village in the bush to live here. They say she will set up a stall at the front gate to sell vegetables and eggs. I believe her sisters have nine children who will also come to live here.'

'I'm not having a rural village move in next door.'

'Yes, Madam, but what can we do?'

'You'll see what I can do. The boss and I have connections.'

Frida smiled. She'd planted the seed in Dorothy Mapfumo's mind.

* * *

Two days later, as Mary packaged vegetables into bags for sale to her customers, a loud banging on the front door interrupted her. It wasn't Winston, Andrew, or George's usual knock, but it sounded urgent, so she hurried to open it. There, confronting her, stood three police officers. She recognised the one in front as the inspector who arrested her when Julia was away overseas in London.

'Mary Moyo, I'm arresting you on suspicion of the murder of Mrs Julia Watson.'

'No, how can you say that?'

'You have two minutes to lock up the house.'

'Where is Inspector Kutumela?'

'Kutumela is on leave, and Mrs Watson can't save you with a hundred-dollar payment this time.'

As the police officers led Mary out to the waiting police car, George Benson from next door raced across to the group.

'What's happened? Where are you taking her?'

The police officers ignored him, but Mary called out. 'George, please tell Winston and Andrew, they've arrested me for Julia's murder.'

'What? What rubbish! Don't worry, I'll tell them straight away.'

As the police car drove off, George rushed back into his house to phone Winston and Andrew.

Winston wasted no time in getting to the police station to announce he represented Mary. Andrew Jones took in a box of KFC chicken and chips for her to eat. He remembered the last time when she almost starved in the police cells.

The inspector told Winston it was too late to apply for bail today, so he would need to apply tomorrow, but he, the inspector, would oppose it.

First thing the next morning, Winston Smith stood in front of Justice Michael Murwira for Mary's bail application.

'Inspector Chasi, why do you oppose the granting of bail?'

'The accused is a dangerous woman, Your Honour. We arrested her once before on suspicion of two separate attempted murders, but we dropped the charges because we could not trace the victims. One attempt was against a burglar and the other against her former boss. They both disappeared after lodging complaints. She attacked them with a garden hoe. Now there's a death whereby the accused profits by inheriting the house and property of the victim. It is too coincidental that three unconnected individuals suffered life-threatening crimes committed by the accused.'

'She is also a flight risk, Your Honour. Her village is in the remote south-west of Zimbabwe, where it would be a simple matter for her to slip over the border to South Africa or Botswana.'

'Thank you, Inspector Chasi. Now, Mr Smith, what have you to say on behalf of your client?'

'Your Honour, Ms Moyo was Mrs Watson's protégé. In that role, she received all the benefits, as if she was Mrs Watson's granddaughter. The deceased was the accused's mentor and benefactor. Ms Moyo was protective of Mrs Watson, whose death has put her in a difficult position. Although she has inherited the house, the estate leaves her little money to keep it.'

'As regards the attempted murder charges, she did not attack the accusers with a garden hoe. She chased them off the property with the threat of using the hoe.'

'We are not here to decide her innocence or guilt, Mr Smith. This is a bail application.'

'Yes, Your Honour, my apologies. Aside from the house, there's little of the deceased's possessions that Ms Moyo can convert into monetary value, so I don't believe she will be a flight risk.'

'But how then can she raise bail, Mr Smith? Is probate completed?'

'It is on the verge of completion, Your Honour.'

'Very well! Subject to probate and Ms Moyo surrendering her passport, I will grant bail against the value of the house.'

'Thank you, Your Honour.'

* * *

Mary was fortunate that probate completed two days later, and a reluctant Inspector Chasi released her from custody.

Winston Smith and Andrew Jones met with her to discuss the way forward.

'Why are they accusing me of murdering Julia?'

'As I understand it,' said Winston, 'the whole thing started with rumours among the maids. And it goes back a long way. They claim you got rid of your husband's number one wife and then your husband. The police are bringing up the two dropped charges of attempted murder, and now Julia's death as a possible poisoning. There was no autopsy, so no one can prove or disprove Julia was poisoned. They're suggesting you'll stop at nothing to improve your circumstances.'

'I will get Julia's cardiologist to give me a letter confirming that in his expert opinion, her death was neither unexpected nor suspicious,' said Andrew. 'I saw no evidence of poisoning when I examined her, though I didn't look for it, of course.'

'Don't say in court, you didn't look for it.' said Winston.

'But if I say I looked for evidence of poisoning, it will suggest I suspected Mary of having a hand in Julia's death.'

'No, all you say is that checking for poisoning, accidental or otherwise, is part of your normal routine before you issue a death certificate.'

'OK, I get it.'

'And what about you, Mary?' said Winston. 'Any ideas?'

'My neighbour's maid, Frida, has always been jealous of the way Julia treated me. She thought she missed the opportunity to get a better job and regretted introducing me to Julia.'

A loud knock on the door interrupted them. It was George Benson. 'Have you all seen today's paper?' George handed a copy to Winston. 'There on the third page, next to the piece about children missing from villages in the area around Figtree and Marula.' George pointed to an article headed, 'Bulawayo Housemaid Accused of Employer's Murder.'

CHAPTER 34

The Preliminary Hearing

To be named in the Bulawayo Chronicle was a blow for Mary. The article didn't give her address, but in a small city like Bulawayo, gossip and conjecture could soon narrow down the area where the accused housemaid lived. It would be a simple task for any determined person to find her.

Mary valued her privacy. The people in her village thought she was visiting the spirits, but now the newspaper was broadcasting she may be a manipulating housemaid, scheming to take possession of her employer's property. But she wasn't just a housemaid. She was a companion and Julia's treasured best friend. Mary inherited Julia's property, but she needed to convince others of her bona fides.

Winston Smith and Andrew Jones were handling her legal and other matters and told her to carry on as normal. That was difficult for her, but the two men promised to keep her informed.

Mary cleaned the house as usual and looked after the vegetables and garden. A casual observer would notice no difference in the neat, well-maintained property, and would be unaware of the occupant's torment. Mary couldn't face cooking alone. She needed to eat, but kept meal preparation to a minimum. She loved the evenings when she and Julia prepared and ate their meals together, chatting and planning their next adventure.

* * *

The big black Mercedes pulled up at the gate, and two well-dressed African men got out, buttoning their suit jackets. Mary wondered who they might be. They didn't look like police officers, Jehovah's Witnesses or Mormons, and she wasn't expecting any visitors.

The men appeared hesitant, hovering at the gate. Just then, Mary noticed Frida near the corner of the garden, where she always smoked. Frida said something that caught the men's attention. To Mary, that represented a risk. She opened the front door and strode down the driveway towards the group. Frida saw her coming and hurried back to her house.

'Ms Moyo, Mary Moyo?'

'Yes, I'm Mary Moyo.'

The men introduced themselves as Jonathan and Timothy.

'We have important news for you. May we enter?'

Mary showed them into the lounge, and they all sat in the armchairs. She offered to make them tea, but they refused, explaining they needed to go to another appointment before lunch.

'I'll get straight to the point,' said Jonathan.

Timothy smiled and nodded, as if endorsing Jonathan's statement.

'Our boss noticed you were having legal difficulties and asked Timothy and I to help you. It is difficult when they accuse you unjustly.'

'What makes you think they accused me unjustly?'

Jonathan smiled. 'Well, weren't you accused unjustly?'

'Yes, but—'

'Our boss knows everything,' said Timothy with a broad grin.

'Who is your boss? And how can you help me?'

The men ignored the first question.

Jonathan continued, 'We believe you cannot afford to keep this house going and may have to sell it. The boss will help you with your case if you agree to pay him twenty percent of the proceeds from the sale of your property.'

'Twenty percent! How can he help me?'

'By making the charges against you disappear.'

'How can he make the charges disappear?'

'The boss has connections.'

'You'd be surprised what he can make disappear,' said Timothy.

To Mary, that sounded like a thinly veiled threat. 'What makes you think I'm selling the house?'

'That's what Chasi told Jacks—'

'Chasi? Inspector Chasi, who arrested me?'

Jonathan frowned at Timothy. 'Our boss has a lot of connections.'

'But I may win my case without your boss making the charges disappear.'

'Do you want to take that chance? When you sell the house, the estate agents and lawyers are expensive. If you pay us instead, you will also get your case withdrawn. It's a good deal for you.'

'I already have a lawyer, and I've not yet considered selling the house.'

'How can you keep the house if you don't have money?'

'I can try.'

'Are you willing to risk both your house and the case against you?'

'My lawyer says my case is strong.'

'They all say that. It's how they get you to use their over-priced services.'

'I'll risk it.'

'You would be foolish to reject our offer. Just as our boss can make the charges disappear, he can also make them much worse.'

Mary turned to Timothy. 'And you believe Chasi when he says I'll not be able to keep the house?'

'That's what Chasi told Jackson.'

'Shut up, you fool,' Jonathan snapped at Timothy.

'Ah, so Jackson Mpofu sent you.'

'Fifteen percent of the selling price to drop the charges. It's our last offer.'

'Tell Jackson I wouldn't give him even five percent.'

'You're making a big mistake. Jackson can make life difficult for you.'

Mary's calm exterior belied the chill that ran down her back. 'I don't need to worry about Jackson. His time is near. The spirits know his mind and his evil deeds, and he must answer for them.'

Jonathan seemed lost for a suitable reply. Timothy was wide-eyed and mopped his brow, though the house was cool. The men rose from their chairs, stating they needed to move on to the next meeting. The charm and friendliness they displayed on their arrival evaporated.

Mary showed them out, and stood at the front door, watching them until the black Mercedes disappeared behind the trees. Her hands shook as the pent-up tension struggled to leave her. Her calm demeanour and brave words hid her nervousness. In her mind, the picture of Julia was a constant presence, and it helped her to keep control of her nerves until the men departed.

Suddenly, she could visualise the missing words Julia spoke as the plane hurtled down the runway at Victoria Falls airport. Mary was nervous then, on her first flight. All she heard above the scream of the engines was, 'I'll... side.' She often pictured Julia mouthing the words and wondered about them. But now they seemed clear. Julia said, 'I'll always be by your side.'

Mary worried Jackson Mpofu somehow found out where she lived. She left her village to escape his menace, but now he'd traced her. Jackson was superstitious, and that's what she banked on when she gave Jonathan and Timothy her message for him. But would her defiant message keep him at bay, or would it spur him into a vengeful act? It all depended on how he interpreted it, and if he still feared her connection to the spirits.

Jackson Mpofu might be less fearful of Mary, now that he learnt she worked as a housemaid. Though taking possession of her employer's property may convince him, she still worked through the spirits. But she needed to be careful and watch her back.

* * *

Inspector Kutumela was back from leave. He'd read about Mary's case in the Bulawayo Chronicle and spoke to Chasi about it. 'I've read the bail application, and I see you told the judge the last time you arrested Mary Moyo, you dropped the charges because you couldn't trace the victims. But you dropped the charges because Mrs Watson paid you the one hundred US dollars you demanded.'

'So?'

'So, it's not true. You took a bribe.'

'Keep your nose out of my affairs, Kutumela.'

'How will the judge react when he finds out the truth?'

'He won't find out.'

'I won't stand by and let you jail an innocent woman for a contrived murder charge. You arrested her on trumped-up charges before, and now you're doing it again.'

'You're getting mixed up in something you don't understand. Last time, Mrs Watson paid me to drop the charges, but this time I'm getting paid to press ahead with the charges.'

'Who is paying you to do that?'

'A government bigwig. Nobody is silly enough to cross him.'

'I'll take my chances.'

'What's your problem? What's that woman got over you?'

'Nothing, but if you're listening to her nosy neighbour, you're making a mistake.'

'It's more than the nosy neighbour, now that the chefs (bigwigs) are involved. And it wouldn't surprise me if they have influence with the judge.'

'No matter. If you don't withdraw the charges, I'll make sure the judge finds out about the payment you're getting. Then what will happen to your case?'

'When trouble comes your way, don't say I didn't warn you.'

'It's time we stamped out all this bribery and corruption.'

'Kutumela, you're a fool. It'll be your funeral if you take on the bigwigs. Mind your own business if you know what's good for you.'

* * *

The morning of the preliminary hearing dawned clear and bright. Mary dressed in the more conservative of the two outfits Julia bought her in Johannesburg. She ate a little breakfast as her stomach churned at the prospect of facing the judge again. Winston Smith arrived on time to drive her to the hearing. He sensed her tension and tried to ease her mind.

'Don't worry, Mary. Justice Murwira is a fair judge. He won't let the case go to trial unless Inspector Chasi provides compelling evidence, and how can he do that?'

Mary's brave smile in response was not convincing. Two hurdles stood in her way, and she needed to clear them both. She'd not told anyone about the visit from Jackson Mpofu's men. Could he really influence the judge and make things worse for her? As they drove up, the sight of Inspector Chasi standing outside the High Court didn't help her confidence.

'All rise' said the clerk of the court, as Justice Murwira entered the courtroom through a door near his bench.

The judge looked over the rim of his glasses and spoke. 'Inspector Chasi, are you ready to outline your case?'

'I am, Your Honour.'

'And if we go to trial, do you intend to call any witnesses?'

'Yes, Your Honour. There are two complainants who will testify how the accused's aggressive and manipulative behaviour traumatised them, causing pain and suffering. A witness will confirm the events and will also detail an attempt by the accused to poison other maids in her street. There are several more witnesses who can corroborate their accounts.'

'What charges relate to the two complainants?'

'One complainant was drunk and came to the wrong house by accident. As he tried to open the back door with his key, the accused charged at him with a garden hoe. The complainant would be with his ancestors if he wasn't able to outrun the accused.'

'And the other?'

'The other is Mrs Watson's former partner, who will testify how the accused became close to her lady employer and undermined his relationship with her. He will also ask the court to confirm that he is the true heir to Mrs Watson's estate.'

As Inspector Chasi paused for breath, someone opened the door of the public entrance. Chasi turned to see Inspector Kutumela walk into the courtroom. 'Your Honour, my colleague has arrived late. May I have a moment to confer?'

'Make it quick, Inspector. We don't have all day.'

'Thank you, Your Honour.'

Chasi hurried to the back of the courtroom to talk to Kutumela in private. He spoke in hushed tones. 'Kutumela, what are you doing here?'

'You know what I'm doing here. I warned you.'

'Listen! I've spoken to the government bigwig. If you back off, he's agreed to pay you the same amount as he's paying me. Ten thousand US dollars!'

'I didn't join the police to take bribes, Chasi, no matter how much he offers.'

'Don't be a fool. If this case doesn't go ahead, we'll both forgo any payment.'

'No deal, Chasi. Withdraw, or I'll speak to the judge about what you're doing.'

'You'll regret this, I promise you.' Chasi returned to the front of the court. 'Your Honour, my colleague advises me the witnesses wish to withdraw from this case, so we cannot proceed.'

'This is most irregular, Inspector. You and your colleague should have resolved this issue before wasting my time. This matter is now closed. Ms Moyo, you are free to go. The case is dismissed.'

'Thank you, Your Honour,' said Winston Smith. 'My client is grateful for your ruling.'

Chasi's face was a dark mask as he glared at Kutumela. Winston Smith was a picture of delight, and the relief on Mary's face was unmistakable.

While they let the moment flow over them, Inspector Kutumela slipped away as quietly as he arrived.

'Now, Mary,' said Winston, 'you must make plans for your house. There's not enough cash in the estate to pay for its upkeep. Expenses will roll in, and you haven't enough income to pay for them. I'll select a good estate agent to come and talk to you about selling it.'

Those words melted the euphoria Mary felt from the dismissal of her court case. She'd considered several ways of keeping the house, but none seemed realistic.

* * *

Jackson Mpofu raged when he heard the news. 'That damn woman says my time is near? She's bewitched that Inspector Kutumela. Imagine, the fool of a man, rejecting my generous offer. Jonathan, I want you and Timothy to deal with those two. I want them gone.'

'Sir, we are inexperienced in such things, and it would be bad if someone traced their disappearance back to you.'

'It would be even worse for you, Jonathan.'

'What I mean, Sir, is I know a Bulawayo man who works for someone in Harare who specialises in disappearances. They say people disappear like magic, and no one sees them again. Perhaps I should speak to the Bulawayo man and see what's possible.'

'All right, but don't mention my name. Leave me out of it. Do you understand? It has nothing to do with me. It's your idea Jonathan.'

'Yes, Sir.'

CHAPTER 35

The London Visitor

THE phone rang, and the distinguished looking African man dressed in a Gieves & Hawkes light grey suit picked up the receiver. 'Yes.'

'It's me, Sir, Khumalo.'

'Do you imagine, after all the time you've worked for me, I don't recognise your voice? Credit me with a bit more intelligence, man.'

'Yes, Sir. Sorry, Sir.'

'What do you want, Khumalo?'

'Sir, someone has asked me about doing a job for them.'

'Who asked you?'

'I just know him as Jonathan.'

'Is he the one paying for the job?'

'I don't think so. He didn't say who would pay, but when I first met him in a bar a few weeks ago, I overheard him telling others he worked for Jackson Mpofu, the government man.'

'I know Mpofu from the Bush War. He's a bully and a coward. What is the job he wants done?'

'He wants a woman, Mary Moyo, to disappear. Also, a police inspector who supported her in a recent court case. The rumour was the woman murdered her lady employer to get her house and money.'

'Yes, I heard something about that. Why can't Mpofu handle it himself?'

'They say the woman is close to the spirits, and one lives in her garden to protect her.'

'Hah! So, they want us to face the spirits? How much are they offering?'

'Twenty thousand US dollars, Sir.'

'Listen! That Jackson Mpofu is a rapist and a murderer. He was a coward in the Bush War, and now he's afraid of women too. Tell him that woman is most dangerous, and we wouldn't dare touch her, even for ten times the amount he's offered. It's too dangerous.'

'Yes, Sir.'

'Mpofu is a superstitious fool. If he already fears Mary Moyo, my message will make it much worse for him.'

Khumalo chuckled at his boss's cunning plan to scare Jackson Mpofu and his men. If they thought his boss was afraid to tackle Mary Moyo, then who would dare? Mpofu's problem would now be even worse. Twenty thousand US dollars was a lot of money to forgo, but his boss was a wealthy man and could afford it.

Of course, Mpofu was not alone in being superstitious. Many Africans were superstitious. Only his boss appeared to have broken with tradition and risen above the old fears. The boss never spoke of his background. He was a mysterious man, and Khumalo often wondered what life's blows moulded him.

* * *

The rap on the front door brought Mary out of the kitchen. She'd been paging through Julia's old cookbook; not for a recipe for a dish she planned to cook, but to help take her mind off Winston Smith's last depressing words to her about selling the house.

Mary recognised Winston Smith's knock. No doubt he'd tell her what arrangements he'd made for the sale. But she had resolved not to sell Julia's house. They might cut off the electricity and water, and cut off the phone, but somehow, she'd get by. She'd raise as much money as possible to pay the rates, and she'd try to fix things herself, but she wouldn't sell. She realised her determination to keep the house was a gamble and perhaps unrealistic, but she would give it a go.

Mary opened the door, and Winston stood there with a stranger. Her heart fell. This must be the real estate agent Winston said he'd find. The men seemed overly cheerful, as if celebrating the imminent sale of her house. No matter how sensible it was, for her it was heartbreaking.

'Mary, meet James Grant.'

'Pleased to meet you, Sir.'

'Please call me Jim.' The man shook her hand.

'We're dying for a cup of tea, Mary.'

'Yes, please come in.'

Winston and Jim sat in the armchairs in the lounge while Mary stepped into the kitchen to prepare tea. She heard them talking and laughing in the lounge. Didn't they appreciate how heavy her heart felt? They'd try to force her into deciding on something she didn't want to face.

Mary walked into the lounge, interrupting the men, who laughed and chatted in an excitable manner. She put the tray down on the coffee table and poured the tea.

'Mary,' said Winston, drawing her attention.

She looked at him as he paused, as if waiting for her full attention.

'Is Jim from the estate agents?'

'Er, no. Jim is from Penfold and Collins, Julia's lawyers in London. Perhaps, Jim can explain.'

'Well, I was in Kenya on a safari vacation when my office in London called me. They said, seeing as I was already in Africa, I should come to Bulawayo to meet you.'

'Oh! Is something wrong?'

'No, no. In January, Mrs Watson came to London to settle her late sister's affairs.'

'Yes.'

'Well, Mrs Watson's widowed sister was married to a wealthy man who died three years ago. That made Mrs Watson's sister a wealthy woman, and when she died, Mrs Watson inherited her estate. Sadly, Mrs Watson has now passed on, and as her only heir, you will now inherit the estate.'

'Oh!'

'You're very calm about this news, Mary,' said Winston.

'Does that mean I can keep this house?'

Jim laughed. 'This house and the apartment in London.'

'Apartment?'

'Yes, that's what you call a flat or townhouse over here.'

For the first time, Mary gave an uncertain smile. She wouldn't have to sell Julia's house.

'Mary, I don't think you yet appreciate what you've inherited,' said Winston. 'You better tell her, Jim.'

'Well, Mary, the estate comprises two principal parts. The liquid assets that are quite easy to convert into cash amount to around fifteen million pounds sterling. That's about twenty million US dollars. And heaven knows what the apartment is worth! That depends on the market. When we last checked, it was worth about three million pounds sterling. If you hold on to it, it will become much more valuable in time. The apartment is in Belgravia, one of London's most exclusive suburbs.'

Winston jumped in. 'It's London's equivalent to the Suburbs here in Bulawayo, Mary. The poshest place in town.'

With Jim Grant and Winston both firing excited comments at her, Mary found it difficult to take in the unbelievable news.

'You are rich, Mary,' said Winston. 'Do you understand how much money you've inherited?'

Mary's mind was in a muddle. All that mattered was she could keep Julia's house. 'Was that how Julia paid for our trips to Victoria Falls and Johannesburg?'

'No,' said Jim, 'she didn't have the chance to spend a cent of her inheritance. I understand she planned to visit London soon to see us and complete all the formalities.'

'Yes, she said we'd go to London soon, but she didn't tell me why.'

'To take possession of her inheritance,' said Jim, 'and sign off on the paperwork. Now you'll have to do that. Why don't we go out tonight and celebrate?'

'Sorry, I have another engagement,' said Winston, 'but you two should go.'

* * *

Dinner with a male stranger was a concern for Mary. She'd always gone to restaurants with Julia and once with the group of mourners at Julia's wake. It was a pity that Winston Smith couldn't make it that evening. She would also have welcomed the company of Andrew Jones or George Benson next door, but Jim Grant invited her, and it was not her place to add to the guest list.

Mary tried on the outfit she wore to court, but no, too conservative. Next, she tried on a yellow floral dress with a flared skirt, but it looked too flirty. In the end, she chose a patterned, navy blue and purple, slim-fitting dress with a row of buttons at the high collar. It gave her an alluring, oriental look, with material just thick enough to keep out the cool, unseasonal, late-evening breeze that sometimes cropped up at this time of the year, in the era of climate change.

After six-thirty, Mary went to the lounge window several times to check for any sign of Jim Grant's arrival. Seven o'clock, he'd told her, but she began checking early, just in case. She'd already locked the doors and shut the windows, but she checked them again, to make sure. In her black clutch handbag, she carried a small amount of cash in case she needed to pay for her own dinner. Julia always paid, but Jim Grant said nothing, and she wasn't sure what the correct niceties were.

At last, car headlights at the gate. Jim Grant stepped out of the car, wearing a light brown jacket and open-neck white shirt and navy trousers. In his late fifties, he cut a neat figure with a receding hairline and lived-in face. Mary found his mature appearance and manner reminiscent of her late husband Josiah, which helped reassure her and settle the butterflies in her tummy.

Jim Grant walked up the driveway as Mary stepped out the front door. 'Wow! Wealthy and beautiful. What more could a man want?'

Mary blushed at the unexpected familiarity. Jim held open the passenger door for her to get into the car. He jumped into the driver's seat, reversed the car, and they were on their way. 'I've booked a table at The Garden Bistro. Is that all right with you?'

'I've never been there.'

'I found it by accident this afternoon, driving in the Suburbs, looking at the nice houses. The garden is a beautiful setting, and the restaurant looks cosy, so we can talk in peace.'

'It sounds nice.'

'Hopefully, the food is good.'

* * *

Mary said little as Jim chatted on their drive to the restaurant.

'How lucky can a guy get? I was having a wonderful safari holiday in Kenya, and now I'm experiencing this in Zimbabwe, in the company of a beautiful woman.'

Mary couldn't help but feel flattered by the compliments from the urbane Jim Grant. She was unaccustomed to such direct charm, as most of the white men she'd met maintained a polite, businesslike distance. Andrew, Winston, and George were always respectful and made no personal comments. They all behaved as if she needed guidance and protection, which to a degree was true. As Julia's companion, Mary inherited a ready-made group of friends besides the estate.

The waitress showed Mary and Jim to a table on the restaurant's veranda, open to the balmy night air. There was no sign of the cooler breezes Mary expected. The waitress brought the menus, and Jim helped her choose her meal.

'This place is known for its curries. Do you like curry?'

'Oh yes, Julia and I often cooked curry at home.'

'Next time, we should try the fish and chips.'

'Next time? How long will you be staying in Bulawayo, Jim?'

'Unfortunately, I'm booked to fly out tomorrow, but I'll soon return for fish and chips if you'll have dinner with me again.'

Mary laughed. 'Yes, I will, but don't you have fish and chips in London?'

'I'd really be coming to see you. The fish and chips are just my excuse.'

'Are you married, Jim?'

'No, I've waited to meet the right woman.'

Mary laughed again. 'You're funny. So, when will you come back again?'

'Well, I'm sure you'll need a bit of advice on your investments and other assets. I'll need to make another trip soon. Perhaps I can come at Christmas.'

'Christmas! That will be nice.'

The balmy evening and exotic fragrances from the garden setting joined the chilled white wine and tasty food to make for a heady night out. It was the first time since Julia's death that Mary could smile and enjoy herself. Jim Grant proved to be entertaining company, causing her to laugh at his quips and flirtatious comments.

She found it easy to chat with Jim, and the time passed quickly, and soon it was late. He paid for the dinner and tipped the waitress. At the front gate of Mary's house, he kissed her on the cheek with a promise to see her soon at Christmas. He was flying out early the next morning, and neither suggested a coffee or nightcap to complete a perfect evening. Mary watched his car drive down the road, and pause for a moment, before turning right onto Burns Drive.

Already, Mary looked forward to Jim's return, a little over a month away. In the cloudless night sky, a myriad of stars twinkled. She and Julia loved these black nights when they'd sit outside watching for shooting stars and satellites. Mary wasn't in the least bit tired and stood in the garden, breathing in the fresh night air. It was the first time she'd done that in weeks. She looked up at the stars. *Julia, which one are you? What are you thinking?*

CHAPTER 36

Anticipation

OVER the next four weeks, each Thursday night at nine o'clock, Jim Grant emailed Mary. There was no special news, just chat about the weather and the developing pre-Christmas rush in London. He promised to show her how to use Skype when next in Bulawayo. She may have worked it out for herself, but hesitated to appear live on the screen, so soon in their relationship.

The days passed at a crawl. Mary couldn't wait to reacquaint herself with Jim again. Even she thought it odd, as she'd been in his company for just a single day—in the morning when they met, and the dinner date later that evening. But he'd been charming and attentive. His sense of humour and his mature manner disarmed her, and his entire focus upon her helped her relax. It proved an irresistible mix.

Mary was grateful Julia made her practice her long vowels and focus on the way she spoke. To Mary, at first it sounded affected, but soon it became second nature, in the same way that she'd got used to calling Julia by her first name. Her developing accent and manner made her appear more educated than she was, but her voracious appetite for books helped in that area too; just as Julia promised it would.

It also helped that most of her conversations were with Winston, Andrew, and George, who, like Julia, all spoke with educated accents. Somehow, her speaking voice enabled her to fit into the group and get her relationship with Jim off to a good start.

Winston, Andrew, and George often dropped in for morning coffee. At first, it was to ask if she needed help, but in due course, their visits became more social, chatting about the weather, local politics, or international events. The men rallied around her because of their friendship with Julia, but soon, a friendship with Mary also developed.

Mary became conscious of the change in her status when Winston invited her, Andrew, and George to his house for a pre-Christmas braai (barbecue). Winston and Andrew's wives chatted away with Mary like old friends. Again, those long vowels helped her fit in well with the company.

George's maid, Eveline, glimpsed Andrew Jones arrive to pick up Mary and George for Winston's braai. She couldn't contain her excitement, waiting to tell Monica and the other maids how wonderful Mary looked, dressed in Julia's clothes. The news set tongues wagging in the mouths of the excited women. Mary's mystique was growing.

When Mary chatted with her friends amongst the African maids, she took care not to slip back into her former accent. The other maids didn't seem to notice, or at least didn't comment, but they all treated Mary with deference. None of them knew the size of Mary's inheritance, and she didn't plan to tell them.

Everything seemed to fall into place. The vegetables grew in abundance, and the chickens provided more eggs than Mary needed. She gave her surplus food supply to the other maids, who wondered why Mary no longer sold the vegetables and eggs to make a little money. Henry kept the garden in pristine condition with the aid of the rainwater tank.

Frida kept her distance, and her employer, Dorothy Mapfumo, did her best to ignore Mary. That suited Mary fine, as she was sure Frida and Dorothy spread the rumours that led to her arrest on suspicion of murdering Julia.

Soon, Mary was back in the kitchen, honing her cooking skills. She'd stopped cooking anything new or experimental after Julia died, but now her passion to improve her dishes returned. By the time Jim arrived at Christmas, she'd be back in full swing, and no doubt he'd enjoy a traditional Christmas dinner. In fact, she'd invite the entire gang, though before now, she'd only ever cooked for two. Her confidence ballooned, and she was eager to try something more ambitious.

* * *

When you're busy, time flies, and so it did for Mary. Two weeks before Christmas, she received flowers from Jim with a card saying, 'See you soon. Love, Jim.' The prospect of furthering her acquaintance with him excited her. Would anything come of the relationship? After Josiah's death, she never intended to involve herself with any other man, but the similarities between her former husband and Jim Grant struck her.

Two days later, an email arrived from her London lawyers, Penfold and Collins, with a simple message advising Mary that their representative would visit her at eleven o'clock on the Friday before Christmas. It further stated he'd deliver documents relating to the estate, and it would be advisable to have her local lawyer present to witness her signature.

* * *

Friday dawned—a beautiful, bright morning. The gang was coming for a pre-Christmas dinner, and Jim would be there. Mary made sure everything was ready. Winston arrived fifteen minutes before the scheduled meeting with Jim, and she started getting the morning tea prepared.

'He's here,' said Winston, as a car pulled up at the gate.

Mary hurried to open the front door. 'No, it's not him. Who is this?'

A serious-looking young man walked up the driveway, carrying a briefcase. 'Ms Moyo? Mary Moyo?'

'Yes, that's me.'

'I'm Tony Williams from Penfold and Collins. I have all the documents detailing your inheritance for you to sign and take possession.'

'Uh! I thought Jim Grant would do that.'

'Oh! I'm sorry. Didn't my office let you know? On Monday, a speeding vehicle ran into Jim Grant. It was a hit and run, but the police caught the drunk driver. He'd been celebrating Christmas a little early and a little too hard.'

For Mary, it was a blow. 'I just got a message from him on Tuesday last week. Is he all right?'

'I'm afraid not. Apparently, it happened just outside a florist. As he stepped off the pavement to cross the road, a car came racing around the corner, straight into him. He died at the scene. The poor guy wouldn't have known what hit him. It's such a shame. He was a nice bloke.'

'Yes, he was.'

'He'd already booked the flights, so the office asked me to take his place. I changed the itinerary because he planned a month-long holiday in Zimbabwe, but I must return to London for Christmas. Anyway, we'd better get down to business. I'm on the afternoon flight to Johannesburg.'

After Tony Williams left, Winston asked Mary if she'd like to cancel the evening dinner, following the dreadful news about Jim. 'Everyone will understand if you'd like to cancel.'

'No, no, let's continue. It can be a dinner in honour of Jim.'

'OK then, see you this evening.'

After Winston left, Mary busied herself with last-minute preparations for the evening dinner. Although she barely knew Jim, the news devastated her. The prospect of a close relationship or romance evaporated in an instant. It wasn't as hard to bear as Julia's sudden death, but it was a terrible shock after she'd built up hopes of a possible future with a charming new partner. At least, she thought, I won't be alone this evening. As she sliced the red onions, she wiped the tears from her eyes.

* * *

The news about Jim Grant hung heavily over Mary. Only Winston shared her sadness as he'd met Jim. The others enjoyed her dinner and commented on her cooking and what a gracious host she made. But the terrible news overshadowed what should have been her triumph. The company helped lift her mood a little, and she hid her emotions well.

She led a toast to Jim Grant and the good health of her friends at the table.

Later, when the guests left, Mary washed the dishes and thought about her situation. She felt a little guilty that she'd allowed Jim Grant to occupy her dreams in recent weeks. So soon after Julia's death, she'd allowed her feelings for Jim to put her grieving for Julia in the background. But meeting Jim helped her to not dwell on Julia's death. It was almost as if Julia had sent him to her.

Mary walked into the back garden and looked at the flourishing vegetable beds she and Julia planted. Heavy clouds hung low in the night sky. One cloud formation looked like Julia's face smiling down at her. The night breezes soon blew the clouds over the trees and out of sight. But that imagined smiling face in the sky strengthened Mary, giving her the resolve to carry on and fulfil her promise to Julia to continue educating herself.

As Mary's thoughts went this way and that, she struggled to sleep. Her entire life had been a challenge with its ups and downs. She wondered if she was a curse to her loved ones—first Josiah, then Julia, and now Jim. Hmm! All *Js*, she thought. That's a coincidence. It was well into the early hours before she drifted into a fretful sleep.

* * *

The next morning, Mary arose with a new determination. Her thoughts turned to her sister, Lulu, and the smooth talking Joller in Francistown. It was almost two years since she last saw her sister, and she wondered if Joller kept his promise to divorce his wife and marry Lulu. It was time to find out.

But first, the question of Christmas dinner two days hence. Winston Smith and Andrew Jones were both busy with their family celebrations, but George Benson was at a loose end. Mary invited him, his maid, Eveline, and the other two maids, Monica and Clara, for the Christmas celebration.

The little group enjoyed themselves. The two days since the news of Jim's passing helped Mary to come to terms with it and relax a little. Unaccustomed to socialising with a white man, Eveline and the other maids were shy in George's presence. It amused Mary to note how the evening began with them calling him boss and ended with them calling him George. She wondered how Eveline would address her employer the next morning, once the effect of the champagne wore off.

Mary's Christmas dinner proved a fresh start for her neighbour. George invited the same small group to his house for New Year's Eve. The timid Eveline called George by his name, as did Monica and Clara, who exchanged hugs and kisses on the cheek upon their arrival. It was unlikely old George Benson would ever be lonely again.

* * *

George, in his younger days, drove the length and breadth of Zimbabwe on impromptu safaris in his old Land Rover, which stood idle in the carport next to his house. Mary sought his advice on a suitable vehicle to travel on Zimbabwe's deteriorating roads. Winston would help her complete the formalities of importing the vehicle from South Africa.

The first significant purchase with her inheritance was a brand new, white Toyota Land Cruiser Safari. The new car smell struck Mary, and she would never forget it. At first, the size intimidated her, as she made a cautious trip home in the large four-wheel drive. Previously, she'd only driven Julia's little blue Honda, which she'd reserve for running around town. It would take time to familiarise herself with her new vehicle.

Now an avid reader of the Bulawayo Chronicle, Mary kept abreast of all the local news in Bulawayo and Zimbabwe. An article about a missing five-year-old boy caught her eye. That's odd, she thought. It's the same article in the paper as when they published news of my arrest. But no, it said the boy disappeared only two days ago, also in the Figtree area. So, it must be a different boy.

Then Mary noticed an advertisement for the sale of a second-hand Toyota Land Cruiser at a higher price than the new one she imported.

She laughed at the funny ways of the world. She took the old tin box from the bedside table drawer. Mary opened it and carefully unfolded the piece of paper with Lulu's Francistown address. Soon, she would drive to Francistown to find her sister. Winston would tell her what formalities she must follow to take her vehicle over the border.

CHAPTER 37

The Reckoning

TIMOTHY jumped into the driver's seat, and with a big grin, he waved goodbye to Jackson Mpofu and Jonathan. The car, with its precious cargo, disappeared in a spray of water as it raced down the road through puddles from the previous night's rain. 'Sir, was it a good idea to give Timothy such an important task?' asked Jonathan.

'Well, he must learn to take responsibility.'

'Yes, Sir, but he's a boastful fellow. He might even let slip what he's up to if he goes to a beer hall and gets chatting with others. You saw how he drove off at speed. He's all show.'

'He wouldn't say what he's got in the boot.'

'It's because of him that Mary Moyo found out your involvement behind the offer we made her. And I know he told Silas what she said. What if he loses his nerve going through customs? Those customs men will soon notice someone who's acting suspicious.'

'You're not jealous because I gave him the job, are you?'

'No, Sir, I'm glad you didn't give it to me.'

'Jonathan, if something goes wrong, I can afford to lose Timothy. But you're my main man. I can't afford to lose you.'

'But four jobs in two years, Sir?'

'Yes, that's why I didn't want you to do it. Each time, it gets riskier.'

'Perhaps we should give it a break for now.'

'Perhaps, but the money is worth it. We procured the goods over a wide area, so no one will link it back to us.'

'Unless Timothy talks.'

'You're too cautious, Jonathan. To become a success, you must take chances. Being timid will only hold you back.'

'Yes, Sir, but can't we sell them in Zimbabwe? Why always over the border to Botswana?'

'Because the best bid comes from our customer in Botswana. He pays double what the locals offer. In Zimbabwe, we'd need twice the number of jobs to make it worthwhile, and that would attract attention.'

* * *

Jackson Mpofu was used to getting his own way. Ever since he joined the governing party, doors opened for him. And he didn't need to knock hard. Competence was not a requirement for members of parliament. Self-serving greed and loyalty to the president were all that was needed. Jackson found no difficulty in qualifying, as he found himself amongst like-minded colleagues in the national parliament in Harare.

He demanded absolute loyalty from his men, and for that reason, he recruited them from outside Matabeleland. That ensured there'd be no divided loyalties.

His ego could not bear the idea that a woman would challenge him. If his men had not been aware of Mary's challenge, he'd ignore her defiance. But now, he must save face. When Jackson heard the response from Khumalo's boss in Harare, he shook with rage. Upon discovering Mary worked as a maid in Bulawayo and was in front of the courts accused of murdering her employer, he thought the spirits had abandoned her. Now he saw he was mistaken, and neither he nor his men possessed the courage to tackle the woman who spoke to the spirits.

There was nothing stopping him from eliminating Inspector Kutumela, but he was only second prize. Jackson wondered how to deal with Mary. Perhaps he could find someone from outside who didn't hold with African superstitions. Maybe his contacts in Harare could introduce him to someone.

* * *

It happened the same night Jonathan brought back Khumalo's message. Outside was pitch black, with no moon and thick clouds hiding the stars.

Jackson sat on his back veranda, sipping a scotch. When he first noticed the rumbling, it sounded like distant, rolling thunder, and he scanned the horizon for signs of sheet lightning. It was early in the rainy season. Heavy storm clouds built each day, and thunder and lightning threatened each afternoon and evening.

A sudden flash of forked lightning followed by an ear-splitting crack of thunder made Jackson jump in alarm. An angry trumpet came in response. Jackson grabbed the torch from the table on which his tumbler of scotch sat. He flashed the beam into the darkness. Elephants! A large herd! They'd never come onto the farm before now.

'Jonathan, get the men! There're elephants in the maize field and vegetable gardens. They'll destroy everything!' A dozen of Jackson's workers raced out, beating drums, shouting, waving brooms and rakes—anything they could find.

It was not a good idea. The hungry elephants wouldn't move. Two bolder young ones charged the advancing men, who scattered like twigs in the wind. The trumpeting hastened their retreat as the beasts caught two of Jackson's men and crushed them like snails on a footpath.

Jackson ran into the house as an elephant charged towards him on the veranda. Another beast ran to the front garden, searching for the terrified men, but they'd scattered and hid in the bush. The angry elephant paced around before venting its rage on a vehicle parked nearby. It was Jackson's new Toyota Land Cruiser, which he'd driven for only one month. In the meantime, the rest of the herd stripped the maize field and vegetable garden of everything they fancied.

When the elephants left, Jackson called for his men. Only Jonathan and Silas appeared. 'Where are the others?'

'I don't know, Sir,' said Jonathan. 'They all ran from the elephants, and we haven't seen them since then.'

* * *

The next morning, Jackson surveyed the damage. The men had reappeared, milling around the front garden, muttering about evil spirits disguised as elephants. Abraham and Elvis were the unfortunates who the elephants caught and trampled.

'Jonathan, get this mess cleared. We'll achieve nothing by the men standing around grumbling.'

'Yes, Sir.'

Jackson walked back into the house and called for his maid to make his breakfast. 'Florence, where the hell are you?' Only silence greeted him. 'Jonathan, where is that damn maid? Why is she late?'

'I haven't seen her, Boss. I'll check her hut.'

A short time later, a breathless Jonathan reported back to Jackson. 'Boss, the men say Florence and her husband left during the night. They believe it was Mary's spirits who visited and caused the destruction. The men want to leave.'

'That's nonsense! Get the men together, and I'll talk to them.'

'OK, Boss.'

Only five men gathered to hear Jackson. 'Where are the others?'

'They've gone, Boss.'

'Gone! What's wrong with them?'

One man from the group spoke. 'They say Mary is coming and bringing more spirits with her. No one wants to work here anymore.'

As Jackson tried to speak, the wide-eyed and restless men slipped away one-by-one to gather their belongings and leave.

'Come back, fools! Cowards! Come back here!' Only Jonathan and Silas remained.

Jackson surveyed the scene devoid of his men, and an ominous silence took hold. 'Where's Timothy? He should be back by now.'

* * *

Jackson looked in the pantry and found a packet of cream crackers. He was hungry after missing breakfast. The fridge and the pantry looked bare, and Jackson cursed the idle maid under his breath. As he spread margarine on the dry biscuits, he was glad it wasn't butter that went hard in the fridge. Just then, the phone rang.

'Hello.'

'Jackson Mpofu?'

'Yes.'

'This is Inspector Dube from the Figtree police station.'

'Yes, Dube, what is it?'

'I've just received a phone call from the Botswana police. They have your man, Timothy, in custody.'

Mpofu swallowed. 'Why?'

'Smuggling a live child across the border to sell for body parts.'

'I was wondering where he was. He disappeared with one of my cars, and I was going to report it stolen if he didn't return by this evening.'

'Is that so? Timothy is claiming you are behind the scheme.'

'You don't believe that nonsense, do you?'

'Well, the villagers in the area do. They're coming for you.'

'What do you mean?'

'The villagers caught one of your runaways this morning. He said Mary Moyo was coming with her spirits to punish you for abducting children for body parts. They say the elephant raid last night was the sign of her imminent arrival.'

'You can't believe those superstitious fools.'

'I am told you are also superstitious, Mpofu.'

'Yes, but—'

'Listen, there's no time to argue. If I were you, I'd leave as fast as possible before the villagers get to your farm. I'm leaving the police station now to give you convoy protection. I can only hope we're there in time to help you.' The phone went dead.

'Jonathan, get the car! Silas, we must leave!'

The new Land Cruiser was undrivable, so they jumped into the old Land Cruiser and charged down the road, heading for Marula. They raced past the boom gate that the deserting men left open. At the point where Jackson's private road joined the road to the village, a crowd of villagers gathered. Angry shouts of 'Here he is,' rang out.

Stones and clods of earth hit the car, and a large rock smashed through the windscreen. Someone hit a side window with a knobkerrie, spraying shards of glass onto the rear seat next to Silas. Jackson put his foot down, ignoring the risk he presented to the angry villagers who ran in all directions. 'Imagine those fools thinking they could stop us from passing.'

'Look, Sir, there's another group ahead.'

Jackson looked in the direction Jonathan pointed. A crowd from another village stood on both sides of the road, waving knobkerries and sticks. A boulder sat on the road. To swerve would mean the ditch. Too late anyway. Jackson drove straight over it, creating a massive, crunching thud under the Land Cruiser. The vehicle almost stalled before picking up revs again and racing onwards. Rocks showered the Land Cruiser, adding further dents to the body.

The speeding vehicle bounced along the rough dirt road, shaking its occupants. Two or three villages remained in their path before reaching Marula. Jackson hoped the information extracted from his runaway was yet to reach those villages where one of the missing children lived. 'How did that stupid runaway know we abducted the children?'

'I warned you, Boss. Timothy talks too much. He must have boasted about his new task to the others.'

'And then that fool gets himself caught by Botswana customs.'

Jonathan remained silent. Another 'I told you so' might draw the boss's fury onto him.

A looming vehicle ahead proved to be Inspector Dube and Sergeant Sibanda in the old police Land Rover. The vehicles stopped nose to nose, and Inspector Dube jumped out and hurried over to Jackson Mpofu's window. 'Villagers are gathering down the road, so we better hurry. I'll put the siren on to warn the villagers to move aside. You better drive close as possible, but don't drive into us. We're going to drive fast, so be careful.'

Sergeant Sibanda made a three-point turn in the Land Rover and switched on the siren before racing down the dirt road. The speed of his acceleration caught Jackson by surprise, and he put his foot down hard as he struggled to catch up with the police vehicle.

The news of gathering crowds ahead spurred Jackson's efforts to keep up with the Land Rover, which seemed determined to leave them behind. Jackson was unaccustomed to driving at speed, and the blood drained from Jonathan's face as he turned a shade of grey.

Rocks and clods of earth struck both the police Land Rover and Jackson's Land Cruiser as they raced past angry villagers along the dirt road. But to Jackson's relief, the police escort discouraged the gathering villagers from presenting too much of a threat.

At the police station, Inspector Dube placed Jackson Mpofu and Jonathan under arrest and locked them in a cell.

'The commissioner general will hear about this,' Jackson shouted.

'It's for your own protection,' Inspector Dube replied. 'I wouldn't like to be in your shoes if those villagers catch you.'

'Well, let us drive on to Bulawayo.'

'What, in a car in that condition? You'd be a danger on the roads.'

* * *

Dube always arrived at the police station early, before the others. But on this morning, as he opened the door, the loud bellow of the officer-in-charge, Chief Inspector Ernest Mlambo, greeted him. 'Dube, my office, now!'

'Yes, Sir?'

'What on earth do you think you're doing, arresting Jackson Mpofu? Have you gone mad? You know he's a government member of parliament.'

'Yes, Sir, but he's not a minister.'

'But he might be soon. What if he's made the minister in charge of police? Have you thought of that? Your career would be finished.'

'He won't be re-elected, Sir, judging by the mood of his constituents. But I'll make him a morning cup of tea before he gets even more irritable.'

'He's not here, Dube. I've withdrawn the charge for his arrest. He and his men left for Bulawayo ten minutes before you arrived.'

Dube spluttered in indignation. 'You can't do that! Didn't you read the charge sheet? He's accused of abducting and selling children across the border for body parts.'

'Don't be naïve, Dube. You know how things are. Let the government handle it. It's not up to us. Have you not wondered why I'm in so early this morning? The chief superintendent was not pleased to be woken at five o'clock by the commissioner's phone call. The orders to release Mpofu have come from high. There's nothing you can do about it.'

Dube stormed out of the chief inspector's office. One law for the villagers, another for the bigwigs. He doubted justice would prevail in Harare.

CHAPTER 38

Francistown

MARY set out early for her drive to Francistown after a quick breakfast of Jungle Oats and a hot cup of tea. She headed down Hillside Road towards the city and turned left onto 14th Avenue. At six in the morning, the city streets were quiet. She didn't want to drive her new Land Cruiser in rush-hour traffic, though she would only clip the edge of the city matrix. Six blocks farther, she turned left again and headed out on the Plumtree Road.

The drive took Mary past the idle, decaying factory buildings abandoned by companies, following the government's drive to move industry to Harare. Soon, on the right, she passed the huge Dunlop tyre factory, overgrown with long grass. It was many years since the last tyres rolled off the production line. A lack of foreign exchange and raw materials brought the manufacturing plant to an end.

A small area of old, low-cost housing preceded scattered African townships on the right before Mary drove out onto the open road. Figtree, only thirty-six kilometres, was a short drive from Bulawayo, but the condition of the road meant it would take about forty minutes. She should make it by seven o'clock.

Mary passed pedestrians, a handful of cars, bicycles, and donkey carts. It was her first experience of driving outside the city limits, and so different from driving in the suburbs. The city, with its stop-start driving and ninety-degree corners, contrasted with the long straight sections and gentle curves of the country road. Somehow, she needed to concentrate harder on her driving on the open road with its potholes, occasional pedestrians, and other slow-moving traffic.

As she drove into Figtree, Mary noticed a single police Land Rover in front of the police station. Perhaps Sergeant Dube was there? She pulled up next to the vehicle, being careful to lock her Land Cruiser before entering the building.

On the front desk, a young police constable sat yawning into his clenched fist. 'Can I help you, Madam?'

Mary noted with satisfaction, her fine clothes brought her a new level of respect from strangers and friends, alike. 'Yes, I'm looking for Sergeant Dube.'

'Sergeant Dube is an inspector since last year, Madam. One moment, please.' The young constable noisily pushed back his stool on the wooden floor and walked down the passage to an office near the cell Mary slept in two years earlier, on her way to Bulawayo.

A stout figure with a neat moustache came up to the front desk. 'What can I do for you, Madam?'

'Inspector Dube, you don't recognise me?'

The inspector stared for several seconds before responding in an uncertain voice. 'Mary? Is that you?'

Mary smiled.

'Good heavens, it's you! I can't believe it! What's happened to you?'

'I've met good fortune since we waited outside together for the Bulawayo bus.'

'You look wonderful! Constable, put the kettle on for tea! Come to my office and tell me what you've been doing. Those trumped-up charges about murdering your employer turned out well for you.'

'Yes, they did. I loved my employer. She was my best friend and like a grandmother to me. I would have done nothing to harm her. All my good fortune is thanks to her.'

'Are you going to visit your village? They often ask about you, but I tell them I know nothing.'

'No, I can't visit the village, in case I bump into Jackson Mpofu. Somehow, he found out where I live, and sent two of his men to say they'd get the murder charges dropped if I gave him a share of the money from the sale of my house.'

'You don't have to worry about Jackson Mpofu anymore. The villagers drove him off his property because they suspected he was behind the missing children. Mpofu left for Harare two days ago. I doubt he'll be back here or contest the coming election.'

'Oh! Well, I may visit the village on my way back from Francistown.'

'Francistown?'

'Yes, I'm hoping to find my sister Lulu. She's with a man who owns a menswear shop there. He said he'd divorce his wife and marry Lulu, but I didn't trust him.'

'A friend of mine is a police inspector in Francistown who's investigating the missing children's case. If you need any help, just call me.'

'Thank you. I better go now, before it gets too late.'

'Francistown is about one hundred and fifty kilometres. Almost a three-hour drive on these roads, but crossing the border takes time.'

Mary glanced at her watch. 'Hmm, half past seven, so I should be there around lunchtime.'

Inspector Dube watched Mary disappear into the distance in the shiny white Land Cruiser. He marvelled at the change in the village woman he once knew.

Mary switched on the radio to listen to the music and rolled down the windows to let the warm country air embrace her. It was an exhilarating experience. No wonder Julia wanted to accompany her to Francistown. She always said she loved driving on the open road.

Within half an hour, she passed through Marula and the turnoff to her village, and thirty minutes later she passed through Plumtree. Now it was only a sixteen-kilometre drive to Vakaranga Siding on the Botswana border. As Dube predicted, passing through the border post was a dreary one-and-a-half-hour process. But the ninety-minute drive from the border to Francistown passed in a flash.

The size of the city surprised her. It was bigger and busier than she expected. Nothing like Bulawayo, but it was lively with a sense of business activity. Francistown was a city-on-the-move, while Bulawayo's atmosphere was one of a faded past.

Mary found a small, bright cafe to stop for an early lunch. Tea and a toasted cheese sandwich would perk her up to face the afternoon. While she waited for her order, she checked her phone. There was no service. The lady who served her gave Mary directions to the address Lulu scribbled on the scrap of paper when she visited her village with Joller.

The shop on the north-eastern edge of the city stood separated from its nearest neighbours by a dusty two hundred metres. Its unusual location in the middle of scrubby open ground made it look forgotten, yet conspicuous. There were two shops on the site. Dante's Menswear on the right, and Dante's Hairdressing on the left. Splitting the shopfronts was a passage leading to a high, wide wooden door resembling a barn.

Mary surveyed the area to make sure no unsavoury individuals loitered nearby. There was no sign of anyone, but she locked the car, just in case. She expected the shop to be deep because of the fifty-metre exterior wall stretching back from the entrance. But once inside, the shop was tiny, like the barber shop it mirrored.

A small, bespectacled, balding man stood behind the counter. 'Can I help you?'

'Is this Joller's shop?'

'Yes, but he's not here. You'll have to come back later.'

Something about the tone of his voice put Mary on her guard. 'I'm not looking for Joller. I want to see my sister who works for him in this shop.'

The man gave a derisive snort. 'No women work in this shop. I work here every day.'

Mary looked past him through the open doorway behind the counter. A short flight of steps led down to a dusty courtyard. Rooms on either side gave it the look of a former motel. Half-a-dozen women milled around in the courtyard, while others sat in rickety chairs on the narrow verandas that ran the length of the building. 'My sister's name is Lulu.'

'No one here has that name.'

'Can I speak to the women? They may know her.'

'No! There's no one called Lulu. You must go now!'

'Then I'll wait for Joller to arrive. He knows her.'

'No! You must go! Rocky, come here!'

Mary heard the shop door open, and a huge African man loomed up beside her.

'This woman must leave now. Make sure she goes.'

Mary was about to object, but then glimpsed a familiar figure in the courtyard. 'There! That might be her! That might be my sister, Lulu.'

The little man slammed the door shut. He snapped at Rocky, 'Make sure she leaves!' The shop assistant's blazing eyes and shrill voice sent a shiver down her spine. His snarling mouth exposed yellow, rotting teeth, reminding her of the village dogs. 'It will be bad for you if you return.'

Mary felt Rocky's huge hand grab her upper arm and drag her from the shop. He waited, arms akimbo, until she got back into her car. She slammed her foot on the accelerator, creating a spray of dust and stones aimed at the big man and the shop front.

After she was back in the town centre, she parked and thought about her next step. The little man's aggressive manner was most alarming. Mary returned to the cafe where she'd eaten lunch earlier and asked the woman where she could buy a prepaid sim card.

In the next block, the helpful assistant fitted the prepaid sim card into her phone. Now she returned to her car and phoned Inspector Dube to tell him what had happened.

'It sounds fishy to me. I'll call Inspector Mogotsi and tell him what you've said. He's a good man. I'm sure he'll help you. Give me your new number so he can contact you. And I'll give you his number, just in case there's an unforeseen problem.'

Mary waited in the Land Cruiser, checking the time every few minutes. Perhaps she should call Dube back to ask what was happening. But a minute later, the phone rang.

'Mary, Inspector Mogotsi here. Where are you? I'll come and get you.'

Within minutes, Inspector Mogotsi's Land Rover pulled up in a parking space next to her. A police constable sat next to him. Another police car with four occupants found a parking nearby.

'Right, Mary, get in the Land Rover. We must move fast before Joller moves the women. He's a slippery customer and somehow always persuades the court we've misjudged him. Dube told me what happened. This time we may have caught Joller on the hop.'

Mary jumped in the back of Mogotsi's vehicle, and they sped off towards Dante's Menswear. The inspector needed no directions as the other police car raced along behind them. Within two or three minutes, the police cars slid to a halt in front of Joller's building. The police jumped from the vehicles and raced through the shop to the courtyard, startling the bespectacled shop assistant who tried to shrink into a corner. There was no sign of Rocky. The courtyard stood deserted, but the police entered the rooms and brought the women out. Someone said Joller was on his way, but the little shop assistant dared not try to warn him of the police presence. He could only stare daggers at Mary, who waited impatiently for the sight of Lulu.

A small crowd of women, some with babies, gathered in the courtyard. When the police emptied all the rooms, Inspector Mogotsi invited Mary to enter the courtyard and check if Lulu was there. Mary's knees trembled as she descended the steps to the dusty ground. The women were hushed as they watched her approach. What could she want of them?

Mary walked down the line of women, most with their heads bowed, not wanting to meet her gaze. With no sign of Lulu as she neared the end of the line, a sense of panic rose in her throat. Then the last one, holding a toddler, looked directly at her and gasped. 'Sister, it's you!'

The two women flung their arms around each other, and the tears flowed. They barely recognised one another. Lulu, the 'modern, city woman' from two years earlier, now looked tired and worn, but the former poor village woman now resembled a wealthy city madam.

'Leave this place! Come home with me.'

'Yes, I will, but I must bring my little boy, Charlie.'

'Yes, of course.'

Mary felt the tug on her arm. 'It's me, Mary, Agnes, Mechanic's daughter.' Agnes began to cry. 'I don't like it here, Mary. Can I come with you?'

* * *

The police interviewed all the women and took notes. They arrested the little shop assistant and the barber next door, who angrily protested his innocence. The constables led them to a police van that arrived to help in the proceedings.

Inspector Mogotsi dropped Mary, Agnes, Lulu, and Charlie back at the Land Cruiser. Darkness was falling as Mary drove her group to the Diggers Inn Hotel, where they would spend the night. The three women and Charlie were famished, following the afternoon's excitement. Afterwards, a comfortable bed awaited them.

In the morning, the group was to drive the half-dozen blocks to the police station for a debrief with Inspector Mogotsi. Also, there was the 'small matter' of their repatriation to Zimbabwe. The police recovered Lulu's passport from the safe in the menswear shop. But Agnes and Charlie possessed no travel documents.

It was early to bed, and neither Lulu nor Mary spoke about the intervening two years since they last met. The long drive to Bulawayo would give them the opportunity for that.

CHAPTER 39

The Homecoming

AFTER the debrief, and an interview with Lulu and Agnes, Inspector Mogotsi followed Mary's Land Cruiser to the Vakaranga border post with Zimbabwe. They found Inspector Dube waiting at the border when they arrived. The two inspectors helped smooth their path through immigration, as Agnes and Charlie didn't have any papers or identification.

While the stony-faced immigration officers completed the formalities, the inspectors huddled in a hushed conversation. This time, Mary's passage through the border post proved quicker than on her way into Botswana. Soon, she thanked Inspector Mogotsi for his help and waved him goodbye.

Outside the Zimbabwean border post, standing by the police Land Rover, the former Constable Sibanda now proudly wore sergeant stripes. His jaw dropped when he caught sight of her.

'We've all progressed in the world, Madam.'

'Yes, Sergeant Sibanda, we have.'

Inspector Dube joined them. 'Mary, may I suggest Sergeant Sibanda takes the others in the Land Rover, and I come with you? We need to discuss a few things.'

Mary and Inspector Dube drove out of the border post parking area, with Sergeant Sibanda and the others following them.

'It's good you got your sister out of there, Mary. Inspector Mogotsi gave me interesting news.'

Mary switched off the radio to give Dube her full attention.

'Mogotsi said they caught one of Jackson Mpofu's men, Timothy, smuggling a young boy through the border post.'

'Timothy came to my house with Jonathan. They're the ones I told you about when I dropped in to visit you on my way to Francistown.'

'Well, Timothy says that Jackson was behind the whole missing child business, and he also implicated Jonathon. But you'll never guess who their customer in Botswana was.'

'Don't tell me it was....'

'Yes, the man you know as Joller. This was his fourth attempt to smuggle a child into Botswana to be sold for body parts for making muti (medicine). Most of the children he sold, he found in the local area, but people got suspicious, so he switched his attention to Zimbabwe.'

'I knew that man was evil.'

'But that's not all. The women working in his brothel gave birth to babies who disappeared soon after they could walk. The women believe Joller stole their babies for the same muti trade. If you waited any longer to rescue your sister from that man, her baby may have also gone missing.'

A shiver ran through Mary at the thought of the body parts trade and the likely fate that Charlie eluded. Fortune indeed favoured her.

The miles melted away between the chit chat with Dube and her thoughts of the evil men she'd encountered.

Dube continued. 'Mary, in Africa, news travels fast, doesn't it? Despite the lack of cell phone coverage or other modern means of communication, the villagers found out you passed through Figtree yesterday. They're expecting a visit from you.'

'We must return Agnes to her family, and with Mpofu gone, it's an opportunity for me to see the village again.'

'Let's stop at Marula for tea and sandwiches, and afterwards, we can go on to your village.'

* * *

Mary drove down the familiar road she walked on over two years earlier. Her anticipation got the better of her. A lump rose in her throat as she passed the turnoff to Jackson Mpofu's farm. A short drive further, she emerged from the forest onto the sweeping road, circumventing the undulating grassy valley. There on the hill stood her village with its huts silhouetted against the blue sky. As she ascended the rise to the village, the huts momentarily blended into the backdrop of the ridge.

The two vehicles rolled into the village centre, where an excited crowd waited to welcome them. Several shouted Mary's name. The numbers suggested many must have come from nearby villages as news of her pending arrival spread.

'How did they know I'd come here today, Dube?' said a surprised Mary. 'No one's had time to warn them.'

'Who can say, Mary? That's the magic of Africa.'

Mary got out of the Land Cruiser and the villagers rushed forward to greet her and touch her. 'Mary's back! She's back!' they shouted. Even Nancy, her fair-weather friend, sheepishly welcomed her.

Mechanic was overjoyed to see his daughter, Agnes. When the exuberant gathering calmed, Mechanic gave a small speech, welcoming Mary's visit to the village. 'The spirits told Mary my daughter needed to be rescued. They told her where she would find Agnes, and Mary took up the challenge and saved her for our family.'

A party atmosphere enveloped the village, and from nowhere, food and drinks emerged. Mary's homecoming excited the people, many of whom she didn't recognise. She addressed the crowd. 'The spirits expect me to return to them, but I will visit here more often. That is my promise.'

In a quiet moment, Mary spoke to Dube. 'Why are they all treating me like someone special? This reminds me of the time when Dennis Nyathi came to see me to ask for my support for his political campaign.'

'They heard you predicted the end of Jackson Mpofu and then the elephants came. Everybody said you asked the spirits to send them. When the rumours of your return started, Mpofu's men deserted him, and all the villagers in the area rebelled against him. If you're wondering why they think you're special now, wait until the villagers find out your part in ending the child abductions. You truly communicate with the spirits, Mary.'

Mary took the door key from her purse, where it lay since the morning she left for Bulawayo. She opened her hut door with trepidation and entered the musty room. It was an emotional moment, and her breath caught in her throat. She'd been happy here with Josiah, but only now she realised how far she'd come since she left the village. Tears welled up in her eyes.

It shocked her to see how she once lived. She remembered it, of course, but being back felt so different. She was now a wealthy, apparently educated lady, but she knew how much she still needed to learn. Her appearance and speaking voice made others deferential towards her. But she felt a fraud, playing a part like the days she gave advice to people while mumbling over the magic book. She whispered to herself, 'Julia, I promise you I will become the person people think I am. All thanks to you.'

Mary sensed the sudden presence of someone standing in the room behind her. It was Lulu. 'Mary, when I visited you here before, I said I was a modern, city woman, and I'd never live like this. But now, I thank The Lord, he has freed me to join you as a village woman.'

Mary laughed. 'Lulu, I don't live here anymore. I live in Bulawayo, and so will you. You will again become a modern, city woman. I suppose, much like I am. And Charlie will go to the best schools and become a modern, city gentleman one day.'

* * *

The celebrations showed no signs of ending, so Mary said goodbye to the villagers, and the two-vehicle convoy headed down the hill, around the sweeping dirt road, and disappeared into the tall trees.

After her departure, the villagers remembered the purpose of their gathering and drifted down to the burial plot near the river where they'd left poor old Aaron's body beside the freshly dug grave. He'd no close relatives, but the villagers came out of respect to lay him to rest.

A murmur ran through the shocked crowd when they discovered Aaron was missing. Rumours of Mary's return were rife, so when someone glimpsed the approaching vehicles in the distance, the mourners all rushed back to the village and forgot about him. Where could he be?

Mechanic suggested a crocodile may have taken the body. The bare rocks between the grave and the river made it difficult to find evidence to support his theory, as no obvious drag marks could be seen. But then, someone said the spirits that surrounded Mary may have taken him. From there, the imaginations ran wild. Some swore they'd seen him walking off with the spirits, and one or two others swore they'd seen him in the Land Cruiser, sitting next to Mary as she drove out of the village.

* * *

Dube promised to keep Mary updated with any developments around the missing children and Jackson Mpofu. She waved goodbye to Dube and Sibanda and drove off with Lulu and Charlie, heading for home. Dusk soon descended, and by the time they reached Bulawayo, the city's twinkling lights glowed in the darkness.

Mary left home only yesterday morning, but the events of the past two days made it seem much longer. Back in her kitchen, she made a light supper before preparing her old room for Lulu and Charlie. Mary would now sleep in Julia's bed for the first time since her dear friend died.

'Can we stay here?' said Lulu, looking around the house with her mouth open in awe.

'Yes, it's my house.'

'Your house! How is it your house?'

Mary and Lulu were yet to exchange their stories and experiences since they last saw one another. The excitement and long drive proved draining and gave them little chance to discuss things.

'It's a long story, Lulu. I'll tell you tomorrow.'

* * *

The rainy season was ending, but warm days would continue for the next month or two. Lulu and Charlie settled in fine, though Mary's sister faced a culture shock. She marvelled at Mary's circumstances and struggled to fit in with her circle of friends. How could her uneducated older sister be so close to these people? Both she and Mary never attended school, yet Mary's friends: the doctor, the lawyer, and the neighbour, seemed to idolise her.

How would she, Lulu, socialise with them? Now that she thought about it, even Mary spoke funny—all this talk about long vowels, and constantly correcting her pronunciation. Lulu found Mary's efforts to improve her speech irksome. But isn't it what older sisters are for—to be irritating?

Mary's friends accepted Lulu without question, and soon Lulu and Charlie were a regular part of the gang. Diversity worked well in Bulawayo, but Lulu realised she needed to follow in Mary's footsteps to fit in this new world. Charlie would soon adapt to this environment, but she'd have to work hard to reinvent herself. Perhaps Mary's older-sister act would be helpful after all.

Lulu looked to make friends amongst the housemaids, where she hoped to relax and speak Ndebele without worrying about her accent or whether she used the right words. But she soon discovered Mary's friends amongst the housemaids, Eveline, Monica, and Clara, always seemed to include the neighbour, old George Benson, in their get-togethers, so they ended up speaking English. Now Lulu understood why Mary referred to the three as 'George's girls.' The other maids suited Lulu better, but even they held Mary in awe. Lulu was appreciating her sister's talent for gathering the support and love of those around her. Yet Mary insisted she was nothing special and seemed oblivious to the way others viewed her. 'I was just lucky to meet someone like Julia.'

* * *

The phone rang, but Lulu hesitated to pick up the receiver. Mary insisted she learn the proper way to answer the phone, though Lulu didn't see the need. 'But why do you insist I learn the right words for answering the phone? The calls are never for me,' she'd argue. Lulu rose from her armchair with a sigh, dropping the magazine she was reading on the coffee table. Mary wasn't nearby, so Lulu answered in her own way. 'Hello.'

'Hello, Inspector Dube here. Is Mary there, please?'

'I'll call her.'

Lulu walked to the vegetable garden to find Mary. Her sister always seemed to be digging, planting, or harvesting something. Why did her wealthy sister do that? It was village women's work. Lulu avoided those tasks as she feared chipping her painted nails. Since her arrival, she'd taken on the more genteel indoor duties of dusting and polishing, leaving most of the physical work to Mary, who possessed an inexhaustible energy for such things. 'Phone call for you. It's that police officer.'

'You mean Inspector Dube?'

'Yes, that's the one.'

'Well, you better keep an eye on Charlie here. He enjoys helping me in the vegetable garden.'

Lulu watched Mary disappear into the house and shook her head. With all her money and looks, Mary should frequent nightclubs and restaurants and enjoy life. She shouldn't waste her time reading books and doing village women's work.

Mary hurried to the telephone table by the front door, slipping off her gardening gloves to pick up the receiver. 'Good morning, Inspector Dube.'

'Hi Mary, I have interesting news for you. Inspector Mogotsi confirmed Joller was the customer for the missing children, but his wife was the mastermind behind the entire scheme. She would send Joller out to charm young women with promises of marriage and a job in his menswear shop. When they arrived, the pair would force them into prostitution, with threats of dire consequences if they refused.'

'That's what happened to Lulu.'

'Yes, the women were trapped, often far from home, with no money or support. So Joller and his wife made money from their brothel and from selling the women's illegitimate children for making muti from body parts. The menswear shop was a tiny part of their business and used as a cover for their illegal activities. The hairdresser was legitimate and only rented the shop from Joller. So they've released him, but Joller and his wife remain in custody. They've confirmed Jackson Mpofu was one of their suppliers of abducted children.'

'Any news of Jackson?'

'No, nothing.'

'Who's looking after the farm?'

'No one. It's deserted since Jackson's men all left. The villagers won't go near the place. They say it's cursed.'

After Dube said goodbye, Mary put down the receiver and then picked it up again and dialled Winston Smith's number. He answered the call almost at once.

'Winston, I wonder if you could do me a favour, please?'

'Of course, Mary. What is it?'

CHAPTER 40

Family Ties

MARY fussed about dusting the books on the bookshelf while her sister sat in an armchair reading a magazine, whilst 'keeping an eye' on Charlie, playing on the carpet near her feet.

'Lulu!'

'Uh-huh.'

'We should visit our father and find out how he's doing.'

'What! Why?'

'I haven't seen him for over five years, and you, over four years.'

'So?'

'Well, he's getting older, and we don't know his condition. It's our duty to check on him, and we should introduce him to Charlie.'

'Father and his second wife made me unwelcome at home. He never stood up for me against her. He's a weak man.'

'You were old enough to leave home.'

'Yes! And look what happened!'

'It'll only be a brief visit. We won't be staying there.'

'If you must go, I'll come, but I don't like the idea.'

'OK, we'll go tomorrow.'

Lulu grimaced. 'Whatever!'

* * *

Next morning at breakfast, Mary wore a white T-shirt and conservative pants. Lulu came to the table dressed in one of her best dresses and bright red painted nails.

'We're not going there to impress them, Lulu. I don't want them to realise how we live. It will seem like we're boasting.'

'Father's second wife never stopped telling me how well-off she was.'

'Well, we'll soon find out.'

After breakfast, Mary put a plastic bag into the little blue Honda's boot.

'What are you doing?' said Lulu.

'Taking meat for father.'

'Why are we travelling in that thing? I thought it was only for running around town.'

'Father's village is closer than my village, and the road is better.'

'The Land Cruiser would be more comfortable.'

'Lulu, I told you, we don't want them to see how we live.'

'That old car will make it a slow, tiring journey.'

'I've already put the child seat in for Charlie. This car will be fine.'

'You're funny, Mary. Everyone with money likes to show others how rich they are, but you want to keep it a secret.'

'It's better that way.'

Lulu rolled her eyes. 'Well, I better strap Charlie into the child seat, then.'

* * *

The little blue Honda buzzed along the Plumtree Road, eating up the kilometres.

'Don't you think this old car goes well, Lulu?'

'It's OK, but imagine their faces if we drove up in the Land Cruiser.'

'Hmm, maybe another time.'

The well-maintained little car purred, with the windows wide open and the radio playing. Lulu was silent, and after a time, Mary noticed.

'Is something wrong, Lulu?'

'I don't like this road, with all its bad memories. First, me leaving home, and then going to Francistown with Joller.'

At Figtree, Mary turned right, circumvented the tiny village, and headed into the bush. A little further on, she turned right again onto a familiar narrow dirt track.

'Didn't you say this road was better than the one to your village?'

'Well, isn't it?'

'Not much better.'

Soon, they got close to their childhood village. 'Must we do this, Mary? Can't we just turn around and find somewhere for lunch?'

Before Mary could answer, they rolled into the village centre, attracting a small crowd of children. A stern-looking woman watched their arrival with unwelcoming eyes.

'That's Winifred, Papa's second wife.'

Mary got out of the car while Lulu unstrapped Charlie from the child seat.

'Winifred, this is my sister, Mary, and my son, Charlie.'

'I'll call your father.' Winifred turned and walked into her hut, with no word of greeting to Lulu or Mary. The sister's eyes met with Lulu's expression saying, I told you so.

A tall, grey man emerged from the hut and stared at the visitors. He was much heavier than Mary remembered.

'Papa, it's us, Mary and Lulu, come to visit you. This is Charlie, Lulu's son.'

The man grunted. There was no smile or welcoming hug for his daughters.

'How are you, Papa?' said Mary.

Her father didn't acknowledge her question but said, 'Come, we can sit under that tree on those logs.'

'How are our sisters, Papa?' said Mary.

'Meredith, your middle sister, ran off soon after Lulu.'

'I never ran off,' Lulu said. 'You and Winifred didn't want me here.'

'But you knew I needed lobola for the two youngest.'

'You only saw me as a source of money. I didn't want to be married off to someone I'd never met.'

'Ah! Here come your two youngest sisters.'

The girls walked up and stood behind their father. One appeared shy, but the other looked hostile.

'Both are doing well at school. Olga will go to university to study to become a teacher. Carol wants to be a nurse.'

'They'll have a better chance of achieving their dreams than we did,' said Lulu.

Her father ignored Lulu's comment and turned to Mary. 'So, why have you come here? Don't expect us to give you money.'

'Mary flushed. We came to see you. We don't want your money.'

'Now that you see we are fine, it's better you go.' The girls' father stood up, signalling the end of the meeting.

'Papa, I've brought meat for you.' Mary hurried over to the car and retrieved the bag from the boot.

Her father looked in the plastic carry bag and grunted. 'Do you think we are short of food? Winifred is wealthy, and she has enough money for all of us.' Then, turning towards the little blue Honda, he said, 'Is that your husband's car?'

'No, my husband is dead. It's my car.'

Her father turned and walked into the hut, followed by his two youngest daughters. Mary and Lulu waited for several minutes, but no one emerged from the hut. The sisters exchanged glances in disbelief. Lulu strapped Charlie into his child seat and got into the passenger seat next to Mary, who waited with her hands clenched on the steering wheel.

'I can't believe it,' said Mary. 'He didn't even acknowledge Charlie, or invite us into the hut, or offer us something to drink.'

'I warned you,' said Lulu. 'That woman has him under her control. She never said one word to us and just stayed inside the hut. And our two sisters never spoke to us either.'

'Papa seemed to resent us. He hasn't forgiven you for depriving him of lobola from your marriage.'

'If I'd stayed, Father would've married me off to any fat old man who offered the highest lobola.'

The women drove back to Bulawayo in silence. Each lost in their own thoughts. Lulu, rebellious to the end, and Mary, subdued. There was no opportunity to make their peace with their father. The family seemed irretrievably split.

'You were right not to show them how we lived,' said Lulu. 'If they realised how rich you are, they'd have been much more welcoming. And it would've been a false reconciliation. At least now, you know their true feelings. There's no room for us.'

Mary wiped a tear from her cheek. What happened to that jolly, loving father she remembered from her childhood?

'Can you remember when I visited you in your village? I told you Joller suspected Papa was involved in Mama's death. Joller was a bad man, but people couldn't fool him. Bad men are quick to recognise evil.'

'Lulu, I can't believe Papa did anything like that.'

'Then how do you explain his behaviour today?'

Mary couldn't answer that question. There was no rational explanation for the way he rejected them.

By the time they reached Bulawayo, flashes of lightning and loud thunder rocked the sky, and the air smelled of rain. Mary was pleased to be home after the longer than expected return journey, which emotionally drained her. Mary's cosy, modest house gave no hint of the wealth of the occupant, but she loved it. It was home.

CHAPTER 41

Action Ma'am

MARY drove her Land Cruiser with a relaxed ease. She no longer viewed every other road user with nervous anticipation. Her passenger, dressed in khaki shirt and shorts and grey Bata veldskoens, was not in the least bit apprehensive as he enjoyed the passing view. 'It's been a long time since I've passed this way. Do you drive out here often?'

'Yes, but only recently,' said Mary. 'Bulawayo is my home now. Everything changed for the better when I moved there.'

'How did you find me?'

'I didn't. My friend Winston Smith found you and gave me your number. There are few whites in Bulawayo, so I knew he'd soon track you down.'

'Yes, most whites left Zimbabwe for South Africa, the UK, and elsewhere. I was planning on making the move myself, but now I'm glad I stuck around.'

'What have you been doing since you left the farm?'

'Nothing much. Just odd jobs and trying to preserve what little money I kept under my mattress.'

'It couldn't have been easy for you.'

'It wasn't, but I was lucky I had friends in Bulawayo, and that helped.'

'Any family here?'

'No, they've all gone to the UK and Australia.'

'And you never married?'

'No, I never got around to it.'

Mary drove through Figtree without stopping and continued for another twenty-five minutes to the turnoff at Marula. The first part of the dirt road was easy going, but after they turned onto the narrow dirt road leading to Mary's village, the track became bumpy, and the sea of yellow grass closed in on both sides of the vehicle.

It was a beautiful, sunny day, with a gentle breeze pushing the tall, yellow grass one way and then another. A clear blue sky with scattered puffy white clouds in the distance. The top-of-the-range Land Cruiser dampened the effect of the rutted dirt road, formed by the lingering impact of vehicles in the rainy season. But now the dirt road was as hard as concrete under the African sun. Only time and traffic in the winter months would help smooth out the ruts.

Just before the forest of tall trees, Mary followed the right fork in the track, heading to Jackson Mpofu's farm. They drove past the open boom gate and on to the rambling farmhouse. To the right lay the crushed wreckage of Jackson Mpofu's new government-supplied black Land Cruiser.

'Well, here we are, John. How does it look?'

'Not too bad from the outside. Let's go in and check.'

Mary and her companion walked up to the front door and tried it. It was unlocked.

'Not too bad at all, Mary. Jackson didn't live like a pig. He's looked after the place. There's even stuff in the fridge. Too bad the milk is off, or we could've made tea.'

'We'd need to start the generator first. There's no electricity.'

A walk through the house confirmed it was in good condition. In the hallway, a rack of fishing rods stood along one wall. Under the stairs was a locked gun cupboard. The keys hung on a nail, high in one corner. John reached for them and found the key that opened the cupboard. Inside were two rifles, two shotguns, and boxes of ammunition.

'Let's inspect the gardens,' said Mary.

They walked through to the back veranda that looked onto the maize field and vegetable gardens.

John whistled through his teeth. 'This mess needs a lot of work. It almost looks like those elephants were vindictive, with an agenda to punish Jackson for his crimes. No wonder he left in a hurry.'

'He was running from the villagers, not the elephants.'

'Yeah, maybe he was running from both.'

'Well, what do you say? Are you interested?'

'Yes, I'll sort things out here. But what about labour? Didn't you tell me the villagers thought the place was cursed?'

'Don't worry, they'll be keen for jobs once I lift the curse.'

'You? How can you lift the curse?'

'The villagers are superstitious. If they believe I put a curse on this place, they'll believe me when I tell them I've removed it.'

'And the elephants?'

'We'll need to build an electric fence around the key areas. We can get more generators and import the fuel from Botswana.'

'What if some other government bigwig lays claim to the farm?'

'The villagers got rid of one tyrant. I don't think they'll accept another. The local population will be the new owners of this farm, so it won't be easy for the government to tell them they are giving it to someone else. And you know, the government did not award this farm to Jackson. He just moved in with his thugs, claiming he was taking over the farm from a white man. He couldn't have done that so easily if the local population owned it.'

'I wouldn't be so sure about that, but OK, I'm happy to try it. When do you want me to start?'

'The quicker the better, before some government official realises it's lying abandoned.'

'Right, I'll move in on the weekend.'

'Let's go to the village. I'll tell them the curse will end on Sunday. The news will spread fast, and there'll be plenty of willing workers. Several farmworkers from before Jackson's time are still around, so you'll have trained workers available.'

* * *

Winston Smith sat opposite Mary, across the coffee table, with papers spread out in front of them. 'Well, Mary, you seem to have worked out almost everything. There's little for me to do. I'll put it into effect.'

'But do you accept the appointment?'

'I'd love to join the board of The Mary Moyo Trust. It will be my most exciting project in years. What did Andrew Jones say?'

'Yes, he's semi-retired now and is keen to set up the Julia Watson Clinic at the farm. He will recruit and support an experienced nursing sister to run the clinic, and will carry out minor procedures in the clinic surgery two days a week.'

'Two days? Will he stay overnight?'

'He'll stay at the farm until the lodge is ready. After that, he can stay at the lodge if he wants.'

'Have you found someone to manage the lodge?'

'Not yet.'

'And what about the school?'

'I'm still looking for a suitable person to run the Julia Watson Primary School. Qualified people are reluctant to move to the bush. It's the middle of nowhere. Once the lodge is open, and they can see where they'll live, it may be easier to find someone.'

'You're putting a lot of faith in that lodge.'

'Yes, I am.'

'So, who are the trust's board members?'

'You, Andrew Jones, Inspector Dube and myself as chairperson.'

'When will these projects be ready?'

'By the end of the year, I hope.'

'And what about your house in London? Are you going to sell it?'

'No! The London lawyers put me in touch with real estate agents. They say I should keep it and rent it out. They believe the value of houses in that area will increase fast.'

* * *

Over the next few months, Mary was a frequent visitor to the farm. The farm manager, John, did a good job, and soon the farm returned to its former state. Already, food was available to the local villages. The farm would pay for itself and fund the medical clinic and school, which would both open early in the next calendar year. The lodge was coming along well and accepting bookings for the Christmas holidays.

Mary was in her front garden when Clara passed. She seemed breathless with excitement. 'Have you heard the news? Mugabe has sacked Mnangagwa as vice-president. What will happen now? There's going to be trouble.'

Clara was right. Mnangagwa tried to escape from the country, first by air and then by road. But when that failed, the army smuggled him to South Africa.

Nine days later, army tanks and personnel carriers entered the Harare city centre. The army occupied the state broadcaster and announced it had taken control of Zimbabwe. Mugabe was placed under house arrest, and the country held its breath.

After an anxious wait of four more days, ZANU-PF, the governing party, sacked Mugabe as party leader and appointed Mnangagwa to replace him. Still, Mugabe wouldn't resign his position as president, and tensions grew. Two days later, his party began impeachment proceedings against him, but during that debate, Mugabe sent in his resignation letter.

In Harare, ecstatic crowds welcomed Mnangagwa and Chiwenga, the head of the army. In Bulawayo, the celebration was more muted because many blamed Mnangagwa for his part in the Gukurahundi—the Fifth Brigade's genocidal assault on the Ndebele people. Despite reservations, the populace hoped for positive change, and an air of expectation took hold.

What impact might the political developments have on Mary's investments? She was not one to wait for events to dictate her course. She saw the changes as an opportunity and made plans to secure the trust's future.

CHAPTER 42

Déjà Vu

THE Land Cruiser slowed to a halt at Marula. Robbie got out and raised his arms to the sky and stretched his tired back.

'Why are we stopping here?' Moira asked.

'I'm girding my loins for the next part of the drive. You should do the same. If you reckon it's been a long, hard drive so far, wait until we hit the dirt road.'

Moira and her husband, Mark, in the front passenger seat, got out of the vehicle and walked around in circles, stretching their legs.

'How much longer?' asked Moira.

'About an hour and a half to the campsite, I reckon,' said Robbie.

'Campsite? I thought you said it was a lodge?'

'Well, campsite, lodge, what's the difference? In Zimbabwe, that can mean a couple of tents and a long drop toilet.'

'Why then did you say we should bring smart-casual clothes with us?'

'I don't know. That's what the advertisement said. They can exaggerate sometimes, but I'm sure it will be OK.'

'Jeez, I hope you're right, Robbie. We've brought all our cossies and stuff, but I'm not swimming in a Zimbabwean river. There might be crocodiles.'

'At least this time, Mark won't be sleeping with The Lady.'

'I am a lady, Robbie.'

'Yeah, Moira, you're a lady, but not The Lady.'

'Trust Mark to confuse me with a lioness. A man-eater, of all things!'

'That's why you wouldn't let him come alone this time. Heaven knows who he'd be sleeping with next.'

'Yes, I couldn't trust you two to stay out of trouble.'

'Do you reckon The Lady might still prowl the area?' said Mark.

'Let's hope not. I don't fancy traipsing through the bush looking for half-eaten bodies.'

The three friends hopped back into the Land Cruiser and turned onto the dirt road to their destination.

'This road isn't so bad,' said Moira.

'Wait until we turn off onto the narrow track. Then I'll have to hold on tight to the steering wheel.'

'Would a road like that encourage visitors?'

Soon enough, they arrived at a turnoff. 'It's this one, isn't it?' said Mark.

'There's a sign saying Impisi Lodge, so maybe that's the one we want,' said Robbie.

'Don't you know the name of the lodge where we're staying?' said Moira.

'It was something like Impisi. I forgot to check the booking slip. But this must be it.'

'I don't suppose there'll be too many lodges out here.'

'We'll only find out if we try it, so here goes.'

Robbie turned the wheel of his Land Cruiser and eased the vehicle over a hump onto the narrow dirt road.

'Is this a road?' said Moira. 'It's more like a farm track. This long grass is so close. It's spooky.' Robbie and Mark laughed.

'This is the real Africa, Moira,' said Robbie. 'No soft civilisation here.'

'So much for smart-casual,' said Mark.

The Land Cruiser bumped and jolted along the rough track, and Moira and Mark held onto the grab handles above their doors. 'This old bus is showing its age,' said Robbie. 'It doesn't glide over the dirt roads like it once did.'

Puddles on the track were evidence of the previous night's storm. 'If it gets us there and back,' said Mark, 'it'll be fine.'

The Botswana dust on the Land Cruiser looked streaky as the wet grass stroked the sides of the vehicle.

'Somewhere here, we bumped into Jackson Mpofu last time,' said Robbie. 'I wondered why he was so accommodating about us staying at the campsite. The bastard was aware the man-eater roamed the area but kept it from us.'

'Oh no, not him again,' said Mark, as a white vehicle headed towards them.

'I doubt it's him,' said Robbie. 'These government bigwigs like black cars. It gives them a menacing air.'

'Snap again,' said Mark, as a sparkling white Land Cruiser pulled up in front of them. An African woman wearing a red bandana over her hair looked at them over the steering wheel of her vehicle.

'I'll ask her if we're on the right track for the resort,' said Robbie, as he slid off his seat and out of the vehicle. 'We may be heading for the wrong place.'

The woman stepped out of her vehicle and met Robbie part way. She wore figure-hugging khaki pants over brown leather boots, and a white long-sleeved shirt with button-down breast pockets.

Robbie was taking his time, and Mark was getting impatient. 'Why's he taking so long? I mean, are we on the right track, or aren't we? It's a simple enough question. He doesn't need to discuss the weather.'

'Relax, Dear. We're on holiday. There's no hurry.'

Robbie returned to the vehicle and jumped into the driver's seat. He eased his Land Cruiser into the grass to allow the other to pass.

'That's obliging of you, Robbie, getting right off the road to let her pass,' said Mark. 'You didn't do that for Jackson Mpofu.'

'Wow, what a beauty!' said Robbie.

'Yes,' said Mark, 'a brand-new Land Cruiser Safari!'

'No, I mean her. A real looker!'

'What was the long discussion?'

'I can't remember. I was just looking at her. Beautiful and educated, with a cultured speaking voice. How come we saw no African women like that when we lived in Zimbabwe?'

'She must've lived overseas. A lot of the educated ones did.'

'Come, you two,' said Moira. 'We're not here to discuss the local population. Let's get to the campsite, or lodge, or whatever it is. Did she mention any other lodges around here, Robbie?'

'No, it's the only one, so we're OK.'

Robbie took care driving on the dirt track. He didn't want to risk sliding into the long grass, which could conceal large rocks. Long muddy puddles looked threatening, but the Land Cruiser splashed through them without difficulty. He also needed to keep an eye out for any oncoming vehicle that the tall grass might hide.

'Is this a road to a luxury lodge?' said Moira, again labouring the point.

'Don't forget, Moira,' said Robbie, 'here is the real Africa. It's not a place for sissies. The road would be easier in the dry season.'

The Land Cruiser bumped and splashed its way along the track. An irritating rattle set up in the glove box. But try as he might, Mark couldn't find the cause. 'It might be loose wiring behind the dashboard, he said.'

After what seemed like an age, Mark pointed in front of them. 'There's the turnoff for the boom gate.'

'What's the boom gate for?' asked Moira.

'Jackson Mpofu has armed guards there to stop unwelcome visitors.'

Soon, a densely wooded area with tall trees appeared in front of them. Four kilometres into the forest, Robbie slowed the four-wheel drive. 'There's the campsite turnoff. We're almost there.'

'It doesn't look so overgrown now,' said Mark.

'I expect they must have cleared it when they built the lodge.'

The Impisi Lodge sign on the roadside stood next to the statue of a hyena. Robbie turned the Land Cruiser's steering wheel to the right and headed down the graded road. A kilometre farther on, like a mirage, a cluster of low, thatch-roofed buildings appeared in front of them. Giant aloes separated the hard, sandy surface of the carpark from an enormous wooden deck attached to a large, open-sided central building. On the deck's right-hand side, a welcoming bar sparkled with an assortment of alcoholic drinks on mirrored shelving. On the left-hand side, a large, light blue infinity pool reflected the sunlight.

'Wow! This is more like it,' said Robbie.

A man, sitting on one of the tall barstools, stood up and approached them.

'Hey, that looks like John Boyd,' said Robbie.

'Welcome to Impisi Lodge,' said John, shaking Robbie's hand. 'Long time, no see.'

Mark shook hands and introduced himself and his wife, Moira.

Robbie slapped John Boyd on the back. 'What are you doing here?'

'Farmer's lunch break.'

'I thought Jackson Mpofu kicked you off the farm. Have you got it back now?'

'Sort of! I'm the farm manager. The surrounding villages own the farm.'

'But you're the boss, right?'

'A trust runs everything here. The farm is just one of four businesses the trust operates.'

'Do you run the lodge as well? I mean, this was your campsite.'

'No, I support the lodge, and I'm here a lot. You can see why,' said John, moving his hand in a theatrical sweep. 'Lulu is the lodge manager. I'll introduce you to her when she arrives. This is our bar, come reception counter. Behind the bar is our lounge and dining room.'

'How many visitors can you accommodate?' asked Mark.

'We have twelve ensuite rondavels with queen-size beds.'

'So, what's this trust that runs everything?'

'The Mary Moyo Trust. Mary's my boss. You may have passed her on the road. She was driving a white Land Cruiser.'

'Your boss,' said Robbie, 'Wow! I'd like a boss like that. Yes, we stopped to ask her if we were on the right road. Is she from the UK or the US?'

'No, she's from the village over that ridge.'

'No way! Are you serious? We visited that village, and I can tell you, nobody looked like that.'

'Yes, she was the housemaid for a retired English teacher who taught her how to speak proper English.'

'Far out, man! Things have changed a lot since we lived in Zimbabwe.'

'Yeah, and she's got a good business brain. She named it Impisi because that means hyena in Ndebele. You'll hear them calling at night. If you're lucky, you might also hear the resident leopard coughing, when it comes snooping around the rondavels. One night, three weeks ago, hyenas killed a kudu on this deck. After dark, a guard will escort you to your rondavel, and if you want to leave it for any reason, you must phone reception for a guard to fetch you.'

'It all sounds very well organised,' said Mark.

'Yes, Mary designed the lodge and oversaw the building work. That entire time, she stayed in her old hut in the village. In the meantime, she sent her sister, Lulu, on a hospitality and bar tender course in Joburg. Mary chose all the furnishings and decor herself—everything you see around you. She's talented and has heaps of energy.'

Moira and the boys looked around them, admiring the exposed beams and thatched roof of the open-sided lounge and dining room. Elevated walkways led to each rondavel, ensuring guests wouldn't walk any mud or dirt into the rooms. African themes, and teak and wickerwork furniture, gave it the air of a luxury hunting lodge.

'She's thought of everything,' said John. 'If you didn't bring your own fishing rods, no worries. There's a fishing rod cupboard in the lounge for guests to take their pick. You can't see it from here, but in the shade of those trees, she's built a raised platform on the river's edge to keep anglers safe from crocodiles.'

'The road's not great,' said Moira.

'Mary's going to have it graded after the rains finish. Ah, here comes Lulu. She'll check you in and make your welcoming cocktails.'

Lulu flashed her big round eyes at the visitors. At check in, Robbie bemoaned the fact that Mark would share a bed with Moira, but he was alone. Lulu possessed a great sense of humour and offered to find someone from the village to keep him warm. 'If she's as pretty as you, I might be interested,' said Robbie. Lulu laughed.

* * *

After dinner, sitting around the brazier on the large wooden deck near the bar, the friends chatted about their experiences since leaving Zimbabwe. Robbie's engineering business was going well, and Mark enjoyed his role as finance manager of an import export business in Johannesburg. Moira taught part-time at a nearby junior school.

John related how Mary found him and gave him the chance to return to the farm, following Jackson Mpofu's dramatic departure. 'I'm not the owner anymore, but it feels like I am. I make the decisions and run things pretty much as I want. The villagers get free vegetables, and the farm also serves the lodge. Mary's a generous and caring boss.'

'It must have taken her ages to achieve all this.'

'No, only three years, I believe. She tells great stories about her life in the village. At one time, there was a man-eating lioness terrorising the area. Two scruffy white men stayed overnight at the campsite. In the morning, they drove to the Figtree police station to report the lion's presence. A village woman was missing, and the police suspected the men may be responsible for her disappearance and reported the lion to divert suspicion from themselves.'

Robbie and Mark looked at each other. 'Scruffy whites!' said Robbie, raising his voice in mock indignation. 'That's a cheek! We weren't going to stick around once we saw the lion's paw prints, so we just dumped everything in the Land Cruiser's back seat. There wasn't time to pack everything neatly. We didn't even have breakfast. We wanted out of there, ASAP.'

John laughed at the perplexed expression on his friend's face.

'Then,' said Robbie, 'this village woman in tatty clothes turns up and asks us for a lift to the Figtree police station. She couldn't speak much English, but we understood someone from the village was missing, and she wanted to report it. So that's when we went to the police station to alert them to the lion's presence. I mean, what if it had taken the woman?'

'Well, I guess you had no choice,' said John.

'Driving to Figtree took us out of our way, and it ended up causing us a lot of problems. The stupid police sergeant said our lion story might just be our cover for the woman's disappearance. He insisted we return to the campsite with him. We ended up spending a night in that damned village, and the lion came after us, scratching at our hut's thatched roof.'

'Hah!' said Moira, laughing. 'You sound defensive there, Robbie. I'm sure you two looked like a pair of scruffs.'

'You're right about your boss telling great stories, John. She wasn't even there! Someone must have told her about it,' said Mark.

'Well, she said she was there, and she mentioned the two white men stayed in her village overnight.'

'She couldn't have been there, otherwise we would've remembered her. If she was there, she didn't come out of her hut.'

CHAPTER 43

Pareidolia

THE fortnight leading up to Christmas was a busy time for Mary. On the Saturday, two weeks before Christmas, she and John Boyd organised a party for the farmworkers and their families, together with the residents of Mary's village. The farm supplied the vegetables, and Mary bought the meat and cool drinks. The workers placed several lit braziers in the parking area in front of the farmhouse, and nobody needed to wait in line to cook their meat.

A surprise guest was the popular politician, Dennis Nyathi, who, three years earlier, solicited Mary's support for the upcoming 2018 elections. She agreed, but after Jackson Mpofu threatened her for supporting his rival, she left the village for Bulawayo. Nyathi gave a short, rousing speech about working for the people and not for personal gain. The villagers, who only recently got rid of the tyrannical Jackson Mpofu, responded enthusiastically.

Several villagers brought their home-brewed beer, and before long, everyone was merry.

* * *

On the following Saturday, Mary held a Christmas dinner at Impisi Lodge for her sister Lulu, John Boyd, Inspector Dube, his wife Mirella, and Sergeant Sibanda. Little Charlie stayed until six o'clock, when the nanny took him off to bed.

'And where is your wife, Sergeant Sibanda?' Mary asked.

'No, she won't come here, Madam.'

'Why not? Wouldn't she like a nice dinner?'

'She's too shy.'

'You must bring her next time. We'll soon cure her of her shyness.'

Sibanda smiled but said nothing.

Visitors staying at the lodge filled less than half the tables. 'The lodge has been open for two weeks,' said Mary. 'This time next year, I expect we'll be full. John has done a wonderful job at the farm, like Lulu has done here at Impisi. Once we grade the road, there'll be a lot more tourists willing to drive here.'

'Where did you find the chef?' said Dube. 'The food is excellent.'

'She's from a local village. She's always been interested in cooking and speaks good English, so I sent her to a cookery course in Johannesburg, where she did very well.'

'And when will the teacher arrive?'

'She's expected in the week before term starts. It's taken a long time to find a suitable person. I wanted someone who spoke excellent English with a good accent. When our students leave for other schools in Zimbabwe or overseas, they'll be able to fit in well. We wouldn't want them to be teased because of their accent.'

'Who is this teacher?'

'Mrs. Anne Cleary. She taught in a good primary school in England. Anne can teach all subjects, but her first love is language and elocution. When her husband died, she came to Africa to help young children from poor families. It seemed a perfect fit for us. As the pupils advance to higher grades, we'll need to employ more teachers, but that's a problem for the future.'

'And, Mary,' said John Boyd, 'have you thought how you'll handle a greedy government bigwig if they set their eyes on this place?'

'Yes, I'm going to invite whoever wins the presidential election to open the project, including all its related business endeavours. With their name on a plaque at the entrance to our various ventures, I doubt they'd want to see the place invaded by someone like Jackson Mpofu, again.'

'And if they don't come?'

'Then, they might send one or more of the relevant government ministers for agriculture, health, education, and tourism to stand in for them. I'll ask the new president for approval to put up the plaque, stating his support and approval for our endeavours and naming him patron of our project. Do you imagine either presidential candidate's ego would allow them to reject that offer?'

* * *

Mary planned to hold a dinner at home on Christmas Eve. The guests would include Andrew Jones and Winston Smith and their wives, George Benson and his girls, Eveline, Monica, and Clara, and Henry the gardener. Mary decided it was time they all met. She intended to cook the dinner herself and didn't fancy holding two separate celebrations for her friends.

On Christmas Eve, during the day, George's girls came in at various times to lend a hand. A Christmas dinner for ten was quite an undertaking, and Mary appreciated the help. The table looked splendid, and everyone commented on it. For Henry, it was a first. He'd seen nothing like it in his entire life. But Andrew, Winston, and both their wives said they'd seen nothing as beautiful in years.

'I'm doing it the way Julia used to do it,' said Mary.

Her cooking had come a long way since her attempt to make mash from unpeeled, boiled potatoes.

'How's Lulu doing?' asked Winston.

'Oh, she's happily settled in at the lodge.'

'Doesn't she find it boring, out there in the middle of nowhere? I mean a young, attractive woman who likes the city lights. She told me so, herself.'

'No, she loves Impisi. There're always interesting guests coming along, and she loves chatting with different people.'

'But what about her days off?'

'If she's not at the lodge, I can always find her at John Boyd's farm. John has taken to Charlie, and the little boy follows him everywhere.'

'Doesn't Lulu worry when Charlie is out and about with John? I mean, he's busy trying to run the farm, so he can't keep an eye on Charlie all the time.'

'No, Lulu also follows John everywhere. And when John's not at the farm, he spends all his time at the lodge, helping Lulu.'

'So, they spend all their time together?'

'Yes, it looks that way.'

'It sounds like Lulu might have ambitions to become a farmer's wife,' said Monica.

Everyone laughed.

'I wouldn't know. They say nothing to me,' said Mary. 'After the New Year, I'm taking Lulu and Charlie to London to inspect the house. It's furnished, so we'll stay there and make a list of everything. While Lulu's away, John Boyd will manage the lodge. Perhaps he's spending a lot of time there to learn how it operates.'

'Yeah, sure!' said Winston with a wink. 'Do you believe that?'

Henry sat between Andrew and Winston's wives and was at his charming best.

'So, what work do you do, Henry?' asked Andrew's wife, Gayle.

'Mary says I'm a horticulturist.'

'Oh, how interesting! My garden could do with help.'

'Mine too,' said Winston's wife, Veronica.

Mary smiled. She'd teased Henry about his work, cutting the grass and tidying the garden. She never realised he'd taken in what she said.

Someone put on an old Acker Bilk LP, and George and Clara glided around the parquet floor. Old George was light on his feet, and Clara impressed everyone with her ballroom dancing. Soon everyone took turns on the floor, and Mary made a mental note it was a social skill she needed to master.

The chatter and the laughter made it a fun evening. They all said how much they enjoyed themselves and left with broad smiles on their faces. Mary refused offers of help with the dishes. She tidied up the lounge and dining room and washed the dishes and scrubbed the pots and pans while daydreaming about her first Christmas with Julia.

There were lots of dirty dishes, but she worked steadily, and soon they were all sparkling clean and back in the cupboard. There was nothing left to do. An intense loneliness suddenly settled on her.

Mary saw the threatening clouds racing across the darkened sky. She walked into the back garden and sat on the bench where she and Julia so often sat, admiring the stars. Then there it was again. Julia's face in the clouds, like the one she saw on the night following news of Jim Grant's death.

The thumping of her heart was so strong it shook her slender body. In a trembling voice, she said, 'Julia, I hope I have made you proud of me. Everything I am, and everything I have achieved, is because of you. Thank you.'

Julia's face in the clouds turned into a smile that warmed Mary's heart. But the night winds soon carried the cloud away. 'Until next time, Julia. Until next time.'

MAP OF ZIMBABWE

Sʜᴏᴡɪɴɢ towns, roads, railway lines and national parks.

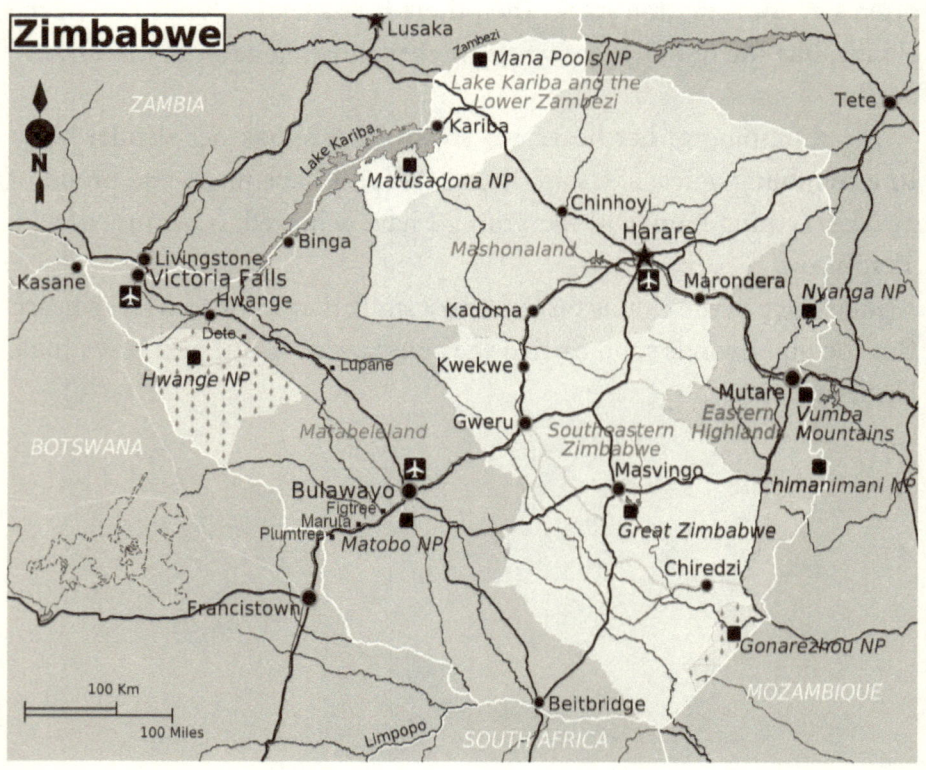

By (WT-shared) Shaund [CC BY-SA 4.0-3.0-2.5-2.0-1.0 (https:// creativecommons.org/licenses/by-sa/4.0-3.0-2.5-2.0-1.0)], via Wikime-dia Commons. Amended to include Dete, Lupane, Figtree, and Marula.

Author's Note

Anyone who has lived in Southern Africa will recognise several of the characters in *The World of Mary Moyo*. The secret to living in Zimbabwe is patience, adaptability and making do.

Zimbabwe's infrastructure continues in a state of decay. Health, education, and roads are in desperate need of funding, and the country's utility services are in danger of collapse because of a lack of maintenance, corruption, and diversion of funds.

Most of the country's population lacks access to potable water and relies on shallow wells and boreholes, with many contaminated with sewage. Tap water is not safe to drink, and often the taps run dry. Cholera and typhoid are an ongoing threat.

Electricity outages are common, with power often unavailable during the day, coming back on briefly in the early hours.

The fragile local currency continues to lose value against the US dollar, and this has condemned many citizens to unforeseen poverty.

I wouldn't like my novels to give readers the impression Zimbabwe is best avoided. It is one of the safest countries in Africa and well worth a visit. But like anywhere else in the world, it depends on the company you keep and the areas you visit. Most of the locals are welcoming and helpful.

L.T. Kay
Author website https://ltkay.com

ABOUT THE AUTHOR

Bulawayo was my home town. That's where I grew up and got my first job. Anyone who has lived in Africa, even briefly, will confirm you can never really leave it. No matter how far you travel, like the grass seeds that stick to your socks, Africa goes with you.

I lived and worked in Zimbabwe/Rhodesia and South Africa for over thirty years, alternating between Bulawayo, Salisbury (Harare) and Johannesburg.

The Bush War got serious while I was living in Hong Kong, and on my return to Rhodesia, I was called up for military service in the army.

Professional qualifications in accounting and marketing helped me secure senior management positions with companies in diverse fields, including engineering, textiles, clothing and cosmetics manufacture, and service industries.

Today, I live in Melbourne with my wife Maggie and write fiction set in Southern Africa, principally Zimbabwe. Since the turn of the century, that country has led a dark, surreal existence that keeps many people shaking their heads in disbelief. It would be funny if it wasn't so sad.

L. T. Kay
Author website https://ltkay.com

Other Books by the Author

The Leopard Series is a trilogy of novels set in the troubled years of Robert Mugabe's dictatorship in Zimbabwe. *Honey and The Leopard* is book 3 in the series.

Feeding the Leopard
Book 1 in The Leopard Series
When going back home is nothing like you imagined…
It is 2008, and the global financial crisis sees Ian Sanders out of a job in Melbourne. He flies to Africa, the land of his birth, to follow his dream of writing a novel set in the wilds of Zimbabwe.

In his twenty-year absence, much has changed. The country is in turmoil. A new power-sharing government is imminent, but the political situation remains volatile. People fear the police, and violent crime goes unpunished. Supermarket shelves are empty, and essential goods are scarce. Cholera rages and the Zimbabwean dollar is in free fall.

Ian plans to focus on his novel and stay out of trouble, but slowly he is drawn into a web of conspiracy and fear that pervades the lives of so many of the country's people. He is in peril, but who should he most fear: the police, the secretive COU, the wildlife or the enigmatic Sarah?

He and those around him find their values, beliefs and prejudices challenged in their fight for survival. Nearly thirty years after independence, many Zimbabweans still wait for their promised freedom.

L. T. Kay
Author website https://ltkay.com

BETRAYAL. PREJUDICE. DESIRE.
A STORY OF AFRICA

FEEDING THE LEOPARD

L. T. KAY

The Bulawayo Boys' Club
Book 2 in The Leopard Series
When there's nothing to lose, you can afford to play fast and loose. But what if someone raises the stakes?
Alan Drake, formerly with the Australian Special Forces, drifts aimlessly, chasing the good life in Melbourne. For him, that means bars and clubbing.

When his wealthy controlling father, George, sends him on a mission to Zimbabwe, Alan has no idea what's in store for him. He regards the venture as a crazy plan and doesn't take the task seriously. Alan has no interest in Zimbabwe, and he's never heard of Mthwakazi, let alone the sinister figure known as The Leopard.

Zimbabwe is a land of shortages, and Bulawayo lacks the bright lights that so appeal to Alan. He can't wait to get back home. He soon discovers the city can generate more than enough adrenalin to keep his blood racing, but not in the way he might have hoped.

The mission takes Alan into the national parks where he sees the plight of the wildlife and the hardship endured by the nearby rural population. It leads him into an unintended war with an unknown foe. How can he fight a faceless enemy? People are relying on him. Has he left it too late to leave?

Alan soon realises someone wants him dead. And to make matters worse, the people he's come to help are now also on a death list. The ambitious project has become a fight for survival, with unexpected consequences. His father never warned him of the dangers of the mission.

How could his simple role in the venture lead to this?

Can he extricate himself and his colleagues from the mess he's created?

What can he salvage from the fiasco?

Can Alan resist Africa's many temptations?

L. T. Kay
Author website https://ltkay.com

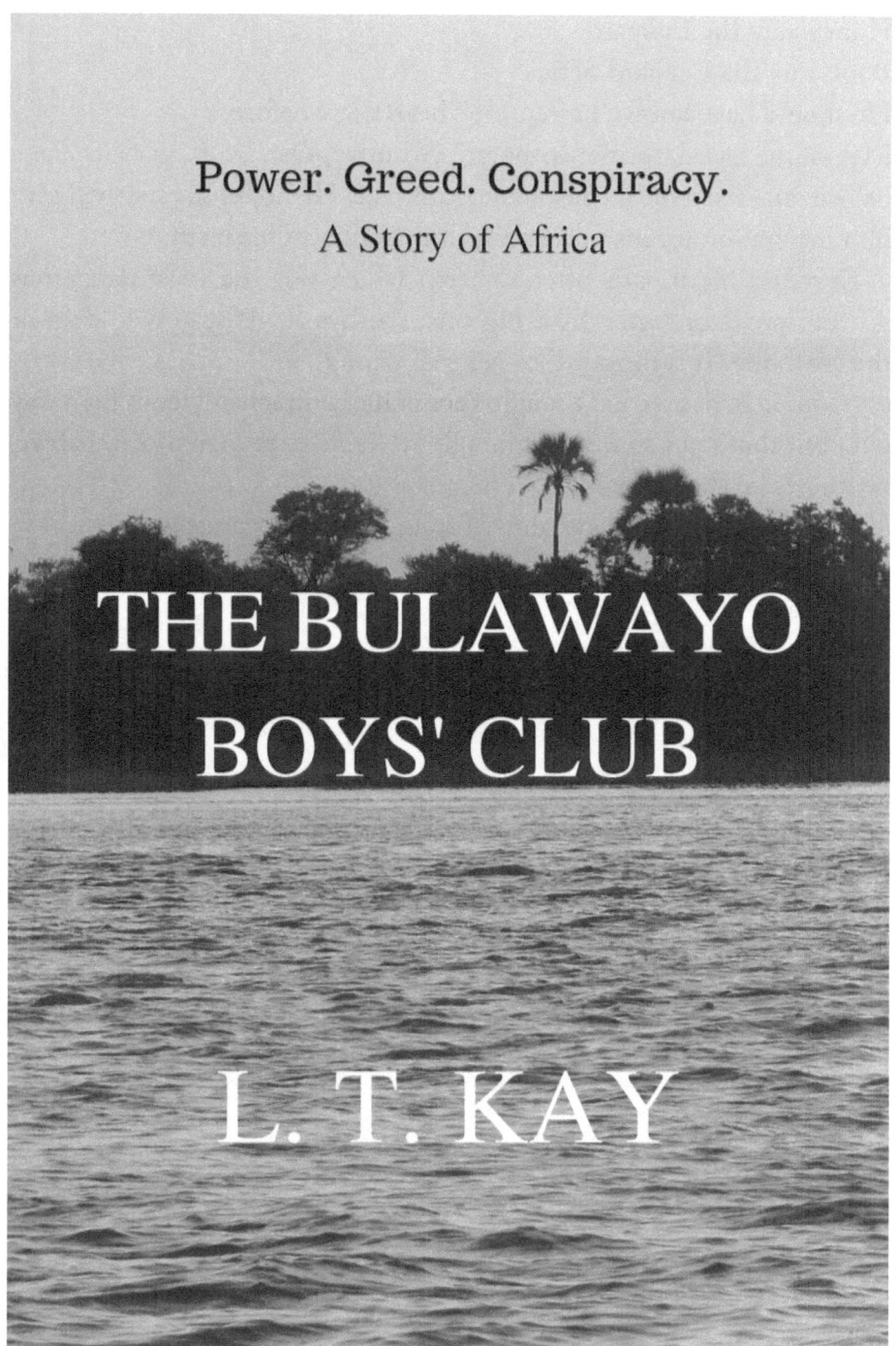

Power. Greed. Conspiracy.
A Story of Africa

THE BULAWAYO
BOYS' CLUB

L. T. KAY

Honey and The Leopard
Book 3 in The Leopard Series
He should have known better. He's been there before.
Melbourne based, former corporate executive, Dan Scott, goes to Zimbabwe on a six-month consultancy contract. He hopes his stay will give him inspiration for his novel set in the country of his birth.

Dan and his friends often debated which was the most dangerous African predator: one of the big cats, the hyena, African wild dog, or the crocodile. It turns out they were all wrong.

Soon, Dan has second thoughts about his contract and looks for a way out. But that's not so easy. Although he wants to remain in Zimbabwe, he knows he should leave.

Must he kill to extricate himself from his dire circumstances?

L. T. Kay
Author website https://ltkay.com

FEAR. XENOPHOBIA. REVENGE.
A STORY OF AFRICA

HONEY
AND
THE LEOPARD

L. T. KAY

www.ingramcontent.com/pod-product-compliance
Lightning Source LLC
Chambersburg PA
CBHW020258120726
47904CB00001B/245